ORPHANED

AN ELKRIDGE SERIES NOVEL

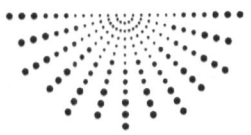

LYZ KELLEY

Belvitri
Services

ORPHANED

**She's attracted the attention of the last man
to see her sister alive.**

Jenna is desperate to find her younger sister.
Ripped away from her when she was seven
years old, Jenna believed Caitlyn the lucky
adopted one.

Yet, Caitlyn has vanished under eerie
circumstances.
Does Grant know where her sister is?

Grant has returned to town to take over his
ailing father's law practice. He craves a settled

life, and Jenna seems the perfect fit. His plan is to marry the adorable baker, and no one will change his mind—not even Jenna.

Yet a stranger brings a shocking surprise that test Jenna and Grant's trust.

If you love a sensual contemporary romance novel, with deep emotional topics, a thread of suspense, and a cozy happy ending, then ORPHANED is for you. Get ORPHANED to unlock the emotional tale today!

PRAISE FOR LYZ KELLEY'S WRITING AND A SPECIAL GIFT JUST FOR YOU.

I have a present for you…your very own ebook exclusive: *Regrets, the prequel to BLINDED* when you sign up for my newsletter.

Newsletter Sign Up: http://lyzkelley.net

The Molly: Award for Excellence
"A writer who will go the distance."
"Masterful dialog."
"I look forward to seeing this book on the bookshelves."

The Sheila: Finalist
"The story has great bones! The plot is interesting, the characters are unique...there are so many things to love about this story."
"H & H are both very appealing and certainly not cookie cutter characters."
"Your opening is a grabber."
"This is one of the best books I've read in a good long while. CONGRATULATIONS."
"Prose is sleek, polished and smooth, a near frictionless read."

The Marlene: Finalist
"You have a lovely writing style with dialogue and scene setting."
"The sensory details are rich, and I was able to visualize the scenes. I chuckled several times at your turn of phrase and thought they were very sassy and smart."
"The plot seems to have it all: conflict, a

mystery and a romance. So kudos for creating an interesting story."

The Golden Network: Finalist
"The setting is painted well and the characters are engaging with very different voices."
"The manuscript is clean and tightly written."
"The manuscript reflects beautiful writing."

CHAPTER ONE

Why, oh why was Grant Newhall standing in the café's kitchen looking more delicious than one of her chocolate cream pies?

Jenna Dolcy grumbled to the bread dough gently yielding beneath the heel of her hand. She released a puff of air to get her overgrown bangs out of her eyes. "You're going to get your suit all dirty."

"I don't mind getting a bit dirty."

The corners of his mouth quivered, then rolled slowly into that heart-stealing smile.

Oh man...I'm in trouble.

Grant dropped a red rose on the maple butcher block table, which was covered with a dusting of flour. Its floral damask wafted and danced with the fragrance of buttery yeast. She closed her eyes and exhaled, trying to forget how handsome Grant looked in his elegant charcoal suit, crisp white shirt, polished leather shoes, and a brand spanking new periwinkle tie. Why did she tell him her favorite color was periwinkle?

He slid an arm around her waist and pulled. His mouth skimmed over hers, and her brain went blank. Tingles zipped across her skin, and her heart skipped along, until…wait. *What am I doing?*

"Whoa." She pushed him back. "You can't just walk in here and kiss me."

"I like kissing you."

I'm in double-trouble. "We don't do that."

"Yes, we do." He leaned in again, and she braced her palms on his chest. "You were the one who kissed me after I won the dart tournament."

"That was different." She stepped out of his grasp. *I had one too many beers and wasn't thinking straight.*

She set a bread round on a baking sheet and grabbed another hunk of dough to shape. "It's Mrs. Bainbridge's birthday tomorrow. Why don't you give her the flower? She's sitting at her usual table."

"This one's for you. I'll bring her flowers tomorrow."

His persistence and the fact he looked downright scrumptious in his business suit kept punching holes right through her determination to remain indifferent.

"You should go before Maggie busts you for being in the kitchen."

"Don't worry about me." He glanced around the small space as his half-smirk expanded. "When are you going to get one of those bakery convection ovens you want so much? I know you've been looking at them. It doesn't seem practical for you to be splitting your time between the café and your bakery."

Your bakery. Dreamy Delights. Her dream.

A coffee-and-croissant warmth seeped into her, and she savored the happy moment for a few seconds before a cold shiver deflated her bliss. What if she couldn't make a go of the business? What if she couldn't make enough to pay off her loans?

"I'll get an oven when I find one for less than five grand. For now, baking breads here and the other stuff at my shop works."

"I could lend—"

"No!" She rolled her shoulders back, squeezing to suppress the building tension, wishing the local macho magnet would find someone new to lavish his attention on. "I know you Newhalls have bulging bank accounts, but I'll purchase one when I have the cash. Until then, Maggie's fine with me splitting my time." She grabbed another piece of dough. "Weren't you supposed to be going over case files this morning?"

"Mom called to tell me Dad isn't feeling well. We rescheduled for tomorrow."

"Is everything okay?"

"I think so. Mom said he just needs rest."

"Yesterday I overhead Dr. Brennan say quadruple bypasses can take up to four months to heal. I hope your dad isn't pushing too hard."

"He's getting bored, so I doubt he'll follow the doctor's orders."

"Last night it sounded like you're thinking about staying on after your dad is well enough to manage his clients. Are you really thinking of staying?"

Please say no. Please say no. Please say no.

"I'm planning on it."

Bummer. That makes things messy.

"This is my home," he said, "and I want to settle down, build my life here. Once I get my permanent Colorado license to practice law, I plan to take over my dad's practice."

Uh-oh. I hope you're not planning to add me to that settle down bit.

He moved closer and leaned his backside against the butcher block counter. "Hey, meet me at Sparky's after you get off. I'm tempted to barbecue up some ribs."

Oh, no. Your yumminess is way too tempting. "I'll have to pass. I'm already exhausted, plus I have a lot of baking to do. I got up late because you kept me up past midnight chatting on the phone. You guys have fun without me."

"You can't work all the time, you know. You'll burn out."

"I don't work *all* the time. You know that, since you popped out of the bushes and scared the poop out of me the other night. Promise me if we go running you won't do that again."

"You shouldn't be running alone on that ridge, especially at night. That reminds me. I picked you up some bear spray. It's in my car."

She pushed on the dough again and again and again, trying to get her pitter-pattering heart to remember why even being friends with Grant Newhall wasn't a good idea, much less doing the friendly-kissy kind of thing.

"What did you decide about adventure racing?" he asked, then tilted his head to get a better look at her face. "We'd make a good team."

"Sounds like a blast, but again, between getting my business up and running and helping out here, I don't have the time to commit to anything beyond putting a smile on every face in this town."

"Still think you don't fit in?" Grant's manly brow arched higher, demanding an answer.

Dang the man. He could read her like a book, which frankly frightened her more than a scary movie.

Besides being quite the walking Wikipedia, a couple of times she'd wondered if he could read minds. Why the man was all gung ho to hang out with the likes of her, though, she hadn't quite figured out. He was way too fancy for her lifestyle. Plus, being in the presence of a Newhall stirred up all sorts of angst, and brought back suppressed childhood memories. Memories she'd been doing her best to muzzle.

Grant took a step further into the no-customer zone. "Why don't you take a break? Let's get some coffee."

Why do you keep pushing? Jenna glanced over her shoulder but kept working. "Sorry. I've already had my quota, and still have a good caffeine buzz going." She pointed to the black liquid in the container sitting on the hot burner. Its strong, bitter scent wafted around the kitchen, confirming the four-am brew should be tossed. "If you want some coffee, Maggie's got a fresh pot out front."

His finger-licking grin gave her innards a lurch of uneasiness. Determined to ignore him, Jenna focused on pounding the buttery dough into submission. Ten seconds passed, then another ten, then another. His lack of response, and the tickling feeling he was staring at her boobs made her glance up to confirm her suspicions.

He wasn't gawking.

He never did.

That's the thing. The guy was perfect in every way. His dark brown hair had the perfect amount of fuss, and his mouth formed a perfect made-you-look grin. Even his dimples were perfect.

Dratted man.

Grant pushed remnants of powdering flour into a pile with the tip of his finger. "How about I meet you at your place after work, instead? We can go for a quick run. I'll bring takeout."

His voice was so soft and sensual her stomach wadded into a bite-sized knot. The Newhall family history should be enough to guarantee she never forgot where she came from: she didn't have time for such foolishness, or additional complications. She didn't want Grant Newhall crashing into her life, even if he was the best-looking lawyer this side of the Continental Divide.

She took a long, weary breath. "Really, I'm

exhausted. An early night is what I need. Why don't you ask what's-her-face out to dinner?"

"Do you mean Rachelle Clairemont?"

Who else would I be talking about? "Yeah, her."

Grant leaned in, his warm, sweet-smelling breath caressing her neck and sending shivers skittering across her skin. "Now why would I do something stupid like that when you're the prettiest in Colorado?" His baritone triggered a shower of goose bumps.

Prettiest? Not even. "Grant. I'm just a simple, ordinary gal who just wants to make her customers happy."

Surprise sparked in his eyes. "Jenna, ordinary you are not."

"Whatever you say," she said brushing his words away with a wave of her hand.

Jenna patted the ball of pastry before glancing at the café's wall clock, confirming the time was, indeed, marching toward the breakfast rush hour. She turned back to Grant. "I've got a lot of baking to do. Maggie's gonna take a large chunk out of my ass if I don't get this bread in the oven."

As if on cue, Maggie, the café's owner,

pushed through the kitchen door—her flustered face peered around the corner.

"Grant, get the hell out of my kitchen! You can't pester Jenna whenever you feel like it," Maggie's voice reverberated off the pots and pans like a kick-started vintage Harley. She retrieved a tray of apple spice muffins before glancing Jenna's way. "Hon, I need some help out front. Sheila's kid is sick again, and food's stacking up at the grill. Oh, and, everyone is raving about your new orange rind muffins. Mrs. Bainbridge said you were sweet to make them. She said they are her favorite."

I know. "I wanted to bake her something special for her birthday."

"That's my sugar girl, always thinking of others." Maggie's gaze swung to Grant. "Newhall? Why are you still standing there?"

Jenna shook her head at the rumbling force of Maggie Connor, who'd already disappeared, leaving only a swinging door in her wake. Three-plus years ago, Maggie's leather layer of gruffness hadn't fooled Jenna. The oversized, quick-witted woman had a heart wider than an interstate highway. She'd given Jenna a job, a place to live, and more importantly, space.

Jenna tucked a piece of plastic wrap around the dough so snugly she could have been swaddling a newborn. "Go ahead, Grant. I'll be out in a minute."

"How about we go over your marketing plan?"

Thank goodness her back was turned to the man, or he might have experienced the most amazing Guinness-Book-worthy eye-roll ever. "Grant," she turned up the sweet in her voice as high as it could go, "Would you pretty-please take a seat in the café before Maggie decides to find another baker?" She pulled her latex gloves off with a snap.

"You know Maggie won't fire you."

His fixed, lawyerly stare triggered a gut-gripping panic. It was like he could see her fears, her flaws.

"Why won't you accept help?" he asked gently.

His tone conveyed disappointment, and made her reconsider his offer for a split second, but she didn't like accepting handouts. And she couldn't accept help—not from him— even if the local church suddenly offered him sainthood. "I'm not good at accepting handouts."

"Helping each other isn't a handout."

It is where I came from. "I appreciate the offer. I do. But I've got everything covered."

Grant pushed away from the counter and made his way through the thick steel door. The door swung back and forth while Jenna rolled her head in slow circles and dropped her shoulders to help release the tension.

Too bad he had the last name of Newhall.

The first time she heard his full name she almost dropped a tray full of plates and glasses. Figures he'd be related to *that* family. Her stomach folded over like dough in a mixer. So, no, she wouldn't accept his help, no matter how sweetly he offered. He might insist on running with her, or she might bump into him at the café, or they might watch the sun set together, but that's where she drew the line.

Donning her River Creek Café apron, she made her way to the grill area, trying to shake the afterimage of those broad shoulders.

In a matter of moments, she delivered ten meals, stopped to say hello to several regulars, refilled four coffees, and took two orders—all to avoid the sizzling source of testosterone sitting on the far side of the café.

Turning from the counter with a fresh pot of coffee, Jenna took a deep, lung-filling breath, glued on her best customer-friendly smile, and walked the twenty feet toward him. She filled his coffee mug and spun to grab a fresh cream pitcher from the back counter. Before she could release the cold metal, his warm fingers brushed her hand. She broke the trace of heat rolling up her arm by grabbing the closest rag to wipe the counter. If she could, she'd wipe away her increasing infatuation.

Grant swirled the spoon in his coffee, creating a whirlpool of creamy brown.

"Want some breakfast?" She picked up an empty plate while wiping the counter and waiting for a response.

He retrieved the menu from the metal holder. "Sure."

She turned toward the kitchen to avoid the eyes full of interest that made her squirm.

"Hey," he waved the menu at her. "Aren't you going to take my order?"

Setting the empty plate in the dirty dish bin, she rotated and placed a fist on her hip. "Omelet, egg whites only, no cheese. Mushrooms, green pepper, ham. Wheat toast buttered lightly. Fruit, no home fries. And a small orange juice. Did you want something different?"

He stared at her for a long, wordless moment. "You an undercover FBI agent?"

"Doesn't take much to figure out what a guy eats for breakfast—especially since it's mostly been the same the past three months."

His sunshine happiness made her feel guilty, but the guilt wasn't enough to squash the urge to rumple his pricey caviar perfection.

She jotted down Grant's order, and took several more on her way back to the grill. More plates of food piled high with Ted's delicious cooking waited under warmers for delivery.

"Ted, your grub smells delicious. Save me some bacon, would you?"

The cook didn't say a word, only lifted a spatula to acknowledge her praise.

The smell of bacon, waffles, and

strawberries mingled in the air to create a concoction of aromas enveloping and comforting her. The same way her foster mother's kitchen stirred up a feeling of security. Fun memories of Kathy briefly surfaced. Jenna spotted a little girl with icing stuck to one of her red pin curls, giggling with joy, and licking the creamed sugar off a saucer-sized cinnamon roll.

Laughing, Jenna inhaled an abundance of joy. She loved Elkridge—the rhythm, the feel, the flow of people through the café and her bakery.

She hadn't meant to make Elkridge her home, but the town had everything she ever wanted.

"Order up," Ted shouted from the kitchen.

Jenna pulled Grant's omelet from under the heat lamps, bustled down the aisle, shoved the plate and a bottle of ketchup in front of him, and then turned to leave.

"Did you hear the latest on Randall Clairemont's park expansion idea?" Grant grabbed the ketchup bottle, pounding the lid against his hand.

Oh, boy. "No. And I don't want to hear

anything Clairemont has to say. That man has an agenda." She snagged the coffee pot to refill Sheriff Joe and Harold's mugs, and dropped a few extra creamers on the counter.

"You should. Clairemont's a successful businessman. This city needs to expand if it's going to grow and attract new families, teachers, and businesses." He leaned back in his chair, with a spark of goading excitement shining in his eyes. "A new park will help."

"Yeah, 'cause that's what we need—more city folk coming up here, tromping through the woods, getting lost, or running people off the road. Most of 'em don't know even how to extinguish a fire properly, and one spark could light this whole town on fire."

Don't you dare laugh.

He laughed. "The only spark the expansion plan will ignite is this town's tourism."

Dang her mouth for matching him, grin for grin. She waggled her finger at him. "Who says a park will bring in more business? Or that the business owners can afford the tax increase? Or that we should fill Randall's pockets with more money? He's got plenty already."

"You tell him, Jenna," came a cheer from the other end of the counter.

Jenna smiled at Harold, who owned the general store, and didn't like Clairemont's plans any better than the majority of the locals. If she had a stack of Ben Franklins to spare, she'd buy that parcel of land behind River Creek Café and put a bullet in the stupid park expansion idea. Grant had no right getting town folks riled up.

No right getting *her* all riled up.

The corners of his mouth began curling, and the sparkle of mischief in his eyes set off alarm bells. The high-pitched, irritating kind that made her feet pedal in the opposite direction.

Grant slid his mug across the counter for a refill. "So, when are you going to move out of that wooden box you call a home? I've seen the plans. The park will bump up against your cabin's property lines, and guarantee you some unexpected visitors."

"Well, then I guess I'll have to invite them in for coffee. I love where I live. I don't intend to move, so don't start your nagging."

"Fill his cup, willya, hon?" Maggie interrupted, tilting her head toward Grant.

Jenna would fill something, all right—his lap full of scalding coffee, if he didn't stop being so flirty. She topped his cup and then worked her way down the counter, taking orders and refilling drinks. A niggling feeling tingled the hairs on her neck, and then began settling in. After delaying the inescapable as long as possible, she worked her way back to Mr. Irritation.

She tried for a take-no-prisoners glare, watching for his reaction. "Grant, you wouldn't happen to know how my Jeep's tire got repaired?"

That devilish grin reminded her of a mischievous little boy who'd gotten caught with his hand in the cookie jar, and gave her an answer she didn't like.

Yesterday, Nellie's flat tire and the two-plus mile hike back to her place created the perfect ending to an already challenging day. She left Nellie parked, keys in the ignition. With the crime in the town escalating, surely someone would steal the rusted hunk of junk. And darned if this morning, Nellie wasn't in the driveway, all pumped up like a courting blue jay, ready to go.

Irritating man.

Jenna squared her shoulders. "Thank you. It's mighty kind of you, but I wish now I hadn't said anything about Nellie's tire. I don't need a Helper Harley. I'm perfectly capable of taking care of myself, you know."

Grant touched an index finger to the left part of his chin with a double-tap. His eyes glimmered with laughter. "You've got ketchup on your chin."

She tugged a napkin from her apron pocket. He pointed. "No up, over... There, you got it."

"Why don't you have a slice of my cherry pie?" she offered, working hard to maintain an air of pleasantness. "It'd occupy those hands and stop you from fixing things that might need to stay broken."

"Jenna, when it comes to my hands, I can imagine a few more exciting activities."

Dang those butter-melting dimples. They did funny things to her innards, but she refused to allow the lawyer to leave a lasting impression.

She tossed the soiled napkin and his

comment in the trash. "Like I said, I don't like taking handouts. I'll pay you for fixing Nellie's tire."

"Not necessary—just being neighborly."

"Better watch that neighborly business, Mr. Newhall," Sheriff Joe said while pulling out his wallet. "Might land you in jail one of these days. I would think a seasoned lawyer would be keenly aware of the definition of property theft." The tall man stood and handed Jenna his check and a twenty-dollar bill. "Keep the change."

Grant winked at Jenna. "Yeah, but I had no intention of depriving the owner of her Jeep. In fact, the intent was the exact opposite."

Joe chuckled while slapping on his wide-brimmed hat before heading for the door. "Lawyers and their technicalities."

Jenna repositioned the sugar and creamer before wiping the counter. "I pay my debts, Newhall." Jenna motioned toward the pie stand. "Take a lemon meringue pie when you leave—*my* way of being neighborly."

"If you're talking paybacks, how about dinner?"

She turned her back and started counting.

When are you going to stop? She released a discouraged breath.

The guy deserved a heap of credit for his tenacity. But she wanted her simple life to remain that—*simple*. No front-page excitement, just baking, some charity work, and hiking the trails when time allowed.

"I'm busy. I'm working two jobs. So why do you keep asking?"

"There must be something you like to do besides bake."

"I like watching the needles grow on the evergreen outside my cabin. You know, that place you say is dangerous and want me to move out of." She sighed and her shoulders dropped a few millimeters. "Why don't you ask Rachelle to go? She's more your style."

She'd heard all about him being seen with Miss Rachelle Clairemont from no less than three different customers. Randall Clairemont's daughter had most of the men in town wrapped around her little finger—that included Grant. Personally, Jenna considered Rachelle to be rather thin—physically and mentally.

"My style?" He put his elbows on the

counter and playfully tossed a wadded-up napkin in her direction. "I don't think so."

Oh, that sexy grin is going to kill me.

"Then you had better talk to your mom. Sounds like she's already planning your wedding."

"Do you always listen to gossip?" Grant waved her closer and leaned in. "You have to eat. How about I take you to the Culinary Art Institute in Boulder on Saturday?"

Man. He could sure deliver a blow to a vulnerable spot. As much as she wanted to, she'd never spend big money on the hard-to-come-by tickets. She nibbled her lower lip, imagining the sculpted radishes and carrots, the savory reduction sauces, and the pureed raspberries. An image of the starched white tablecloths and weighted silverware shimmered in her mind. An intimate table for two....

She grabbed the water pitcher, hoping to douse the temptation. "I take it Rachelle's busy."

"I haven't asked her. Nor do I intend to. But the look on your face says you're interested."

Encouragement sparked in his eyes. Jenna became dimly aware customers had quieted to hear her answer. Unaccustomed to holding center stage, she turned her back to the crowd while an embarrassed heat skimmed her cheeks. Her mind scrambled to gain control.

Jenna pushed a strand of her hair behind her ear in a losing battle to keep the French braid tidy. A long, unsteady breath escaped from her lungs. "You know I don't do fancy."

"Jenna, it's just dinner."

"Fine. I'll go, as long as I'm home early. I need to get up before sunrise to get my baking finished."

"Done." He tossed a twenty on the counter. "I'll pick you up at five on Saturday. That way you have time to close shop, get home, and change."

When his delighted grin framed his perfectly white teeth, she realized too late she should never have agreed to go anywhere so intimate.

The Newhalls were bad news. There were a thousand reasons she should never get involved, but only one reason she should.

"Don't forget to take a meringue pie out of the case on your way out."

"Sure thing."

Sure thing? She didn't need to go on some deluxe, get-all-snazzy type of date.

And what in the world was she doing, agreeing to go anywhere with *him*, the cherished son of the one family she'd sworn to hate.

CHAPTER TWO

The late-night crowd in Mad Jack's pub erupted in a celebratory roar.

Grant unzipped his jacket and studied the closest large-screen television to catch the baseball score. License plates hung on the walls. The aroma of beer, the peanut shells on the floor, and the initials carved in the chairs took him back, but he spotted the passage of time. He recognized fewer faces, and the place sounded different. Louder, more chaotic.

Jack Burke, the bar's owner, lifted his chin in greeting. "Look, everyone. The dartboard champion is here." Some things hadn't changed.

Several people turned with smiles and shouts of *congratulations* and *happy to see you, man.*

Grant nodded and provided handshakes, smiles, and waves in return.

"Thanks for donating your winnings." Jack pointed over his shoulder to the playing lanes. "The townsfolk will love getting new dartboards. Ale or stout? Your choice. On me, as a way of saying thanks."

"I'll have a stout, but put it on my tab. The tournament was a lot of fun. It's been a long time since I played in a competition that fierce. We finally beat the crap out of that Loveland team."

"Because of you, we also got a few new members."

"That's great."

Grant scanned the room while Jack poured his beer. Memories of playing foosball, shooting darts, and doing his best to avoid trouble flowed through his mind with a tang as dark and rich as the stout Jack poured. Grant leaned his elbow on the antique bar and considered the clientele. "Those kids old enough to be in here?"

The bear of a bartender peered past Grant's shoulder and chuckled. "Older than you were when you joined the men's team."

"I don't feel thirty-one, but damn if kids aren't looking young these days." He shook his head.

"Wait until you get to be my age."

Grant chuckled. "Back then, I swore you had eyes in the back of your head. I never could sneak a drink."

"Still can't."

Grant smirked, then caught his buddy Erik's wave and acknowledged with a hand signal to let him know he was waiting for a beer, then looked up at the game on the large screen TV.

"Here you go." Jack placed a bubbling glass of liquid richness on the counter.

He grasped the full glass and nodded a silent thanks to Jack. As he approached the booth, Erik Sparks nudged a plate of hot wings in his direction. "If you canceled again, I was gonna drag your sorry ass out of your office. Especially since you're working for your dad."

Same ol' Sparky.

"Sorry I'm late. I was meeting with a new client. Once I take over the practice, I'll be able to manage my time better." Grant howdy-slapped Erik's shoulder, then slid into the booth.

Erik pushed a side plate and silverware in his direction. "Have a hot wing. They're not as good as yours, but they're edible."

"I don't care. I'm starved. I was too busy trying to decipher my dad's case files. I never found time to eat lunch."

"And you wonder why I choose construction and pay someone to take care of the office details." Erik gave Grant a sly grin. "Your brisket the other night was the bomb. When are you going to open a food truck or something? The guys at the site would fight over your ribs."

A zesty satisfaction gave him a zap of energy. "Beats the heck out of updating case files. If I had files that looked like my dad's, I would have been fired. It will take me weeks to get the files properly documented."

"You picked the wrong profession, buddy boy."

"Like I had a choice," Grant responded before chomping on another wing.

"I still think you should have told your old man to shove it."

Grant slumped into the brown leather, letting the buffalo sauce mix with the beer's barley. The combination left a savory aftertaste in his mouth. "Yeah, right. You're well aware of how persuasive my parents can be."

"You mean downright controlling. I remember when you wanted to go on that class field trip instead of Paris? I still can't believe your mom hauled you off the bus. We got in more fights that summer."

"At least the snide comments stopped."

Erik gazed at the big screen to watch the pitcher fire a fastball toward first. He pulled at the edge of his beer's silver label before turning to study Grant. "I still don't get it. Dude, you were out of here. Free. Why, after all these years, did you agree to come back? Last I checked, Chicago is still a top-ten place to live."

Grant lifted his hand as if to swat the question like a fly, an irritant, a question he wished would stop buzzing around in his head.

"What don't you get? When Buck and Vivian call, you jump, or end up being tortured for months until you cave." The self-loathing made the acid in his stomach churn. "Besides, city living can be exhausting. I never felt right there. I was always waiting for someone to stab me in the back, figuratively and literally." He shrugged. "Here things are more...predictable, easy."

"Like Rachelle dropping Stupid Stu as soon as you entered the city limits. That woman has plans for you, my friend."

People connected Rachelle's name with his like they were two Lego pieces. The whole town assumed they snapped together, but history proved they didn't even belong in the same plastic tub.

"Rachelle's like a deer—always looking for greener meadows." Erik tossed a wing bone onto his side plate.

Erik's odd expression made him curious. "Tell me you didn't start dating the hairdresser again."

"Sandy? Nah, she moved to Arizona."

The way Erik's eyes wouldn't meet his produced a flippant, "Dude, tell me you didn't."

"I don't want to talk about it." Erik shifted uneasily.

"Connie? Again? You're a glutton for punishment. She's nothing but drama."

Erik conveniently turned back to the baseball game seconds before Grant shot him a questioning look. Fifteen years of dancing around each other, and the two high school sweethearts still hadn't been able to make the relationship stick.

"Same ol' Sparks. I bet Connie will drag your sorry butt down the aisle before the year's end."

"Bugger off. Besides, I'm still holding out."

"We'll see how long that lasts."

"Just because you're in love with Jenna doesn't mean everybody's ready for the ball and chain."

Grant grabbed one hot wing, then another, then another...and then one more.

Erik stilled, his beer bottle frozen midair. "What the hell? I was just kidding." He dropped his arm to the table. "You've only been in town—what?—two, maybe three months?"

"Keep it down. I don't want rumors to get back to my parents."

"Dude, you sure Jenna isn't just some passing fixation?" Erik dipped a wing in a cup of blue cheese sauce. "Is this like Burcham's Corvette?"

Grant sighed as he remembered the cold November morning. "The instant the tarp was pulled back, I was in love. I'd still have her if my brother hadn't wrapped my beauty around a pole."

Erik pointed at Grant. "Then there was that redhead in third grade." He snapped his fingers in the air in quick succession, squinting as he tried to recall a name.

Memories of the freckle-faced, pigtailed bully made Grant chuckle. "Sally Haynes."

"That's it." Erik smacked his fist on the table. "You sulked for a month after her dad was transferred to Dallas."

Grant remembered the innocent thrill of his first pucker-lipped kiss. "Who knows? I might have been forced to marry her by now if she hadn't moved. She was at the top of my mom's most-eligible list." *At least Jenna isn't on my mom's damn list. That puts her at the top of mine.*

"I don't know how you do it, man."

"Do what?"

"How you fall so fast. I've been dating Connie for years and I'm still not sure."

"The second I saw Jenna, I knew she ticked all my boxes and then some. It was instinctual. Besides, there's something about her...I can't put my finger on exactly what *it is*." *She pulls on me like a bungee cord, snapping me closer...but I ain't gonna tell you that.*

Erik pulled on each finger, making the knuckles crack. "You said that about Sassy Sally."

The nickname made him pause. "Yes, I did, but I was eight."

Erik sat back, his eyes watchful. "So tell me why you want to marry *this* woman."

"She's kind, funny, non-glamorous, generous, spunky, athletic, outdoorsy, energetic, smart, independent...she just fits."

"Does she have a sister?"

A feeling of contentment washed through Grant. "Nope. Out of luck there, buddy."

"Then I'd suggest you put a ring on her finger before your mother decides to drag your sorry butt down to the courthouse with a wealthy debutante in tow." Erik popped a peanut in his mouth, tossed the shell into a half-filled bucket, and reached for another.

"I know, right?"

Erik cracked a smile. "You'd better be careful. Rumors have already started flying around town. I know you've been trying to keep your relationship quiet, but the beauty salon crowd is starting to buzz."

"That's what I've been afraid of. Wait a minute. Are you telling me you're hanging out with the blue hairs now?"

Erik's shoulders jerked while he snorted with laughter. "You should be afraid. Very afraid."

Grant's cell phone rang. He glanced at the screen and then shoved the phone across the table. The town's first beauty pageant queen filled the screen.

Erik pointed at the phone, recognizing Grant's mother. "As I was saying…you should be very afraid."

A few days, maybe less, that's all he had. He

could already imagine his parents' razor-sharp comments once they got a whiff of any girlfriend rumor. Erik was right. They'd arrange a marriage of their choice faster than he could figure a way out.

Grant leaned forward. "You wouldn't happen to be in touch with that redheaded chef?"

"You mean Ginger?" Erik tipped a beer to his mouth, taking a long pull.

"That's the one. Do you think she can score me tickets to the Culinary Art Institute in Boulder?"

Erik choked and pounded his chest, then sputtered some more. "Those tickets sell out months in advance."

"Yeah, I know. I need a pair for Saturday."

"Holy shit. Only you would ask for the impossible like it was no big deal."

Grant could almost feel the bets being placed on the table, the dice shaking in his hand while the odds simultaneously tallied. "I need those tickets, and I need your help getting them. I figure Saturday's a good day to pop the question."

"I..."

A waitress paused at the table's edge to collect Grant's empty glass. "Sparky, want anything else?"

Grant noted Erik's three-quarters empty beer bottle. "Another beer for my friend."

The young blonde nodded, made a note, then turned and left. Erik's gaze followed her retreating form to the bar.

"Hey, Erik. Tickets?"

"Gotta admit that waitress has a mighty fine figure. I bet she's got a few surprises hidden around the bends of those curves."

"If you're not careful, you'll get yourself arrested. The Judge won't appreciate you going out with his daughter."

"Doesn't she remind you of Rachelle?"

"Rachelle?" Grant followed Erik's line of sight. *Ohhh, yeah.* "Please tell me you're still not all wound up over Rachelle. Dude, you just said she reminded you of a deer and greener meadows."

"Yeah, I know, but there's something about her I can't quite shake. I felt like such an idiot when she turned me down for the prom—in the cafeteria, no less."

"I still don't see what everyone sees in the

woman, but I'll tell you what. You get me in, and I'll get you a date with Rachelle."

Erik's eyes snapped to his. "What fantasyland did you fly in from?"

"I'm not joking."

The bar erupted in cheers, and Erik pushed out of the booth, reaching for his coat at the same time.

Grant checked the sports scoreboard. "It's only the fifth inning. Where are you going?"

"To get you those tickets." Erik pulled on his coat and pointed a finger at Grant. "And don't set up one of those sissy coffee dates. I want the whole shebang."

"You get me those tickets, and I'll make it happen."

"You positive about popping the question over dinner? It's public and risky."

A risk. Yep. But he wanted to go for it. Nothing in life was a sure thing. After his brother's death, he promised himself never to wait for things to happen.

He hoped she'd say yes, because for the first time in his life, he felt full.

During their long conversations into the night, he told her things he'd never told anyone. She made him laugh. Challenged him. Made him believe he could have the future he dreamed about. She brought out his protective side. He wanted to give her things.

Be the man to stand by her side.

Be all the things a husband should be.

She loved him. He could tell. She showed him in so many ways. Remembering what he ordered. Baking his favorite treats. Listening to his dreams. Teasing him about everything.

They were such good friends. He wished he could figure out what held her back from embracing her feelings.

He had to figure out the riddle, and fast, before his parents stuck their noses where they didn't belong.

Since he returned home, every conversation with his parents circled around to marriage and the fact he was the only remaining child.

Sure, his parents had guilted him into coming home to keep the law practice afloat until his dad recovered, but what he wanted was to settle down. Find a wife. Create a family of his own. Build a life. He refused to allow his family's snobbish prejudices taint what felt so right.

On the outside, his family appeared pristine, like powdery snow, sparkling under the wintry sun. Then, one small unpredicted disturbance, and the whole hill would start to slide—a sheet of death racing down the hill crushing, burying trees, animals, and people in the slide's path.

He needed Jenna to get to know him before his mother's claws came out. Vivian was perfectly willing to use her ever-so-devious beauty queen ways to torment anyone who stood between her and what she wanted. He'd protect Jenna. No matter what.

"You get me those golden tickets and let me worry about the rest." Grant caught Erik's smirk as he turned toward the door.

A list of all of Jenna's favorites rolled through his head. Running. Baking. Making people happy. He would support her, make her feel safe, throw in a little spice, and then Jenna would come around. If she didn't, his goal of having a real family—a supportive family, a family filled with dozens of kids and dogs and cats and gerbils—would be forfeit.

CHAPTER THREE

Instead of focusing on her dream, all Jenna could think about were Grant's fabulous, forest-green eyes. *Dratted man.*

That morning, he stopped by Dreamy Delights for his favorite, her chocolate-covered bear claws. She tried again to convince him she didn't have anything to wear for a fancy date, but he hadn't believed her. He just smiled and offered to take her shopping—probably to one of those specialty boutiques in Cherry Creek, where she couldn't afford a pair of socks, much less a dress. Heck, she couldn't even afford hair ties at those prices.

She shook off the agitation and reached for

the bakery's phone, dialing by memory. "Hey, Kathy."

"This is a pleasant surprise," her foster mom's light, cheery tone made her miss the woman even more.

The tension in Jenna's neck eased. "Do you have a reliable way of gracefully backing out of a date?"

"Is this the date with Grant?"

Jenna's mouth fell open. "Have you been talking to Maggie again?"

"You rarely call. Besides, I hear he's a nice boy."

"He's more than just a boy, but that's not the point. The point is he's a Newhall."

"Ahhh. I see. But you did agree to go, right? Jenna, you can't keep avoiding conflict. You were given the tools to communicate. Ask for what you need. Use the skills the foster counselors gave you."

"Never mind. I'll figure something out." *Because theory and reality are two different things.*

"What are you afraid of?" Kathy prodded.

"I'm not afraid." Jenna snagged a stray wire twist-tie from the counter, bending it back and forth, then tying it into a knot.

"Why do you think I'd be afraid of going on a date?"

"You're calling from the bakery in the middle of the afternoon, and you tend to bake when you're trying to sort out a problem. You're hiding. Knowing you, you'll bake until you run out of every ingredient in the place."

A yucky, sour milk taste crept into her mouth, and she forced herself to swallow. "There's always some charity or club or someone who needs cookies."

"You could give them to Grant. Cookies are a great way to ease into a conversation." The hope in Kathy's voice made Jenna march in a circle around the butcher block worktable.

"He doesn't like cookies." Jenna cringed, hoping Kathy wouldn't ask how she'd gleaned that personal preference.

"He must like you. Maggie says he stops in to see you every day."

"Maybe he has a sweet tooth."

"Maybe you're making excuses. When's the last time you went out with someone?"

Jenna mentally scrolled the calendar back months, then years. "I'm too busy to date." Jenna cringed as soon as the statement was out of her mouth, because it sounded too defensive, and most likely raised Kathy's BS sign.

"Then maybe it's time you stopped working so hard. How are your sugar levels? Is your diabetes under control? Are you still running?"

"All's good, but it was a busy week...only thirty-one miles so far. And—"

The welcome bells on the door jingled. Jenna glanced toward the storefront. Ashley's round, pregnant belly preceded her into the shop.

"Kathy, I have to go. Ashley's here."

"Love you, baker girl. Call anytime."

Jenna's heart squeezed at hearing those special words, the words she could never bring herself to say aloud. "Take care, Kathy."

She tossed the phone on the counter.

Jenna faced her best friend, her annoyance expanding at the sight of what dangled from Ashley's finger—a little black dress carefully wrapped in plastic. The kind you wear on a fancy date. "Absolutely not. Turn around and take that back to your car."

Ashley ignored her and rotated in a slow

circle, her eyes expanding to absorb the bakery's transformation. "Holy lickin' toads! Look at this place. I take off for two days, and look what you've done. I wasn't convinced the artwork would look good on the burnt orange walls, but the pictures are perfect. Good choice."

A rooster painted in earthy yellows, reds, and browns drew Jenna's attention. "The artist finished the last painting yesterday." She pointed at the art groupings. "He suggested I hang the pieces high to prevent sticky fingers from ruining them."

Ashley approached the counter's glass barrier. "And look at the display. When you told me you wanted to screw candlesticks into plates, I questioned your sanity. Never again. Promise."

Jenna followed her gaze. "I'm glad Bill Masson insisted I let him help when I stopped by to purchase some screws. He must have known I didn't have a clue what I was doing. I would have made a mess and gotten frustrated in the process."

"Chase or my dad might have been able to help out." Ashley's brows creased. "I still can't get used to calling Chase my husband. Seems weird."

"Good thing I don't have that problem. I've got my hands full with this place. I wouldn't know what to do with a husband."

A slow smile lit up Ashley's face. "I bet you could figure it out."

Her insides puckered like a dried-up prune. "A girl doesn't need a ring on her finger to figure out how to do the horizontal." Jenna pointed at the cupcakes and pastries filling the cabinet. "Did you see the three-tiered stand? It's amazing what you can do with thrift shop junk."

"I'm so glad Gwen was able to talk you into opening this place."

Phew, at least the change of subject worked.

"Me too. She was right. I just need to get creative and stick to a budget. Gwen promised me she'd look for more candlesticks and plates on her weekly scouting trips to Denver. Last week she found a couple more at a secondhand store."

Ashley pointed with the hand holding a snazzy black dress on a hanger. "This place is brilliant. Fabulously brilliant."

"Nice try." Jenna waggled her finger as Ashley lifted the dress she was holding a bit higher. "I appreciate the compliments, but even though you are my best friend in the whole world, you're not getting me into that dress."

Her friend's mood abruptly sobered. She rubbed her stomach, her face losing color. Jenna held her breath while scrutinizing her friend's movements. "Are you okay, or are you just trying to win sympathy so I'll try on the dress?"

"If the guilt's working, I'll take it."

"Sit. Can I get you something?" Jenna pulled out a chair.

Ashley folded the garment bag over the chair back and dropped her purse on the table. "What I want is you in that dress. I'll wait here while you change."

"You know a fancy outfit won't help."

"It'll look beauteous. Trust me, I fit in the dress once upon a time, and it looked great," she released a heavy sigh. "I can't believe it was only a couple months ago I fit into my mom's wedding dress. Now, my big toe wouldn't fit." Ashley placed her hands around her swollen baby ball. "I wished I had figured out I was pregnant sooner. I was sure it was a stomach virus."

"Stop beating yourself up. You weren't showing—just a little weight gain—then kaboom, there you were."

"I was so busy dealing with dad coming home and Chase's rehabilitation and the wedding, I just didn't have time to think." She held up a clear plastic bag with silver earrings and a black clutch inside, before sinking her oversized, baby-swollen body into a chair. "Look, I even brought you shoes and accessories."

"Doesn't matter. I'm not going."

"You've heard of lucky jeans. Well, that's my lucky dress. Mr. Newhall will be squeezing your muffins in no time."

Jenna squirmed. "If he wants to be squeezing something, I'll send him a loaf of bread. I'm still not going on the stinkin' date."

"I'll even do your hair and makeup."

Stop! She wanted to scream. To Jenna, makeup was the hundred little boxes, tubes, and jars other women carried and stuffed in drawers. Other women. Not her. "What word in *I'm not going* didn't I enunciate?"

Ashley grabbed her large belly. "Come quick. The baby's kicking." She seized Jenna's hand and jammed it against the baby bulge. Jenna wondered if this was another ploy until the mound swelled and rippled underneath her fingers. A quick, firm press against her palm startled her, making her jerk back her hand with a sense of awe before she extended her hand to feel the moving, living, responsive infant again.

Her friend's eyes sparkled with hormonal tears. "I'm going to be a mom."

Jenna squeezed her hand. "And a wonderful one at that." She stared at the protruding belly again. "Have you and Chase picked out names?"

"If it's a boy, Aidan. If it's a girl, we're thinking Anne."

"My middle name's Anne. Please tell me you're spelling it with an *E*."

"There are a few special people with that name in my life, and of course Anne will be spelled with an *E*." For some reason Ashley's cheeks blushed red, but Jenna figured with the heightened hormones in the pregnant woman's body, it was a wonder she didn't turn purple.

Anne was a nice, simple name. Melancholy touched Jenna. She, too, became reminiscent. Her mother's name was Anne. She remembered her mom telling her the name was rooted deep in their family tree. A thrust against Jenna's hand brought her back from the past.

"I should get you some herbal tea." Jenna unfolded from her crouched position and moved to the counter area. "Maybe we should also talk about you reducing your hours so you don't have to do so much standing."

"Maybe you should hurry up and get pregnant so our little ones can play together."

"Pregnant?" Jenna paused, panic compressing her lungs. "I think you forget I'd have to find a guy I'm willing to put up with first. Besides, what would I know about raising a child?"

"I have books I can loan you."

"How do you know I can read?"

Ashley snorted a laugh. "Shut up. You're

better educated and more well-traveled than most folks around here."

The town's folks liked what she baked, but none of them were aware she'd been trained by some of the best chefs in the world, and had won prestigious awards. Only Ashley and Maggie had a small inkling of her past. The rest she worked hard to keep hidden.

The fragrance of sugar, lemon, and cinnamon wafted in the kitchen when Jenna dropped a cookie in the center of a napkin and extended her hand. "I'm running Fred through his paces."

"Fred?" Ashley tilted her head back and to the side.

Jenna pointed a thumb over her shoulder. "Fred, the old oven. I finally named him. I'm testing him, and trying out a new recipe for Labor Day. Taste this and give me your opinion."

"Labor Day?" Ashley accepted the cookie. "I can't believe it's the end of August already. Another few weeks and the baby will be here," she said before biting the edge and catching the crumbs in her hand. "Ohhhh, these are fan-freakin-tastic." She popped the crumbs into her mouth and licked her fingers.

"Keeper?"

"Definitely."

"Awesome. What about calling them... hmm...Ashley's Luscious Lemon Drops?"

Ashley perked up. "About time I got a cookie named after me. I think you've about exhausted the rest of the town. I love Maggie's Marvelous Muffins. She resem—"

Both women's heads turned when the bells on the door jingled, and a cool breeze blew in.

"Hello, girls." Rachelle Clairemont's heels clicked across the freshly washed tile floor. The socialite dropped her cell phone into her bag and held the purse at the perfect angle to display the label.

Jenna lifted her chin. "Hey, Rachelle. What brings you to this side of town?"

"Just wanting to check things out," she said, setting her designer sunglasses with the opposing, interlocking C's on top of her honey-blond hair.

Ashley rotated in her chair, her expression skeptical. "Check what, exactly?"

Jenna gripped the back of Ashley's chair,

using it as an anchor. The last thing she needed was a pregnant Ashley getting into a hair-pulling contest with Rachelle.

"A woman always needs to know where she can get things." Her contact-enhanced violet eyes skimmed with disgust over the dress hanging on the back of the chair.

Jenna's palms itched to adjust Rachelle's perfectly lovely and oh-so-apparent sneer.

"What can I do for you, Rachelle?" She managed to keep her tone bland.

Rachelle picked at the tips of her pastel pink nails. "I came to place a special order. I'm having an intimate get-together this Sunday, and stopped to order some tempting nibbles."

"By special, I suppose you'll demand something Dreamy Delights doesn't already make." Ashley supplied, with lashings of snark which made Jenna cringe.

"It's okay, Ashley. What did you have in mind, Rachelle?" Jenna didn't need to read the recipe to understand what type of trouble Rachelle was baking up.

"Rich, dark chocolate. Possibly some brownies."

"I think I can manage something." Jenna

retrieved a pen and order pad. "How many will be in your party?"

"Just two. Grant likes chocolate. I'll pick up the strawberries and whipped cream later."

Ashley grunted, drawing Rachelle's dagger-like gaze. "You couldn't get Grant's brother down the aisle, so you decided to settle for number two."

Jenna took a protective step forward, placing herself in front of Ashley. "I'll have your order ready Sunday morning around ten."

When Rachelle's gaze connected with hers, Jenna saw pain, or maybe it was regret simmering behind the contact lenses. Then she blinked, and the false gaiety slithered back into her expression. "Do yourself a favor, Jenna, and purchase a dress that doesn't look like it was found on a salvage rack at some discount store. The Newhalls have standards."

"So nice of you to offer fashion advice, Rachelle." Ashley bristled.

"I'm always helpful. Besides, I wouldn't want Grant to ruin his family's reputation by socializing with...well, you know."

Ashley pushed her five-four body out of

the chair belly first. "No, I don't know. Please explain."

Rachelle lifted a toothpick-thin wrist, displaying her diamond-faced watch. "Oh, my. Look at the time. I'm running late for my tennis lesson. Can't stay to chat, girls."

With a perfect pirouette, Ms. Clairemont whirled toward the door. Jenna focused her energy on not caring about Rachelle, but it didn't work.

"You okay?" Ashley's voice sliced through the fog of anger clouding Jenna's mind.

"I'm fine." Jenna swept past Ashley. The mental YouTube video of Rachelle's weekend plans with Grant still played in her mind, whether she wanted it to or not. Jenna began transferring lemon cookies into a tin to busy her hands and mind. "What was that about Grant's brother?" she asked, loathing the fact she was even curious.

"You don't know? I thought everyone knew."

Hurtful feelings surfaced before Jenna could smack them back. "Obviously, I'm not everyone."

"Don't take it that way." Ashley shuffled

back to her chair. "Grant's brother, Jason, always liked making headline news. However, this one wasn't so appealing." Her eyes glittered with humor. "It was all supposed to be hush-hush, but supposedly Jason took some woman up to the family condo in Vail for a ski getaway. While he was there, he played chicken with a tree and lost...guess who his fiancée was at the time?"

"No way."

"Yep. Jason and Rachelle were supposed to get married in less than a month. The invitations had been sent, the cake ordered, everything."

Jenna reflected on Rachelle's reactions. "That must have hurt."

"She got what she deserved."

"Don't say that. No one deserves that kind of pain."

Ashley opened her mouth, her cheeks turning pink, then paused before proceeding. "You're right. My comment was unkind, and uncalled for. She's just so irritating sometimes." Ashley rubbed a hand in a circular pattern over her belly. "It's weird how Jason and Grant are so different. I never could understand what Rachelle saw in the jerk. He treated her like a trophy, only taking her out when he wanted something sparkly on his arm."

"A trophy? She is so...so perfect." Jenna concurred. "Perfect makeup. Perfect wardrobe. Sometimes I don't think the wind blows when she's around. It would mess up her perfect hair."

"Perfect is what you will be in that dress. So...are you going or not?"

"I can't very well back out now, can I? The fashion expert will have it all over town I chickened out. I don't have a platinum card or belong to an elegant country club, but I'm no piece of poultry."

"True statement. Now, how are you going to wear your hair?"

"Not going there. You need to get out of here and rest. And if I'm going to get Maggie's pies baked, I'd better get started."

"All right, Ms. Workaholic. I'll see you tomorrow."

Ashley grabbed her purse and waved her fingers over her shoulder while waddling to the front door. The bells tinkled a few times before settling, and then the silence closed in. Claustrophobia spun a web around her, squeezing tighter and tighter, to the point Jenna wanted to scream—until she realized she was standing in the middle of her store. Her dream. A place where she could start a pseudo-permanent family. A place she could finally call home.

From around her neck, she lifted her cherished metal medallion and rubbed the engraved surface. The mental image of her sister on a swing set, her feet pumping toward the sky, her butter-blond hair trailing in the breeze, brought her comfort.

She extended her arm to pick up the accessory bag. Jenna studied the little black rhinestone clutch. "I guess now I'll have to shave my legs."

CHAPTER FOUR

"I forbid you to see that, that...that girl." Vivian Newhall's lips scrunched together in a scowl of haughty distaste. She paced the length of a formal living room adorned with generations of family portraits and handcrafted furnishings.

"You would think," Grant unfolded from the burgundy leather couch to stand and force his practiced legal mask into place, "after all these years, I would be able to choose my friends, or whom I date."

"Son, be reasonable." Buck Newhall chimed in from his favorite high-back chair. "A girl like that doesn't belong in a family like ours.

Think of her. She wouldn't be comfortable with our style of living."

"A girl like that?" Grant rubbed the coins in his pocket together, grinding the edges against each other, over and over again. "I suppose you think Rachelle, or some other woman who strategically matches your ideal would be better suited, but I don't. Forced marriages are illegal in this country, or have you forgotten that fact?"

"You're making a huge mistake." His father rubbed his chest, but the act to gain sympathy wouldn't work, not this time. "Your mother would be heartbroken."

As if I care. "Mother will adjust if she wants grandchildren. After all, as you both keep reminding me, I'm the only one left."

"I will not have the likes of that woman in my home." His mother's contempt iced the room.

"I assumed as much. That's why I've decided to move into grandpa's cabin next week."

"Don't be ridiculous." Vivian grabbed the back of the wingback chair. "Buck, say something. Tell your son he will never be granted partnership in your firm if he keeps pursuing this insanity."

Grant's breath hitched. He'd counted on receiving his promised equity share.

The room started to spin, but he fought for control. The disappointment etched on his father's face was not there solely to manipulate. The disappointment had developed over the years, because Grant had never met his parent's expectations. His father remained silent.

"Let me know what you decide. If you want me to move today, or stop working on the case files, I'll be fine with your decision."

Grant locked down the anxiety squeezing the air from his lungs. He grabbed his coat jacket and lengthened his strides.

Jenna. He released a decisive breath. *I need you.*

For the past hour, his mother's venomous pronouncements had choked him to the point where he could hardly breathe.

Practice and discipline kept him from slamming the front door. In seconds, he was shifting into fourth gear and accelerating down his parent's long drive. Seconds ticked by as every word, every emotion, every threat replayed in his mind.

An ominous cloud of dust billowed out behind his silver sports sedan.

She has to marry me, now, before I drown.

Rocks bulleted up from under the tires, and in a few minutes his car skidded sideways and rounded the corner into Jenna's drive. Ten seconds later, he hit the brakes and slid to a stop in front of her log cabin. Pushing the car door open, he gasped for air, fighting the poison of his parents' hour-long lecture.

Maybe I shouldn't do this. Shouldn't get Jenna involved.

If he was smart, he'd get back in the car and leave. If he was smart, he wouldn't be standing on her porch, knocking on the door. If he had any intelligence at all, he'd offer Jenna an apology and get the heck out of there. Yet he needed to see her. She didn't make demands of him, or apply guilt. She made him laugh, and allowed him to be real—unlike his parents.

A breath later the door opened a foot. Jenna squeezed her body into the narrow space. "Didn't you get my message?"

He stood, transfixed, his gaze ensnared by her gorgeous face. Then he blinked and his observations drifted lower to her form-fitting T-shirt and faded jeans. "Guess not," he said, dejection wrapping around each word. Her gaze locked onto his hand. He pushed the bundle of red roses into her midsection, prompting her to accept them. "For you."

The tick-tock of time sounded like a base drum thrumming in his ears.

"You don't look so good. Are you feeling all right?" she asked, while her eye color darkened with concern.

"Honestly, I could use a stiff drink."

"I don't have any alcohol, sorry." After an eternity of seconds, without a word, she pushed the door open and stepped back with an invitation. "Thank you for the flowers, but you shouldn't have. We're keeping things simple, remember?"

"Yep, I remember." He allowed his heart to celebrate a mini-victory but braced for another battle. He hadn't let his parents change his mind. Jenna wouldn't either. She didn't know it yet, but he could outdo her stubborn any day of the week. He wanted time, time for her to get to know him—know the guy, not the man with the last name Newhall. Then she wouldn't pull away.

The misperceptions he would eliminate.

She removed a rusted coffee can from a narrow shelf above the stove and filled it with water. Her hands shook while settling the flowers. He realized her nerves were as rattled as his.

A cool breeze brought with it the fragrance of cedar, drawing his attention. The open window behind the potbellied stove, which was sandwiched between a small table and a couch, allowed a breath of scented air into the cozy room. A double bed and oak dresser filled the room to the right, with a kitchenette to the left. The intimate space offered no extras, no television, no little boxes or pictures most women collected and set out everywhere. But the simplicity didn't make the cabin any less comfortable. Nothing, not one thing, struck him as out of place—except for the black dress hanging from the top of the bathroom door, still wrapped in a plastic dry cleaning bag.

Determined to change her mind, he needed

to gather facts, lots of facts, because everyone knows the lawyer with the most facts wins.

"What about dinner?" He asked maintaining a neutral, unassuming tone.

"Grant, I—"

"If you don't want to go, we can stay here and...talk."

Her face paled to the color of his cream shirt when he took a step toward her bed.

"Let's not do this today. Maybe some other time," she said, but her statement had a thread of indecision woven through.

"Why not? I'm here. You're here. We have the evening free."

"Yes, but—"

"It'll be fun. I haven't spent an evening hanging out since my sister and I..." He stopped to avoid unearthing painful memories.

"You never talk about your family. What about your sister?" Her voice practically vibrated, under tight restraint. Her eyes latched onto his mouth, waiting for a response.

Her intense reaction reminded him of a deeply troubled client, waiting, wanting him to promise them everything would work out fine. He took a step closer to assess her interest. "I felt sorry for her. When my parents wouldn't let Caitlyn go out, we'd hang, listen to music, watch a little TV, sometimes read. She used to recite her poems and tell me about her day."

Jenna's arms folded across her stomach. "You hung out...with your sister?" she asked, with such disbelief she could have been wearing a pin saying "you're full of crap" attached to her T-shirt.

"Yes. I did. Caitlyn was my..."

"Your...a...your what?" The tone of her voice and brows both arched up at the same time, with a not-so-subtle hint of accusation that he didn't like.

"One of my best friends, actually," he said with enough conviction to shut down her suspicions.

"Friend. Good. That's really good." She walked toward the counter creating distance. "Brothers and sisters should be friends."

"You remind me of her."

She twirled around so fast she almost dropped the sponge she picked up only moments before. "How so?" she asked, studying his face, every feature, one at a time, before turning back to clean an already-spotless counter.

"You both are smart, have a good sense of humor. And for some reason you both have this underlying sadness." Afraid he'd revealed too much, he looked away to study the edges of the design on the small area rug. "Then again, what do I know?"

"Maybe you have a point. If I remind you of Caitlyn, that would be like dating your sister and that's sort of gross. And because you brought me those nice flowers, you apparently consider this a date. Maybe we should skip dinner—just be friends."

Somehow the way she said *friends* didn't work for him. Not at all. He needed to turn the conversation around, and quickly, to get her headed toward the bathroom to change. His empty stomach rumbled, giving him an idea. He loosened his tie, before taking off his jacket.

She scanned the wool coat he tossed over the back of the kitchen chair. "What are you doing?" she asked.

"While you remind me of my sister, you also have quite a few additional traits I'm rather attracted to. Your love of food for one, and the fact you just plain won't accept my help." *Your luscious lips, and the way you blush when you're embarrassed.* "I want to know everything about Jenna Dolcy." He stretched out on her bed, plumped the pillows, and folded his hands behind his head. "Why don't we call the café and get Maggie to deliver a dinner for two? It's nice outside. We can have a picnic. Hang out."

Her lips thinned. "That's not a good idea."

Donning his best Bradley Cooper imitation, he tilted his head. "Okay. We can skip dinner if you like."

"If this is about sex—"

He swung his legs over the edge of the bed, and rolled to a sitting position. "It's about spending time together, but I'd hoped for dinner. I'm starving."

"I've always wanted to experience dinner at the Institute, but...it's not..." She lifted her hand to her mouth to nibble on her already-short nails. He allowed the seconds to tick past in silence. One thing he understood about

Jenna—beyond anything else—she lived by her rigid rules. He'd have to learn to be patient until she decided to change her requirements. "It's not what you think," she finally responded.

"A beautiful baker, a fabulous waitress, and a mind reader. Quite the resume."

"Funny." She scrunched her nose, as if smelling something sour.

"I was serious, Jenna. You are beautiful."

She lifted his jacket, searching one pocket, then another.

Grant braced his elbows on his knees. "What are you looking for?"

"There must be a pair of glasses in here somewhere, because you obviously can't see very well right now. I'm not beautiful."

"You are beau—"

"Did you know I worked on a cruise ship as a baker?" She laid his jacket over the chair. "The guys—the other chefs—they liked to play practical jokes to get a reaction. I thought...I don't know...." She pulled at the end of her French braid twisting it around and around on her index finger. "Why couldn't you find another date? Why me?"

"Did it ever occur to you that I value good food and wanted to dine with someone who appreciates quality as much as I do? Jenna, you're not a consolation prize. If you had told me you couldn't go, I wouldn't have gone to the trouble of getting tickets."

Her eyes brightened like the sun coming out from behind the cloud. "Wait, you said you already had tickets."

"I said the Institute had their monthly student dinner. I said nothing about having tickets."

"Sweet fudge." Her laughter expanded and bounced off the wooden beams. "You're serious."

"Considering how many favors I had to call in and IOUs I had to sign, yes, I'm serious. Can you at least pretend you want to go?"

Her gaiety sobered. "I've always wanted to go. In fact, that reminds me, I need to pay for my ticket. How much was it?"

Not telling because you couldn't afford it. "Always? You always wanted to go?" The unconvinced grin spreading across his face couldn't be helped.

She observed the disbelief for a smidgen of

a second, before deciding the stain on her T-shirt was more interesting. "Okay. You're right. Maybe I didn't want to go at first. The timing isn't the best."

"Perfect timing is never perfect." He waited, but got no reaction. "You don't have to worry about the ticket. Especially since we aren't going," he said, sensing a change of subject was in order. "Are you still excited about your bakery?"

Finally. There was the 100-watt flicker of joy he loved to see.

"Excited? I'm thrilled one minute, then petrified the next." She flung her hands in the air, then let them fall again, only to lift her hands again in a flurry of movement. "I already have a wedding order. Can you believe it? I thought I'd have a few months before people approached me for specialty items."

"Who's getting married?"

"Out-of-towners getting married at the Elkridge Lodge."

He didn't care who was getting hitched. He wanted to see the hands-in-the air, non-stop, chattering, infectious Jenna. The confident

Jenna. The Jenna who'd captured his interest and refused to let go.

He wanted her. She didn't need him. That was a good and bad proposition. He reveled in the fact she didn't cling, or text him every two seconds, but once a day would have been nice. At least then he would know she was thinking about him.

She twisted the hem of her T-shirt around her finger until it knotted into a ball and then she began to pace.

"I found a magazine article with a frosting chart. Using just four colors, you can make over forty different hues. I want to see if the chart is any good. I was thinking...." Her pacing feet paused suddenly, and the words spilling out of her mouth died like a whistle running out of air. She leaned over and picked fluff off his jacket.

"Why did you stop?" he encouraged.

"You don't want to hear about the bakery. Maybe you could tell me a little more about your family. You never talk about them."

"I'd rather hear about the bakery."

"I'd rather hear about your family."

"I'll make you a deal." He pointed at the

LYZ KELLEY

bathroom door. "Go in there and put your dress on so we can leave for dinner, and I'll tell you anything you want to know."

Jenna hesitated, as if weighing the options. "Anything?"

"Anything," he said, before she could change her mind.

She glared at him, and then the borrowed dress, before taking a few steps and lifting the hanger off the door. "Why don't you start by telling me more about your sister? Caitlyn... isn't it?" she said, walking into the bathroom, leaving the door cracked open so they could continue the conversation.

There was no way she could know how much talking about his family would hurt—their sudden disappearance from his life—however, he was more than willing to pay the price to get her to dinner.

"Don't you want to hear about my outrageous and fun brother, Jason...how wonderful he was, how he was perfect in every way, how he could do no wrong?" Grant swallowed the strangling sarcasm creeping in, and cloaked with the black resentment he'd never been able to shake off.

"You didn't get along?" Her tone held no judgment, only curiosity, which helped ease the tension.

He adjusted his position on the bed to horizontal and settled in to wait. "We tolerated each other in order to give a good impression."

A movement made his mind pause. Just beyond the door, a sliver of bare, shapely ankles led to a hint of lime green cotton covering the gentle curve of her ass. When the T-shirt lifted up off her peach skin to reveal the rest of her sweet body, he could only stare at the tiny bit of Jenna he could see through the door. The craving to touch, smell, and sample every inch became agonizing. His hand gripped the comforter into a tight ball to hold himself anchored to the bed.

"What about Caitlyn?" she asked while a curtain of black fabric cascaded over her slender frame.

"Caitlyn? Oh…my sister."

Grant forced his gaze to the ceiling and shifted on the bed to ease the thundering visions and sensations the sight of Jenna's tantalizing skin triggered.

He pinched the bridge of his nose to

concentrate. "I was about ten when my parents brought Caitlyn home. She resembled a little porcelain doll with blond hair and blue eyes— a duplicate of my mother at the same age. Looking back, I can only assume when my mother couldn't have more children, she adopted a girl to mold into the picture-perfect socialite."

A loud crash came from the bathroom. Grant bolted up to a seated position. "You okay?"

"Fine. Everything's fine." Her compressed voice sounded panicked. "Just dropped something. Go on."

He noted the wobble in her words. "You sure you're okay?"

"I'm good. Just dandy. How did Caitlyn take to being groomed?"

Grant pressed his thumb into the palm of his opposite hand to ease his building headache. "She did okay, I guess. At first, she struggled, but after a while she got used to the rules. My parents are demanding and very controlling. They call it influencing, but it's more than that. I had to put almost a decade and a thousand miles between my parents and me before I could find the balls to stand up to them. Some people shouldn't be parents."

Grant gritted his teeth. The steel he'd emotionally implanted in his spine had been tested and bent over the past several months. A spark of pent-up frustration returned, but evaporated when Jenna opened the bathroom door.

The contrast between the woman who went into the bathroom and the woman standing in front of him forged a how-did-I-miss-that awareness. Though he'd always found her attractive, and she met all the criteria on his list, he had a keen sense that he hadn't seen her fully until this moment.

The black silk against her flushed skin did something astounding, something that heightened the contradiction between the pony-tailed, fun-loving baker and this high-heeled, take-me-seriously woman who robbed him of breath. A mass of soft curls hugged her shoulders, and made him want to bury his hands in the thick mass, letting the strands sift between his fingers. When she stepped closer, a light floral smell wafted through the air, reminding him of the botanical gardens he often visited in San Francisco while on business. She emerged fresh as a lily, and more alluring than he could have envisioned.

"You look stunning," he managed.

"Thank you." From the top of the dresser, she retrieved a black clutch and turned back. "Do you think Caitlyn was happy?"

Her trembling fingers and tense shoulders provided insight into her nervous questions. "Happy?" he again pinched the meaty part of his hand. "I...ah...I guess. I wish I'd been there for her. It's my fault she left."

Jenna paused, a loop earring halfway through her ear.

He replayed what he'd said, and realized how careless he'd been, and what conclusion she might have drawn. "I'm sure you've heard my sister disappeared several years ago. But if you're thinking I had anything to do with Caitlyn's disappearance, I didn't."

"You just said it was your fault she left."

He winced. "I meant if I'd taken the time to listen to her, maybe she wouldn't have left."

"What happened? Was she upset?" Jenna's voice sounded uneven and shaky.

He released a slow exhale, thinking back

over every significant and insignificant memory or action, trying once more to put pieces together that never fit. "Honestly, I don't know. We were as close as two siblings with a five-year age difference can be. Then I went to college, and we drifted apart."

"I get that, but I don't see how her leaving was your fault."

Grant nodded, letting the slice of blame sink deeper into his skin—a bleeding regret that had hounded his actions for years.

"My parents had planned a ski trip for us and three other families. I flew in that afternoon. Caitlyn had come home from college several days prior. When she picked me up at the airport, I could tell something was wrong, but she wouldn't talk to me. When we stopped at the house to get my skis, Caitlyn said we needed to wait for her best friend."

He measured and weighed his words before continuing. "The day before, I finished work on a huge case and was exhausted, and wanted to get going. She insisted we wait. I was tired, and the argument got ugly. We said some nasty things to each other—stuff brothers and sisters say, but usually forgive each other for later." His fingers dug into the bed. "She told me to go. I only left after she said her girlfriend was on the way. We were staying in different condos, so I had no idea she hadn't arrived until she didn't show up the next morning for breakfast."

All the details about the search—the police investigation, the news reports—the entire nightmare came pouring out. He couldn't stop the flood of words. The guilt shredded his skin, his heart.

He hated his parents for wanting to keep the disappearance private. The not knowing ate at him, gnawing away day after day—an open, unhealed wound.

"Was there a boyfriend involved?" Jenna asked tentatively.

"She was dating James Hunt—one of my mother's choice picks. The Hunt family came from oil money. My mother somehow managed to weasel her way into Charlotte Hunt's inner circle. Apparently, James got to the lodge several hours after I did, and although police couldn't prove he had contact with Caitlyn that night, he had no alibi. Although James was outed for having several other girlfriends, plus a Meth habit neither set of parents was aware of." He wrapped a hand around his neck to massage the aching tension.

"Did James appear upset over Caitlyn's disappearance?"

"Relieved is a more accurate description. Neither he nor Caitlyn was all that thrilled with the match. Like I said, Caitlyn was being groomed for bigger and better things—so was James—which is why the parents considered the match remarkable."

"What happened to her?" Her anguish forced him to meet her gaze.

"I wish I had a clue." Frustration frayed the edges of his thoughts. "I'm sorry, I don't mean to get so..."

"Emotional?" Jenna dropped her hands to her side. "You loved her. I can hear it in your voice."

The statement pointed out a truth he couldn't deny.

"She might have been adopted, but in all the ways that counted, she was my sister." He released a long, steady breath. "She used to write these poems and send them to me at school. Most of them were funny, but there was this one about Monarch butterflies. It was raw and touching." Sorrow added weight to his already burdened shoulders. "I never got a chance to ask her what that poem meant, and assumed it was about her being tired and wanting to rest...but who knows? She was good at using words to hide her true meaning —a puzzle, in a way. There was this one poem about the sun, but if you interpreted the words correctly, the story was actually about the moon. It was cleverly done."

Jenna lowered into a kitchen chair and stared straight ahead. "Someday I would like to read her poems, if you're willing to share them."

Her serious, concerned expression touched him deeply. Her willingness to let him drone on about his sister moved him. "Caitlyn had such kind heart, a vulnerability that made everyone around her want to protect her." Yet he'd failed Caitlyn. And that failure still haunted him, and probably would for the rest of his life.

The silence between them thickened.

Jenna's contemplative gaze turned his way. "Did she leave any clue?"

"No. Nothing. It's almost like her disappearance wasn't planned."

His demanding stomach grumbled, filling the room. Her mouth curled. He followed the drift of the mood and laughed, releasing the emotional tension. The room suddenly felt warmed.

She stood. "If we're gonna go, we'd better go now. It's past time for me to eat."

"It would be a waste of some hard-earned tickets." He stood and walked toward her.

"Yes." She moved back and bumped into the counter. "A waste."

CHAPTER FIVE

Approaching the hostess stand at the world-renowned culinary school, Jenna unclenched her hands to allow blood to flow to her fingers.

Grant paused to give the attractive, twentysomething hostess his last name and tickets before resting a hand on the small of Jenna's back. The heat from his palm centered her awareness on a six-inch section of her spine that hummed with energy, and robbed her of rational thought. The fact that this man had finally allowed her past his hard, external shell both excited and terrified her at the same time.

A high-pitched squeal jerked her back and expanded her awareness.

"Grant?" A brunette surged forward, flinging herself into his arms before he had enough time to do more than turn.

He rocked back, absorbing the impact as his arms circled around the woman. A rush of unexpected jealousy unbalanced Jenna, and that warm spot on her back competed with the new arctic blast cooling her senses.

The flying dynamo swayed back, rubbing a thumb against Grant's cheek to remove the lip-smack red imprint she'd left there. "When did you get back?"

The woman's energy, flawless skin, and half-clad form drew attention, which obviously was her intention. Even Jenna stared. Admittedly, she was more concerned about Grant's hands and how they fit so snugly around the brunette's needle-thin waist, than the woman's chic hairstyle. But she couldn't help noticing how their noses almost touched. Even in her three-inch heels, Jenna barely reached Grant's chin.

A few feet away, the brunette's bored companion's attention turned her way. The man's indifference morphed into curiosity while his gaze swept over her. He made it obvious he liked what he saw.

Grant leaned back. "Tiffany, what are you doing here? Why aren't you on a Caribbean shoot, or traveling across Paris, or on some runway?"

"If I had any inkling I'd run into you, maybe I'd come home more often."

Grant managed to unlock his stare from the beauty and extended his hand toward the man. "You're her manager...Tim, isn't it?"

"It's Troy, and as of six months ago, I'm also her husband."

Tiffany giggled and slid her arm around Troy. "We're the bomb. Get it? Tiffany and Troy. Like TNT." Her eyes sparkled with mischief. "And who's your little friend?"

Tiffany's gaze slid over Jenna like she was a pair of worn shoes in a donation box.

Grant turned to Jenna, finally remembering she existed. "This is Jenna. Jenna Dolcy."

"Jenna. Nice to meet you." Tiffany screeched like an owl preparing to attack its prey.

Suddenly, Jenna's vision began to narrow, the edges going gray, as a shaky feeling ran from her chest down to her fingers and back again. *Oh, no. Not now.* Her body swayed with the all-too-familiar diabetic signs. She needed food—and now. She slid her fingers into the borrowed purse for a glucose tablet to curb the sugar low. The desire to turn her back on the socialite snobs and leave was no longer an option. Jenna reached for something to steady her and found Grant's muscular forearm.

Tiffany coiled a finger around her hair extensions. "Let's eat together. Troy, honey, see if you can get a table for four so we can catch up. Wouldn't that be fun?"

"Actually," Grant placed a hand over Jenna's, "We can't join you. Jenna and I are here to discuss her business."

"Grant, you naughty boy. Isn't taking your clients to dinner against some law?"

Client? I'm not a client. Like Grant had no choice in being with me? The way Tiffany summed her up and brushed her off as a nobody stung.

The hostess stepped forward. "Mr. Newhall, your table is ready."

Troy's gaze swept over the petite hostess and discarded her with one practiced sweep. The impression he liked to possess, use, and destroy came across so clearly, the idea even registered in Jenna's sugar-depleted mind. If the model wasn't careful, she might be the next casualty.

Grant stepped back, allowing Jenna to move past. "Perhaps another time. Tiffany, Troy, nice to see you again."

Jenna slipped another tablet into her mouth and followed the perky hostess. *Come on, glucose. Kick in.*

Accepting his deep burgundy napkin, Grant took the seat to her left before releasing his jacket button and repositioning his silk tie. Oblivious to her physical condition, and the hostess's overzealous personal appreciation, he accepted his menu.

With the sugar tablets finally doing their thing, Jenna observed how casual he seemed in the elegant surroundings, a level of comfort she could never achieve. He examined the set menu, analyzing the options as if his worldly fortune depended on selecting the right dish.

"How do you know Tiffany?" Jenna asked,

expecting a blush and an ex-girlfriend confession.

"Our parents belong to the Colorado Mile-High League. It's an exclusive group of business owners who started this mastermind group back in the 80s. You can't apply to join. It's by invitation only, and it's made up of the biggest group of snobs I've ever met. Tiffany's not so bad."

I wonder what you consider a snob, then.

"I met her and her older brother at one of the Christmas parties before she took off to Europe." Lowering the leather binder, he asked, "Have you made a selection?"

Not about to tell him she wasn't able to read the menu because she couldn't fully comprehend the words yet, she offered a simple, "I can't decide."

"The duck tatin appetizer and the rack of lamb look good."

She blinked, while her sugar-depleted brain struggled to decipher the tiny script. "I think I'll order the...the a..."

"I bet the butternut squash soup and halibut selection is fabulous."

"Then that's what I'll have."

"The unoaked Chardonnay might be the best wine pairing."

"Says the foodie," she managed a puff of a laugh that sounded as fake as Tiffany's eyelashes.

"What can I say? I like to reverse engineer fabulous meals and pair them with fine wines. That's how I came up with my barbeque sauce recipe. You would have laughed. My first attempt was pretty bad."

"Your sauce is awesome now," she nodded. "I still think you should package some and sell it, or ask Claudia if she would help. She likes filling the grocery store with local stuff." His devastatingly handsome smile likely melted the butter on the table, making her sigh. "Would you order for me, please? I need to visit the restroom."

Before he could respond, she retreated toward the reception area.

If she didn't need to eat, she would have disappeared out the front door. *A business client? Nice of you to imply to the whole world I have legal problems, Newhall. A friend...a cousin... anything would have been better than a client.*

She pushed the bathroom door open and

discovered a dimly lit seating area with leather chairs far nicer than most Elkridge folks could afford. She sank into the first chair she came to, laying the borrowed clutch in her lap, skimming her cold, shaky fingers over her forehead to wipe away the perspiration.

You can do this. Don't rush.

Spreading open the kit and placing it across her lap, she removed an alcohol packet and tore the edge.

"Do you always carry a personal stash?" Tiffany purred from the doorway.

Jenna's hand jerked, and the sterile pad hit the floor. *Crap.* She reached for another alcohol swab from the case, repeated the process, and then disinfected her middle fingertip. "It's not what you think."

Tiffany rubbed her nose and stared intently at the syringe in the kit on Jenna's lap. "That's what they all say."

The bouncy, bright-eyed, cover model Jenna glimpsed in the lobby had transformed into a she-cat ready to pounce. Tiffany licked her lips with a nervous twitch, but continued hovering by the towel rack.

Jenna raised her glucose meter to check the

readout. Not bad. At least the tabs had done their job.

She shifted slightly to address Tiffany. "I'm a diabetic. My drug keeps me alive. It looks like you take yours to get numb." She uncapped a syringe and jabbed the point into the insulin bottle.

"To get numb, be thin, stay awake, fall asleep, you name it." Tiffany's mouth flattened, probably because she realized she'd said too much.

Holding up the bottle to the light, Jenna drew the proper dose. "I don't get it."

"Get what?"

"You're beautiful and intelligent—and don't deny it, I can tell you've got smarts. You can be anything you want. Yet you choose to laugh away your brains and talent. Why?" Jenna lifted her dress hem and plunged the tiny needle into her upper thigh.

"What do you know about my life?"

"Good point." Jenna's impression that Tiffany threw herself at other men because she wanted her husband's attention, or the attention a father never provided, solidified easily. Tiffany craved to be the center of everything, but she couldn't stand to be herself around other people. And, Jenna was willing to bet, Tiffany used drugs because she didn't like who she was.

Jenna slid her logbook and syringe back into place. "You're right. I know nothing about your life. What I do know is life is hard, it sucks some days, and the only thing each of us can do is try our best. I bet one day I'll be picking up groceries and see you on one of those fashion magazine covers, that is if you decide to take care of yourself."

Tiffany pushed away from the wall and moved to the sink. The model aggressively scrubbed her fingers with suds, whether to wash away the words or something else, Jenna couldn't tell.

Tiffany smoothed her eyebrows, rolled her lips back and forth, and plumped up her breasts before her half-lidded eyes connected with Jenna's reflection. "Where did you find Grant, anyway?"

"I didn't. He found me."

"You're not his client, are you?"

Jenna placed the insulin kit in Ashley's loaner bag and stood. "Why do you ask?"

"Because the way he looks at you. Protects you."

Looks at me? What's with you people? You all need your eyes checked.

Jenna shrugged and shook her head. "I'm the flavor of the month. Grant will move on when something new catches his interest."

Tiffany rolled lip gloss over her full lips before looking at her again. "Nope. Wrong brother—that was Jason. He was the one who liked a new girl on his arm every week. But your opinion of Grant tells me you don't know him very well." Tiffany turned and leaned back against the counter. "As long as I've known him, Grant never dated, or at least not casually. Believe me, I tried to get his attention. Back then, sports and career were his only loves." Tiffany placed a hand on the door handle, then paused before pulling open the door. "I'd better get back before Troy collects all the waitresses' phone numbers."

"Tiffany?"

The glamorous model turned slightly, swaying on her four-inch heels as she peered over her shoulder. "Yeah?"

"I meant what I said. You're stunning *and*

smart. You have that special something that draws people to you. I honestly believe you deserve better. You don't have to settle."

Tiffany's expression clouded, then cleared. "You know, when I saw you with Grant, I really didn't want to like you."

The model disappeared through the doorway faster than the words could register.

JENNA APPROACHED the table just as Grant set his wine glass down.

"Is everything okay?" He asked, unable to wipe away the concern with his napkin.

"Fine. Why?"

"I saw Tiffany leave the restroom. She had a strange look on her face."

Jenna noted the questioning lift of his brow. "Yes, she was there, but it's not what you think."

"Ahh. I forgot. You're a mind reader. Okay then, tell me, what am I thinking?"

She folded her arms in front of her on the

table and tilted her head to the side. "Something about two women clawing and hissing at each other."

His mischievous sentiment turned serious. He caught her wrist, turning her hand over. "You have blood on your arm."

She pulled back, but he wouldn't let go. She looked him in the eye. "It's not Tiffany's."

Her expression, the way her body moved, her direct, soft eye contact, made him believe she told the truth. Searching for lies was a natural side-effect of being a lawyer. He released her hand.

"It's from testing my blood. My sugar's low."

He leaned in without hesitation, "Why didn't you say something? Are you okay?" he asked softly, his gaze tender and searching.

Diabetes. She hated *that* word, hated feeling like a freak. The fuss. The inconvenience of it all. She rubbed at the smear with the edge of the napkin. "Please don't make a big deal out of this."

His fingers caressed the callused surfaces of her fingertips, smoothing over the trail of tiny holes, slowly moving down to her open palm, and making calming circles against her skin.

The waiter approached the table with a basket of warm bread, saving her from foolishly cooing over his lavish touch.

The assortment of breads and rolls—rosemary, garlic, cracked wheat, sourdough, and rye—looked amazing, and was enough to distract her from the tingly warmth his touch created on her skin. Counting to three, Jenna waited for Grant to select his preference before she ripped open a hot, yeasty ball, feeling the steam snake across her skin, lifting it to her nose to inhale the buttery scent. Yummy. She pulled off a piece and folded it into her mouth, closing her eyes as the taste slid across her tongue. The urge to slather the bread with butter consumed her, but she resisted, tempering her hunger.

"Amazing," Grant said, holding a knife in his closed fist.

"What is?"

"Watching you enjoy the roll."

Heat touched her cheeks. She shrugged. "Hazard of the job, I guess." She gave into temptation and slathered the butter on the second half, even though she shouldn't be eating the carb-filled roll. But she would allow this night to be an exception.

"Can I ask you a question?" she asked and waited. He nodded, since he was busy chewing. "Don't get me wrong. I appreciate this, but still…I'm not like you, or Tiffany, or Troy, I don't fit—"

"You fit fine," he said, cutting her off, yet working to get the words out around a mouthful of bread.

"In my borrowed dress and shoes." A pfft puffed out on a breathy scoff. "I'm a jeans and clogs kind of gal." She gestured, indicating the table settings. "There's more silverware on this table than in my entire kitchen." She set the knife on the edge of the plate. "Why can't you see it?"

"That's all upholstery fabric." He waved his hand, dismissing her concern.

She dropped her chin and stared at him. "Upholstery fabric?"

"Yep. Every few years my mom reupholsters the antique chairs in our living room. But whether she changes the color from red to gray or black, it doesn't make a bit of difference, because the chairs are still bloody uncomfortable." Grant wiped the corner of his mouth. "Jenna, you're comfortable. I like that. I like that you're kind, fun, and smart. I don't care what you wear, what job you have, or whether your plates match. I want to be with *you*."

"You do? Huh, that's odd." Jenna nudged her bread plate an inch toward the middle of the table. "If you want to be with me, then why did you introduce me as your client? Like the only reason you'd be with a woman like me is for business reasons."

"My client? I never...Ohhhh." Awareness crossed his face with a firecracker pop.

"Never mind."

"No, not 'never mind.' I turned down Tiffany's offer so we could have a pleasant, private dinner together. If you would prefer, we can go over there now and spend the evening listening to all things Tiffany. Your choice."

"I...ummm..."

Waiters approached the table, conveniently saving her from having to respond. The two appetizers were served simultaneously, in a coordinated, almost theatrical production of elegant gestures and pristine napkins. She stared lovingly at her soup bowl filled with a golden broth, a swirl of cream and some roasted pumpkin seeds. She slid her spoon into the generously-sized bowl and lifted the steaming liquid to her mouth. The smell of nutmeg enhanced the blend of butter and squash. She closed her eyes, relishing the swirl of flavors on her tongue.

"I guess you don't like the soup much." Grant chucked, his voice rich with affectionate sarcasm while pointing at her bowl with his fork.

"You have to try this." She dipped her spoon to offer him a taste. Halfway to his mouth, she wanted to withdraw the offer, but Grant's mouth closed around the silver. When his eyes also closed to savor the taste, her mouth dropped open and she fought the urge to lick her lips. Ecstasy transformed his face.

"Man, that's good. Here, try the duck."

A second and a half later, a fork hovered in front of her mouth. She accepted the gift and found joy in the sensations rolling across her tongue. While studying the texture, the flavor, the warmth…each building response made her think of Grant's warm lips around her spoon. The image made swallowing rather difficult.

"That's so yummy. The sound you heard… that was an angelic choir belting out the *Hallelujah Chorus.*"

"Hallelujah. I've finally met someone who loves food as much as I do."

The thrill and unsolicited praise made her uncomfortable to the point where she couldn't hold his gaze. While his approval stimulated her sense of belonging, she refused to be fooled into a false sense of well-being.

"Is that chocolate I taste?" She rubbed her garnish between her fingers to release the scent of thyme. The herbal fragrance soothed her muscles and senses.

"Well done. The description said the duck contains a hint of cocoa, but I didn't pick up the flavor."

She rested her spoon on the serving plate while the servers presented dinner.

"Strange," she took another pinch of bread to clear her palate. "I understand you're a big fan of chocolate."

"Not really. Only sometimes." He offered

her a bit of lamb, but pulled back when her mouth twitched.

Her shaking shoulders must have given her away, because Grant set his fork back on his plate. He brought his napkin to his lips, slowly wiping his mouth. "Let me guess. The rumor mill has been buzzing about me."

"A rumor? More like someone taking poetic license."

His hand bunched into a knuckle-cracking fist. "First and final guess —Rachelle."

"Rachelle," she confirmed.

"Let's get one thing settled—there is nothing between me and Rachelle. Never has been, never will be." His annoyed glance sent her a chilling warning. "And don't believe anything you read in the papers, either."

"What's that supposed to mean?"

"Just that my parents posted my brother's engagement announcement before he popped the question, effectively forcing him into a corner. My parents are manipulators, and like to control everything they can touch. I want to be clear. There is nothing—I repeat nothing— between me and Rachelle."

"You might want to tell Rachelle that, because she made her plans clear."

"Plans?" Grant placed a forearm on the table and concentrated on remaining calm. "What type of plans?"

Under Grant's cross-examination stare, she shuffled her feet under the table. She pushed on her thigh with the palm of her hand, to keep her leg from vibrating, because she absolutely refused to let him intimidate her.

"Rachelle stopped by the bakery for some 'nibbles.' It seems you'll be busy tomorrow."

"That's interesting. My mother told me to keep the afternoon open. I assumed she was inviting me to discuss family matters." His jaw muscles pulsed. "Apparently, I have a sudden need to become extremely busy. What are you doing tomorrow?"

"Baking nibbles."

"Ah. I guess I'll have to catch a cold, then." Grant pounded his chest and rubbed his throat in jest.

A giddy sensation tap-danced its way up her arms, and the airy excitement remained. Maybe it was the glass of wine, but throughout the dinner courses, his sense of humor captivated her, tempering the professional, serious side of his character. While she listened and watched, a collage of images emerged, mixing the ingredients of his life.

He leaned back, allowing the waiter to remove his dessert plate. "I'm stuffed."

"You should be. You hogged the dessert."

"You said you only wanted a bite."

"When do men listen to what women want?"

"When a woman is clear and concise, and doesn't change her mind a dozen times a minute."

His puckered frown made her laugh. "Typical man," she teased. "It's always the woman's fault." She placed her napkin on the table with a playful grin. "We could do this Mars, Venus thing all night, but I need to get up at four to bake for the café."

He rolled his wrist, checking the time on his expensive gold watch. His eyes widened. "I didn't realize it was so late."

He'd somehow failed to notice most tables in the restaurant now sat empty. He raised his hand to call the waiter. She expected a check or their coats, but a small tray of chocolates suddenly appeared with a black box sitting in the middle of the delicate swirls of raspberry puree.

A sliver of dread ran up her arm, as her eyes met Grants.

"What this?"

"I know we've only know each other for a few months, yet every day is more special than the one before. We connect. I've fallen in love with you. I want to marry you. Spend the rest of my life learning every facet of Jenna Dolcy."

The beating of her heart and the screams in her head drowned out all sound. Why had she let her relationship with Grant go so far? It was her heart's fault. Every dang time he came around, her heart sighed with possibilities— possibilities that couldn't thrive.

"Grant—"

"Say yes."

"Grant, I—"

"At least think about it. I want to marry you, Jenna. I won't change my mind."

"You don't understand."

"Then tell me."

"It's not you. It's just that I've never wanted to get married."

"Why not? You would make a great wife and mother."

"That's the thing. I wouldn't. As a diabetic, I shouldn't have kids, because it's too risky. And there are other reasons."

"Those are?"

Grant leaned in and touched her hand. The warmth did nothing to ease the turmoil burning hot and causing all sorts of friction. She fought to think. "Social status—for one. Lifestyle —for another. You name it."

Please don't push.

"We can work through all of those things. Jenna, I've fallen in love with you."

Oh, no.

"Please say yes. I want to make this work. I want to make you happy."

Double crap. "Grant—"

"Give me one good reason why we can't be together."

"You want a good reason?"

"Yeah, I do."

Fear and resentment and compassion coiled into her soul. She couldn't let Grant believe she was a good person. She had lied.

Lied to everyone. Well, to everyone who mattered.

"Because I'm…because I'm Caitlyn's true sister. I came to Elkridge to find her."

The illusion of who he believed she was faded from his eyes. Replaced with a hurt so pure, so piercing, she did the only thing she could think of…she ran.

CHAPTER SIX

For all of ten seconds, Grant sat dumbstruck.

Caitlyn's sister?

Wow. Didn't see that coming.

Without waiting a second more, he tossed a couple of twenties on the table, grabbed the little black box, and breathed in a renewed sense of determination.

Her excuse didn't work. Not for him. He wanted to know more. He searched the empty parking lot.

No movement.

Nothing.

Damn it. He clicked his fob to open and start his car.

The moonlit night offered at least some help. He backed out of the parking space and pointed his car west. In the headlights, a figure cloaked by the night flung her arms wide seconds before the unforgiving ground greeted her up close and personal. He pulled up behind Jenna, retrieved the first aid kit from the glove compartment, and was out of the car and running toward her in a heart-pounding second.

She rolled to a sitting position and raised her hand against the intense beam of the headlights bouncing off the dust particles hovering near the ground. Propping her elbows on her knee, she dropped her head onto the palms of her hands.

"Were you planning to run all the way home?"

Jenna poked at the scrape on her knee. "I was thinking about it but I don't seem to have the appropriate shoes."

He tilted his head back toward the sky. "It's a lovely night. Maybe we can sit and look at the stars for a while. The moon is full."

"Newhall, why can't you be normal? Why aren't you mad? You should be mad. I would be mad."

"Why? Because you left out some personal details about your life? No, I'm not mad. Disappointed, maybe. I was telling the truth when I said I love you, Jenna. I meant it. What type of man would I be if I let something like this get in the way?"

"You're a good man, Grant."

"But?"

"No. No, buts. It's a fact. Too good of man, in fact. I wish you would believe me when I tell you I'm not marriage material."

"Let me decide."

She shook her head before pulling a white packet from her purse.

"Here, let me help." He knelt down and opened the emergency kit.

"I wish you would stop being so nice. I feel guilty when you're nice."

He pushed her hand aside to help. "I wasn't always nice. I grew up in a privileged home, with a first-rate education, knowing that my grandparents left me a trust fund which would make my life easy. At school, I was arrogant. Proud."

"What changed?"

"I got a wake-up call. My senior year, several buddies were skipping school, and asked if I wanted to go boating. I wanted to go. I would have gone, but I had a test the next morning, and my parents were riding me about my grades. The next morning all four of my friends were dead. They were driving too fast for the conditions and rammed into a brakeaway wall. That could have been me."

"How old were you?"

"Seventeen. I knew then that I had to change my life." He handed her a bandage. "Let's get you patched up so I can get you home safely."

"Grant..."

"Shhh." She smelled delicious—a combination of coffee and toffee cheesecake—and the urge to taste became so intense her lips mesmerized him. He noted the tiny scar on the corner of her left brow, and wondered why he never noticed it before. All sense of urgency to get her to safety evaporated as his lips met hers in the most mind-erasing kiss.

When she finally pulled back, his hands slid down her arms, reaching for her hands. "That kiss was amazing, yet somehow I feel I should apologize for it."

What am I doing? Trying to convince her I'm the right guy, that's what.

She touched her lips with her fingertips, while he waited for his circuits to come back online. He'd never experienced a kiss. Not like that. He wanted to have another go, but decided to take it slow. He'd scare her, and it was the last thing he wanted.

"I...um..." She licked her lips. "Wow."

"Yeah, me too." *Screw it.*

He dove in again. A long, slow burn spread through his body like liquefied sugar. She slid her hands inside his wool suit jacket. He pulled her closer, deepening the sensations. A low groan escaped him before he circled an arm around her waist. His thumb rubbed against her pulse line on her neck with the perfect amount of pressure.

For a single moment, the fact that his last name was Newhall, that she objected to his social status, that she was his sister's sister, and that she'd probably kick him to the curb come morning, didn't matter. For once, he wanted to be selfish, and revel in the sensation of being appreciated by a female who didn't give a damn about the balance in his bank account. Blood pounded in his ears. He accepted what Jenna had to give. She leaned into the warmth of his jacket. He let the sounds of the night fade around him. When his tongue reached for hers, her lips parted, allowing him in, opening to him. Their breaths mingled and evoked a longing so strong that his body rebelled when she held him away.

Her eyes opened slowly, almost sleepily. He relished the tingling sensation her lips had left behind. A vision of an early morning forest, with dew on the flowers, birds calling to their mates, came to mind. She opened her eyes fully. He remembered eventually to draw in a sustaining breath. Her hands drifted lower down his shirt and splayed to feel the rapid rise and fall of his chest.

"I liked that even better the second time." Jenna's voice, frothed with feeling, elicited a superhero sensation.

"Let's get you home. You have a busy day tomorrow."

"Grant, I meant what I said about not making a good partner for anyone."

"Let's get you in the car. We can talk about it on the way home."

Time and facts. That's all he needed. If he could convince even the most skeptical jury to change their minds, he could convince Jenna to marry him. After that kiss, he was sure of it.

He opened the car door for her and tucked her skirt inside. "Before I forget to tell you again, you look stunning tonight."

"I warned you about needing glasses. Why are you so nice?"

"If you prefer me to be an asshole, I can do that. I have the knowhow, but I'd rather not."

"I never want you to be something you're not."

He shut the door and made his way to the driver's side to slide behind the wheel. "You're the first person I've met who thinks that way. Everyone else expects me to be perfect. And you wonder why I fell in love with you."

"Grant..."

He waited for a car to pass and then pulled into traffic. "There's no pressure. My parents are always pressuring me into doing things. I won't tell you how I feel if it makes you uncomfortable. Instead, I'll show you. You being Caitlyn's sister makes so much sense. She had this haunting fear that people she loved would disappear. She remembered you, and wondered what happened. What did happen?"

Jenna tugged at her seatbelt strap and let it snap back into place, then started playing with the hem of her dress. "Nothing, actually. After your parents adopted Caitlyn, I got stuck in an overcrowded children's home. No one wanted the hassle of a socially awkward kid or the expense of a juvenile diabetic. As the months went by all my friends found forever homes. I was left behind. It was about that time I decided to stop making friends."

"It must have been lonely for you." He reached for her hand, and released a breath he'd been holding when she didn't pull away.

"By then, I'd convinced myself I didn't need anyone. When Kathy took me in, I was extremely lacking in the social skills department. I didn't fit in, and I was okay with that."

"Honestly? I don't know of anyone who doesn't want to fit in, at least a little."

"I couldn't even if I wanted to. I stuck out like a pink M&M. The only thing I owned was a pillow, a wooden treasure box my mother gave me, and a handmade quilt some lady gave me. I came with two sets of clothes: one too big, the other too small. Every pair of jeans or shoes I wore belonged to the children's home."

"Kathy, she's the woman you talk with on the phone sometimes."

"When have you heard me talking to Kathy?" Her brows stitched together. "It doesn't matter. Yes. She's my foster mom. The first person in my life who saw beyond my anger. I was lucky to finally get a family. The Dolcy family lived in the center of the community, but I never did make friends. I hated being odd, different, always an outsider. When Kathy asked if I wanted to take her last name, I gladly accepted the offer. The change was supposed to make me like everyone else. But it didn't."

Grant squeezed her fingers to capture her attention. "You have a lot of friends in this town. Maggie would be lost without you."

"I do like it here. For the first time, I've found a place that feels like home. This community is becoming more and more like family. That's why whatever this is between us —it can't happen. I might be a lot of things, but I'm not naïve. The social class you live in will never accept me. Look at Tiffany and her reaction. I'd be a misfit toy that no one wants. I might be the buzz today, but tomorrow I could be a squashed bug under some vindictive woman's three-inch spiked heel. I have no desire to be more than I am. I certainly don't want to be a target for social bullying."

His brows locked together. "Has something happened?"

"No, but it will. I've spent my whole life knowing when to keep my head down."

Grant turned off the highway and headed for Elkridge. "I don't want you to take this wrong, but I don't think you'll ever see how special you are. You don't have it in your character. You don't dwell on where you live, or what car you drive, or the clothes you wear, but focus on being a real person. You're special in the best kind of way. You're lucky."

"Lucky?" Her cheeks puffed out with a skeptical smirk.

"Yes, lucky. When people look, they see you...and only you. Not a name to live up to, or dollar signs."

"You're right. I like my life. No one has any expectations, and that suits me."

Score. A small victory for him.

She pulled her hand from under his and crossed her arms before looking at the mountain ridge ahead. "You'd better go hiking or something early tomorrow, or you'll get caught in Rachelle's trap."

"Why do you do that?"

"Do what?"

"Change subjects when you're uncomfortable."

She considered his too-accurate observation. "Because I'm tired, and after the events of the night, I *am* uncomfortable. I appreciate that you aren't mad, but I can't marry you. I have nothing left over to give anyone right now. I'm trying to open a business, running on fumes, and—"

"That's just it. I don't want you to feel like you have to give anything. All I'm asking is for you to let me in, let me help, let me support you once in a while. Marry me, Jenna. We can figure out the rest later."

"I told you before I'm not good at accepting help."

"I've noticed." Disappointment tromped in and left some serious boot marks on his soul.

She drew her shoeless feet up to the edge of the seat and wrapped her arms around her shins. "Ever since I can remember, I've worked hard. My foster mom told us kids it was better to have capable hands than a pretty face, because there were people in the world who take advantage of pretty girls. From the day I entered Kathy's house, I learned to cook and clean—to stand on my own. She opened a savings account in my name, and I learned to work hard, save money, and dream big. She taught me to be independent and careful, since I would have to live in this world with very little support."

"You're not alone. And, that's another thing, why won't you believe me when I say you're pretty?"

She pulled at the seat belt to loosen the strap. "From what I've seen in magazines,

Chicago is full of gorgeous women. Maybe you worked too hard, or didn't take the time to look around."

"I looked, all right. I'm a guy. But there's only so much silicone and Botox a guy can stand. I'll take a real woman in a T-shirt, her hair in a ponytail, and ketchup on her chin any day." He leaned in and reached for her hand again. "Why do I make you so uneasy?"

"You don't know me."

I now know you're Caitlyn's sister. "I'd like to."

"Can we please change the subject?"

"Here we go again." *Why didn't I see the resemblance before? She has the same nose, the same freckles, the same chin.* "Caitlyn used to talk about you sometimes. She said you took care of her."

"I promised her I would, but I didn't keep my promise. I let her be taken and molded into something she didn't want to be."

Oh shit. Molded into a doll. My stupid and careless words. He gripped the steering wheel tighter as regret circulated. "Jenna, Caitlyn got a first-rate education, designer clothes, piano lessons, a room filled with white lace. She didn't want for anything."

"Except she wasn't loved. Not unconditionally. From what you are saying, she was forced to associate with people she didn't like. Our parents loved us. Even though we were different. They loved us as we were, and gave us choices."

"You remember your parents?"

"I was seven when they died in a car accident. I was watching Caitlyn while they ran an errand." Jenna rubbed the top of her thumbnail like she was trying to rub off the pink polish. "I heard them talking the night before. They were racing to pick up a bike for my Christmas present, because they thought that I still believed in Santa Claus." She rubbed and rubbed some more. "One of the policeman at our house said they slid on a patch of ice and hit a pole." He placed a hand on top of hers. "For the longest time, I believed it was my fault. I didn't want a bike. I wanted my parents."

He was undone by the ache in her voice. He wanted to absorb it, relieve her of the pain, but he couldn't. He'd learned that lesson with the passing of his friends, Jason, and others. Each person had to somehow find their way through the grief process, or let it shrivel the soul.

That's what she'd done.

A part of her had died with her parents, and again when Caitlyn was taken from her. She'd ratcheted her heart closed with a four-inch bolt, locking out all possibilities. She didn't know it yet, but he intended to do everything in his power to break open that lock.

"I know how you feel. Losing my friends, then my brother, I realized how precious life is."

"But you don't know." Her grinding tone caused him to shift towards her. "Losing friends and a brother is one thing, but imagine one minute living in a house full of familiar things, a dad, a mother, a sister, and the next living in a large room with rows of cots, and a single suitcase containing the only things left of that life. Top that off with an inconsolable sister, because the nuns, in their infinite wisdom, decided to take away her beloved stuffed teddy bear. No one understands."

He accelerated up her drive, parked in front of her cabin, and cut the engine. When she reached for the door, he touched her arm. "Wait."

She eased back into the seat without looking at him.

"You're right. I can't possibly understand." He closed his eyes, pondering what he could say that might make her hear what he so desperately wanted her to understand. "Maybe I failed Caitlyn. Maybe I should have protected her from James Hunt. I tried protecting her to the best of my abilities. She was my sister, and we became close friends. If Caitlyn were here, I would hope she'd tell you I did my best. I see *you*, Jenna, but I can't understand what makes you sad, happy, feel safe, unless you help me to understand."

Jenna pulled her purse closer, using it as a shield.

"Please, hear me out." Determination and stubbornness came to a raging boil. "Being Caitlyn's sister. Being diabetic. Not being able to have children. All of those things, I'm good with. Give me a chance to prove it to you."

"Don't you get that I'm trying to protect you from me? You're funny, and kind, and the poster boy for any woman."

"Any woman…just not you, is that it?"

"You can have a big life, Grant. You can do anything you want. All I want to do is bake, and possibly put a smile on some people's faces."

"Why can't you do that with me by your side? You'll need help soon anyway."

The nuance of his statement made her head twist in his direction.

Shit. Why did I say anything?

"What you are talking about?"

"It's unofficial, but you'll find out soon enough." Grant played with his key fob, and prayed he hadn't just stuck a foot in it. "Clairemont's secretary told our paralegal that Randall's making Maggie an offer to buy her River Creek property so he can combine the parcel with the rest of the land. He wants to expand the park's footprint."

"That's ridiculous. Maybe those middle-aged gossips don't have their facts straight. Maggie would never sell this land or the café."

"Apparently, Maggie's receptive. I think she needs the cash."

Jenna opened the car door, and launched from the car. After a step, she turned back and leaned in. "Are you certain they were talking about this property? The one where my cabin sits? Not the empty lot next door?"

"The offer is for the whole thing, land, cabin, café. All of it." He got out and rested his forearms on the car's roof. "Clairemont wants free access to the creek. He's willing to offer a hefty sum of money to get it."

"And you support this?" her voice bubbled with heat and rose to a crackling stage.

"I'm not the enemy here, Jenna."

"No you're not, and I'm grateful you told me."

A lump lodged in his throat. He was well aware of her store loan. There was no way she could afford to move. She walked to work most days as it was.

She propped her hands on her hips. "Maybe this is all a rumor, or some vicious lie someone made up."

"Not likely. From what Peggy Sue told me, Clairemont's drawn up some plans. Besides, why would someone lie about this?"

"Ha. Politicians lie. Cops lie. Everyone lies. People even lie to themselves if it suits them."

"I wouldn't lie to you. I've checked. The offer

to purchase the land isn't a rumor. Look on the bright side. You don't have a garbage disposal, no phone, no central heating—maybe moving wouldn't be such a bad idea. Winter's coming."

He didn't blame her for the skeptical look on her face. At least she knew now, so she could talk to Maggie before it was too late.

She shrugged, holding on to indifference. "At least I have hot water."

"Great." He moved around the hood of the car to her side. "That's really great."

She pointed at the front door. "I had better go take care of this knee properly."

"I don't suppose you would accept my help."

A slow need grew, and he slid her arms around his waist and pulled her closer, but she pushed him back.

"Grant, I—"

"Don't tell me you don't feel something. You'd be lying to yourself. And to me." He needed to change the big, bold determination lodged in every angle of her face. "I've made up my mind, Jenna Dolcy. Do us a favor. Give me time. Give us a chance."

"I can't. All I can offer is friendship. If that's not something you can live with, I can just be your friendly neighborhood baker."

Grant shoved his hands in his pockets. "Okay."

"Does that mean you're okay with being friends?"

"Friends? Yeah. Sure." He rocked back on his heels, and then leaned in. "Sooner or later, Jenna, you'll figure it out."

"Figure what out?"

"That you can't get rid of me that easily." Grant moved toward the driver side door. "Someday I hope you'll realize we both want to create a home here—support this community. But a word of caution. Learn from my brother's mistakes. Don't keep pushing away those people who only want to help. Because one day they might stop offering." He yanked the door open. "Not everyone in your life will leave you, Jenna, and I'll prove it to you."

The slamming of the car door reverberated up his arm as he started the car.

He didn't look back, because if he did, he

might turn the car around. He pushed on the accelerator.

"Friends. She wanted to be *just* friends."

One way or another, he'd get a ring on her finger.

Because failure wasn't an option.

CHAPTER SEVEN

"Fff-fudgy-frosted-fruity-funnel-cakes, that hurt." Jenna cursed and licked her finger. "Another paper cut. I didn't know folding coupons was dangerous. I hate to ask again, but why are we doing this?" She sucked on her fingertip and glared at Maggie and Gwen, who were quietly folding Labor Day fliers.

"Because you had a brilliant idea." Maggie gave her a don't-test-me glare. "The kids will love bringing their moms in for a free cookie. And what mom isn't going to buy a cookie for her kid? This will give all the businesses a nice boost."

"I'm hoping to move some inventory." Gwen placed a flier on her teetering stack of paper. "I hope the thirty percent off coupon will get people shopping."

"I'll be by, for sure." Maggie gave Gwen a smile and winked at Jenna. "And, you, young lady, did such a nice job getting your bakery open. You should be proud, and want to show it off. I love the cozy feeling. The openness, the case display, and the art will tempt people to come back. You just need to be discovered."

"Thanks." Jenna inspected her finger a bit closer. "For a while there, I wasn't sure the opening would happen with the inspections and clearing the list of findings. By some miracle, it came together." Jenna straightened her pile of folded paper. "I'm planning to bake nine dozen giveaways. Do you think that's enough?"

"Nine sounds like a lot." Maggie handed her another stack of paper to fold. "Six should be enough, and if you run out, so be it."

Six sounded more reasonable, especially since she was officially running on fumes—and most likely the reason Maggie and Gwen had stepped in to help. Ashley had agreed to reduce her hours at her doctor's request, even though she still had stopped by twice during the week.

"I think you're right. I can always throw in another couple dozen if needed. Plus, the smell of warm cookies always makes people stop in."

Maggie put a rubber band around her stack of fliers and set them in the box. "Are you gonna sit there and suck on your finger all day, or get back to work?" Maggie grabbed Gwen's stack to rubber band. "The cut's your fault, anyway. If you and Gwen weren't so gung-ho to see who could get the most done in the shortest amount of time, then you wouldn't be cutting your fingers."

"Me? Competitive? Noooo. Where did you get *that* idea?" Jenna giggled.

Maggie's exaggerated eye roll made her laugh until the thought of all her to-do's and extra baking bogged her down. Mondays were slow days reserved for catch-up and deliveries, not flier-folding. Where was her dang deliveryman, anyway?

Gwen nudged her shoulder. "Maybe Grant will kiss your finger and make it better."

Jenna rocked sideways from the friendly nudge. The motion reminded her of how Grant's kisses had rocked her senseless. Somehow, after their ten-mile run, he talked her into letting him cook her dinner, which led to talking, and eventually other things. "That's the third time you've mentioned Grant today. Are you having mental hiccups, or what?"

"I feel sorry for him," Maggie interrupted, without bothering to look up.

"And now you're starting." Jenna paused mid-fold, her brows creasing with questions. "Why would you feel sorry for Grant? He's got everything he needs and more."

"Hon, you know having money doesn't equate to happiness. Grant and his sister came in often enough for ice cream, hot fudge, and whipped cream. The poor kids." Maggie's observations drifted and her hands dropped to the table, "Every time those two showed up, I suspected trouble at home. Grant's always been the protective type. He treated his sister kindly, even though he was mostly grown by the time little Caitlyn came along."

Interesting. Jenna muscles tightened. She didn't dare look at Maggie. She should have told the woman a long time ago about looking for her sister, but Maggie never asked, and Jenna never found a reason to pry open her history book. Grant had promised not to say anything. She trusted him at least that far.

Gwen snapped her head to the left. "Holy craps, Mags. Are you trying to freak Jenna out or something?"

"I'll admit, Grant and Caitlyn are the exceptions. The rest of them Newhalls, I'd leave in the trash heap."

"Careful, Maggie, someone might think you're being witty." Jenna teased. Maggie's fierce loyalty and protectiveness gave Jenna an endearing sense of peace. Grant, however, made her feel a profound sadness. If he wasn't so perfect. "To be honest, I'm not worried. Grant will figure out soon enough that we don't belong together and move on." Jenna hoped the conviction in her voice would sway even the biggest skeptic.

Bam. Maggie slapped the table. "Baste me

up and carve me stupid, then, because it sure looks like that man's stuck, and stuck good."

But it won't last. Everyone I've ever loved has disappeared from my life.

Jenna rolled her shoulder to release the tension, then inhaled enough courage to ask the question she'd been too afraid to ask till now, especially since the opportunity had presented itself.

"Grant told me his sister had a boyfriend— a James Hunt. Do you know anything about him?" She kept her tone light and semi-interested.

Maggie placed another stack of flyers in the box. "That idiot strutted around this town like an elk in rutting season. Sure, he came from a wealthy family, went to the best schools, played sports, but Caitlyn saw right through his act. Smart girl. Rumor has it Harold witnessed an argument between the pair a couple days before she disappeared."

"Did anybody tell the deputies?"

"The sheriff's department investigated. I was certain he'd be arrested, but no warrants were issued."

"Arrested? You think he had something to do with the disappearance?"

"Something or someone made her run." Maggie's gentle gaze turned her way. "You remind me of her, Jenna. You're both kind and caring women. Both of you stand against the wind, but I'm convinced neither of you were prepared for the tornado-force blast of the Newhalls."

"I can't help it if Grant keeps coming around."

"Same as you can't stop the elk from mating every fall. That man's in love, and there isn't much you can do about it."

In love? The sound of those words made her squirm.

Gwen's muffled laughter tripled her uneasy factor. "Always the double-doubter."

"It's called being careful."

Maggie scoffed. "Hon, if you were any more careful about allowing people in your life, you'd have all your clothes made of bubble wrap. You need to take chances. Believe. Trust a little. Have some faith. Live a little. Grant Newhall is a good man, who simply happens to have an inconvenient last name."

Dozens of little voices in Jenna's head started talking at once, every one telling her not to listen. Jenna mentally swatted at the noise and kept folding paper. "My plate's full, and he's already enough of a distraction."

"There's always room for love if you're willing to compromise. You just need to give it a try." Maggie said without looking up.

Jenna ran her finger down the edge of the paper, creating a crisp crease. "I feel like my life's a five-tiered cake that's already tilting. Adding one more layer will cause the whole thing to collapse."

"Sugar girl, a relationship doesn't have to be a burden. Sometimes it's nice to have someone to depend on, someone to lend a hand, add a little stability where needed. Don't you get lonely?"

Lonely? Every day. "Wasn't it you who said it's better to be alone than with the wrong person?" Jenna asked, doing her best to avoid Maggie's penetrating gaze.

She wanted to avoid talking about trust, loneliness, or love. Especially love. Everyone she'd ever told she loved them had died or disappeared. No. She didn't want to love anybody. It hurt too much.

"Are we done?" Jenna leaned back, looking for more paper stacks, and didn't find any. "How about I call to check the ETA of my delivery, and then we can celebrate with some lunch?

"I'll have to skip lunch." Maggie's voice held a basketful of disappointment. "I promised Ted I'd review the new specials menu with him today." Maggie picked up the box with all the fliers and set it on the table. "Why don't you call Grant? Ask him to join you ladies for lunch."

"When're you gonna quit?" Jenna gave Maggie a narrow-eyed back-off stare.

"When you have some sense knocked into you. He's got some baggage, but it's not often a man like that comes along. He's a good catch." Maggie retorted.

Jenna laughed. "You make him sound like a piece of fish."

"Well..." Gwen shifted. "He's definitely a prime piece of mea—"

"Gwen Keebler!" Maggie's head snapped in

Gwen's direction. "I didn't expect that from you."

The friendly banter faded into the background while Jenna's mind whirled—a photobook of childhood memories—then Grant, her bakery, and various other fragments collided and overwhelmed. She needed to find a way out from under the pile. Even if she admitted Maggie and Gwen were right, she had no idea what to do with Grant. He couldn't love her. Heck he'd only been in town a few months.

"If you two want to stop by for an early discount day, feel free," Gwen said pulling down the sleeves of her shirt.

Jenna blinked back to the present. "Now all I have to do is figure out how to get rid of a thousand of these things." She stood and folded the tops of the box closed. "Gwen, would you be willing to help me load the fliers into Nellie? I want to drop some fliers off at the B and B and the Elkridge Lodge, to see if they are willing to help distribute them to their guests. I made up a goodie box to sweeten the deal."

"Be glad to." Gwen threw her purse over her shoulder.

Jenna scribbled her prepaid cell phone number on a post-it note for the delivery guy to call when he arrived. "Where do you want to eat lunch?"

"How about Mexican?" Gwen lifted a stack of boxes. "I'm in the mood for a good chile relleno."

"Sounds awesome. I've been craving Mountain Mex." Jenna's stomach rumbled with anticipation. "Maggie, you sure you can't come with us?"

"I've got to check on the café." Maggie slipped her feet into her sandals and stood. "You two have fun."

Gwen let the front door close behind Maggie before turning to smack Jenna on the arm with the back of her hand. "Did you hear Erik Sparks went on a date with Rachelle Clairemont?"

"When will you stop listening to gossip?" Jenna picked up a box of baked goods and her purse. Gwen lifted the other before moving toward the bakery's back exit. "Half of it isn't true."

"Yes, but half of it is."

"Rachelle wouldn't date..." Jenna stopped outside the metal door.

The remainder of her sentence fading away as her gaze centered on the handsome guy leaning up against Nellie. Grant looked casually delectable in his jeans and flip-flops. The way his casual, button-up shirt framed his shoulders, then fell untucked, gave him just enough of a spontaneous look to make her innards all gooey and mushy.

"Newhall. What are you doing? You fix Nellie's tire, and now you think you can get all cozy with her?"

He crossed his arms and leaned back against the bumper. "Why? You jealous?"

Dang it if her cheeks didn't flush with a sensual heat—not embarrassment. "No. I'm not jealous of Nellie, but I think there are other women in this town you could be rubbing up against."

"Are you volunteering?" He moved in closer, so close his breath warmed her face.

Gwen provided a fake cough as the boxes disappeared from her arms. "I'll store these and be on my way."

Jenna ripped her gaze from Grant's "Gwen...I a—"

"Don't mind me." Gwen took several steps toward the Jeep. "Just keep doing what you're doing."

Heat crept up to Jenna's scalp and made her ears buzz. Suddenly she remembered the post-it in her hand. "I need to put this note on the door, and then Gwen and I are going to lunch."

Gwen peered around the back of the Jeep. "Are you insane?" Her face turned serious, and she shook her head. "If I had a man with a body like that," she pointed at Grant moving her index finger up and down, "I wouldn't hesitate to tell you to find another lunch date. Scratch that, I wouldn't be talking at all."

"Wait. Don't go, I'm—"

"I'm leaving." Her friend closed the back hatch and disappeared around the corner.

"Gwen, wait." A familiar rumble made Jenna turn. "Dang it." The roar of the delivery truck making its way down the alley emphasized her exhaustion. "Perfect timing. Just what I needed." Her frustration over the late arrival whistled out like a boiling teapot.

The truck brakes squealed as it came to a stop.

"Sorry I'm late. Did my dispatcher get ahold of you?" The driver asked while swinging out of the cab. Jenna's shoulders slumped in defeat while she calculated the hours it would take to check the order.

Jenna pulled out her phone to look for missed messages. "Nope."

The driver mumbled some colorful words under his breath. "We have a new dispatcher. Not only did she double-schedule me, but she mixed up the paperwork so I had to reload the truck, and apparently she doesn't know how to use the phone."

She turned to Grant. "I guess lunch will have to wait."

"What if I help?" he offered, with a heavy layer of apprehension, most likely expecting to be turned down.

Don't keep pushing away those people who only want to help. His words invaded her mind again for the hundredth time.

"Sure," fell out of her mouth before her brain fully engaged, because that darn sexy smile of his kept making her mouth say things she didn't mean.

"Come on, then," he nudged her shoulder and winked. "Give me instructions before I make you mad by taking over."

"I have everything labeled in the storage room. I'll inventory if you'll stack."

Without a word, he rolled up his sleeves and followed her into the storage area.

"The town newspaper should do an article on Dreamy Delight." He pointed at the wire shelving filled with ingredients, with corresponding recipe substitutes if supplies were low. "You run a tight shop. Other businesses could learn from you."

"This is nothing compared to the cruise ships I worked on. Every bag of flour and sugar was measured against what was produced, eaten and tossed. I was trained by some of the best."

"You have flour on your face." Grant brushed the back of his knuckle down her cheek and leaned in, his lips descending, and his arm wrapping around her waist, pulling her closer. Her mind went silent.

He tempted her in every possible way.

The driver's approaching footsteps made him take a step back.

"Remind me to kiss you later."

Yeah, like I really need to remind you of anything.

"Thanks for pitching in."

"No problem. For a minute there, I wasn't sure you would let me help."

For a minute there, I wasn't going to.

Oh, how she wanted this sexy man.

CHAPTER EIGHT

"Those bags of flour were heavy. I'm glad you let me help." Grant brushed a hand down his jeans to dust the remains of the white powder off his pants, and scooped up Jenna's car keys when she dropped them loading the back of Nellie with a box crammed full of paperwork.

"You know I'm not good at asking for help."

True, but there were so many things he liked about her. The way she supported the community. The way she made special gifts for people. The way her suntan lines peeked out from underneath her tank top, her petite toes painted with blue polish...essentially the whole package made him yearn to touch—to feel—to sweep her into his arms and breathe the freshness. Jenna reminded him of a carefree butterfly, who unconsciously seduced him into taking a break from his predictable, controlled life.

His parents had suffocated any independent thought into a robotic response. The constant text messages and phone calls and lectures from his parents dragged him down, down, down, into a dark hole.

He leaned in to smell her sugary essence. "Everything takes practice." *I'm practicing living my life, not the life my parents planned.*

Her mouth did that funny little scrunchy thing he so dearly loved. He had to grit his teeth to stop smiling. "How about we get some lunch?"

"I should have eaten an hour ago."

"Do you mind if I drive? I want to show you something."

Jenna's lips pulled into a half-smirk. "I'd warn you that Nellie's rather finicky, but you two certainly have developed a thing."

"You sure you aren't jealous?"

"Maybe. Can we go?" She walked around to the passenger side and used the side rails to leverage into the passenger seat.

A slow grin expanded across his face. "Yes, ma'am." Grant climbed in and started the car, then put an arm over the back of the passenger side bucket seat and reversed into the alley.

"I want you to know, I heard what you said...you, know...about letting people help."

Grant shoved the Jeep into gear, then placed his hand on hers. "Jenna, you give to so many in this town. You deserve to get a little something back."

"I don't—"

Grant placed a thumb over her lips to caress their tender softness. "It's a small town. I know about the pillowcases you make for foster kids. I also heard about the meals you delivered to Ashley when her mom was sick, and the cookies you donated to the Boys and Girls Club. Why do you keep trying to convince me you're something you're not?"

She shifted uneasily under his penetrating glance, and then released a heavy sigh. "I'm glad you're not mad about the other night. When I found out my sister had disappeared, I wanted to get as much information as I could, and I didn't know who to trust."

His brows knitted together. "Therefore, you didn't trust anyone. I get it. I hope you know you can trust me." Grant slowed to stop at the traffic light.

"You're the first man I've let into my life in a very long time. I'm not good at trusting people, especially men."

"I want to kiss that doubt right off your face."

"You've got a mighty fine kisser, Newhall," She could feel the beginnings of a cherry-red blush before she turned to study the passing landscape for no particular reason.

"That's good to know, but I think my kisser could use some fine tuning. Would you mind helping a guy out? I'd like to shake out some of the cobwebs. It hasn't been used for a while." He reached for her hand again and winked.

Her mouth curved up and made his heart do that throbbing thing.

Her fidgety shifting, he suspected, was her being unaccustomed to riding in the passenger seat and not being in control. He loved that she was so protective of anything she christened as hers. Including cars, people, and now bakery equipment.

Yesterday he overheard her talking to someone named Fred. Glancing around the empty bakery, he figured she'd lost her mind… until she opened the six-foot oven, the one that took half the kitchen space, and appealed to Fred to treat her muffins kindly before closing the door.

Grant wished she'd christen *him*, because then he would know for sure she'd accepted him as part of her life.

He drove in silence, allowing the sunshine and blue skies to work their magic and ease the tension. A few minutes later, he turned off the highway onto an unpaved back road, and headed up a sharp, rutted incline. He shifted gears and eased Nellie around the muddy curves.

"Where are we going?"

"Just a few more minutes and we'll be there."

The road turned east, then west, doubling back every quarter mile, and he passed through a decrepit metal gate. Nellie's tires spun on the steep, graded gravel road, but there was no question the Jeep would make it. Rounding the corner, he rolled to a stop and shifted into neutral.

She turned to him, questions popping up on her face like gophers out of their holes. "I've poked around these mountains a lot since I landed here, but I've never seen a view this spectacular."

"I agree." Grant leaned over the steering wheel. He pointed. "From that grove of aspen, down the valley to that clump of evergreens, is private property." He shifted Nellie into gear. "But this isn't what I want to show you."

"What are you up to now?"

"Patience."

After a few more minutes, he turned back onto a paved, curved road. Within a couple of switchbacks, he'd be able to show her what he'd shown no other woman. He gripped the steering wheel harder. *Would she understand how important this was to him?* He pulled up the long drive circling his home.

Not his parents' home.

His home.

The place he wanted to plant trees, watch the wildlife roam through his garden, maybe one day have a snowball fight with his adopted kids, since she couldn't have children.

Like a pendulum, her attention bounced back and forth between him and the log home nestled in the semicircle of towering pines. "What is this place?"

"My little slice of paradise. Come on, let me show you."

He rushed around the hood of Nellie to meet her, his excitement and apprehension building in tandem.

Walking up the entrance path, she stopped to pick up a pinecone, and gifted him with the ordinary item as if the tree's seed pod was a precious gift. Absentmindedly, she stroked the needles of the pine, running her fingers along the ancient branch before bringing her hand to her nose. Her fascination spilled over into him. He loved experiencing life through her perceptions.

Grant unlocked and pushed open the front door to let her precede him into the large, open space. He could smell the lingering scent of fresh paint. Ten feet in, she bent down and stroked her hand over the living room hardwood floors, and then stood to trail her fingers along the worn leather couch before moving into the kitchen.

From her facial expressions, he got the idea the butcher block island upped the house several notches on her impressed scale. He could so easily imagine her rolling out piecrusts or spooning cookie dough in his kitchen. He followed at a distance while she moved back into the living room to the built-in bookshelves beside the fireplace.

She dropped her patchwork bag on the table next to the couch. "Is this yours?" she asked.

"Jason didn't want it, so my grandparents left it to me."

"And the land?"

"All of it. In his greed, Jason demanded the stock funds, because he considered the paper a better investment. I'm not so sure. My parents took control of the portfolio after he died, but my hunch is it hasn't appreciated as much as this land."

She ran her hand along the wood panel. "Is this all original?"

"Most of it. Until a few years ago, the structure remained empty, and by the time it was mine, it needed a lot of repairs and TLC. Sparky needed a place to stay, and I needed the work done, so I swapped for free labor."

"Erik does such great work."

"He finished improvements several months ago, but asked if he could rent the place while I was gone. It's not good to let a place sit. I think I got the better end of the deal."

"I'd say. The craftsmanship is wonderful."

"Want to see the rest?"

"There's more?"

He held out his hand. When her warm fingers touched him, the peaceful caress spread up his arm. He tugged gently and walked with her through double doors into the master suite.

He released her hand to allow her to explore. "I added this room and the garage."

She approached the wall of windows overlooking the valley. He came to stand beside her. A squirrel gathering food stopped to chatter at her, twitching its tail, chastising her for the interruption. She laughed and tracked the little imp up the side of the house until the greyish-brown little fella scampered away.

She met Grant's gaze in the window's reflection. "If you have this, why are you living at your parents' place?"

"Living at my parents isn't by choice. Erik needed time to find a place. He moved out last week and sent a painting crew in."

"So you really are staying."

"You sound surprised."

Crossing her arms, she turned. "I didn't think this little town would be enough for you. You have some mighty big ideas, Newhall."

"Just because I want to push for modernization doesn't mean I'm unhappy here. I've always loved these mountains. It took moving away to realize how much. When I'm here, I feel full, if that makes any sense."

"It's like living in a little protective bubble with nothing but happiness inside. You're shielded from the mean, ignorant world. Nothing can harm you." Her eyes met his. "Because you feel safe." She took a couple of steps toward him and placed her hand on his arm. He could feel the warmth of her fingers and the undercurrent of tension. "It's a beautiful home, Grant. You should feel proud."

"Not as beautiful as you."

"Grant...I'm telling you, you need to get glasses, plus you need to improve your pick up lines. If you think you'll get lucky with that line, you need to think again."

He loved her teasing smile. "I already consider myself lucky. You're here." The tension he'd been feeling all morning dissipated. "That's all that matters."

Her cheeks pinkened. "You sure? 'Cause it seems to me, I'm here, your bed's there, and you're trying really hard to convince me the two don't have anything to do with each other," she teased.

"Nope. There's no connection...unless you want there to be." He reached for her waist, homing his fingers in on what he hoped would be a ticklish spot. "Come here, you. I want to show you how lucky I am."

Bull's-eye. She pogo-jumped into his arms, until his lips touched hers. Instantly, all residual resistance ceased. Her soft, warm lips allowed him to explore new territory. A sensual moan vibrated in her throat. The heat of her hands sank into his skin, sweeping wide, like a wildfire burning out of control.

"I need you, Jenna," he said, fighting for breath.

She dropped her head back, exposing her throat. A soft, indescribable sound escaped from the lips he adored. He indulged, inhaling the scent of mountain spring, skimming his thumb down the blue, pulsing vein, past her collarbone. The urge to taste her sweetness consumed him. He gently nibbled at her earlobe with his teeth. When she arched back in his arms, he lifted and cradled her. Her sultry eyes searched his.

Grant gazed at the face he could look at for a lifetime. "Be sure this is what you want, because once we start, I won't be able to stop."

"I want you, Grant. I just don't want to be married—to anyone. I've already explained my reasons."

We'll see about that. "Yes, you have, and I heard you. But I want to be with you, and I only want to think about today. You think you can manage to tuck away your doubt for a little while?"

She laid a hand on his top button. "Do you have a condom?"

He lifted and laid her on the bed, then opened the top drawer to his dresser, then the next, then the bottom drawer.

Come on, Erik, buddy. You must have left some here.

He raced toward the bathroom, pulling the cabinet doors open.

Please. Please. Please. Damn.

He unzipped his shaving kit, and dumped the contents on the counter.

Score.

His legs trembled as he stopped in the framed doorway, out of breath, with a wad of foil packets gripped in his fist.

She smiled, then flopped back onto the bed with a tentative, yet husky, laugh.

He took a running leap onto the bed, trapping her beneath him, and she squealed with glee. After cupping her breast, he used the tip of his thumb to trace the rigid peak beneath the thin cotton. She let out a sigh.

Mine, all mine.

Her lips trailed across his neck while he settled into the cradle of her hips, his knee parting her legs. She smelled delectable—lemon, possibly vanilla, with a bit of sugar. He released the band holding her braid, unraveling the thick mass of hair one loop at a time.

"You're so beautiful." He kissed the tip of her nose.

Her gaze flicked away from his, quick as a bird, darting to the window, then the door, looking everywhere but at him. He nudged her chin with his finger. "Don't argue. To me you are ravishing." The doubt rolled across her face like a big rig.

"You won't say that when you see all the bruises from my needles."

He was enlightened enough to understand the discomfort. The testing. The injections. The hassle.

"You're sexy on the outside, but even more breathtaking on the inside. A few bruises won't taint what I see."

He reached under her shirt, skimming his hand over the soft surface, lingering, the heat building. He wanted to take her to a place where she didn't think about how she looked —a place where her body took over and allowed the good things to come. He went to push her shirt up, but she stopped him by holding his hand still.

"What if I do something you don't like?" The panic tightening her face made him even more determined to prove she didn't have to worry.

"You can't."

"But—"

"It will be all right. All you need to do is stop thinking so much."

He continued to slide her shirt higher, placing feather-light kisses on her skin while he did. A fierce battle raged inside. He could see the struggle on her face, but he'd conquer those insecurities, show her how much power and strength she had. He'd been in that place of indecision, plagued by self-doubt. But not this time. This time he didn't want to hold back. To him, Jenna felt right. Perfect, in fact. He wanted them to climb the emotional mountain side by side.

"Lift your arms." The command boomed out more sternly than he intended.

When she complied, he lifted the thick cotton tank top off over her head. He trailed his lips over each rib to appreciate every spot. Her hands bunched the fabric of his shirt and pulled higher.

He laughed. "Not very patient, are you?"

Her fingers worked to free his top button. "You're taking too long." She smiled, a hint of shyness still lingering in her eyes. She lifted an admonishing brow. "Are you going to help me, or what?"

Reaching an arm over his head, he pulled. The whole shirt came off in his fist. The scramble was on to see who could undress fastest. He beat her by a breath, the cool air making his skin pucker with goose bumps. Yanking back the bedcover, he rolled both their bodies beneath the cotton sheet and down duvet.

"Now, where was I?" He trailed kisses down her neck, and she giggled. He toyed with the silver chain she wore, flipping the medallion over in his palm. An echo of a memory touched his mind, but Jenna tugged the necklace out of his hand, refocusing his attention. Grant placed a kiss where the medallion had been, then laid a trail of kisses down her belly.

The sun streaming through the window warmed them, and allowed him to see the powerful pleasure his touch created. His mouth drifted lower, crossing her abdomen. Her muscles quivered in anticipation, and sent an electric thrill bouncing from cell to cell. When she relaxed a bit more, he moved lower.

Small moans escaped her, encouraging him to delve deeper. He surged his tongue in and out, like a hummingbird searching for nectar, feeling her flesh swell, feeling her need grow. He wanted to push her higher, higher than she'd ever been. Cupping her bottom, he lifted, allowing her to fully open and let go.

With each touch, tickle, and lick she opened to him more, little by little, a time-lapse of a flower bud opening with the heat. Her folds swelled, turning from pink to red. Her fingers balled and pulled his hair, then a glorious ripple raced through her. Her fingers slid to his shoulders and pulled. He shifted and reached for the foil packet. Sliding on the condom, he returned to her.

"Look at me," he demanded.

When her head turned, he lifted and positioned her, and then pushed forward, inch by inch, until they were fully joined. *God, you're beautiful.* The surrounding warmth made him weak and strong at the same time. Weak—because one negative word and she could pulverize his heart. Strong—because one request and he'd move boulders to protect her.

Her hips lifted to meet his, as though seeking to find fullness and a perfect rhythm. *You're mine. All mine.*

Within seconds her body moved with his, carnal instinct taking over. Driving. Pounding. Ecstasy danced across her face. He almost couldn't believe she was his. He thrust deeper to prove she was. Her eyes closed, and her mouth opened. Her neck arched, pushing her head back into the pillow. She surged up, taking him to the peak and into the clouds and beyond.

She held him, teetering on the edge of limbo, for seconds, then minutes, until time didn't matter. Only she mattered.

A tiny quiver flowed across her skin, then her muscles clenched again and again, driving him toward a new high. Having sex with Jenna wasn't sex. He loved her. Her euphoric touch pushed him into the stratosphere. An intense convulsion rocked him, over and over, before he began descending down the slope into paradise. When he reached the bottom, he rolled, pulling her with him. He wanted to feel her skin. Her breath mingling with his.

For today.

For always.

He'd waited such a long time to find this bliss, stuck in the living hell of self-doubt and torment his parents created. She swept those tortured doubts away. Finding her freed him from his past.

He craved her.

Wanted to take care of her.

And now that he'd gotten a taste of her essence, he couldn't let her go.

His quivering muscles started to ease, and he was drifting, listening to her breathe, when she began pushing and pulling at the covers, kicking her feet.

He reached for a tissue to dispose of the condom, then turned back. "Are you all right?"

Jenna kicked her feet again. "I'm good."

He didn't like the tentativeness in her voice, and lifted up on his elbow to see her face. She yanked, and the covers trapped beneath her body flew free.

She relaxed back into his arms. "How can you sleep with so many layers?"

He dropped his head to the pillow, laughter building inside him until the sound filled the room and tears leaked out of the corners of his eyes. He couldn't have been more content.

She nudged him in the ribs. "What's wrong with you?"

"I've just had the most mind-blowing sex with the sexiest woman in the world, and the first words out of her mouth are about my bedding. My ego's taken hits over the years, but this one surpasses them all."

Her mouth curved into a tender smile, melting away his misgivings. Her generous, delicate kisses scattered across his skin relieved his anxiety.

"That was"—she kissed him again—"the most"—and again—"incredible"—and again—"amazing"—and again.

"I get it," he laughed.

She pushed hair off her face. "I hope so." Her small hands slid down his face, then trailed down his torso. "Too bad you only had one condom."

He didn't bother telling her he'd found three. There were better, more satisfying ways to announce the good news.

He'd let her be surprised.

CHAPTER NINE

Jenna awoke with panic spreading like a swarm of locusts across her mind.

She demanded her eyes open, but her body was slow to cooperate. In the dark night sky, little lights twinkled happily while her skin tightened, became chilled. Her vision blurred and moved in and out of focus. A blanket of muscle cocooned her cold, clammy body until she couldn't move. She pushed at the mass, fighting to escape. Fighting to calm the screams in her mind, and release her tangled feet.

Trouble. Need sugar. My kit.

Warmth eluded her, yet her racing heart

pounded. A loud roar in her stomach reminded her she should have eaten something. Taken her insulin. She pushed upright and stumbled out of the bed, tripping over something on the floor.

Sugar. Need sugar.

She extended her arms to brace the fall. Grant's aftershave tingled her senses. She crawled and homed in on the smell, a lifeline, until she found her bag, her jacket, something holding the tablets she so desperately needed.

Reaching the edge of the wool carpet, she crawled on hands and knees on the wooden floor. The floor chilled her palms and knees as she dragged herself toward the couch. In the darkness, she blinked. The room blurred into a fuzzy shadow.

Move.

Don't stop.

Stay conscious.

Leaning toward the fireplace, she hoped her limbs would respond to the forward motion. Her body vibrated, and beads of sweat swelled on her forehead and drained into her eyes.

Not far.

She pushed and dragged her legs and arms to the table until she could reach up onto the empty, flat surface, where she swore she'd left the satchel carrying her essentials. No bag. *No bag! Where's my bag?* She weaved, trembling in defeat. Her muscles collapsed.

Think.

Strands of hair hung in her face, drenched with sweat from her panicky quest for the only thing that would calm her body. With every ounce of energy, she badgered her mind to configure a solution that kept dissolving before fully forming.

Come on.

Each arm weighed more than she could lift. She urged her limbs to move. A sound of defeat escaped her lips. She shivered from the cold. Tears welled and began to fall.

A blinding light made her squint and heave an arm across her eyes.

"Jenna?" Grant's voice echoed through the room. "Jenna?" he called more urgently. "Shit!"

Strong arms lifted her body from the floor. A blanket of warmth surrounded her. Grant smoothed damp hair from her face.

Need sugar.

She threw her arms wide and screamed glucose in her mind, even though the word came out a weak whisper.

Grant settled her on the couch. She rolled her head. He ran toward the kitchen, pulling open a cabinet, and returning seconds later with a bottle. One hand wrapped around the cylinder while the other cupped her jaw, and he squeezed the liquid honey between her lips. The golden sugar mingled with saliva before sliding down her throat. She opened her mouth for more. He repeated the process twice more before she turned away when he offered. Grant sat back on his heels, naked and clearly shaken, yet refusing to leave her side. His ashen face and white lips told of his regret.

She struggled to lift her chin far enough to meet his eyes. "It's okay. I'm good," she mumbled to ease his concern.

He disappeared, only to return moments later with what appeared to be the whole bed. He scooped her into his arms and settled her against his body, pulling and tucking the blankets to swaddle her in warmth. His heartbeat pounded in her ear, and his chin rested on the top of her head.

She curled her fists under her chin while the shivers subsided. "I…I'm really sorry."

His arms tightened. "No. This is my fault."

"It's not," she mumbled, wanting to ease Grant's misplaced guilt. "My…My low blood sugar has no…nothing to do with you." Her teeth chattered. *I should have asked for your help, but I just couldn't.*

"You missed your lunch with Gwen. When we got here, I should have made you something to eat. Type one diabetics are supposed to eat regularly."

"How do you know that?"

"Same way I knew to use honey. After our dinner date, I did some research. The web has lots of information about diabetes."

He'd taken the time to look up the information. Gratitude eased the tension in her shoulders and neck. "I carry protein bars in my purse to keep this from happening. You're not responsible for me forgetting to eat." *I'm not good at taking care of myself.* "And this could have been because of the stress of running the bakery, or overdoing my exercise the past couple of days. All the above might have impacted my sugar levels."

"You sure you're okay?"

Yes...well, no. "I need to check my blood and get something to eat, but I should be fine in a minute or two." *I hope.* She took a frustrated breath. "My blood sugars are going to fluctuate big time for the next several days. I may have to change my running schedule and reduce my carbs. Diet and exercise are about the only things keeping me stable. This is what I get for being careless." *And not taking the time to take care of myself.*

Grant rubbed the palms of his hands up and down her arms. "You're still cold."

"I should get dressed and go."

He pulled back. "That's a bad idea."

"I told Maggie I'd cover a shift at the café tomorrow night, so I need to get the baking done in the morning. I've had to reduce Ashley's hours, so I'll have no one to cover the cash register."

"I guess it would do no good to offer my help."

"You have your dad's business to run. Tell you what. If I need help, I promise to ask." She released a slow steady breath and pulled at the edges of the cover.

"I'll set the alarm. You're hungry, tired, and not functioning properly. I'm not letting you out of my sight until I've remedied all three." He pushed on her shoulders and scooted from behind her, replacing his body with pillows behind her back to support her.

He dropped her insulin kit on her lap. "Give me a minute, and I'll whip something up. Eggs okay?"

When she looked at him, his naked strength and ease of motion reminded her of the wonderful things his tongue and his hands and...she blinked to reset her mind. "You'd better put something on if you plan to add bacon to the menu."

He glanced down, then winked with an affectionate smirk. He didn't move or hide his body—just watched her with raised brows. "Funny."

Funny. No, nothing was funny. "I...I didn't mean..." She trembled with the need to curl into a ball and hide. She pulled the comforter higher as hateful tears welled in her eyes.

"Hey?" Grant rounded the table and lowered onto the couch. "What happened?"

"I know better." Tears tumbled down her cheeks. "I do. It's just that…I just…I don't have an excuse."

Grant smoothed the lines of tears with his fingertips. "Don't be so hard on yourself. I was here."

She scrunched her nose in repudiation. "Yes. You were right beside me. I should have asked for help, but I didn't. Like you said, if I don't start accepting help, I'll be all alone. I don't want to be alone. I'm not good with people. I'm socially inept…" *I'd be a terrible wife.*

"Shhh." Grant leaned forward and kissed her forehead. "You are not terrible at anything. You just need a little practice with the trust thing. Habits are hard to break. It takes time to make changes."

Change. She wasn't good with change. She reined in her self-defeating attitude before it pushed her over the edge again. "I can try, but letting people in my life is scary. Everyone I've ever loved has disappeared."

He kissed her forehead, and slid his

knuckles down her cheek. "Okay, then what does a guy have to do to win your trust?"

She stuck out her stubborn chin. "Stick around long enough."

"That should be easy."

"This from a guy who could live anywhere in the world."

His eyes flashed a communiqué she didn't quite understand. "I could. Just because I could, doesn't mean I will. I've rediscovered a taste for Elkridge since I found something delectable and sweet to sink my teeth into." He closed the distance and leaned in again, savoring her lips. "I'm not leaving, but you don't have to believe me. Sooner or later my actions will prove my intentions. Now, be good and stay put while I rustle up some grub."

He ran his knuckles lightly down her cheek before going to the kitchen. The way the muscles in his butt cheeks and thighs flexed generated a hunger, a deep hunger, for something more than eggs and bacon. Her mouth watered. He moved so effortlessly. The whole domestic thing made her nervous.

This wasn't how it was supposed to go.

Getting information. Finding Caitlyn. Wasn't that her goal?

Getting tangled up with Grant was downright stupid.

Oh, Caitlyn, why didn't you warn me I was in trouble?

CHAPTER TEN

T*wenty minutes to go.*

Jenna pushed her knuckles into her lower back, twisting to ease the muscle tension, wishing she could do the same to her feet. The intense ache tempted her to flip her open sign to closed early, find Grant, and crawl into bed until her alarm clock rudely jolted her from a deep sleep. Her skin could put up with being encrusted with flour and sugar until morning.

Sleeping with Grant the past week had been heaven.

He made her coffee, bought her a lunch pail, and loaded it with all her favorites. At night, he loved her into oblivion, or talked to her until she fell asleep in his arms. She told him things she'd never told anyone. But between standing all day, walking through the park handing out fliers, and the lack of sleep, everything between her toes and ears hurt.

Every single day, she forced her body to keep working until she could collapse in Grant's arms. Today was the first day she might be able to fit in a few hours of uninterrupted baking. Fingers crossed.

Spatula in hand, she groaned when the phone rang. If one more person ordered dozens of anything, she might burst into tears. And she tried hard never to cry.

"Dreamy Delights Bakery, how may I help you?" Jenna answered in the calmest voice she could manage, given the chaos of the day.

"Hey, sugar girl," Maggie said, in a distracted, hurried tone. "Can you add another three chocolate cream and two Dutch apple to my order?"

Jenna's hand shook as she grabbed a pen and rotated the order pad. "That's fifteen pies. Are you having a pie-throwing contest over there, or what?"

"We got hit with a group of bikers who stopped in for some grub on their way up the hill. Also…do you have some extra toilet paper I can borrow?"

Jenna scanned the orderly shelves and racks of baking and business supplies, tallying when the next shipment of supplies would arrive.

"I think I have enough TP. I'll bring over what I can spare after I close, and top you up on desserts tomorrow."

"Perfect. You're a doll."

"See you soon," Jenna said before returning the phone to the cradle.

She noted the time, then retrieved a carton of eggs from one of the double-wide industrial refrigerators.

With the leaves starting to change, motorcycle groups traveled up the canyon every weekend, causing pies, cookies, and sweet bars to sprout legs and walk off the racks faster than she could make them. The cake pops didn't last long, either.

A tonsil-stretching yawn made her pause before her mind drifted back to the heavenly hunk of man who'd been keeping her up nights. For the fifth time this week, she awoke in his arms before dressing in the shivering cold, accepting a travel mug of coffee, and heading out to open her shop.

After the first day, she learned to avoid Grant's kisses. If she got within arm's reach before she got out the door, she wasn't able to get her baking done before the morning rush.

In the process of pulling cinnamon and nutmeg from the alphabetized spice rack, she heard the entrance bells' happy chime. Setting the large jars on the counter, she turned, her cheerful customer greeting fading when she saw who was waiting.

Vivian Newhall was standing regally in the center of her bakery with a scowl that would frighten most people. Her shoulders were pinned back. Not a hair dared move out of place. She didn't acknowledge Jenna's greeting, only stood dead center in the store, inspecting every surface of the spotless bakery with a critical eye. "What a little shop," the woman said stiffly.

Jenna walked to the counter, her hand automatically seeking a towel to brush away a single crumb, possibly the only crumb in the entire place. "Yes, friendly and cozy. It provides a more intimate, personal feel, don't you think?"

"That sounds about right—you wanting to deliver an intimate feel."

The town's most famous member twisted Jenna's words purposely, but Jenna refused to let the woman deflate her spirit. "Can I interest you in a peach and apricot pie? I understand they're Mr. Newhall's favorite."

"My husband is on a strict diet. I'm afraid he won't be eating any more desserts."

You mean any more of my desserts. She twisted the cloth in her hands. "Yes, well, I wish him a speedy recovery." Jenna replaced the towel on the assigned hook and tapped her fingers on the stainless steel counter. She managed to get to the count of seven before the next volley of grenades started going off around her.

"I hear you've been seeing my son."

Kaboom. Figured that was coming. "If you mean that he's visited the café, or stops in for a bakery item now and then, then yes. He's quite fond of Maggie's meatloaf, and gets a hankering for an apple spice muffin on occasion."

"Don't play stupid with me." The woman widened her stance, her knuckles whitening as she clutched her purse handles, her mega-diamonds sparkling in the overhead lights. "You know why I'm here."

The urge to cross her eyes, relax her jaw, and let her tongue hang loose, to mock the woman's stupid label was getting hard to resist.

Mrs. Newhall adjusted the alligator leather purse on her crooked arm, and then carefully pushed a plastered piece of hair off her face, only to have it rebound seconds later, due to the seven layers of hair spray that made her head a bulletproof shield.

Jenna tilted her head slightly to the left. "It's a bakery. I assume you stopped in to buy something."

"I figured you for a gold digger," Mrs. Newhall huffed in a superior tone. She pulled out a checkbook. "Fine. Tell me how much."

Jenna fought to remain calm. "I think you have it backward, Mrs. Newhall. First, you need to pick out what bakery items you would like to purchase, then I ring you up and provide a total, and only then do you pay me."

The woman marched to the counter. "You little slut. Don't you dare pretend to misunderstand me. Tell me how much it will cost to ensure you will never see my son again."

Jenna tugged on the hem of her baking jacket, twisting and pulling the thick fabric. Then she lifted her chin to a confident level. "You may buy a muffin, a cookie, or a loaf of bread, but you certainly cannot buy me, Mrs. Newhall," Jenna enunciated each word with a careful measure of precision.

The woman's eyes narrowed to slits. "Everyone in this town has a price. You'd be surprised at how cheap some people are," Vivian's cool demeanor dropped the temperature three degrees. "I bet you're a real bargain."

"What's that supposed to mean?"

"My family's been part of this community for generations. My great-grandfather developed this area, and my father expanded it to what it is today. Grant has been raised to carry on family tradition, and nothing will prevent him from taking his rightful place—especially some little twit with no breeding who doesn't know her place. People like you don't stay long in Elkridge, and those who foolishly decide to stay don't last."

Caitlyn, how did you live with this woman?
"Aren't you forgetting something?"

"What's that?"

Jenna hesitated, choosing her words carefully. "Grant is a grown man, and this is the twenty-first century. You can't force him to your bidding. He's quite capable, you know."

"Grant will do what I tell him to do. He knows the consequences." Vivian snapped shut her checkbook. "If I were you, I'd be careful. You don't live in a very safe area, Ms. Dolcy. Tell me this. Have you slept with my son?"

Jenna's jaw dropped before her mind engaged. "That, ma'am, is none of your business."

"You little bitch. Are you pregnant?"

Jenna squeezed her shaking hands into fists. "I wouldn't tell you even if you asked nicely. Please leave before I call the sheriff."

"I demand an answer." Red blood vessels popped on Vivian's cheeks.

Jenna crossed her arms. She'd been bullied, and on occasion physically abused. This woman couldn't spit enough vinegar to sour her milk.

The bells on the front door jingled, but Jenna didn't move or take her eyes off the puffed-up peahen in front of her. Settling in for a fight, she pressed her shoulders back. "I won't be intimidated. Again, I ask you to leave."

"Mother?" A familiar voice caused the woman accosting her to turn.

"Grant. So nice to see you, darling." Vivian's voice dripped with sticky sweetness.

At that moment, Jenna understood something important. Grant hated false, plastic women for an excellent reason. The perfect example stood in front of her.

Grant moved closer, and his size cast a shadow on the woman, who stood a foot below his chin. "What are you doing here, Mother?"

The woman's eyes swept past Jenna as if she didn't exist. "I'm getting a little something for tomorrow's ladies' charity meeting. Would you like me to get you something?"

Grant searched Jenna's face. She refused to allow either Newhall see how the confrontation had unnerved her. She should have listened to her inner voice of warning. Being with Grant had attracted trouble. She wanted them gone. Both of them.

Jenna took a deep breath. "If you're not interested in anything, I would like to close the shop. It's getting late, and I have baking to do."

"We should go, Mother." Grant cupped the woman's elbow.

"I suppose you're right, son. There's nothing of interest here."

Assaulting the woman with a barrage of croissants held a certain appeal. Thank goodness Grant escorted his mother out of range before the temptation became too great. Jenna massaged the back of her neck, trying to get the tense muscles to release. *Holy hell.* Her hand jerked when the front bells sounded again. She leaned sideways to see around Grant's tall frame.

He pointed a thumb at the door. "Don't worry, she's gone."

"You should go, too," she said, dismissing him, and fighting the instinct to run before slowly walking to the back of the kitchen.

"Why are you angry with *me*?" Grant's question carried a heavy layer of surprise.

She spun on her toes, grabbing the counter for support. "Why?" she demanded. "Why?" She wanted to thump him in the chest. "I run a business here. I can't have your mother, or Rachelle, or anyone else for that matter, coming in here and scaring away customers. I told you this town was too small for the two of us."

"Jenna, be reasonable."

"Reasonable?" Hot, burning rage flooded her. "You aren't the one who's just been called a slut and bitch to her face, and told to be careful because I 'live in an unsafe area.' I shouldn't have to put up with those kinds of threats.

"I'm working extremely hard here to start something, something good, something I've wanted for a long time. I don't need my dream tainted because some guy's mother doesn't like who he's spending time with."

She pointed to the door. "She tried to pay me off. She threatened me, Grant. I don't want to have to worry she'll try convincing everyone in town I've poisoned my baked goods, or that my wedding cakes aren't up to standard. I don't want to have to look over my shoulder all day every day, wondering when a vicious, threatening bitch will walk through my door again. I can't handle *that* right now."

"Would it help if I said I'm sorry?"

She heard the hurt in his voice, but couldn't allow herself to surrender. "I don't want you to feel sorry. I want you to leave."

Grant stood, his feet planted, his face flushed and livid. "Jenna, don't do this. What we have is real. I need you to see that."

"It's real, all right. Today, your mother made it all too real. I got her message loud and clear. And to think you wanted me to marry into...into that."

He grimaced, straightened his shoulders, and rubbed his forehead. "Don't you see? Separating us is what she wants."

She asked herself why she was so scared

and angry, but her pit-bull stubbornness had served her well over the years, and she returned his direct look. "I asked you to leave."

"Fine. I'll go. But know this. I'm only going so I can divert my mother's attention. I told you—I'm not going anywhere, and I mean it. I'll earn your trust if it's the last thing I do."

When the silence became so thick a blender couldn't crush through it, he turned and walked out the door. Unable to stand one more surprise customer, she followed and secured the deadbolt, and turned to rest her back against the door.

Her heart thumped the walls of her chest in synch with the bakery timer reminding her she didn't have time for this nonsense. She returned to the kitchen and retrieved a lemon from a wire basket, rolling the fruit between her palms and squeezing it while pacing the length of the counter. Her mind replayed the conversation again and again. Dozens of things she wished she'd said, but hadn't, came to mind—if only she'd been faster on her mental feet.

Channeled rage conquered her exhaustion and provided motivation.

Thanks to the surge of adrenaline, she could probably bake enough pies to supply both the bakery and café for weeks. Turning the order pad, she prioritized and then lifted the cinnamon.

One thing was certain. Tomorrow would be a better day.

At least it couldn't get any worse...at least she hoped it couldn't.

If life was determined to deliver lemons, she'd just have to make lemon zest.

CHAPTER ELEVEN

"Figured I'd find you here," Erik said, dropping two beers on the table before sliding into Grant's booth. "Don't worry, I had Mad Jack put them on my tab this time."

Grant popped a carrot with some ranch dressing into his mouth. "Do I look worried?"

"No. You look like someone ran over your dog, and you don't even have a dog."

Grant turned to watch a soccer player dribble the ball toward the goal. The rage over his mother's interference boiled in his gut, and he was trying to maintain an outward calm he didn't feel. In fact, he wanted to drive over to his parents' house and release thirty-one years of pent up anger. But he'd matured enough to know *that type* of reaction wouldn't work. Not with them. If he wanted to take his life back, he needed a carefully laid out plan.

His phone vibrated on the table. He picked it up. Noting his mother's image, he powered off the device and tossed it back on the resin tabletop.

"I heard your mom threatened Jenna. Don't tell me you're going to let her bust in on your business like that. Dude, that's not right."

Yeah, and I didn't protect her, like I didn't protect Caitlyn. Grant leaned back in the booth, his body tingling on high alert. "Where did you hear that rumor?"

"I stopped at the café to get a bite and overheard a couple of women gossiping, saying how they saw your mom talking to the owner on their way to the café. After that, you can probably guess what happened."

"Great. No, my mother won't get away with what she's done. But right now I have to cool off."

"Did you ask Jenna to marry you?"

"I told you I was going to. I love her. My mother can't change that."

If only I could get her to love me back.

Every morning, his first thought was of her. Throughout the day, images of her with flour on her cheek, or interacting with customers, or sleeping with moonbeams tickling across her face, made it almost impossible to concentrate on his work. She was infectious, like a euphoric drug. She made him want to inject her essence into his veins so he could become completely addicted—not that he wasn't already totally smitten. He turned back to the television, because he didn't want to deal with Erik's WTF reaction.

"Okay, then." Erik leaned over and clinked his beer glass with his. "Good on you, buddy. What did she say?"

I'm not admitting defeat. "Let's just say it's complicated."

Erik picked up a carrot stick, dipped it in the ranch dressing, and munched. "Man, I hear ya."

The memory of Jenna standing in the middle of her bakery, and the fury on her face after his mother's visit, burned a hole in his stomach. He'd been making progress. He'd been granted a peek behind those formidable walls, built with bricks of mistrust and mortar crafted from anger, only to have them refortified. Now he'd have to start all over again.

Grant was suddenly curious to find out if Erik had fared any better. "So how was your date with Rachelle?"

"I don't know what I was thinking. I'm a brick-head for wanting that date."

"Maybe you should start a list. I'm telling you, it works," Grant smirked, "and I bet Rachelle won't have one tick next to any of the boxes."

Erik grunted and turned toward the TV screen to watch a soccer player score a goal. When an erectile dysfunction commercial began, Erik shook his head, pulled the peanut bucket closer, and grabbed a handful.

A tossed peanut shell bouncing off his forehead centered Grant's attention.

"What's your next step, buddy?" Erik asked.

Grant retrieved the peanut from his lap, cracked the shell and tossed the nuts in his mouth. "First off, I'll have a heart-to-heart with my parents, and hope it doesn't turn into a fist-to-fist. I'm done playing their little

Pinocchio. My puppet strings have been permanently severed. Never again will they interfere in my life. And, I mean *never*, this time."

"That sounds easy, though I expect it will be much more challenging than gutting and refurbishing your entire cabin. You're gonna have to rip down those walls, 'cause I suspect your parents won't change."

"My parents keep telling me they only want what's best for me. Now that I'm the only child, and their legacy, I have some leverage. All they care about is wealth, position, and continued dominance. I need to live my life, not theirs. I'm happy with the woman I've chosen. I just have to figure out how to make it work."

Jenna had gifted him with a determined purpose to carve out a life he wanted, and damn it, that included her.

"What's next, then?" Erik asked.

"I've decided I need to make a change, do some soul-searching, figure out what I *want* to do with life rather than just reacting. Like you said, paperwork gets to a person after a while. First, though, I'll settle and clear the caseload my dad turned over to me. I finish what I start."

"Man, I never could see you as a lawyer, even though you worked hard at becoming the best."

"Maybe, I'll open a food truck like you suggested."

"Hell, yeah. You should serve those meat-thingies. What did you call them?"

Grant searched his memory, trying to remember what Erik was talking about. "You mean hobo pockets?"

"Yeah, those things."

"Gourmet? Hardly. Dude, it's tinfoil-wrapped hamburger, a packet of onion soup mix, and vegetables. Even you can manage that."

"Nope. I couldn't cook like that. Tried and failed."

Erik couldn't make a pot of coffee, much less a full meal. "If you like that," Grant drew Erik's attention away from the soccer game, "You should try my buffalo tacos. Spiced buffalo chunks with a blue cheese cilantro sauce. Throw on some chopped romaine and avocado. Delish."

"If I hang around you long enough, I'm hoping some of your big city experience rubs off. Lately I've been thinking I can't keep doing renovations without help. Falling off that roof last summer busted me up. Maybe you can help me figure out how to structure my business, you know, legal-wise." Erik cracked open another nut and tossed the small orb into his mouth. "Do you know what I was thinking about when I was out with Rachelle?"

Grant shook his head. "I'm almost afraid to find out."

"Funny." Erik gave him a friendly sneer. "I thought maybe I'm stuck, too focused on reminiscing about the good times we had in high school. I can't keep thinking I'm eighteen."

Huh. Grant felt stuck. Not in high school, but in life. Every time his parents tightened the screws and applied guilt, he did anything, everything he could think to escape the choking feeling, often caving to their demands just to get the pressure to stop. He hated regrets. What-ifs. The debilitating guilt.

For years, he wanted to leave, avoid the emotional games, the drama, yet all it took was one phone call to drag his obedient butt back into the fray. He needed to unravel the thread of parental compliance. No, actually, he needed to sever it entirely, cut it out of his life. He needed to find a way to live on his terms.

So what if his parents got mad? So what if they threatened to disown him? He didn't need their money anyway. Power and prestige weren't his thing. He could live a simpler life. Yet they could so easily make him feel guilt— guilt for not being more like his brother, guilt for not getting the unwanted promotion, guilt for living so far away. The ginormous guilt list went on and on and on. Bitterness burned the back of his throat.

Grant tossed Erik a smirk. "You do tend to distort reality."

"Shut up. You ain't no better. Your parents still have you squirmin' under their thumbs."

"Maybe you have a point."

I've ignored the problem long enough. I've got to make a change. Right fucking now.

He didn't have a plan, but he was done with his parents' suffocating influence. His dad could shove his law practice up his ass. He could open a restaurant, or purchase a gourmet food truck. Maybe he'd help Jenna run her bakery. Bottom line, he moved back to Elkridge to start a family. His parents couldn't force him to leave.

He wanted to build something solid. Whether his parents liked it or not, Jenna would be a part of his future. That decision was already made.

Loving her didn't scare him.

Convincing her to love him back scared the crap out of him.

Because what if he couldn't?

CHAPTER TWELVE

J enna hadn't expected Grant to stop by the bakery. After all, he said he'd stay away, but he hadn't visited the café, either.

The lonely echo of his missing presence triggered a deep melancholy. She waited. She expected to hear something from him. Anything.

She didn't want to admit to overreacting, but she missed him—his positive influence on her mood, the banter, the way he coaxed out grudging smiles. Sure, she didn't want to deal with Vivian Newhall, but maybe it wasn't fair to have forced Grant to deal with her all alone.

Friends stood by each other in hard times. Wasn't that how Kathy raised her?

She hadn't been a very good friend. She didn't know how to be.

She went so far as to look up the definition and essential elements of being a good friend at the local library. She scored a four out of thirteen. Socially awkward...that's what her adoption file stated in big, bold, black, permanent ink.

She closed her eyes to quiet the abusive voices of the nuns, teachers, caseworkers, and so many others who felt entitled to belittle the unwanted orphan who heard and dwelled on every negative word spoken. She dug deep and did what any proper baker would do, and loaded up on enough sweets to bribe even the most stubborn of men, and then texted him.

"I'm sorry for overreacting."

"I know. What my mother did was wrong," he messaged back.

"Are you busy?"

"Busy thinking of you."

Oh, how sweet. She could almost feel her heart sigh in a new puppy lick-the-face kind of way.

"Where are you? I have something to give you," she messaged.

"Sounds interesting. I'm at your place. I figured you'd be tired after a long day."

My place? "I'll lock up. Be home in five."

She took a step, then grabbed the counter, a searing pain jabbing her in the side.

Jenna folded over. Her midsection burned. The cramping raced across her abdomen and down her legs.

Fighting to stop the merry-go-round, she reached for the floor.

Jenna fought to catch her breath.

Then nothing. *Odd.*

The pain. The dizziness. All gone. It had dissipated, leaving behind a freezing chill. The sensation created a hollowing emptiness, a feeling of desolation and disconnection she hadn't felt before.

The vacant space felt different.

Weird.

Frightening.

Jenna looked outside to see if an earthquake might be the cause. The windows hadn't rattled. The tables and chairs hadn't moved. Reaching out with shaky hands, she grabbed the counter for balance, then stood upright and brushed her hair from her face. *I'm not pregnant. I can't be.*

Rubbing her abdomen, she thought back over the past several weeks. She and Grant had been careful. She couldn't be pregnant, yet the searing pain hadn't been a figment of her imagination.

The late afternoon sun brushed casually through the display case, highlighting the splendor of the fancy sugary designs, yet a foreboding chill settled around her heart and encouraged her to lock up quickly and get into Nellie. "Okay, girl. Let's go see Grant."

Minutes later, she turned off the main road, then bumped and bounced and skidded around a sharp corner. Calmly, she righted the wheel and continued up the incline, crunching rocks beneath the sturdy tires. She pressed the accelerator, forcing the Jeep to slide sideways into her drive, hoping to create a mini-thrill and dissipate some of the eerie sensation plaguing her.

The setting sun painted the clouds with shades of orange, pink and purple, easing her growing anxiety. The tufts of fluff floating in the air from the nearby cottonwoods encouraged her to ease off the accelerator. Nellie rolled to a stop next to Grant's silver Audi before she cut the engine and lights. The sight of Grant's vehicle should have made her tense, but all she experienced was a great relief, and a need to be engulfed by his strong arms.

Retrieving the pie from the passenger seat, she noticed the odd, soft glow through her cabin windows. A few seconds later, Grant emerged, the interior light casting his body in shadow. She paused at the bottom step, reluctant to know why he was at her cabin, yet hopeful the reason a positive one.

When she looked up at him, he stood, holding out his hand. Uncertain how he might respond, she hesitated. With his face shrouded in darkness, she had to act on instinct and faith, and lifted her hand, stretching to meet his fingers, to bridge the distance—but a gap remained.

Her heart reached the extra centimeter to connect. His warm hand pulled, helping her ascend one stair at a time. When her foot reached the top step, she wrapped her free arm around his waist with a silent sigh.

She arched back. "Hello."

He pulled a bit of cottonwood fluff from her hair and let it drift away on the gentle breeze. "I'm glad to see you."

"I've missed you." She released him.

"Yeah? How much did you miss me?" He asked, his voice frayed and ragged.

She attempted to move past him, but he stepped in her way. After practically bouncing off his chest, she questioned his sudden movements. Then she got it. He wanted an answer. He was too familiar with the tactics she used to avoid answering questions. Grant remained silent, but the way his body leaned forward, listening, waiting, left her no choice but to provide a reply.

"More than I should. I brought you a pie." She lifted the box in her hand as proof.

"Is that your way of saying you're sorry?"

"I am sorry." An elastic band tightened around her chest, restricting the air to her lungs. She kicked at the dried pine needles gathering on her porch. "You haven't stopped by the café. Maggie was worried."

"Maggie, huh? Maggie was worried about me. And?"

She tried to read his expression, but the night still masked his face. "Okay...yes, I missed you. I shouldn't have told you to go away. I was wrong. Are you satisfied now?"

He turned sideways into the light. A slow, delighted smile crossed his face. "I missed you too."

She nudged him with her shoulder. "You didn't answer *my* question. Why are you here?"

He nodded toward the cabin's interior. "See for yourself."

She leaned into the light and the air entirely emptied from her lungs. Multicolored bouquets in every shape and size sat on every surface. He'd turned her cabin into a virtual mountain valley in springtime. Amazed, she stumbled into the room. Dozens of vanilla-scented candles were scattered throughout the room, creating a glorious combination of light and fragrance, and filling her senses. She placed the pie on the kitchen table and turned. Astonishment tingled and sprinted through every vein.

"Are you trying to burn down my cabin?" she asked with a laugh.

The words were meant to be funny, but came out more in the direction of a slight. Her over-stressed nerves had pushed out the first nervous comment that popped into her head. Figuring he'd get angry, she retreated. He followed, matching her step for step until a log wall stalled her retreat.

He leaned in. "I told you this place was a fire hazard," he said in a deeper-than-usual voice before pointing at the new fire extinguisher now bolted to the wall by the door.

"I—"

His lips captured hers in a demanding yet nurturing kiss. He understood. She didn't have to explain, only accept what he offered. When his mouth lifted from hers, she folded her lip under, tasting a mixture of spices she couldn't quite place.

"That's one way to keep me quiet, Newhall."

"I don't want to silence you, only make you happy." He bent forward, tilting his head sideways, "I told you, I'm not going away."

She snuggled into his arms. "You never let me push you away before. I didn't think you would be gone so long."

His laughter sent tingles every direction. "I had some things to take care of. You hungry?"

She pressed her lips together wanting to ask if he cooked, but decided the time to give a little had come. For years, she'd held tightly to the end of her rope, and she didn't want to struggle much longer. She wanted to let go, ride the wave of abandoned freedom. To trust. To love. To be loved.

"Yes." She could feel her lips slipping into a crescent shape, giving him what he wanted. "Yes, I'm hungry."

He bumped her nose with his. "Your purse, madam."

His terrible attempt at a French accent made her shake her head. She handed over the requested item before kicking off her clogs and seeking the coolness of her flip-flops. A soft excitement set the mood.

She'd missed him more than she would have believed possible.

In the middle of bundling her hair to get it off her neck, she glanced at his buzzing cell phone lying on the counter next to the cutting board. The familiar melody made her pause, then she finished pulling her long strands of hair through the tan band. He punched at the pad, ending the tune mid-cycle, then returned to the dinner preparations. His calm from the previous minutes had vanished.

Jenna approached tentatively and touched his back. A vivid, vibrating anger had tightened the muscles along his spine. "Was that Erik or your mom?"

"Doesn't matter."

She leaned around his stiff body. "Is something wrong?"

His hand tightened on the grip of her best cooking knife, and she hoped the tempered steel could withstand the pressure. "It's my mother. She's been calling all day and driving me crazy."

"If she's called that many times, maybe it's something important."

"The last call, she wanted me to pick up her dry cleaning. The time before that, a case of wine for a party. It's her way of trying to connect—say she's sorry—without taking responsibility for her actions. I'm not going there. Not this time."

"I see your point."

"What she did was completely out of line. She manipulates everyone to get what she wants. I'm not playing anymore. I'm not her errand boy. She has two assistants she runs into the ground. If I weren't waiting for a call back from a client, I'd silence the damn thing."

"You can do that?"

"J-Bird, what am I going to do with you?"

J-Bird? He'd given her a nickname. No man had ever given her a nickname before.

How sweet. She quietly embraced the nickname, pulling and hugging it to her heart.

"Yeah, I need to get a grip on all this technology stuff. How about you be my YouTube video. I've been so busy, I haven't had time to learn all this techy stuff. The world seems to have a love affair with these techy gadgets that, far as I can see, only make life more complicated and crazy."

Impressed he hadn't grabbed her cell phone to show her the latest trending app, she shook off the tension in her shoulders. "Do you need help with dinner?" she asked, hoping to change the subject.

He pointed his knife at a creamy-yellow brick. "You can cut up the cheese. I only need to finish slicing the apples, and we'll be ready." He set and pushed the button on the microwave.

"Peggy Sue stopped in to get her son some magic bars and said you were at the courthouse today."

"I needed to see a judge and file some papers. Nothing important."

She unwrapped the cheese and placed it on the cutting board. "Why do you do that?"

He laid the knife down to set the apple slices on the plate. "Do what?"

"Act like your job, and what you do, isn't valued. People depend on you."

He lifted the dinner plate and paused. "You're right. In Chicago, I worked on big, complex corporate cases. Just because the cases are smaller, simpler, doesn't make them less important."

"Word has it, Mr. Lawyer Man, you're an expert at what you do."

"Is that right?" he said, leaning in. His pupils dilated. "Tell me how good I am."

He continued moving closer, his breath warming her neck. *I'm in trouble.* He nibbled on her earlobe and sent a tingle down her spine. *Big trouble.* Joy exploded from limb to limb. Her body relaxed with a sigh. *Nummm,* she sighed. She leaned in, seeking, and then stiffened when the familiar ring tone broke the moment. She turned to look at the display. "It's your mother again. You should answer it, because she's not gonna stop. We both know that."

Placing the plate of carrots, celery, and red peppers on the counter, Grant grabbed the phone. "Mother," he answered, through clenched teeth.

He held the phone away from his ear. The high-pitched whine emanating from the phone reminded her of a dentist drill. When it stopped, he held the phone back to his ear. "Mother, you're not making sense." He held his arm away again.

"This is why I don't answer the phone when she calls," he whispered, taking a deep breath when the whine stopped. "Mother, I'll call you later."

He pulled the phone away, then immediately pressed the electronic back to his ear. "What did you say?"

His face turned ashen, and his body went rigid. "When?" he asked, becoming very still. He nodded. "Okay. I'll be by tomorrow." The buzz-whine came back. He squeezed his eyes shut, as if in pain. "Mother, I'll be there tomorrow. No... Tomorrow."

His thumb ended the shrilling voice emanating from the phone. He scrolled up and down the black square, then stopped and tossed the phone on the counter.

He grabbed the counter with both hands and stepped back, obviously trying to catch his breath. Jenna placed her hand on his back.

"Grant. What happened? Talk to me."

His watery gaze met hers. "They found Caitlyn."

Jenna retracted her arms and wrapped them around her waist. "Where?"

"At a farm, outside of Sterling. She's dead." He turned and pulled her into his arms. "Caitlyn's dead."

Her arms wrapped around his back to hold on. Jenna mentally checked for that thread— the one connected to her sister.

Oh, God. It's gone. No, no, no, No, NO! It can't be. Please, don't let it be true.

She checked again, and there was nothing.

Just a void.

A dark, scary, empty spot.

Then she remembered. The earlier dizziness. The acute pain.

Devastation swamped her, and the world turned black at the edges. Caitlyn was gone.

Her dream. Her family. Everything... everything she'd ever wanted...gone.

CHAPTER THIRTEEN

Grant stopped pacing and pivoted on his parents' living room designer rug, which matched his mood—black with fleeting specks of gray.

"What do you mean by convenient, Dad?"

From a blood-red wingback chair, his father glared at him over the top of his bifocals, his caterpillar eyebrows connecting. "Simply, if your sister had returned to town, there would have been awkward questions and innuendos, and I would have had to take care of the situation. Our family integrity would have been questioned. The past would have been dredged up again, and we would have needed to spend months trying to clear our name. My law business would have been in jeopardy. This is a sad tragedy, but one that's happened in a way that allows us to avoid intense scrutiny and speculation."

Vivian Newhall sat to the left of the domineering man, a teacup from her grandmother's china set balanced in the palm of her left hand. Her right fingers held a silver spoon, swirling cream into the red liquid counter-clockwise. Her ominous silence marked time. Never once did she look up, maintaining her demure, practiced blank face.

Grant's hands fisted at his side. "But the look on your face, Dad, indicates you had a clue where she was this whole time."

"Your assumption is out of line," his father's reply flashed like a yellow warning beacon, but Grant wasn't about to stop or slow down. He wanted answers.

"But you both knew something. I've been a lawyer long enough to know when someone is not telling the truth."

"If you must know, when Caitlyn didn't return, your mother insisted I hire an investigator. He was able to track her to the train station in Denver, but then her trail went cold. She disappeared. The investigator reported there wasn't any evidence of foul play. I figured she wanted a little freedom and would return home on her own." Buck took a long pull from a crystal water glass, and shrugged. "After six months, when she didn't return, I figured she didn't want to be found."

Grant shoved his hands into his pockets to avoid sending the man back to the hospital. "But why did she leave? She wasn't the type to go places on her own."

"I don't know." The softening of his father's shoulders and his direct eye contact indicated the man was telling the truth. His mother, with her steel-stiff back and clamped tight mouth, communicated the opposite.

Out of frustration, Grant again paced the length of the room, the coins in his pocket keeping beat with the pounding steps. He wanted to hit something, anything, until his knuckles bled and his hand and arm went numb. He painstakingly replayed the conversation in his mind, analyzing each sound bite, endeavoring to find sanity in his parents' whacked-out logic. A conclusion began to take shape. He stopped parallel to his parents, appreciating the barrier the leather sofa provided.

"And, what about you, Mother? Do you know why she left?"

"Why would you ask me such a silly thing?" His mother shifted slightly before regaining her usual rigid poise. *What are you hiding, Mother?* Her eyes connected with his briefly before she found a crumb from her butter cookie more interesting. "Your father said he doesn't know why she left, and frankly, her departure was so upsetting, I had to let your father handle things." His mother gracefully set the fragile cup on the side table before folding her long, slender hands in her lap.

"Handle things? Since when do you allow other people to *handle things?*"

"Grant, don't upset your mother," his father said protectively. "Or me, for that matter. My doctors insist I reduce the stress in my life."

Stress. Right.

He ignored his father and leaned in to study his mother's face. "In case you forgot, Mother, Caitlyn was your daughter, and my sister." Grant's voice raised an octave higher.

"You spent years raising her, grooming her in your likeness. You even forced her to date James Hunt when she didn't want to. She did everything you asked of her."

"Not everything." His mother's eyes widened, and suddenly her expression resembled someone who'd swallowed a cherry pit.

"What do you mean, not everything?" Grant was well aware his tone could have ground pepper.

Sudden tears glistened in her eyes, and she pulled out a hanky to dab the corner of her eye. This entire episode reminded him of a badly acted movie. "You already know the answer, dear." She sniffled to emphasize her point. "By the mere fact that she ran away, she demonstrated her lack of loyalty to this family. We gave her an excellent education, proper social introductions, and she traded our generosity for what?—mucking stalls on a farm. Please." Her head tilted back, her fingers gently nudging the dyed blond hair from her forehead. Her tear-filled eyes reconnected with his. "Grant, release the poor couch before you leave imprints in the leather."

Grant's fingers dug in deeper. "It's amazing how conveniently you forget your grandfather moved here to farm and develop this land. If it hadn't been for him breaking his back, squeezing every ounce of sunlight out of the day, you wouldn't be able to stick your surgically-altered nose so high in the air."

"You're being disrespectful," his mother responded in a shrill voice.

"You live in a fantasy world, Mother. If I were you, I wouldn't be following any little white rabbits down black holes."

His father stiffened. "That's enough. You will not speak to your mother that way."

Grant crossed his arms and rocked back on his heels. "Well, maybe if you hadn't pushed Caitlyn so hard, or punished her for wanting to be a veterinarian instead of a lawyer, she wouldn't have left."

His father's eyes forged a searing hot fire before a mask of indifference shuttered into place, dousing the flames. "I don't know what you're talking about."

"Sure you do. Caitlyn told me how furious you were when she applied to Colorado State's

College of Animal Sciences and got in. You made her life miserable. She—"

"That type of education doesn't produce the kind of social environment suitable for your sister," his mother interrupted. "Certainly, I understand girls don't attend college anymore to find husbands, but a college campus is a perfect environment to make proper connections. We'd already made arrangements at Princeton. Only an Ivy League school would have provided the correct opportunities for her. For such a smart girl, she was rather foolish."

Grant's gut twisted in disgust. "Listen to yourselves. Caitlyn didn't want to get married to some guy with a trust fund and have babies, she wanted to become an animal doctor. That's all she ever talked about."

"Then she got what she asked for, now, didn't she?" His father waved his hand in the air as if flicking away a fly. His accusing gaze honed in on his wife. "Why you let her watch those melodramatic television shows is beyond me. The boys didn't watch that trash."

"How do you know?" Grant challenged. "We were sent away to boarding school at eight to learn discipline—become men. You never visited, except for the obligatory parents' day, of which you both missed half. So, I ask again, how do you know?"

"Don't you dare question me."

Grant squared his shoulders. "It's about time someone did."

His father uncrossed his legs, and shoved up from the chair, only to fall back. His hand clenched the chair's cushioned arms. Beads of sweat formed on his forehead. His mother reached for a medicine bottle sitting on the side table, and struggled to release the lid.

Grant moved around the end of the couch and extended his arm, offering help. His mother hesitated before she relinquished the brown-tinted bottle. Seconds later, Grant opened and extended his palm to allow his mother to select the correct dosage. She gently placed the medication to his father's lips. Color slowly crept into his dad's face, and stalled his mother's frantic efforts to pour a glass of water. Grant returned the remaining pills to the bottle, secured the cap, set the bottle on the table, then walked toward the kitchen to let his temper cool.

The restaurant-sized kitchen, with state-of-the-art appliances, antique white cabinets, and Italian granite, gave him room to pace in private. He pressed his palms on the counter's cool surface, stepping back to stretch the knotted muscles in his back.

"Do you believe your mama knew where *la niña* was?" asked a small, whispered voice.

Grant turned to the Hispanic housekeeper settled in the family's breakfast nook, hand-drying crystal stemware. "Carmelita, I didn't know you were here. Isn't this your day off?"

"Mrs. Newhall insisted I come in today in case people visit."

Grant nodded with sympathy. "How is Javier doing? Did he make an appointment with the tutor I recommended?"

Carmelita rotated the crystal in her petite, work-roughened hands. "My grandson thinks he is a man, and school is not necessary. I try to tell him otherwise, but he does not listen to this old woman."

Grant unbuttoned the top button of his shirt to dismiss the formality his parents demanded. He leaned across the counter for his favorite churro treat. "Not so different from when Jason and I were young, eh, Carmelita?"

Her dark brown eyes studied him, as if seeing a time-lapse movie of photographs compressed into a few seconds, before she picked up another glass to dry. "No, not so much different. You still don't answer questions."

"What que…ah, that question." Grant bounced his fist on the counter. Maybe that's why Jenna's avoidance of questions frustrated him so much. She was his mirror. Somewhere he read people tended to loathe the traits in other people they disliked most in themselves.

"Yes," he turned to face his nurturing, yet gently strict caretaker. "I think my mother knows more than she is saying." He unconsciously kicked the cabinet toe board. "In this case, I think my father resents that one of his children created a spectacle, but instinct tells me he was as shocked as I to learn of her death."

"I should have said something."

The guilt embedded in the age-weathered face made the hair on his arms stand at attention. "About what?"

"Your sister, she was afraid all the time. Quiet. I thought maybe something happened at school, but she said nothing. Kept to herself. When she came home, she would lock herself in her room and rarely come out."

"My parents can drive anyone to their rooms."

She waggled her finger back and forth. "No, no. Back then, your parents were never around. They spent most of their time at the club."

Grant took a few steps closer to the shadowed corner. "I don't understand what you're trying to tell me."

Tears welled in the aged housekeeper's eyes. "I was cleaning, you see. Not snooping," she assured. Carmelita's hands shook so hard she had to set the glass on the counter. "Mrs. Newhall, she always says not to be seen or heard. So I kept quiet." She glanced at him, then away as her hands wrapped around each other in a nervous tangle.

"It's okay, Carmelita. Take your time."

"Time. Out of time." Her sad brown eyes lifted to his and held steady. "It doesn't matter now."

"Will you trust me and tell me anyway?"

"*La niña*, she was pregnant. I heard her on the phone arguing with her boyfriend. I never did like him."

"No one did, except Mother." The air in Grant's lungs released with a hiss. "Did anyone else know about this?"

Carmelita's head slightly bobbed. "Jason knew. He said not to worry. He'd take care of Caitlyn...that everything would work out fine."

Not to worry?

Grant extended his hand to Carmelita's arm. "This isn't your fault."

"Maybe, if—"

"No shoulds or woulds or coulds or maybes. Isn't that what you always taught us? Not to second-guess."

The housekeeper's mouth quirked up as she remembered. "She was such a sweet girl."

"The night she disappeared, you told the police she was home until after six, that you didn't hear her leave."

"That's right. She was waiting for a girlfriend."

"Do you think she lied? Was she waiting for her boyfriend?"

"I don't think so. She didn't like him much, and only dated him to please your parents."

A wad of cinnamon churro dough must have jammed down his throat, because he couldn't swallow, or breathe. Memories of Caitlyn flashed by, one by one, circling in his mind, a whirligig of different places and times. His friend, a person he could talk to, tease, laugh with, share successes and failures. God, he wished he'd done things differently. Stayed home, or stayed in contact. He couldn't quite believe his buddy—his little sister, his confidante—was gone.

Forever.

Jenna's face suddenly appeared, as if one file opened while another closed. Jenna reminded him of Caitlyn—the way she approached life, her cautious optimism. A powerful and profound longing hit him with such force, he had to widen his stance to find balance.

He leaned a bit to the side to see the housekeeper's face. "I'd better go. Will you be okay?"

"You go before your father's nap, or you'll get your mother's sharp tongue."

Grant reached and pinched the old woman's cheeks, a gesture he used since he was a lad to make her blush. "*Mi yaya* still looking out for me, after all this time?"

Both heads turned toward the door recognizing the shrill voice in the hall.

"Go now," Carmelita said picking up a dishtowel and another stem of crystal.

Without a word, Grant leaned in and kissed the soft, wrinkled forehead, then grabbed the kitchen door handle to escape.

Halfway down the garden path, he remembered his jacket, but a little chill versus the frostbite he'd suffer if he returned to the house, was worth the discomfort. After quietly closing the iron gate, he pulled the car keys from his pocket.

He wanted to go home—not to his house, not to his mountain ridge—but to a little cabin sitting next to a creek. A rustic wooden box with no phone service and no heater, only a wood stove, which barely pumped out enough heat to keep the people inside it warm on a cold mountain night, and a double bed that sloped toward the center.

A place where he could hold Jenna in his arms.

The woman who reminded him of where he wanted to be—with her—home.

CHAPTER FOURTEEN

Jenna awoke to a trickle of sunlight dancing through Grant's bedroom window, nudging her from slumber. Sparrows darted from tree to tree, shaking the dry needles off the prickly limbs. She leaned back into Grant's warmth. His arm tightened around her waist, revealing his wakefulness.

Yesterday, Grant arrived at her store late in the day. He seemed lost. Alone. His miserable expression mirrored what she felt. Her sister's death had blasted a hole in her soul. She didn't have the heart to push Grant away, even as exhausted as she was, and agreed to dinner at his place.

Yet that wasn't wholly accurate.

She didn't want to be alone either. In fact, she wanted to be with Grant. No one else. She'd spent the week furiously baking and working on her business plan, trying to avoid addressing the feelings she had shoved into a small emotional jar and screwed the lid on tight.

"Good morning," Grant mumbled, his face buried in his pillow.

Jenna turned her head. "Did you sleep at all?"

He lifted his head to see the clock on the night stand. "Only the past hour."

The thick black circles under his eyes hadn't disappeared. He rolled, and she settled her head into the crook of his arm, the ache of loss surfacing again.

She'd barely eaten or slept in the past several days since her sister's death blew her world apart. She placed her hand on his stubbled chin. "I should go. Maggie's coming by at ten to pick up the cookie trays for the memorial service. I thought I might box a few dozen extra for your parents' reception, in case more show up to the funeral than expected."

"Don't worry about it."

"If your parents run out of food, it will reflect poorly on the café. Your parents will be swift to point the finger. I still don't understand why they didn't use the Elkridge Lodge caterer."

A small, sly grin formed on Grant's face.

Her fingers clutched his chin and wiggled. "What did you do?"

Grant shrugged. "When I overheard my mother's assistant complaining about being unable to book the Lodge or find a last-minute caterer, I might have dropped a hint or two. My parents don't have to know where the food came from. Besides, River Creek's food is better than those places that charge twelve dollars for an appetizer the size of a quarter."

"More like the size of a dime," she huffed out with a dollar's worth of sarcasm. Spontaneous laughter shook the bed. Jenna placed her cheek on Grant's warm chest, wrapping her arms around him and squeezing his sides, before the loss of Caitlyn came tumbling back, and her mood sobered. With her finger, Jenna slowly wrote Caitlyn's name on Grant's stomach. She wasn't quite ready to put her sister in the ground, but today would force her to face reality.

"What are you thinking?" Grant asked, threading his fingers through hers.

"I'm wondering if Caitlyn would have wanted a funeral service. When you're young, you think you'll live forever."

"I get that. My life changed after my friends died. I no longer had the patience to wait for things, and began to focus on my career, burying myself in details. Every day, I took some action toward securing my happiness. Or at least what I thought was my happiness. Turns out I was trying to make my parents happy, not me." He hauled in a deep breath and sighed it out. "Maybe that's why, when I saw you, I knew."

"You knew what?"

"That you are the one."

Jenna lifted onto her elbow. "Grant, please."

"Jenna, I want to spend the rest of my life with you."

But, I don't know how to be loved. I would only

hurt you. "You must be crazy. I've told you before I wouldn't make a good wife."

"Crazy? Maybe. But I want *you.* I know it in here." Grant thumped his chest with his fist.

Jenna flopped onto her back and placed a forearm over her eyes. "This isn't good."

Grant pulled her arm away from her face. "Why?"

An excuse. Any excuse. C'mon think. "Your parents, for one."

"I'll take care of my parents. Since I'm the only one left, if they want grandchildren, they'll learn to behave."

Children? All the air in Jenna's body evaporated. She couldn't breathe, and threw back the covers, launched out of bed, and grabbed her nylon track pants at the same time.

"I can't have children. We've been over this."

"We can adopt."

I can't. I just can't. "Who said I wanted children?"

"You're great with kids."

Great with other people's kids. What if she couldn't care for them properly? What if something happened to her, and they were left alone to fend for themselves—like she'd been? No. She couldn't do that to a child. She wouldn't orphan them.

She pushed her arm into her long-sleeved shirt. "Maybe we should have this discussion in the next century."

He sat up, the sheets falling to his waist. She counted the squares on the comforter to avoid the hot yumminess sitting in bed, and all the roiling emotions this conversation created.

"I didn't mean to scare you." The tenderness in his voice almost made her want to crawl back into his arms.

I know, but you did.

She squeezed her lips together, her mind generating and dismissing several frantic responses, before settling on the generic. "I need to get going. I want to check on those cookies."

Before she could take a step, Grant was vertical, blocking her way. "You're changing subjects again. I don't mean to make you uncomfortable, but you asked for honesty. That's what I've given you. What we have is good, and I'll do whatever it takes to stop my parents from coming between us."

"It's not just your parents."

"Don't run away. I want us to talk this out."

Jenna leaned in, her forehead hitting his midsection. "I thought we understood each other. I want to keep things simple."

"Life doesn't always work out that way."

"Not for you, at least. There are expectations attached to your fancy last name —being seen with the right people, being in the right places. That's not me."

"We can compromise."

Jenna shook her head. "I've made sacrifices and hard choices my whole life. I'm tired of being the one who's always bending to fit in. I don't want to have to try so hard anymore."

"Compromise and sacrifice have two different meanings. I don't want you to have to give up things you love...I'm asking you to meet me in the middle."

"The ingredients for compromise are missing from my recipe book."

Grant pulled his fingers through his bedraggled hair. "Maybe this isn't the right time to discuss it."

Today, next week, a year from now, and she still wouldn't be ready to go where Grant was heading. Permanence wasn't something she had experience with, and she didn't know if she could get there. She'd already taken a big risk with the bakery. Anything more was way too soon.

"I should go."

"Will I see you at the funeral?" The despondency in his voice made her reach out to cup his cheek with the palm of her hand.

"It will be okay. I'll be there. Just a muffin's toss away if you need me."

Grant's eyes welled with tears, and he reached for her again. "I can't believe she's gone." He shifted his weight. "I mean, I know she's been gone a long time, but I always imagined I'd get a phone call one day saying, 'Hey, what's up?' That won't happen now."

The emotional words weakened her resistance and overwhelmed her meticulously crafted defenses.

Jenna slid her hand down and paused above his left pec muscle. "She's here. In your heart, just like she's in mine. She always will be."

Grant's mouth pressed against her forehead, then her cheek, searching for her lips. Once he found them, his wounded passion surged forward. He cupped her head, pulling her closer, before sliding his hands down her back and rounding her rump. His erection pushed into her belly.

"I need you," he whispered next to her ear. "Please, I need you."

She lifted her hands to his chest and pushed. He stepped back. Their eyes met. Hunger and need filled his pleading eyes. Crossing her arms, she clutched the fabric of her shirt and pulled. His hands slid up her sides. His thumbs drew circles around her already aroused nipples.

Jenna placed one foot on the hem of her sweat pants and pushed the waistband to her knees. "Then make love to me like tomorrow doesn't exist," she demanded.

With a deep groan, he stepped back and pulled her with him as his mouth descended.

Envisioning Grant thrusting deep, deeper than ever before, made her shiver with lust. His warm, muscular body made her sizzle. His skin tasted salty, all smooth, while individual parts became swollen and hard. She wanted to touch and feel and explore, and moaned when he slid his hands between her thighs. He nudged her legs apart, spreading them, making room for his prepared body. His erection pushed against her.

"What are you waiting for?"

He didn't respond, only dropped his head to slide his tongue over her erect and waiting nipple. Her body arched to meet him and deepen the sensation. He serviced every centimeter of skin, taking his time.

When she reached for his stiff rod and stroked, he let out a sound that reminded her of a bear coming out of hibernation. The low, throaty growl pleased her, as she pushed and pulled the smooth skin.

"My turn," he whispered, and then reached for the layers of skin, separating, stimulating, until she couldn't wait any longer. She reached for his hips and pulled.

"Now," she commanded, and swore she heard a gentle laugh.

He pulled back, pushed her to the bed. She crawled backward on the mattress. He followed, centered on her, and didn't wait another moment. He took her, surging inward, so devastatingly inward, in slow, slow motion. Impatient, she thrust her hips up to meet him halfway. He pulled back.

She expected careful, but tender wasn't what she got, and she loved it, arching to meet him. Again and again and again, he thrust, pushing her toward the sought-after state of mindlessness. She could hear someone crying and begging for more, but didn't associate the gasp of ecstasy with herself. On one last thrust, she screamed and exploded, and Grant followed shortly after before collapsing on top. She reached her arms higher to pull him closer, but closer wasn't possible.

She panted out a breath, as he rolled to her side. She fought returning to her senses, because she didn't want to think. His fingers drifting up and down her side created only a small distraction, only enough to avoid rational thought.

"Jenna?" he asked while nuzzling her ear.

"Yeah?"

"Thanks for staying," Grant's open expression and raw words packed a powerful punch.

The simple words shouldn't have made her want to roll over and start from the beginning, but they did. The guy made her feel safe and loved, things she was sure wouldn't last. But hope kept her coming back.

Then again, she wanted to feel something.

Anything.

Other than being numb and empty and alone.

CHAPTER FIFTEEN

Cheeriness was everywhere. Birds sang happily. Wildflowers tilted joyfully toward the light. Even the grave markers brightly reflected the sun's warmth. She folded her arms around her waist to ward off the unsettling gaiety of her surroundings.

Caitlyn was dead, and nothing would bring her back.

The pastor's words pounded her into a surreal void. Alone. Lost. Emptiness encased her heart. The detachment expanded, setting her adrift, tumbling down the raging river, bashing her against the rocks, her lungs filling with water, no life jacket, no rescue in sight.

She stared at the casket hovering above the freshly disturbed ground.

An ache filled her so completely the soft wind created an imbalance. Warm, unfettered tears flowed down her face. She wept for the lost and lonely years. She wept for the broken connection, for the future she'd never have with her sister—her only family.

Protecting Caitlyn had been her sole purpose in life until the day she was betrayed by those nuns and the Newhalls. The day her sister skipped down the children's home hall, replayed in her mind. Jenna could still see her doll dangling from one hand, her other clasping the hand of the nun who was taking her to meet some people.

Had Jenna known that moment would be the last time she'd ever see her sister alive, she might have run screaming down the hall, wrapped her arms around her sweet, fragile sibling, and never let go. At seven, Jenna still had a child's uncolored trust. When the nun said her sister would be right back, Jenna had believed the evil woman.

Across the cemetery, a distant movement drew her attention. On the hill to her left, a single elk stood in the tall grasses, watching. The giant male's head swung toward her while at the same time a graceful peace settled in her soul. The sun glinted off the animal's rich chocolate coat. He seemed perfectly comfortable in his solitary existence. Would she ever enjoy that kind of solitude? She stood humbled, observing the mighty animal, clenching and unclenching her fingers, working to increase the circulation in her hands.

Silently she thanked the animal for soothing her spirit, and wondered if Caitlyn had come to her in another form to ease her burden.

When she turned back, people had already started moving toward the line of cars, or around the graveside, like a swarm of black ants surrounding a piece of food. She hung back, wanting to avoid getting caught up in the crowd, not caring, or wanting to hear the words of condolence for a life taken too soon.

"Jenna?" Grant's voice broke through her misery. She swiped a tissue across her face quickly, then shoved the damp ball in her pocket.

She kept her eyelids lowered. "It was a lovely ceremony." She picked imaginary lint off her black slacks.

Vivian Newhall summoned her son in a come-now tone of voice. Grant ignored her. "Are you all right?"

What could she tell him? That her whole world had been put into a jar and shaken until nothing made sense anymore? Her legs wobbled from the stress of the day, and from the lack of sleep.

"You should go before your mother causes a scene."

Grant acknowledged his mother with a give-me-a-minute signal. "Why don't I meet you at the café? I won't be at the reception long."

Jenna shook her head. "I'm not in the mood for crowds."

He lifted and folded her hand in his. "The café isn't a crowd, it's family. A bit of a wacky family, but good people. Promise me you'll meet me there."

"Jenna?" Ashley's voice called from a distance.

Ashley and Chase made their way up the

sharp incline. A throb of sympathy over her friend's distraught, sorrowful face ignited.

But wait.

Jenna's breathing stalled.

Her heartbeat thrummed and thrummed again before she identified the sentiment on her best friend's face, and a certain truth—Ashley had known her sister. Based on Ashley's expression, she and Caitlyn had been more than friends. Best friends, maybe? Worse yet—she knew Jenna's secret—but for how long? How had Ashley found out? Why hadn't she said something?

Ashley stopped in front of her. "I would like to introduce you to someone."

"You knew, didn't you?" The embittered words churned out. "For the past three years, you knew."

Her best friend's face paled to a sickly shade of grey. "Jenna, please, you have to understand, I was her friend first."

"Don't. Just don't make excuses. I thought we were friends. Why? Why would you do this?"

"Why didn't *you* tell me you were Caitlyn's sister? Why didn't you trust *me*?"

The deceit sliced at her wrists making her ache. "Because I didn't know who I could trust."

Grant moved to her side and slipped an arm around Jenna's waist, but she shoved out of his grasp and turned toward the woman she'd believed was a friend.

"I assume you knew where she was. That she was alone. That she needed help. And you didn't tell me...you didn't tell anyone."

Grant placed his body between her and the younger woman. "What's going on?" he demanded.

Ashley circled her hands protectively over her pregnant belly. "I wanted to tell you—I did —but Caitlyn wouldn't allow it. She was stubborn, more stubborn than you are."

"That's crap, and you know it," Jenna took several steps back.

Grant followed Jenna, and placed a supportive hand on her forearm, and then rounded on Ashley. "It was you—wasn't it? You were the friend she was waiting for that night. You knew where Caitlyn was all this time?" Grant accused, his voice raw.

"No. I didn't. Honest." Ashley reached for

Chase with a shaky hand. "She contacted me a couple years ago, but refused to tell me where she was. She said I wouldn't be safe."

Ashley's pleading eyes darted to Jenna, then Grant, then back to Jenna.

An older man she'd seen earlier approached the group tentatively with a little boy in tow. The man's halting breath made her wonder if he might collapse, but he managed to make it the last several feet up the hill.

"May I help you?" Grant asked, his tone clearly conveying *go away, this is a private affair.*

The man looked like someone who'd moments earlier walked off the set of an old western. Jenna glanced at the man, then studied the boy. Her breath hitched. The sweet, innocent face had eyes the color of the Colorado sky. *Caitlyn.* A color she hadn't seen in years. *There you are.* Those eyes had haunted her, reminding her of happier days...before they were snatched from her, never to be seen again.

Family. The little boy. He was family.

The breath she was holding released.

Pieces from her shattered heart knitted back together again.

Renewed hope resuscitated her soul. This boy filled her with something unexpected. He filled her with love, a love she could trust in.

Caitlyn had left a piece of her behind.

The old man pulled an envelope from his pocket. "Sorry to bother you, Miss. But are you Jenna Graden?"

Movement behind her pricked her skin in warning, and she turned to see Vivian Newhall standing less than three feet away. If the woman had a gun, Jenna would have been dead. The hatred in the woman's stare could have punctured her with nails.

"I couldn't place why you look so familiar." Vivian hissed, her words pointed. "I should have known. You wanted into this family. Until Grant came along, you didn't have an in. And to think you've lived here for the past three years, right under our noses."

Grant looked at Jenna, Ashley, the old man, and the little boy, frowning, before turning to his mother. "Mother, don't say one more word."

A slimy, sadistic smile spread across the woman's face.

"Mrs. Newhall, I can explain." Jenna pleaded.

Grant's hand left her arm. "Jenna, there's nothing to explain."

Vivian Newhall slithered to her son's side. "So you knew? How convenient."

As Vivian neared, the little boy's lips trembled, and he pulled on the older man's hand, trying to get free. When he couldn't, he did his best to hide behind the man, his watchful eyes peeking out and tracking Vivian's every move.

Jenna couldn't stand the horrified expression and swooped in to pick him up, wrapping her protective arms around the tiny frame. The little guy reluctantly laid his head against her shoulder, nuzzling into her neck, yet still keeping an eye on the older woman.

Grant moved to block his mother from view.

Vivian took a step around her son. "I'll take my grandson."

"No you won't." Several voices responded at once.

Jenna tightened her grip when the boy whimpered. "It's okay," she whispered. "I won't let anything happen to you."

Blue eyes searched hers. "Are you my auntie?" a little voice asked, spreading and deepening Jenna's terror and indecision.

I am, instantly formed in Jenna's mind. She considered the blond-haired little boy.

"Answer the boy's question," Grant said.

She turned and met Grant's compassionate gaze, and tightened her arms around the tiny frame. Then movement behind her made her turn. Chase, Ashley's husband and shield, had moved in front of Ashley. Jenna took a step away from the woman she once believed was her friend.

"I...a...I...." She tried to swallow, but her tongue didn't budge. Jenna's mouth had gone dry, and she turned back toward Grant.

Vivian smirked at her discomfort.

Surrounded by anger, she pressed her hand into the boy's back, her determination becoming steel strong.

"Yes. I'm your aunt." The conviction in her voice rang loud and clear. "You don't need to be scared. I'll protect you—I promise."

CHAPTER SIXTEEN

Jenna sat peering over Nellie's steering wheel, staring at the activity in the café.

Could she do this? Face all those people she'd lied to for years? Her insides shriveled.

Her dishonesty tasted like unsweetened chocolate. Bitter. Vulgar. So many should-haves and could-haves had clamored in her mind during the past hour, she couldn't keep track of them all.

She considered the proof of identity the old man had asked her to bring. She didn't need proof of Kyle's. The instant she saw those blue eyes, there was no doubt.

Those bright, crisp blue eyes had come to her in dreams, and even in the middle of the day, when least expected. The color she compared to all others, only to find them lacking.

Caitlyn had the prettiest crystal-blue eyes, and the boy's eyes matched perfectly. A knock at the driver's side door startled her out of her whirling deliberations.

When her heart stopped thundering, she rolled down the window.

"Are you going to sit out here and bake your butt off, or will you get your butt inside where there's air conditioning?" Maggie's lack of anger or resentment surprised Jenna.

"I'm coming. Just give me a minute."

"Good. Test your blood sugar levels and take extra insulin. Ted's making you a juicy hamburger with all the trimmings. Comfort food is what you need today." Maggie removed one hand from her hip, reached in her pocket, and handed Jenna a tissue. "There's a cute little boy inside who's very scared, hurt, and confused. He doesn't understand what's happening. He keeps asking where you went."

Oh, no, he thought I abandoned him.

"We let him know you had some things to take care of this morning, and were anxious to see him. So dry those eyes and pluck up your courage. It will be okay."

Jenna gasped at Maggie's generosity. The shadow from the café hid Maggie's expression, but she got the impression the woman was quite pleased with herself.

"You're not mad at me—for not telling you I'm Caitlyn's sister?"

"I'm pretty smart, you know. It took me awhile, but I figured it out. It was your mannerisms and a few of the phrases you used that got me thinking. I figured you'd tell me when you felt comfortable."

"I'm sorry, Maggie, I—"

"No need to be sorry. Just come inside."

"Why's the café so empty?" Jenna stared through the bank of windows at the old man and the blond, curly-haired boy swinging his little legs on the stool at the counter.

"I figured everyone would choose free food at the Newhalls' so I closed early. But let's not change subjects. You've got five minutes to get inside before I come get you." She turned and sashayed those large, round hips back into the restaurant.

Jenna rested her forehead on the steering wheel and groaned.

You can do this. You need to do this.

Living in a small town was a particular hell only the deranged accepted. Palming the keys, she opened the Jeep's door. She might be insane, but at least she was in good company.

She shuffled to the front door, while her limbs seemed to get heavier and heavier with every step. Once at the entrance, she spent time stomping nonexistent dirt from her shoes. When her excuses to avoid the inevitable finally ran out, she opened the door. Heads turned her direction. The temptation to turn around and leave was so intense, she turned and bumped into a massive human wall.

"Going somewhere?" Grant asked. "When you didn't show up here after twenty minutes, I got nervous something happened and came looking for you. Thank God Maggie called to tell me you were here."

"I a…"

He used his chin to point towards the

kitchen. "Don't tell me you're passing on Ted's cooking." She turned to see Maggie holding up one of the cook's famous burgers.

She pulled her purse in front of her, intending to use it as a shield, but Grant latched onto the fabric and took it from her before she could object. She slid into the first booth she came to, the one closest to the door and farthest from the old man. Automatically, she reached for the sugar, salt, and pepper, straightening the condiments out of habit.

Grant slid into the booth across from her, shoving her purse into the corner. "Are you going to tell me what's going on inside that head of yours?"

"Everyone knows now I'm Caitlyn's sister. That I've been lying all this time." She couldn't meet his eyes. "Everyone must hate me."

"People don't hate you. They just want answers. Tell them Caitlyn was your sister, that you came to find her, but when you arrived you didn't know who to trust, so you hid your true identity. End of story."

"You make it sound so easy."

"What are you going to do about the kid?" Grant's prosecutor's tone drilled in.

"He's coming with me."

"You said you weren't sure about having kids."

"That was before I found out I had a nephew."

Something in Grant's eyes flickered with uneasiness before settling on the people at the counter. "Don't you think you should talk to the old man? To learn more? Maggie said he isn't talking to anyone. Just said he'd wait for you."

The cowboy was doing his best not to look at her. They both were working hard to ignore each other. And both were failing miserably.

Grant closed his large hands around hers. "After a lot of prodding, I got my mother to admit Caitlyn's adoption was handled out of state, and closed. The records were sealed. I promised myself I wouldn't ask, but how did you figure out she was here?"

"Kathy, my foster mom, visited one of the nuns who worked at the children's home where I stayed until I was twelve. I wrote to the nun several times over the years, but never got a response. Five years ago, Kathy visited the sister, who'd been moved to a hospice. She convinced her I wouldn't let the past go until I found Caitlyn, and it was her last chance to set things right. Kathy played on the aging woman's guilt until she got a confession. The nun remembered Caitlyn was taken to Colorado by a family with the last name Newhall. The details were pretty easy to figure out from there."

"I thought maybe Caitlyn signed up on one of those adoption registries, but that wouldn't have made sense if she was hiding."

"She wasn't on a registry. I checked." She discovered a small piece of napkin on the table and began rolling it into a tight little ball. Round and round, she synchronized the motion with her churning thoughts. "The day Caitlyn was adopted was the day my heart shattered completely. Losing my parents was hard, but losing Caitlyn was like losing my left hand. Life wasn't the same. The nuns lied to me. My trust was destroyed. I hated everyone."

Grant sat in silence for a few moments before he nodded and slid from the booth. "I think we need to get more answers. It might help us both get past this. I'll keep the boy company while you talk to the old man. Eat something," he said before handing her back her purse and walking to the counter. He exchanged some words with the boy's guardian before he sat next to the boy, and ordered a coffee and dessert.

The older man pushed from the counter and hobbled over, sliding into the booth with great effort. At the last minute, he plopped an envelope on the table.

Maggie brought her hamburger platter, some silverware, and water. Jenna hesitated. Her stomach had decided to twist into a knot, making her appetite disappear, but now she'd taken the insulin, she needed to eat. She reached for a French fry.

"We have things to discuss," she said, pointing to the white mug stamped with an outline of an elk. "Would you like some coffee?"

"No, thanks. Had my quota for today," the man said with a gravelly voice. "Maggie served me a slice of your peach pie earlier. It was sure good." He said pie like it had a couple extra elongated I's in the word.

His generous compliment didn't help quell

her chaotic emotions. "Guess you figured out I'm Jenna Graden...or was, anyway."

"Got some ID?" He met her gaze. "No offense, but I want to be sure. I can see the resemblance to Caitlyn. You're both beautiful, but your blond hair is darker, and your eyes aren't as blue."

Guess I didn't do a very good job of hiding.

She dug in her purse and pulled out her current ID, birth certificate, and change of name papers. After skimming the documents, the old man shoved the envelope across the table, and then leaned back in the booth.

"My name's Duke O'Connell. Drove in from Sterling hopin' to find you."

She leaned closer to him. "No offense, Mr. O'Connell, but you don't look so good."

A burst of laughter set off a series of congested coughs. Jenna reached for a glass and water pitcher. "Should I call a doctor?"

Sad, bloodshot eyes connected with hers.

"No doctor can help me. Not no more." Duke adjusted his skeleton-thin body before leaning forward. "Caitlyn sure missed you."

"If she missed me so much, why didn't she

get in touch? Obviously, she knew where to find me."

Hurt and anger oozed and bubbled. She rubbed her forehead to ease the escalating frustration.

She'd envisioned Caitlyn at a piano recital, graduating the top of her class in college, or getting married to a gorgeous man. But never did she envision Caitlyn dying.

Jenna choked back a sob. "What happened?"

The old man's face drooped. His desolate sadness stilled the air. She reached for his frail hand.

His gaze grew distant. "It was my fault. I shouldn'ta allowed her to work the tractor—that monster of a machine—but I wasn't feeling so good, and the cows needed feedin'. I didn't know nothin' was wrong till the sun started settin'. I warned her not to go near the embankment. When the tractor tipped, she got caught underneath."

Jenna couldn't imagine Caitlyn working on a farm, much less driving a tractor, but her sister had a stubborn streak larger than her childhood dollhouse, which was big as a dresser. Duke's weathered, overwrought face mirrored Jenna's emptiness. The searing pain from a branding poker couldn't have hurt worse.

"You can't blame yourself," she said, squeezing his hand gently.

"When you get to my age, there ain't a whole lot of people left to blame. When my cancer came back, I should'ta sold the farm, but Caitlyn and Kyle needed a home."

Pushing the old man about the details of her sister's death wouldn't help anyone. His haunted eyes told her what she needed to know, and a few extra details wouldn't bring Caitlyn back.

The image of Caitlyn's beloved doll dangling from her hand popped into her head. Caitlyn had dressed her doll and combed her hair every single day. Her plastic companion accompanied her through mud puddles and snow banks and piles of leaves. Despite the personality differences, Jenna adored her pigtailed little sister, and became protective out of necessity.

"And what of the boy's father?" She rolled the straw wrapper into a tiny paper ball between index and thumb to stop her fingers from shaking.

Duke shook his head and reached for the envelope. "She refused to say. I found Caitlyn alone at a bus stop diner on a run into town. I didn't know she was pregnant at the time. I asked if she'd eaten and wanted dinner. She was scared as a mouse in a cat's mouth. She rejected my offer at first. I kept waitin' for a boy to show up—had my shotgun ready—none ever did. When night fell, she decided my offer weren't so bad."

"Odd she didn't mention who she was hiding from."

"She did slip once and mentioned the name James. I figured he was the father. I sure would've liked to give that fool a piece of my mind for leavin' her."

"James. Might be James Hunt, but he'll never get his hands on Kyle."

She had tracked James down on Facebook. *Irresponsible prick.* Based on the pictures and comments, he'd gotten more than one girl pregnant.

Duke fumbled with the envelope clasp for a few seconds before she gently took the plain

manila folder from his arthritic hands, opened
it, and removed the contents, placing them on
the table. Jenna unfolded the first document—
a birth certificate. She scanned the boxes,
noting the boy's name—Kyle—and his May
birth date. He was four. Last name of mother
and son—Graden, not Newhall. The father's
box was blank.

"But something must have made her leave
Elkridge."

Duke nodded in agreement. "I agree, but
most people don't talk about what or who
they're runnin' from."

Running. That's what Jenna wanted to do.
Run for miles and miles to clear her heart of
the ache that wouldn't end.

"Here's her journal." Duke pushed a thick
leather binder in her direction. "I haven't read
it. I figured she didn't want me to, so I
haven't." His aged lips creased at the corners.
His shaky fingers lovingly touched a few worn
pages before he pulled a white cotton square
out of his back pocket to rub his nose.

"After the baby was born, she drove the
eighteen miles to the nearest library as often

as possible to use those fancy computers. I think she was trying to find you."

And all this time, I was right here. "I was looking for her, too."

The opening of the café's entrance door pulled in a cool breeze. She ignored the fact until a human presence made her look up. "Sheriff Joe."

"Jenna. Sir." The sheriff tipped his hat and gave the old man a thorough assessment. "Would you be willing to introduce your friend, Jenna?"

She supposed he was a friend. After all, he'd taken care of Caitlyn all these years. "Duke O'Connell, this is Elkridge's Sheriff. I have an inkling he has some questions for you."

Duke began to stand, but Joe held out his hand. "Do you mind if I sit?"

Jenna scooted across the leather booth toward the wall. "Help yourself." Duke only nodded and finished wiping his nose.

Duke eyed the sheriff, probably wondering if he was old enough to be protecting this town. "Joe is our recently elected sheriff," Jenna said, trying to reassure the man. "He grew up here. You can trust him."

"What can I do for you, Sheriff?" Duke asked firmly, even though his body pulled inward and his eyes held misgivings.

"I hear Caitlyn Newhall had been staying with you for a while."

"Yep. I knew her as Caitlyn Graden." Duke pointed at the packet of papers. "In there are her personal items."

"Understood." Joe must have also noted the mulishness in the stranger's tone, because he proceeded more gently. "Mind if I take a look?"

Jenna pushed the packet of papers toward the sheriff, and then monitored the activity at the counter. Grant and Maggie and Ted, in various combinations, were working diligently to make Kyle feel comfortable.

The automatic acceptance reminded her of when Maggie had, within three hours of hitting town, given her a job and place to stay. A calming optimism swamped her with the bright, uplifting feeling of belonging—of being accepted.

Joe examined the official-looking

documents. "Everything looks to be in order. Jenna, does this picture look like your sister?"

Jenna accepted the driver's license from him. "She looks like my mom, only she has my dad's nose." *Or had, anyway.* "And that's my sister's locket." She pointed at the delicate chain with the heart-shaped pendant. "It used to be our grandmother's before she passed."

Jenna thought of her parents' wedding bands hidden beneath her T-shirts in the toe of a sock. A crushing sorrow pushed past her defenses and threatened to turn into tears. Thankfully, neither Joe nor Duke were looking at her.

Joe carefully placed the documents back into the envelope, and pushed them aside. "Did Caitlyn ever mention anything about being kidnapped?"

"Kidnapped?" Duke's exhausted expression squinted with questions. "Not that I recollect."

Joe tapped on the table as his expression pinched and closed off. "Did she ever say anything about someone wanting to take her baby?"

"You sure got some interesting questions, Sheriff. Nope, she didn't say nothin' directly."

Duke leaned forward. "Although when she first arrived, she had nightmares, always the same, screaming about wanting to keep her baby. The whole first year at the farm, she reminded me of an abused dog, always looking behind her, hiding whenever someone came 'round, rarely going into town. Something or someone frightened her, all right. After a while, when nobody came, she settled into a routine. A farm has a way of helping a soul heal by working the body—making it strong."

"Did she ever give you an indication of who she was running from?"

"Never said a word. Figured she didn't want to stir the past. She was real careful to protect that boy." Duke turned toward Kyle, his expression contemplative. "And she protected him with everything she had. While she never said a word, her actions did. She never let his precious soul out of sight, and taught him to be wary of strangers."

"Strangers? Or, Vivian Newhall," Jenna asked. "At the cemetery, Vivian scared the bejesus out of him, but he accepted me easily enough."

"Possibly so, but I don't know why."

Jenna watched Grant and Kyle's interaction. *But, he isn't afraid of Grant. Interesting.* Kyle appeared cautious, watching and waiting, but wasn't afraid. Not like before.

"Do you know why she stayed in hiding for so long?"

"She wasn't. Not really. She said she loved the farm. The animals. Tending the crops. She loved her life, but I suspect she said that more because I was sick, then because of the farm."

"Mr. O'Connell, may I ask what your role is in this?" Joe asked.

Duke huffed out a puff of air. "I've asked that question myself a time or two. My wife hated farm living. She met a man and took my son and two daughters with her to live in Texas. Never did get to see them much. When Caitlyn came along…I guess she reminded me of the daughter I never really had." Duke coughed and blinked several times, then looked away.

Joe pulled a business card from his breast pocket and passed it to the man. "Thank you for giving me a few minutes of your time, Mr. O'Connell. If you think of anything else, I'd appreciate it if you would share the information. Someone in this town made her run. I would like to know who."

The sheriff pushed from the booth. "Jenna, you know where to find me in case anything else turns up," he said, sounding calm and matter-of-fact.

"You should know, Sheriff," Jenna waited for Joe to turn back, "Caitlyn mentioned the name James. I'm assuming she was talking about James Hunt."

"Interesting." He pulled out his notepad to jot down a note. "If anyone comes around asking about Kyle, or threatens you in any way, please let me know right away."

Like Vivian Newhall, you mean? She supposed the rumor mill had its uses. "Sheriff, do you think my sister was kidnapped and somehow got away?"

"I don't have enough facts to say, but anything is possible."

Something in the sheriff's expression told her he knew more than he was saying, and she wished she could figure out what it was. Bits and pieces from past and present jumbled together until her mind was about to combust.

"Also…" Joe pointed at the car seat, "if you

need help installing the car seat correctly, stop by the fire station. The guys there will be able to help."

Car seats and Kyle's safety should be the first thing on her mind, but at the moment getting answers took precedence. "Appreciate the information, Sheriff."

Jenna shivered in the summer breeze, and turned back to Duke. "I still don't get why she didn't reach out if she knew I was here."

"Maybe she was afraid. After all, you's was separated when young. Who knows what she was told? If it helps, once she got the word you was here, she started planning a visit. She wanted me to come along, but at the time I couldn't leave the farm, and she wouldn't leave without me. Like I said…nothing you say will take away my guilt."

Jenna covered the man's hands with hers. "And we both know feeling guilty was the last thing Caitlyn would want for either of us. She obviously cared for you a great deal."

The man's sad eyes turned away. "I'll be in town till tomorrow, if you need anythin'. I'm stayin' at the hotel up the road. Figure you know the one, since it's the only place I could find. Then I'll be visitin' my little sister in Denver for a while. She sent me this number."

An acidic taste burned in the back of her throat as Duke handed her a scrap of paper with a phone number. A phone number added up to a pile of deer dung. She needed his help with Kyle. She wanted to know more about her sister.

"Wait a minute. You can't leave Kyle with me, just like that. What if I'm a bad person or…or, something?"

His overgrown brows lifted, "That paper there on the top says something about you's being Kyle's kin. Caitlyn never said a bad word against you. Never. Said you took good care of her when she was little. She missed you. I could tell. Tore her apart not seeing you. Now her son needs a home. He needs his family."

She unfolded the paper and read the notarized statement giving her full custody of Kyle in the event of her death or illness. With Caitlyn gone, she didn't have a choice. And she didn't *want* a choice. She would protect Kyle. Period.

"The boy's things are over there." Duke

pointed an arthritis-plagued, jagged finger to the corner.

The small tattered bag sat beside the car seat. *That's it?* Duke's rasping breath mingled with cracking bones as he slid across leather and pushed from the booth. Duke returned to the counter, and Jenna followed. "I'm gonna ride out, little man. You take care of Ms. Jenna, you hear?"

Small, sad eyes looked up. Kyle's shoulders slumped, his ice cream forgotten. He jumped down and looped his arms around the man's legs. "Can't you stay?"

Duke's hand hovered over Kyle's head, his breathing shallow and forced. "'Fraid not. You livin' with your aunt is what your mama wanted, and I need to visit my sister awhile." He gave Jenna a pleading glance as he pulled the little arms away from his legs and stepped back. "You need to stay with your aunt, little man. She'll take good care of you."

Kyle gave her a skeptical look and pulled away. She didn't blame him. In his mind, she'd already abandoned him when she left him with Maggie and Duke to retrieve the necessary paperwork. But, he'd misunderstood. Leaving him wasn't even close to the truth. The instant those blue eyes turned toward her, she'd given him a piece of her heart.

Jenna squatted down to Kyle's level. "I meant what I said, Kyle. I am your mama's sister—your aunt. I loved her very much." *Just as I love you.* "I'll protect you. I promise."

The young boy grabbed the legs of the counter stool, holding tight, while looking at Duke. Duke leaned across the counter to grab his hat, then pressed the worn leather on his head. "You trust these good folks, now. Ms. Jenna's good people." His eyes turned watery. "Behave yourself, little man." Duke turned and limped toward the exit without a glance back.

"Don't go," Kyle sobbed. Jenna circled one arm around Kyle's shoulders to prevent him from running after Duke. "Don't leave me," the boy screamed, while he pulled and wriggled harder.

Just as the old man reached the door, Kyle broke free from Jenna's grasp and chased after Duke.

Jenna raced around the corner of the last booth to find Kyle plastered against the café door, nose and hands pressed flat. A small, soft gurgling cry emanated from the pint-sized form while a green pickup truck reversed out of the parking spot, his little face turned toward the red taillights until they disappeared around the corner.

Oh, Kyle. I'm so sorry.

Her heart broke with the too-familiar ache of abandonment. She moved closer, and gently peeled the little boy off the glass door, turning him toward her. Thin little arms clamped around her legs, plastering the little guy's distraught, sweaty body against her. The lump in her throat made it impossible to speak.

Kneeling down, Jenna put an arm around Kyle's quivering shoulders and tucked his head into the crook of her neck, letting his tears of grief flow. A soft hum sang in her throat, showing him in the only way she could that she would be there for him.

Finally he sniffled and pulled back a little, watery eyes peering up at her. "Is he coming back?"

She wanted to say what he wanted to hear, but she couldn't give him half-truths.

Adults lied.

She'd sworn many years ago she'd never do that to a child.

The deep sorrow-filled eyes almost broke her. "Duke needs to stay with his sister for awhile. Even though he'd love nothing more than to see you again, I don't think he'll be back."

"He promised to take care of me."

Jenna tried to swallow a wedge of pity while stroking Kyle's vanilla cream hair. "He kept his promise to you and your mom. He brought you to me."

Kyle pushed out of her arms and wiped the tears from his cheeks with the back of his hand. His arms dropped to his side, and he became eerily quiet. She wondered if, in his child's mind, he blamed her for Duke's abandonment.

A muffled, strained sob escaped while he stared at the floor. He moved around her, shuffling along the tiled floor, back to the counter, where his melted ice cream sat uneaten. Maggie tried to intercept and comfort the boy, but he shrank from her touch.

Kyle crawled up into the seat, wrapping his

rail-thin arms around his worn backpack. He laid his cheek against it and rocked silently back and forth, back and forth, back and forth.

His world had crumbled, and no one standing in the café could make it completely whole again.

Even her.

CHAPTER SEVENTEEN

D rumming her fingers on the café's counter, she rummaged through her life experiences, trying to think of what this little boy needed, what she could do to help.

What did she know about raising little people?

Nothing.

Fear, stubbornness, and resolve all commingled to create a push and a pull. Life had pulled another holy-crap card out of the deck and slapped it faceup on the table.

Now a stranger had handed her a child—not to babysit or get to know, but to keep, to nurture, to guide—she needed to think. How was she supposed to support and raise another little human when she was barely managing on her own? She'd deal with it, for sure...but how?

Every major speed bump life had tossed her way began pelting her like hail on a car's roof, a deafening roar of destruction, with no chance to recover, no way to get out of the storm's devastating path. An all-out, wracking, breath-stealing panic ripped through her.

She'd been a child once...a moody, wounded one. Being sole provider for a sad, deserted child required a special kind of skill —a skill she didn't have. Clothing, feeding, educating. School? How old was a kid supposed to be when they started school? She had no clue. She'd start a list of things to learn, but had no idea what to put on it.

Sweet fudge. What's Kathy gonna say? On her way home from the funeral, she tried calling, twice, but got voicemail.

Protect him. That's what Kathy would say. Protect the innocent.

Kyle had shoved his half-eaten bowl of ice cream to the middle of the counter, dropped his chin on folded arms, and stuck out his bottom lip. His orphaned-baby-deer eyes made her want to snuggle, but she didn't think he'd let her. Strangers had tried to comfort her after her parents' death. The memory of those unfamiliar arms trying to touch her hair or pat her shoulder made her skin crawl. Kyle had rolled himself into a self-protective ball.

Her mind whirled in a circle, nothing helpful emerged. In the middle of another anxiety attack, a shadow fell across the counter. She lifted her head to see Grant towering above her.

He extended his hand. "You might need these."

The concern on his face disturbed her, even as she accepted the stack of documents from him.

"Thanks," she said, at a loss for what else to say.

He shoved his hands into his pockets. "I looked over those papers. They need to be verified, because papers like those can be easily forged."

The loops and swirls in Caitlyn's signature resembled many of her early drawings. "The papers are good."

"How do you know? In fact, how do you know this kid's truly Caitlyn's?"

"Because I know. And be careful what you say." She tilted her head toward Kyle. Grant gave her an incredulous look.

"I am being careful," he whispered, sounding impatient. "I ask you again, how do you know if this guy's who he says he is?" he pressed, his lawyerly skepticism kicking in again.

Her nephew sat, quietly entertaining himself by pushing his car through melted ice-cream puddles, his face as long as the day. "Look at him. He looks like Caitlyn...and me." The statement drifted off her tongue with a wisp of softness. "You said once that I look like Caitlyn. I want to find out what made her run."

"So do I. First thing tomorrow, I'll start combing through every piece of evidence, and put a timeline together."

"I appreciate that you want to help, but Kyle is my responsibility."

"I think you're forgetting something important. Caitlyn was my sister, too." He moved closer. "I'll ask again, what are you going to do with this little guy?"

She sucked in a sharp breath.

He's right.

Caitlyn was his sister, at least by adoption.

A plan. Right. She wanted to tell him her plan, but she didn't have one. Her rustic cabin, the box Grant referred to, contained little enough space for one, much less two. She didn't have a clue what to do next, and every person in the café knew it.

"I'll figure something out." Jenna gritted her teeth and slipped into her familiar suit of stubborn.

"I can—"

"No." The word came out more sharply than intended. "Whatever you were about to say, thanks, but I need to do this. He's my responsibility, my family. I'll make it work."

Grant rubbed the back of his neck. "Then let me at least show Kyle to the men's room. He needs to go."

The way Kyle clutched the front of his pants and his puckered-lip grimace indeed indicated an urgency. Why hadn't she been watching Kyle? The same guilt she told Duke not to feel came creeping up her spine.

"Kyle, do you have to go to the restroom?" Jenna asked.

There was that skeptical look again. Jenna slid a gentle hand over his baby-fine hair and down his cheek. "I'm not going anywhere. Go with Grant, and I'll be waiting right here for you to get back. Okay?"

He blinked, but didn't say a word, only hopped off the chair.

She moved to allow him to pass, then turned back and nudged the pile of papers, wishing for an instruction guide, something to tell her what to do next.

What was she supposed to do with a four-year-old?

She turned to watch the man and boy. Just as Grant and Kyle turned the corner, Grant leaned sideways, extending his hand. Kyle's hand slowly stretched to accept the gesture. The picture of the two of them took her out at the knees.

There was something profoundly touching about watching a grown man walk hand-in-hand with a child. The little guy summed up the big man while Grant took slow, measured steps to allow Kyle to keep up. The moment touched her more than she wanted to admit.

Just when her life had been thrown into a blender, fate sent the most exasperating and pushy man to her rescue. God, she could see where this was going. He'd already been pushing for a committed relationship—one she didn't know if she was capable of having.

KYLE WALKED into the bathroom stall, and Grant frowned at the little guy's expression. His chest tightened, and a familiar emptiness punched him in the gut, making him once again aware something was missing from his life.

He experienced an epiphany one day while he was walking along the Chicago pier, watching people soak up the sun. A craving for home and family had gripped him hard. He'd been gone a long time. Too long. He wanted to come home to breathe the mountain air and find the part of him that always was a fingertip out of reach. When his mother called about his dad's heart attack, the universe had sent him a message. Now was the time to make a change.

Grant listened for movement in the urinal. "All done, buddy?" he asked, looking at the grey metal door.

Kyle emerged, pulling on the waist of his pants, and looked up at him expectantly, but said nothing. Grant lifted and held him sink level, watching the sullen boy work the soap dispenser, suds overflowing, dripping into the sink. Kyle rubbed his hands under the faucet, over and over again, splashing water across the counter.

"Good job. All done?"

Kyle nodded. Grant lowered the boy to the floor before ripping off a strip of paper towel. The kid wadded the wet towel into a ball and then slam-dunked it into the trash bin. Kyle reached for the door handle, just as Grant reached out, but the tike pushed his hand aside.

The boy tugged and pulled until the door budged. The three-and-a-half-foot stack of stubbornness had to be Jenna's nephew, because Grant had never run into that level of bullheaded pride anywhere but in a Graden... or was it a Dolcy? Kyle looked around the café with a wide-eyed panic, noticed Jenna, and raced to the table and launch headfirst into the booth before righting himself.

"I thought you might like to color." Jenna had placed a cup of crayons and paper on the clean table, Kyle pulled out a red crayon.

"Want me to keep you company?" Grant asked.

"You don't have to stay. Plus, I bet your parents are wondering where you are."

Yeah, but maybe I don't care.

He slid onto the bench seat close enough to smell the sweet cookie dough scent of hers that made his teeth ache from the sugar rush. Grant nudged her foot with his. "Tell me what you're thinking."

Her sad eyes turned to him. "My sister was searching for me, and I didn't know it." Kyle scraped the red crayon across the paper, then switched colors. A protective mother-bear expression crossed Jenna's face.

"What would you have done if you had found her?"

Her eyes narrowed in disgust. "What kind of question is that?"

"A logical one."

She leaned back and crossed her arms. "Maybe for you. Asking what-ifs can only send people running in circles."

A few weeks ago, she told him she wasn't smart, since she had only a GED, but she made a whole lot more sense than most. She wasn't smug, or uppity, just stated things the way she understood them. And, whether he admitted it or not, she was part of this town, part of the core making it run. And he wasn't—not anymore.

He smiled to cover his disjointed feelings. "Well, I guess you've got all the answers." He pushed out of the booth. *Stop pushing me away, damn it. I won't let you break my heart.* "My parents sent me a text more than two hours ago, requesting my immediate attendance. If there's nothing more I can do here, I'd better go."

She followed his movements as he leaned in to rub Kyle's head. "Nice meeting you, Kyle."

Jenna lifted her chin. "See you tomorrow?"

"I have some things I need to do."

"Are you mad at me?"

Mad? Never. Just frustrated.

Her pleading expression made his residual anger evaporate. The sweet softness of her tone and Kyle's sad slump re-ignited his desire to make things better. For her. For Kyle. For him. "I'll be by tomorrow for my oatmeal cookies. Same time as usual."

"I'll see you then."

The pulses in his body did a zip and a zing. "Does this mean you're reconsidering my offer?"

"Newhall, don't push it."

There it was—that scrappy tone. The one he'd come to love. He laughed and grabbed his suit jacket, dropping a few bills on the counter to pay for Kyle's ice cream. "It's only a matter of time, Jenna. I'll change your mind yet."

He was out the café door before she could respond.

CHAPTER EIGHTEEN

Kyle hadn't spoken. Not one word since Duke left four days ago.

Her nephew sat at a table in her bakery making dinosaurs out of colored dough she made the day before.

His lack of voice spawned a panic that was an unrelenting vibration beneath her skin. After the loss of the only two people he'd known his whole life, the normal kid energy had been sucked out, and she couldn't figure out how to stuff him full again. Every five minutes she flip-flopped about whether she was the right person to raise him.

That morning Kathy assured her again that

she'd do fine. "Rely on your common sense," her foster mother suggested. Yet how was she supposed to provide a stable, safe home? Clothes? A good education?

Love and patience trumps all. Wasn't that what Maggie said? Apprehension gripped her gut for the millionth time.

In the middle of her next volley of cascading thoughts the store bell rang. Maggie walked in with her usual friendly, rumbling attitude, all business and all in control.

Envy filled Jenna to the brim and the two-tons of doubt began to compress her lungs.

"Hey, cutie pie," Maggie ruffled Kyle's hair. "Found you another car."

The boy perked up, and puddle-stomping delight lit up his face. He held out his hand, palm up, to accept the gift. The metal speedster held his attention for only a second before he jumped to his feet and hugged the curvy woman's knees.

Jealously seared her heart. Why could Maggie and Harold get a reaction from him, but she couldn't? If Jenna had the extra cash to spend, she'd buy every dang car in the toy store to get that reaction.

Maggie's chubby hand rested on the silky blond curls. "You're welcome. Now get busy. I expect a picture." She lifted Kyle's chin and winked before moving to the counter.

"Hey, hon. How's business?"

"Insane. I think I need to grow another set of hands. Between deliveries, baking, customers, bookwork...I can't find my balance."

"Where's Ashley?"

"Her help isn't needed anymore."

"Why? Because she didn't tell you about Caitlyn?"

"Because, she's about to have a baby and shouldn't be on her feet." *More lies.* More guilt heaped into her overflowing measuring cup. "Right now I don't have the time to find and train counter help."

"All you need to do is ask, and I'll send one of the girls over, at least until you find help."

Jenna shook her head. "Like your staff has nothing better to do than make two dozen cupcakes for the preschool class."

"Sounds like you managed to get Kyle enrolled."

"I did, and Gwen's been so helpful. She

found a backpack for him, and picked up his school supplies when she went to Denver. She saved me a bundle."

"Has he started talking yet?"

"No, not yet." Jenna's heart ached. She understood why his voice had shriveled and disappeared—why saying anything to anybody could trigger paralyzing fear, how silence allowed him to feel a sliver of control. She understood, better than anyone, and didn't push him to speak. "When he's ready, he will."

"I hope so, but seriously, Jenna. If you need help, ask," Maggie repeated.

Help. There was that stupid word again. A stubborn seed planted years prior dug in a bit deeper. She didn't want to ask for help. Even more, she didn't want to depend on others, because leaning on another person would mean opening up, trusting, and she wasn't good at allowing others into her space, her life.

Jenna pointed at the bag still in Maggie's hand to change the subject. "Whatcha got there?"

Maggie set the bag on the counter, an excited glint in her eye. "I thought these might help."

Jenna pulled off her latex gloves before peeking inside to see what Maggie brought. Her fingers clutched a heavy material and pulled.

"Oh, Maggie," she gulped down a wad of injured pride. "These are perfect, you shouldn't have." She held the pair of jeans in the air, while the inability to afford a simple pair stirred up some shame. "Kyle, come and see what Maggie got you."

He walked to the counter, barely lifting his head, avoiding the cracks in the tiled floor.

Jenna dropped the pair of pants into his outstretched hands. "You'll look good for your first day of school, don't you think?"

His fingers caressed the label secured to the pants. He tugged at the plastic sticker, while studying the 3T symbol. The serious and confused expression broke Jenna's heart. She'd had a similar experience the first time she received a brand-new pair of shoes, still in the box, tissue paper stuffed inside. She didn't care that the shoes were too small or pinched her toes. She would wear them, sleep with them, hold them, to make sure they didn't get stolen, or given to one of the other kids.

Jenna nudged Maggie's arm to get her attention. "Thank you," she mouthed.

The store bell jingled a happy customer tune, and both she and Maggie turned.

"Hey, Ernie. What can I get you today? Would you like to have the double chocolate cream or the red velvet today?"

The deputy's normal friendly smile didn't quite translate correctly today. The tall man in a uniform pressed with precision, walked with a heavy burden.

"I need to pass." Ernie tipped his wide-brimmed hat.

Jenna straightened, the hairs on her neck lifting in warning. "Are your boys okay?"

His forehead creased. "They're fine. I'm sorry to say I'm on duty."

Jenna's breath hitched and lodged in her throat. "Then what can I do for you, Deputy Baker?" Jenna said, adding lightness to her tone to unburden the man.

He reached into his official coat pocket and pulled out a folded wad of papers and handed them to her. Maggie craned her neck to see the typed words. Jenna unfolded and scanned the top of the document, then re-read each sentence to fully understand what the papers meant. She dropped her hand to the counter with frustration, anger, and exhaustion, all descending at once.

Jenna lifted her unbelieving gaze. Her body vibrated. "Vivian and Buck have petitioned for full custody of Kyle, and I've been ordered to take a DNA test. I suppose the test is to confirm I'm related to Kyle. There is no way I'll let the Newhalls take that boy!"

A wounded, heart-wrenching wail filled the bakery and forced Jenna to move with superhuman speed toward her nephew, who was practically running backwards.

Kyle grabbed his new backpack and launched under a table, pushing his little body into the far corner. He clenched the bag to his chest and squeezed his body into the smallest ball possible. Jenna crawled into the darkness, pushing chairs and tables out of the way, to pull the stiff, terror-stricken child into her arms.

"Kyle. Oh, Kyle. It's okay." Jenna said rocking the boy back and forth, cooing. She placed her hand on his head and pressed it down to her shoulder, offering the only comfort she could think of at the moment. She appealed to Maggie and the deputy, who'd rushed to the table's edge and appeared as helpless. "Deputy, if you wouldn't mind switching my open sign on the way out, I'd sure appreciate it. I think Kyle and I need a moment."

He touched the rim of his hat for an instant, and then nodded. "I'm sorry, Jenna. I truly am." His long stride crossed the spotless tiled floor and exited, leaving behind only the heart-wrenching sobs.

Maggie pulled the table fully out of the way and collapsed onto the floor. "I'd like nothing better than to rip—"

"It will be all right," Jenna said, effectively cutting Maggie off. She rested a cheek against the cherished boy's head.

"It will be all right." She said again, trying to convince herself. She scanned the freshly-painted bakery, the brightly lit display cases filled with new baked goods, and the kitchen beyond. The place that at one time had been her cherished dream, a dream drifting farther out of reach with each passing minute.

Her bakery was no longer the priority.

She had a child to protect.

A toe-tapping country tune skipped its way through the store, but all she wanted to do was curl in a protective ball around Kyle and cry. Cry for the time she'd never spend with her sister, for missing her nephew's birth, for Kyle's distraught mental state, for feeling like she was drowning.

With Caitlyn's death came responsibilities, and a family she hadn't known existed, and—worse—had no idea how to deal with.

She'd lost Caitlyn.

She wouldn't lose Kyle. Not to the Newhalls, not to anyone.

"I expect the Newhalls will claim I can't provide a suitable home for Kyle. I've been in the system. I know what the courts will look for. I'll need to find a new place to live, one with a separate room for Kyle."

"I bet this is all Vivian's doing. Damn woman." Maggie blew out a breath of frustration. "I wonder what Mara Gaccione did with her apartment over the flower shop?"

"I think her sister-in-law turned it into office space."

"Right. Finding a place will be difficult.

There are so few vacancies. We'll make something work. I wish I had a couple of extra rooms, but I'm maxed out."

"I'm so sorry to be causing problems."

"You, young lady, are never a problem." The indignant look gave Jenna's heart a miniature pump of relief. "Now Vivian Newhall, on the other hand, that woman I'd like to run over with a lawn tractor."

Jenna kissed the top of Kyle's head. "You wouldn't happen to know a skilled lawyer who doesn't have the last name Newhall, would you?"

"Not today, but we'll search this county, and find the best lawyer our money can afford."

CHAPTER NINETEEN

The last eighteen hours must have been a resiliency test.

Between soothing Kyle, getting him off to preschool, keeping a lid on her emotions, the lack of appetite, and no sleep, Jenna might still be vertical and functioning, but just barely.

Passing through the kitchen, she made her way to the front, flipped the "Open" sign, and unlocked the door. She lifted a tray of dough and pulled on Fred's handle. "You treat those baby bites of brownies nice, old man. They need some TLC," she said before closing the door and pulling off her latex gloves.

"Talking to your oven again?"

Startled, she pivoted. "Grant, you scared the pee out of me."

He looked mighty scrumptious in his pressed business casual. The open collar and tweed jacket made her again wonder why, once upon a time, she'd preferred men in jeans.

His smile made her heart patter harder for a second. "What are you doing here?"

"I stopped by the café for breakfast. Maggie gave me an earful. I had no idea my parents filed for custody. I thought you might need this."

At the end of Grant's extended hand, a little white card with black cursive lettering sat nestled between his fingertips. Their eyes met.

"Since your parents are petitioning for custody, don't you think offering to help me find legal representation is a conflict of interest?"

Pushing the tweed fabric aside, he braced his hand on his hip. "Let's get something straight. My folks are petitioning for custody of their grandchild. I'm not involved in their case, but I'd like to ensure they have nothing to do with raising any child ever again. If you're thinking of winning, you'll need a good lawyer. I'd represent you, but family law isn't my specialty, and I'm not familiar enough with the Colorado court system yet."

Jenna scanned the business card still sticking out from between his fingertips. "Sure looks like you're involved." She extended a hand to accept the card.

"You're right," he slid his hands into his pockets. "I am involved with a beautiful woman, whom I love very much, and want to see happy."

Holy crap. Ka-boom. He drops the L-bomb, again.

Jenna bumped into the baking island. Reached behind her to grip the edge for stability.

I didn't think you were serious. I thought you meant fond of, not love, as in L.O.V.E..

No, no, no.

He needed to marry someone who could give him babies, and who was already conditioned for his family's kind of social life. She needed to push him away now, or neither would have any peace.

Jenna tilted her chin up to look into his eyes. "You love me?"

Grant's expression suggested he'd wadded up her question and tossed it in the trash.

"I'm not sure it's love." She pushed to get his attention. "I suspect what you're feeling is classified somewhere between pity and sympathy. There's a huge difference."

"Jenna, it's not pity or sympathy," he whispered, with an underline of hurt.

"Then maybe it's a passing lust thing. Or maybe you're attracted to me because I remind you of Caitlyn. Ever think of that?"

Grant put a hand on the butcher block top and leaned in. She slipped out of his trap, and he turned.

"You remind me of your sister in some ways, but you're completely different in others. She didn't make me laugh the way you do."

A hollowness echoed in her soul. "Grant, I know you want to fix this, but you can't."

"You want to bet?" He reached for her hand. "Marry me."

Why don't you get I'm not the woman for you? I'm not the right woman for any man. "And after

Kyle's hearing is over with, then what?" Tears dripped from her heart. "Please let this go."

"I won't let us go, and I want to protect Kyle. There isn't much time. You and Kyle should move into my place, today if possible. There would be two of us to take care of him. We'll share the responsibilities. Both of us have jobs, a good income, we're young...better yet, we can win against my parents."

Oh, God. He's totally serious. I can't do this.

He grabbed her arm, and she shrugged away.

"Jenna," Grant said, his exasperation clearly nearing the boiling point. "You can't do this on your own. I did some checking. The lawyer my parents have retained is top notch, and he will stop at nothing to get his clients what they want. He will look at your living conditions, your ability to provide, and your emotional connection to Kyle. The fact Kyle isn't talking doesn't look good. Are you prepared for that?"

"Caitlyn specified me—chose me," she pointed at her chest and leaned in, "me, Grant, not you or your parents, but *me* to be Kyle's guardian." Jenna paced away, anger solidifying to a rock-hard state. *You're still a Newhall, and*

Newhall's believe in perfection. "That piece of paper gives me what I need to protect Kyle. Besides, this isn't just about where he lives or the type of school he attends. Kyle needs love, all the love he can get, and he doesn't need to be molded into a perfect little doll like Caitlyn. And he doesn't need your pity. For that matter, neither do I."

Grant puffed his chest and crossed his arms. "Why do you always have to be so stubborn?"

"Stubbornness is what helped me survive for the past twenty-eight years. I cut my teeth on it. Lived on it. I learned how to survive. My stubbornness is what will get Kyle and me through this."

He nodded. "I love that about you. But you don't have to do this alone."

"I'm not alone. I have Kyle, and the support of this town. Kyle is my family, Grant. My blood. I'll do what is necessary for his well-being. Besides, that's what Caitlyn wanted. Me to raise her son."

"Then do what is necessary to keep him safe. Marry me. Help me prevent my parents getting custody of Kyle."

Oh, Grant. Why can't you see I'm trying to protect you from me? She squeezed her eyes closed. "Do you always have to push so hard? I can't marry you. No, I won't."

"Is that it? Do I have a chance? Can I change your mind?" He rushed, speeding up, firing one question after another, trying to change the outcome.

"I'm sorry. It has to be my final answer."

Fred's timer sounded, and she moved to the oven door and grabbed the paddle. She removed the bite-sized double fudge and blond brownies from the oven and placed the treats on the racks to cool. When she closed the oven door and looked up again, the front door bells were swaying back and forth, and Grant was gone.

Lifting the card, her fingers brushed over the fancy raised lettering while her stomach churned with remorse.

I'm sorry, Grant. It's better this way.

Melancholy deflated her cheer. She'd forced her white knight to leave. The only man she could see spending her life with.

If only…

The ultra-thick card stock drew her

attention. The law firm had one of those three-name deluxe titles, one she'd never be able to afford, but she'd cross that bridge later. If she had to, she'd work the rest of her life to free Kyle from a cage of silence, and keep him away from that witch.

At least, she and Grant agreed on one thing.

Vivian Newhall wouldn't be raising Kyle. Period.

CHAPTER TWENTY

Jenna's heart skittered, then fizzled when she spotted the mouthwatering man pushing his way through the crowded city park toward her little group of Labor Day parade watchers.

If circumstances were different—if Caitlyn hadn't been her sister, if Kyle weren't her nephew, if she were just a baker—having Grant in her life might have been easier. But Grant represented a whole container of hurt she'd been trying to keep in the deep freeze, but dang it if he didn't keep defrosting her will to stay indifferent.

The way he homed in on her, like she was

the only person standing on the street, made her stomach flutter and her skin tingle with embarrassed heat.

"Newhall, I thought you were busy today." She raised her voice to be heard above the mass of town attendees, all impatient for the parade to begin.

Kyle's body stiffened underneath her hand, and Jenna realized her mistake. "Kyle, remember we talked about Grant's last name. He's a Newhall, but one of the good ones—just like your mom. Her last name was Newhall at one time. Remember?"

Her nephew nodded and was clearly examining Grant under a magnifying glass, trying to reconcile the name with the man— like she'd been doing.

Jenna tilted her head back to see his handsome face. "What brings you here?"

"Given the fact you and Kyle are in the same place as my parents, I figured it'd be best to make sure nothing happens."

"I haven't seen them." She scanned the crowd. "Where are they?"

Grant pointed with his thumb over his shoulder at the white tent ten feet away. "With the mayor, in the parade tent, getting ready to hand out ribbons for the best float."

Next to her, Maggie stiffened. "Did I ever tell you I was my high school's softball pitcher? We took state that year. I've got an accurate arm, and can hit most anything from forty feet. Kyle's got several metal cars in his pocket. I bet he'd let me borrow a couple just in case." Maggie gave the boy a nudge and wiggled the brim of his baseball cap.

Grant's shoulders shook with laughter. "Good to know. Let's hope it doesn't come to that."

"You're no fun," Maggie's giant, pouty lip made Kyle giggle.

"You remember my dad's a lawyer, right?" Grant asked Maggie with a chuckle, which, combined with Kyle's, and sent a happy thrill zinging around her body.

Maggie pulled her floppy white hat with its stars and stripes bandana lower over her eyes. "Everybody wants to sue somebody for something these days."

Jenna pulled a bag of lemon squares from her bag and handed them to Grant. "Here. Give these to your dad. He hasn't had my treats for a while. They might sweeten his disposition."

"I'm not giving these to my dad. He doesn't deserve something this special. I'll eat them myself, or better yet, share them with Kyle. Speaking of which, where did Kyle go?"

Jenna turned to glance behind her and along the street where Kyle had been standing only seconds earlier.

Her breath caught.

She searched left, then right again. "He was right here."

How could I have let this happen?

"Don't panic," Maggie advised, "he can't go far."

Sheriff Joe, who just walked out of the judging tent, walked their way. "Is there a problem here?"

"My nephew's disappeared. He was just here, and now he's gone." Jenna choked.

Oh, Kyle. Where did you go?

Joe reached for his radio. "All deputies, silent code, amber, Kyle Graden is missing. All deputies keep a look out for a little blond-haired boy, age four, wearing..."

"Jeans, he's wearing jeans, and a red shirt,

with a Mickey Mouse baseball cap," Jenna provided.

The sheriff repeated the information before saying, "I'll call dispatch to prepare a hard amber alert."

Jenna gasped. *Oh. My. God. What if someone took him?*

She scanned the crowd, visually grasping hold of anything red, but on Labor Day, the swarm of people turned into a massive sea of red. Leaning farther into the street, she looked to see if the horse brigade or the old fire truck with people hanging off the sides had captured his attention.

Nothing. *Oh, Kyle. Where are you?*

Joe turned to Grant. "Why don't you check the porta-potties. I'll check the food area. Jenna, you stay here in case Kyle returns."

Maggie grabbed Jenna's hand. "It will be okay. Someone will find him."

"How can you be so sure? He still won't talk. I don't know if he'll call for help."

"Have faith."

Faith? Life had rarely treated her with kindness. She didn't expect fate to start handing out favors at this late date.

"I'll check the playground. He might have gone there," Maggie said.

"No. I'll go."

Maggie's hand clamped around her forearm. "You heard the sheriff. You need to stay here in case Kyle comes back."

The swarm of people watching the start of the parade didn't care that her world was imploding. Panic shortened her breath to the point where she had to take a gulp of air.

Someone shouted her name, and she recognized it as Grant's voice. She stepped toward the curb. Hearing her name again helped her home in on the sound.

Grant stood on the side of a stand of bleachers and waved a come-quick motion in her direction. She took off running.

"'Scuse me. Pardon me. Coming through." She zigged and zagged through the crowd, barely breathing, a calm hysteria taking control of her mind and body. Her pulse drummed in her ears.

Grant met her at the edge of the three-tiered stack of metal bleachers. "I found him. He's underneath here, but I can't get to him."

Thank God.

Crouching low, she could make out a small, dark lump wedged under the steps in the middle section. "Kyle," she shouted, but the little guy only huddled farther back into the metal structure. "Hey, little man, don't you want to see the parade?"

She didn't wait for an answer. She didn't need one. Ducking under the metal barrier, she squeezed through the maze of steel.

Let him be okay. Let him be okay.

The boom-boom-boom of her heartbeat pounded against her chest walls. She gasped for air when the breath she'd been holding expired. Another ten feet and she could breathe again.

Kyle's eyes were drowning in terror.

"Kyle? Kyle, are you okay? Did something happen?"

He pulled his knees closer to his body and wrapped his arms around his shins, clutching his ball cap. After reaching him, she smoothed his delicate bangs to the side to get his attention. "It isn't safe here, little man, we need to go." His fisted hands, lackluster skin, trembling body tore at her heart. "I'll protect you. Promise. Just give me your hand."

Slowly, he stretched his arms and reached out. The tension in her muscles slowly released. "That's it. I've got you."

Kyle slowly unfolded from his cowering position and stood before she helped him past the first metal barrier. Weaving their way back under the cross-sections, she could still feel the tension running through his fingers. As they neared the end of the bleachers, Kyle tugged back and finally she understood.

"You still think you'd make a good parent. You can't even keep track of a single little boy?" The sarcasm in Vivian Newhall's voice made her want to punch the woman.

"You couldn't control my sister, or prevent her from leaving. What makes you more qualified?" Jenna cleared the structure and lifted Kyle into her protective arms. Tremors pulsed through his tiny frame, and her fierce devotion spawned a low-level, growling hum. "Why is it children run at the very sight of you, Vivian?" Jenna responded. "More importantly, what did you do to my sister that made her leave?"

Vivian's face deteriorated into a demonic mask. "How dare you make such accusations?"

"Mother," Grant's commanding tone drew the group's attention. "You're causing a scene, and you abhor public displays, remember? Father looks tired. Why don't you take him home?"

Vivian pulled the bottom of her designer jacket down as her shoulders pushed back. After forcibly restoring her haughty composure, her mouth curved into a slow, sadistic smile. "You're right, son. This conversation isn't worth my time. The situation will be resolved shortly."

"Situation?" Jenna's nephew's small arms tightened around her neck. "Kyle isn't a situation, Mrs. Newhall. He's a precious human being." The child's sniffle reshuffled her priorities. The boy's safety became paramount. She turned Kyle away from the threat.

"Grant will you please inform the sheriff that Kyle's safe?"

Without another word she turned and walked toward the park.

I'll protect you, I promise.

Protect you at all costs.

She pulled him closer. "Kyle, what do you

think about making some of your favorite s'mores bars?" Finally, his arms relaxed their death grip from around her neck. "Yeah? Does that sound good?"

His little head nodded. Movement behind her made her turn. Her arms tightened around her nephew's tiny body, then eased.

"Is Kyle okay?" Grant trotted up next to her, his obvious worry somehow soothing her worst fears.

"He'll be even better after we get away from here for a while." She turned to look at the crowd. "I think he saw your parents and got scared."

"Understandable. I want to run, too, whenever I see my parents." His teasing grin helped ease her turbulent commotion . "It'll be all right."

"I'm not so sure."

"My parents will have no control over Kyle. You have my word."

Maggie made her way toward her carrying an armful of bags. The alarm on Maggie's face made Jenna again realize how lucky she was to have such loyal friends.

Her lifelong angst and knee-jerk insistence

on pushing people away suddenly made her surrender. The almost tranquil feeling startled her, yet made her hold onto the new realization that not everyone demanded she give up a part of herself in return.

She now saw Maggie, even Grant, through a newly altered filter. A kinder, more trusting lens.

Maggie handed Jenna Kyle's backpack. "I saw Vivian and Buck Newhall sprinting out of here like their tail feathers were lit on fire and wanted to come and check on you."

"I hate to leave you stranded at the parade by yourself, but Kyle's had enough for today."

"Don't you worry about a thing. All the fliers are gone, Gwen volunteered to re-stock your cookies in the welcome tent, and there are dozens of people I can pester." Maggie's smile deepened Jenna's newfound inner calm. "Now get out of here, and put a smile back on that boy's face. Grant looks like he could use some fun, too," Maggie said with an exaggerated wink.

Here we go again. Why does everyone trust Grant but me?

Yes, he's a great guy. Yes, he's a dependable

guy. Yes, he's a guy any woman with any sense would marry.

*What's my problem? *sigh* I'm chicken-scared, that's what. Scared something will happen before it happens—when that something never does.*

Jenna adjusted Kyle's weight, shifting him from one hip to another.

"Kyle, how about a piggyback ride?" Grant interrupted the bombardment of thoughts.

The instant change on the adorable four-year-old's face reminded her life didn't have to be complicated. Marshmallows, coloring books, and piggyback rides could make the world better in an instant.

Yep, Grant makes my world better just by being in it.

"Well, what are you waiting for?" She released her grip, and Kyle slid down to the ground. "Here, take your flag." She pulled the foot-long stick from her back pocket.

Kyle placed the gift in his backpack, settled his hat on his head, and then took a run and leaped onto Grant's back. Grant turned back to her, both boys awaiting her instructions.

She couldn't quite decide who looked more adorable, Grant or Kyle.

"What do you want first? S'mores? Maybe we can talk Grant into playing catch in the park. Your mitt and ball are in your bag. Or, we all could plan a wedding."

Grant took a step closer. "What did you just say?"

"You heard me." She swallowed the doubt clogging her throat. "Today has shown me I can't do this alone. You were right when you said I need help. Kyle deserves to be surrounded by people who love him."

"And what does Jenna deserve?"

"I've never expected much out of life, so I can't really say."

For a long moment Grant stood silent, then he turned to look at Kyle. "I recommend we play catch. Afterward, we can make some sweets, possibly barbeque some hamburgers with ketchup, just the way you like. We can even add some potato salad and get your favorite pickles. And then your aunt and I are going to discuss moving into my house. Would you like that?"

Kyle's eyes sparkled with a joy that matched Grant's.

No matter how hard she pushed Grant

away, he always managed to weave back into her life.

He might just be protecting Caitlyn's child, or her, because she might remind him of her sister. But she had to give the man credit. He was persistent. His relentless loyalty was quite astonishing, even to the point of matching hers.

Grant would protect Kyle, but how could she protect her heart from Grant?

She couldn't.

He'd probably break it...just like everyone else she'd ever loved.

CHAPTER TWENTY-ONE

The excitement building over the past three days exploded when Grant opened his front door.

Finally. Jenna and Kyle are home.

A contented jubilation sprinted from one extremity to another, and filled his soul with abundant optimism.

Kyle stopped a foot from the door and looked up at him. His arms were wound around his bulging backpack so tight it might take a crowbar to dislodge the bag.

"Can I carry that for you, bud?"

Jenna placed a protective hand on Kyle's shoulder. "I asked him that. I think he feels safer if he has his things with him. All this moving around has made him uneasy. Is that right, Kyle?"

The little nod, and sadness on Jenna's sweet face tore at his heart, especially because the empathy on Jenna's face gave him an insight to what her childhood must have been like. Moved from place to place. Owning nothing. No stability. He wanted to give them both a sense of permanence, because Jenna wasn't in any better shape than Kyle. A suitcase dangled from each arm. The grimace on her face reminded him of stranded airline passengers waiting for the weather to clear.

He could only imagine the pressure of suddenly having to raise a child. The fear of being let down by people. The reasons Jenna tried to drive people away. Add on top of that the burden of his parents' threats, and opening a new business—basically an avalanche of responsibilities burying and squeezing the life out of her.

He read somewhere about how people who'd been abandoned reject others to avoid being hurt. While he understood the deep-seated belief, fighting against the illogical was both challenging and frustrating.

He'd have to work harder.

He wanted her in his life. He needed her. Plain and simple.

"Here, let me take those. Make yourself at home." He hoped Jenna heard and believed his cheery sincerity. This was her home—his gift to her and Kyle. And he was so glad they were here.

Her grateful yet tired eyes tugged at his heart. Jenna stood in the entryway, briskly rubbing her hands up and down her arms against the latest dip in the ever-changing temperature.

"Thank you for dropping off the moving boxes, and for getting Kyle new bedroom furniture." She lifted her hand, but didn't reach for him. "I saw the car seat in the back of your car, and the books. He likes books and getting to pick out his bedding. Red apparently is his favorite color. And...well, thank you for... thank you for everything. I mean—"

"Jenna." She shifted her weight while her eyes darted this way and that to avoid his scrutiny. Her trembling uneasiness gave his heart another strong tug. "Jenna, it's all good. You'll see."

"I know," she whispered, like she was still trying to convince herself she made the right decision.

He reached for her hand. Several seconds passed before her eyes connected to his. "Did you make an appointment with the law firm I recommended?"

A wary flicker of the unknown caused her eyes to expand, and her usual guarded fragility to settle in. "The meeting is scheduled for tomorrow."

"Do you want me to come with you?"

Jenna pulled inward and found the wood grain on his floor most interesting. "I can manage."

"I'm sure you can."

Grant wanted to ask her if she was prepared, if she'd like him to handle everything, but instead released her hand and walked into his kitchen.

Jenna pointed toward the front door. "I left the groceries outside. I promised Kyle we could make pizza tonight. He's never had pizza. It will be a new home experience. What kid doesn't like pizza?" She babbled on.

Kyle crossed the living room to look out the picture window at the enormous evergreens. Grant pointed to the family of squirrels playing in the branches. "My friends came to say hi. Do you see them? Those are pine squirrels. I named them Alvin and Britney. Someday I'll have to rent the movie Alvin and the Chipmunks. I bet you haven't seen it."

Kyle's enamored gaze followed the animals' every move. The mating pair ran around and up the base of the tree before launching onto the roof and disappearing.

"Kyle, I have a present for you." Grant walked to the fireplace and waited for Kyle. The little boy shuffled his feet, not noticing one of his shoes had come untied. Approaching the bookshelves, Grant unplugged the digital camera to check the battery level. "Fully charged." He handed the small electronic to his nephew and pointed. "This was your mother's."

Jenna dropped the groceries on the counter.

"Your mom liked to take pictures, and had a very artistic eye. Not that you have to know what artistic means. Let me show you how the camera works."

Grant got to his knees beside Kyle, and placed the camera in the boy's hands before sliding on the activation button. Kyle's eyes filled with excitement as the lens shutter opened. Grant pointed to the screen. "See this image here? If you press this button on top, you'll get a picture of what you see on the screen. Sort of like your drawings. Want me to show you?"

Kyle turned the device over and over in his hands, then handed his gift back. Grant centered Kyle's face in the frame and snapped his likeness. "See? I took a picture of you. Now you try."

Accepting the camera, Kyle studied his image. Then he repeated the process, ending up with a somewhat fuzzy picture of Grant.

"Great picture." Grant rubbed Kyle's head. "You even have a fairly steady hand. If you're careful to hold the camera very still while you take a picture, the better it will turn out."

"What do you say to a hike?" Grant pointed

over his shoulder. "I think we can all use some fresh air. There is lots to see, and Kyle can practice taking pictures."

Kyle grabbed his backpack and scurried toward the front door.

"Whoa, there buddy. Do you want to carry all that stuff?"

Kyle raced back to the kitchen table to unload what he thought wasn't necessary, and then sprinted back to the front door.

"I think he wants to go. How about you?" Grant stood to face Jenna.

"A hike sounds perfect."

Her perky, delighted acceptance drained away the last of Grant's tension. "Why don't you grab your coat, and I'll meet you out front."

Grant shoved the groceries into the refrigerator, retrieved his backpack, filled it with water bottles and protein bars, and headed for the front door.

"The trailhead's out back." He led them around to the back of the house, and paused at the trailhead leading to the back of his property to take Jenna's hand.

"Okay, Kyle." The boy turned back with an

expectant look. "I need you to make me a promise. When we are out, you must stay in eye contact with your aunt or I at all times." Kyle's brows knitted together. *Simpler words. You've got to use simpler words.* "That means we have to see you, and you have to see us. Deal? I want you to be safe. The only way I can do that is if I see you."

The corners of Kyle's mouth slowly turned up, and his little face lit up into a perfect picture of sunshine happiness. Then he held out his hand, thumb up.

Grant chuckled, "Okay, we'll shake on it." Grant engulfed the boy's smaller hand in his and gave it a firm, vigorous pump, hoping to produce a giggle to seal the deal. He wasn't disappointed.

"Let's take some pictures, shall we?"

Kyle turned and toddled down and then up a slight incline, his arms held out for balance. Watching an exuberant Kyle explore thrilled Grant in a way he hadn't experienced in years.

Jenna squeezed his hand. "You're very good with him."

"Really? To be honest, I'm terrified

something will happen. I suppose every parent feels that way."

"The first few days, all I did was stay up and watch him sleep. I was afraid if I went to sleep someone would come in and take him away from me."

"That's not going to happen. I'll make sure both you and Kyle are safe."

"I know you will. You're a good man, Grant."

She lifted onto her toes and placed a kiss on his cheek. She lingered a second or two, long enough to convince him the kiss was more than casual. In that moment, he needed to be careful. She could spark a fire and set the whole hillside ablaze. To see if he couldn't control the burn, he leaned in, then paused when Kyle reappeared around the giant pine for the second time.

"What do you see?"

Kyle pointed to a blue and black blur that took flight and landed twenty yards away. "It's a blue jay." Grant explained in case Kyle needed an explanation.

Kyle pointed his camera, and Grant was sure all he got was the tree, but it didn't matter. He'd learn. Grant helped Jenna over a log and let her walk on ahead when his cell phone rang.

"Hey, Erik, what's up?"

"Checking in to see if you want to get together for the Rockies game today."

"Sorry man, I can't. Kyle, Jenna, and I are taking a hike, and I have plans later."

Erik chuckled. "I bet you have plans."

"It's not like that."

"Not like what? Jenna is moving in. You're helping raise your nephew. I'm happy for you, that's all."

Satisfaction settled in, and he hoped the sensation might stick around awhile. "The way I figure it, every boy needs a man in his life. He misses Duke, and I'm positive my dad has no intention of being a proper grandfather, so that leaves me. Not that I mind. He's an awesome kid."

"I've got an old fishing pole sitting in my garage somewhere if you're interested. I still laugh about the time you fell in the lake and your grandpa had to haul your sorry ass out."

"You're sore 'cause I caught seven of the finest rainbow trout ever caught," He teased, remembering his proud adolescent swagger and boasting…until he walked into his family's kitchen. Disgusted by the smell, his mother told him to throw out the fish. He chuckled, remembering how Carmelita served the trout for dinner to spite his parents. "That reminds me, I need to sign Kyle up for some swimming lessons."

"You think he's ready for lessons? He might have enough adjusting to do for now."

"I've thought of that, then imagined how I'd feel if something happened. Elkridge has too many streams, rivers, and ponds. Which reminds me. Come next spring, I was thinking you and I can take Kyle on his first overnight fishing trip. Jenna found a fishing lure in the little guy's things. Fishing might make him feel more at home."

Erik didn't respond right away.

"Erik? You still there?"

"Yeah, I'm still here. Just thinking about what a great dad you're gonna be."

Grant heard the yearning in his friend's voice and could relate. He always wanted a family, but having Kyle in his life was a gift, and he would cherish every second. "Thanks for the vote of confidence, buddy. And I'd better go. Jenna and Kyle are waiting."

"Catch you later, man."

"I'll call you tomorrow."

He trotted to catch up with Jenna and Kyle, who were squatted down next to the path, looking at something.

Grant quickened his steps to investigate. "What did you find?"

Kyle slowly opened his hand to reveal his treasure.

"Hey! You found an acorn. A nice one. Have you taken a picture of it yet?"

Kyle placed his acorn on the ground and studiously and very carefully took a picture. He checked the results and, beaming, showed it to Jenna, who praised him lavishly.

When he was about to reclaim his find, Grant interrupted. "You know Kyle, if you leave the acorn in the forest, a little tree might be born." He swept his arm to encompass the surrounding area. "Same with the flowers and the pinecones. What if you just take pictures of the things you find, and not touch them? What do you think about that?"

Kyle stood still, turned inward for several

moments before he leaned down, picked up the acorn, and walked several feet off the path to set it back down in a safe spot.

He couldn't wait to experience life through Kyle's innocent, eager eyes. Experience a childhood unlike his own. He might even try stomping through a few mud puddles of his own.

But his gut warned him life could never be that simple.

Not when his parents were involved.

He leaned in close to Jenna's ear. "Have you given any thought to when you might want to get married?"

She paled, her smile fading. "The sooner the better, before I change my mind."

"Then maybe we should wait until you're sure."

"I'm sure. I can't lose Kyle."

He was willing to give Jenna everything, anything she would ever want, but something made him pause. "Then I will draw up a prenuptial agreement for you to sign. If you want, we can get married on Wednesday."

"Oh, okay. But, Grant. I would prefer if we kept this quiet. I mean. I don't want your parents finding out before they have to, and people might want to give us gifts and stuff. That would feel awkward, since we already have what we need."

Is it my parents and gifts, or something else?

He didn't want to start worrying about the real reasons behind her request, so he walked over to see what Kyle had just found.

"Anything you want, just ask," he said over his shoulder.

"I'm good."

The way she said those two words flattened him. If he was a gambling man, he'd estimate the odds of her going through with the wedding at about negative ten percent. He'd better get to work upping those odds, or he'd end up alone, nursing a broken heart and a kid who didn't talk. Ever.

CHAPTER TWENTY-TWO

The thirteen-foot-high frosted glass door etched with Henderson, Coffton, and Stewart, Attorneys at Law, looked impressive. If a law office door could actually impress.

She was about to reach for the handle when the door opened. A conservatively accessorized couple dressed in black made their way out the door and to the elevator. She scanned her black slacks hanging off her body, too large at the moment, because she couldn't seem to maintain her best weight. The forty-five-minute commute hadn't helped much either, and her thrift store blouse looked wrinkled, but a tad better than one of her butter-stained T-shirts.

"May I help you?" the receptionist asked before glancing her way with an assessment that measured and then placed her squarely into the unimpressed bracket. A stray hair from Jenna's carefully crafted ponytail dropped over her left eye. She looped the strands behind her ear.

"I'm Jenna Dolcy. I have an appointment."

"Ah, yes." In a robot-like movement, the receptionist thrust a clipboard forward with papers attached. "Here are some forms to fill out," she said, sounding like a tape recorder of miniature sound bites she replayed for everyone who walked through the door. "Someone will be with you in a minute," the droned message continued.

The apparent dismissal didn't calm Jenna's nerves any. She perused the six-page form, a page each for a general case description, financial and personal information, and then a bunch of pages with print she'd need a magnifying glass to read—which was most likely the point of the tiny font. She lowered herself onto the uncomfortable couch's leather surface and dropped her purse to the carpeted floor. Her hand hovered over the name box.

You can do this! Custody. Marriage. Kyle needed her to do it, which meant she had no choice.

Her hand moved, penning her name, then moved to the next box, then the next. Ten minutes later, while she was still working on forms, a woman holding a manila folder called her name. She scrambled to gather her things and the clipboard before following the woman, who wore a perfectly fitted black jacket over her precisely pressed straight skirt, down the narrow corridor.

On her left, six-foot-high bookcases lined the wall as far as she could see. To the right, offices were furnished with matching cherrywood desks, stacks of files, and sometimes a body in a suit sitting behind the desk. The whole setup reminded her of a factory job. Workers processing the same thing, day in and day out, with no break in the monotony. If Grant's job in Chicago was anything like this place, it was no wonder he quit.

The woman stopped at a door and waited

for Jenna to catch up. The office was larger than some of the others, but the format was no different.

A voice to her left said, "Ms. Dolcy. Thank you for coming in. I'm Drew Gertt."

Short and balding, with buttons straining across his midsection, the man fit his name. She always imagined lawyers looked like tall, dark and handsome romance novel heroes— more like Grant. Yet Mr. Gertt more resembled the online dating profile of a man seeking a woman who'd decided to load a picture of a distant cousin to get a date.

Jenna hesitated to accept the man's outstretched hand. She turned toward the young woman at the door. "There must be some mistake. I made an appointment with Leslie Stewart."

"No. No mistake." Mr. Gertt drew her attention. "Mrs. Stewart isn't available, and she passed your case file on to me."

"I see." *Grant won't like the switch. He won't like this one bit.* Her muscles tensed while thoughts whirled in endless circles.

His plain hazel brown eyes peered over the top of his round, gold-rimmed frames. "Thank you, Janice. I'll take it from here," the woman nodded and disappeared faster than a jar of candy on an unoccupied office desk.

The lawyer walked to the round table, obviously only temporarily emptied, because now a large, teetering stack of files rested against a large paned window beside the credenza.

"I'm sorry to meet in my messy office, but unfortunately there's been a scheduling error, and the other conference rooms are booked."

And you're telling me I drew the short straw, she thought, sitting in the chair Mr. Gertt indicated. She placed the clipboard on the desk and her purse on the floor. *I should have asked Grant to come.*

"Tell me your story, Ms. Dolcy." He leaned back, making his paunch drift further over his belt, his too-white teeth causing a distraction.

"Before we get started, would you be willing to tell me how many of these types of cases you've worked on in the past? More importantly, how many you've won?"

Mr. Gertt uncrossed his legs, sat bolt upright, and folded his hands on the table.

"Each case is different, with different circumstances, Ms. Dolcy, it's hard to..."

"Yes, yes, I know. But surely you can tell me how many cases you've won."

The lawyer pushed his rimmed glasses further up his nose. "I...um...around forty percent."

"Forty percent. I see. Is there anyone with a better record in custody petition cases?"

The little man dropped his chin and studied her over the top of his glasses.

She squirmed in her seat. "I'm sorry. I didn't mean my concerns to come out as a criticism. It's just...a little boy's welfare depends on the outcome of this case. You must understand, Mr. Gertt, I can't afford to lose."

The man leaned forward again, picking up a pen and pulling a legal pad forward. "Then I suggest we get started."

"One more question." Jenna pressed on, hoping the lawyer-man didn't groan, because he surely looked constipated. "Do you know the Newhalls?"

A smile made his cheeks pucker, and his overgrown brows droop over his eyes. "Very well. Buck Newhall is a prominent member of the Colorado bar association. Good record. From what I understand, he and his son have a connection with Leslie Stewart, one of the firm's partners."

A questioning suspicion zipped through her system faster than she could shut it down. But she trusted Grant. Well, she had to trust someone.

She tapped her finger on the forms asking her just about every question except when her next period would start. Pushing the growing fear aside, she pulled out Caitlyn's document granting her custody of Kyle. The thin, fragile piece of paper sitting on the table didn't look strong enough to hold up in court.

"I'm hoping my sister's letter is sufficient to win this case."

"As I mentioned before, Ms. Dolcy, custody hearings depend on a lot of different factors. The judge hearing the case, the facts presented during the hearing, even the wishes of the child."

Suddenly there wasn't enough air in Jenna's lungs. "Since Kyle's not talking right now, I don't think he'll be much help."

Mr. Gertt's untrimmed brow lifted. "That

could be a problem. I understand from the office manager's notes that your nephew was talking before he came to stay with you. Is that correct?"

She sat back and crossed her arms. "His not talking has to do with his mother's death and his caregiver dropping him off unexpectedly. He's feeling abandoned. Losing the only two key people he's ever known in such a short period has to have been traumatic. His silence has nothing to do with me, but the Newhalls will find a way to use it as a strike against me. How big a problem do you think it will be?"

The man patted her hand, placating. "We'll work around it. Where's Kyle now?"

"He's at school this morning, and then a friend will pick him up and take him to lunch, and then the library. When I'm done here, I'll pick him up."

The lawyer raised his right brow. "What type of friend? A boyfriend?"

"No. Not a boyfriend. Harold owns the grocery store in town. Kyle took a liking to him when they first met. He started a Children's Reading Hour at the library and offered to take Kyle."

"No need to get defensive, Ms. Dolcy. The judge will ask far more pointed questions, and you will need to stay as calm as possible."

Calm? Right. Jenna's first instinct was to take scissors and trim the man's fuzzy brows while he assessed and condemned her as a client, a person, and parent. Instead, she pulled out a pen and paper and prepared for battle.

For the next hour, Mr. Gertt browsed every piece of documentation Jenna had, reviewing the information from different angles, coming up with theories about what the Newhalls would present, such as no experience in child-rearing, lack of child care or supportive network, lack of stable income...the list went on and on and on until she was so nauseous she barely dared to swallow. At least she had adequate housing. The income calculation sheet the court required showed her in the double-digit-red.

She'd spent every last penny in her coffee jar.

Grant had no need for coins. The income statement accompanying the prenuptial agreement proved he was loaded—in fact, he didn't need to work if he didn't want to.

She didn't want Grant's money, only his protection, which made crossing out the alimony section and signing the pre-nup documents easy.

The only remaining problem was Vivian. The woman meant to see Jenna humbled, or, better yet, destroyed.

Most rational people might give up, probably even some not-so-rational people, but when Jenna looked into the crystal-blue eyes of her nephew and saw her mother, father, sister—her entire family—looking back at her, and she wouldn't let go, no matter what.

Jenna laid the pen down and skimmed the overwhelming list of things she needed to do scribbled halfway down the page. "Is there anything else you would recommend?"

Drew Gertt took his glasses off and rubbed his eyes with the back of his hand, before replacing them. "If I were you, I'd go home and spend time with Kyle to remind you of the reasons you want to do this, because frankly, what you have on your side of the ledger is far short of what you need."

She dug deep for a bit of courage. "You

should be aware, Mr. Gertt, that Grant Newhall and I will be married in a few days. We are not telling anyone at this time. I suspect our marriage will come as a surprise to his parents."

"I'm not a marriage counselor, Ms. Dolcy, but I sense a hesitancy. Are you sure you want to take this course of action?" *Why, because marrying Grant will be like setting a wasp's nest on fire?*

"I'm fully aware his parents' threats can sting. I've been on the receiving end."

"If I were in your shoes, I wouldn't be up for this kind of fight. The Newhalls have mighty deep pockets."

"I'm hoping facts, not money, will settle this case. I can't lose. Caitlyn kept her son from the Newhalls for a reason. What that reason is, I'm not sure, but I aim to find out. Kyle can't be left in their care. He just can't."

"The only way I can see you winning is if you find proof of why Caitlyn ran."

Drained and discouraged, Jenna pushed the notebook back in her purse. She'd believed Caitlyn's custody-papers would be enough. Right there in black and white, it gave her custody of Kyle. She stood, pressing the creases in her slacks down, before pulling her purse over her shoulder.

"We didn't talk about a retainer."

"You've already signed the retainer paperwork. We can talk about a payment plan next time, after I've gone over your case more thoroughly."

Her bank account balance had enough money to buy a loaf of bread and a jar of peanut butter after paying the bakery's rent, buying supplies, and a few things for Kyle. She wasn't about to argue the point, and she wouldn't ask Grant for money. She would pay every cent Mr. Gertt billed, only payment in full might take a while.

Mr. Gertt escorted her to the lobby while mumbling something about seriously considering what was best for Kyle, and staying positive, and wished her a good day. His insincerity rubbed an already itchy spot raw.

Lawyers are supposed to be smart, insightful, and ruthless in defense of their clients. Aren't they?

Jenna walked to the parking lot in a daze. Opening Nellie's door, she tossed her purse into the passenger seat and pulled herself into the Jeep. Keys in hand, she reached for the ignition before her hands fell into her lap and her already-aching forehead landed on the steering wheel. "Caitlyn, what made you think I'd have the courage or the means to face the Newhalls when you didn't?" *Why?*

She'd thrown question after question into the universe over her twenty-eight years, but she never received helpful answers. She hoped for once fate might recognize her desperation and grant her a small favor.

As she drove out of the parking lot, thoughts continued to bombard her. *Why did you run, Caitlyn? Was it Vivian? Your boyfriend? Why?*

Doubts about ever finding the answer churned in her stomach.

Three years she'd searched, and nothing had surfaced. Why she thought she could find a clue now, she didn't know, but she would try —no longer for Caitlyn, but for Kyle.

Pulling onto the interstate, she contemplated the lawyer's advice and speculations. His cautious doubt rolled over and over in her mind while she tightened her grip on Nellie's steering wheel. *What did I miss?*

She'd missed the Ashley-Caitlyn connection, for sure.

Maybe that's where she should start. Ashley had to feel remorseful, because she'd volunteered, several times, to help with Kyle and the store, which Jenna had refused. She couldn't go there. Not yet. Trust never came easily, and rebuilding trust never happened, not because she hadn't tried, but because she'd never succeeded.

With a resolved breath, she glanced at the manila envelope sticking out of her purse.

Maybe she could talk to Sheriff Joe, see if he'd allow her to review the police file from when Caitlyn went missing. Now that everyone knew she was Caitlyn's sister, she could ask for the information directly without raising suspicions. She already read the news articles and the paperwork Duke provided, the most important of which was Caitlyn's diary. The book detailed the last year of Caitlyn's life.

Her glance snapped to the hardbound book peeking out of her purse, its edges worn with use. Memories of Caitlyn started tap-dancing through her mind, an endless collage of places and events. Her mind seized on Caitlyn's frequent entries.

Drawings. Writing. Poems. And random musings about events.

Caitlyn always drew what she was thinking. Why wouldn't she have continued to capture her thoughts?

Jenna skidded to a stop on the shoulder of the interstate highway. She reached into her purse for the cell phone, then opened her wallet to pull out the cherished scrap of paper from Duke.

She rushed to punch the numbers into the pay-as-you-go cell phone, and waited, listening to the dial tone.

"Hello," she shouted. "Hello? Is this Duke?"

"I may be old, but I'm not deaf. Lower your voice before you blow out my eardrum," Duke's grumpy voice responded.

She laughed at the familiar, gravelly voice while heady hope filled her. "Duke, it's Jenna. I have a favor to ask."

"I'm not sure these old bones can help, but ask away."

Relief eased her neck muscles, which had been screaming with tension. "My gut tells me Caitlyn had more diaries. You gave me the most recent one, but I believe she kept more, possibly from the time she lived in Elkridge, and when she first came to live with you." There was silence on the other end of the line. "Duke? Are you there?" she began to panic, thinking she might have lost the connection.

"Yep, I'm here. Just recollectin'." The silence continued. "I remember her showing me some books one day. Said she was gonna put em' in a safe place."

Excitement started brewing. "Do you know where she put them?"

"Nope, can't say as I do." Her whole body sagged. "Well, now wait a minute." The spark of hope reignited. "She had this key, and took it with her to town on occasion. She might have gone to see young Bruster about a box."

"Bruster?" Jenna asked with confusion. "What kind of box?"

"One of those metal thingy-ma-jigs in the bank. Bruster took over from his dad about seven years ago and I 'spect he might have rented her one. I can give him a call. See if she got one to store her private things. Never could understand why people would want to give their money or things to others for safekeeping when you could do as good buryin' them in the yard."

Duke continued to mumble about how times changed. She could envision the old farmer out at night with a shovel, burying glass jars all over his land. She hoped for his sake he remembered where he'd buried his money.

"I would appreciate your help."

Because I'll need all the help I can get. Trust be damned. I'll have to trust somebody at some point.

"You okay, Ms. Dolcy?" Duke's concern soothed her with a layer of comfort.

She considered telling him about the custody suit for about two seconds before deciding he didn't need the burden. He'd done his share of giving and protecting, and now she needed to fight the rest of the battle.

"I'm fine. I want to find out what happened to Caitlyn. I need to find closure."

Duke cleared his throat. "Funny thing about life. Never does quite turn out how you 'spect."

"No," she sighed. "No, it doesn't," she responded, the weight of his words sinking in.

She exchanged good-byes, and disconnected the call.

She drew a long, full breath of air. The first full breath she'd taken in days. She hoped Duke's inquiries would lead to something... anything. With a little luck, she might dig up enough facts to put Vivian in her place.

CHAPTER TWENTY-THREE

"Jenna, are you ready?" Grant stopped at the hallway mirror to pick lint off his best suit, straighten his tie for the sixth time, and adjust his boutonniere. "We need to get going, or we won't make it to the clerk's office and back before Kyle's released from school."

"I'm coming. I just need a second. I can't find my cell phone."

"It's on the kitchen table."

A second later Jenna appeared, sandals in hand, wearing jeans and a cream cotton top. She stopped halfway down the hall. Her jaw dropped, but not even a squeak emerged. She narrowed her focus on his hand. "You bought flowers, and you're wearing a suit."

The bridal bouquet of white roses and baby's breath grew heavy in his hands. "I wanted our wedding to be special. After all, I only intend to do this once."

Her shoulders began to rise as she wrestled with something to say. "I...I'm sorry I misunderstood. I thought you said Colorado law allows couples to complete a form to get married. No minister. No formal stuff."

"Well sure, it's a piece of paper, but it's our wedding. Your wedding. I know it's probably not what you dreamed of, but I want to make this day special for you."

Jenna took a step backwards toward the bedroom. Her face unreadable. "I'll go change."

"I didn't mean to make you feel uncomfortable. I should've said something this morning. Let's go. It doesn't matter what we wear."

But it did matter. Mattered a lot. He never doubted the wisdom—the necessity—of getting married to Jenna until today.

The prenuptial documents were a precaution. An assurance any sensible lawyer would take. Signing documents didn't scare him. Her apathy was what terrified the shit out of him.

Today was about starting their future together. Not about plunking down thirty bucks and signing another piece of paper. He lay the bridal bouquet on the hall table when his hands started to shake.

"Give me ten minutes." Jenna dropped her purse and passport on the floor. "I want to fix this. You're right. Our wedding day should be special."

"We're already late," Grant reminded, without burdening her with the disappointment he already felt.

"Ten minutes. That's all I need," she shouted from down the hall.

"I'll wait."

But should I?

Maybe he should wait—not to switch clothes—but until she was positive this marriage was what she wanted.

Reality hit him upside the head. He wanted to be married to her. No doubt there.

But loving someone who didn't love you back hurt. Hurt a lot.

He'd been raised without the ordinary ruffling of hair or bedtime hug or parents cheering on the sidelines. About the only thing he got from his parents was criticism and disappointment. The one-sided love had created a chilling emptiness.

He could do without that type of love.

His phone vibrated in his jacket pocket. He pulled out the device and checked the screen. "Hey, Erik. What's up?"

"Just calling to see if you're busy tonight. Thought you might be wanting a boys' night out."

"I...a..." *Would Jenna want a wedding night?*

Erik rattled on about work, sports, his day. Grant didn't need to say a word. "So how about it? I thought maybe we could get a burger and play some darts."

"Better not."

"What's up with you? You sound like your place burned down."

Maybe it did, in a symbolic way. I'm supposed to be getting married today, and no one knows... because my bride wants to keep it a secret. How screwed up is that?

"I'm good." *Just got the wedding day jitters.*

"Let me ask you a question. How come you never married Connie? I mean you were together all those years. What was it about her that made you eventually walk away? I know you loved her."

"That's the thing. I'm not sure I ever did. The sex was great, but that's where the connection ended. In the end, it was the little things. I couldn't stand to watch her eat. She gossiped non-stop. Wore too much makeup. Constantly nagged me about finding a different job or my clothes or the decisions I made. She was never satisfied. Why are you asking?"

"No reason. Just curious."

"Does your question have anything to do with Jenna?"

Grant turned toward the hallway corner and softened his voice. "Maybe it does, but she doesn't chew with her mouth open or nag me about my job, clothes, or decisions. Then again, maybe it's because she doesn't care."

"Are you having second thoughts about her?"

"No. Well, maybe."

"Have you ever considered the only reason

you're dating the cute baker is to get back at your parents?"

"Jenna has nothing to do with my parents." *Or does she?*

"I know you want to be Mr. Perfect, but it's okay to be wrong once in a while."

"I've been wrong plenty of times, but I don't think I'm wrong about Jenna. She's giving and kind, and tries harder than any other person I know."

"I hope you're right."

"I am right." He heard the click-click-click of footsteps coming down the hall. "I'd better go. I'm late for an appointment. How about I call you tomorrow?"

"Sounds good." Erik disconnected the call.

Grant turned and the doubt and frustration from the previous few minutes receded. "You look amazing." Her hair was now pulled back, with only wisps framing her face. A soft brush of makeup applied to her cheeks and lips. If he wasn't already in love with her, she would have stolen his heart right then.

"Really?" She smoothed the skirt of her fitted powder blue dress. "It's not white, but when Gwen showed it to me, I had to buy it. I thought maybe someday I'd have a special reason to get dressed up. I think today is that day."

Grant lifted the flowers from the hall table. The sorrow in her expression drew him closer, enough to take her hand. "Jenna, are you sure about this? I told you before I'll wait. I'm not going anywhere."

"You're a good man, Grant. We need to do this. We need to protect Kyle."

"Is Kyle the only reason you're marrying me?"

"Kathy asked me the same thing yesterday." She nibbled on the end of her fingernail. "I don't know why, but I've always believed I'd never get married or have a family. Kathy thinks it's because I've never felt worthy or qualified to be a wife or mother."

"And what do you believe now?"

She reached for his tie, lifting and moving it a millimeter to the left, and then ran her hand down the fabric before letting her arm drop to her side. "I'm pretty stubborn, and I don't trust people. I forget important things like saying thank-you, or I'm sorry. I stick my foot in my mouth a lot, and I'm not very good at the social thing. I don't care about clothes or makeup or fitting in…well, I do a little.

"But that doesn't mean I don't want to try. I can change. You believing in me, even asking me to marry you means a lot—although I don't know how to make a relationship work. Heck, I can't even manage to put on the right clothes, and I know I hurt you just now. I am sorry for that."

He put a finger under her chin to lift her face. Her regretful look met his. "I told you what you wear doesn't matter."

"But it does matter. I don't want to disappoint or embarrass you. Like I said, you're a good man. You deserve good things, and I'll make you happy."

"Come here." Grant needed to feel her in his arms. He needed this woman in his life. Every woman he'd ever met cared about money, career, appearances, just like his mother. Jenna was at the opposite end of the spectrum from Vivian Newhall, and that was a big part of why he loved her. For her, not his mother.

Grant tucked her into his arms, and

pressed a kiss on the top of her head. "You deserve good things too, you know. I don't want anything more than to keep you and Kyle safe."

"I don't know what I did to deserve you, but for once I think I did something right."

Jenna accepted the flowers. "We'd better go if we're going to get back in time pick Kyle up. I wish we didn't have to go so far, but no one in this town can keep a secret. I still think our best option is Eagle County."

"Agreed. You ready?" Unsure why he'd felt compelled to ask one more time, he held his breath, hoping she didn't change her mind.

"I'm ready."

The breath he'd been holding whooshed out in a huge wave of relief.

He hoped she was committed, because her rejection would send him spinning into hell.

CHAPTER TWENTY-FOUR

Jenna swirled the pastry tube around in a circle, hovering above the dark chocolate cupcake. Edible butterflies sat atop the colorful frosting on the two dozen already-decorated rounds. She picked up a delicate wing and pressed the creature into the creamy butter frosting.

"I figured you'd still be here. You got a late start this morning."

"Who's fault was that?" Grant's happy tone and tap of shoes against the floor tile gave Jenna's spirit a lift. She glanced over her shoulder.

"Yours. You're so beautiful, I couldn't stop making love to you last night."

"I still feel bad because I didn't think of doing more for our wedding. The flowers, the photographer, including Kyle in our dinner celebration, it was all…so…so memorable. That's the word I'm looking for." An uneasy joy settled in her heart. "Thank you."

He leaned in and gave her a kiss. "I dropped by to see if you're picking Kyle up, or if I am."

"I guess you didn't see my note. He's staying at Maggie's tonight. Her daughter is in from Texas, and Maggie thought her grandson and Kyle might hit it off. He's all excited. He's having his first sleepover, complete with popcorn and a movie."

A sensual smile stole across Grant's face. "That means we'll be home alone tonight, and you won't have to be quiet this time."

Her body heated to match Fred's temperature—baking hot.

"You're not wearing your wedding band." His forehead knotted as he pointed.

"I didn't want to get it all dirty, or worse lose it. The engagement ring and band are a little loose." *Plus, I didn't want your mom to see it. That's all I need.* "I put them in the top dresser drawer for safekeeping."

Grant nuzzled her neck, dusting light kisses across her skin. "The two-carat is rather impractical. How about I get you a simple band you can wear for everyday."

"I don't need a band to remind me I'm married. You, your caring, your touch, and your body are reminder enough."

Memories of the exquisite wedding night made every nerve ending flash like police cruiser lights. She needed to get a pair of handcuffs. The way he made her feel should be classified as illegal. He made her want to scream. He should be punished, in the nicest kind of way. The intimacy. The feeling of his skin pressed against hers. The explosion of newness.

He was carnally arresting—in every sense of the word.

He cupped her bottom, his mouth descending to her neck. He nuzzled and caressed until her mind started flashing a list of the baking that still needed to be done like a neon sign. She slid the palms of her hands up his chest and pushed.

"Not so fast, mister." To be safe, she moved to the other side of the counter. "I have baking to do. Besides, I'm exhausted. After I finish here, I'll be lucky if I don't fall asleep in the shower."

"You sure you don't want to cover your body with cookie dough and let me lick it off?"

He took a step toward her, but she took several steps back. "No. No. No, you don't. I'm still sore from last night."

The silly grin on his face made her laugh.

"Okay. No cookie dough wrestling. I'll put that one on my wish list." Grant snagged one of the broken cookies she kept in back for samples and popped it in his mouth. The envelope from the lawyer's office sitting on top of the stack of mail caught his attention. "Did Gertt call you back?"

"He did. I don't trust that man. He asked again if I want to fight for custody. I don't know what it is about that guy, but he makes me question if he's the right person to be on this case."

"Just to be absolutely clear. There is no *if.*

We will fight for Kyle, and we will win custody. I'll put a call into Leslie Stewart to find out why she's not available." His eyes narrowed. "I wonder if my father has something to do with her suddenly full schedule."

She crossed her arms to stop the burning anxiety forming. "You don't think—"

"It's possible. My parents have a lot of influence in certain circles."

She tried to swallow, but she couldn't. This David and Goliath thing was getting all too real.

"We could take Kyle and leave. Like Caitlyn. We could get jobs. Learn to be a family."

For an instant, a pained expression crossed his face before he hid the emotion. "You want to be looking over your shoulder the rest of your life? Do possible jail time if you're caught? We got this. We need to stay calm."

"How can you be so sure?"

"Because I can't—and won't—ever allow my parents to raise another child. I can't. They need to be exposed, and it needs to be on record, so they can't adopt Kyle or any other child."

Any other child. She hadn't thought of Vivian wanting to adopt again.

"We have to make this work." He shoved his fingers through his hair and gave her a hard look. "Promise me you won't run."

He was getting to know her too well. Shoving stuff in a suitcase and leaving sounded so easy. "Okay, we'll do it your way." *For now.*

"Good. Then, we're in agreement." He pointed at the tray of broken cookie pieces. "Those are really good."

A frustrated huff leaked out as pride filled her. "I'm playing around with my ginger cookie recipe. I added orange peel to give them a citrusy taste. Did you see the bug cakes I made? I tried making worms, but they ended up looking like Tootsie Rolls instead."

She lifted one of the delicate spiders from the tray. "Maggie said Kyle took an interest in the live worm farm over at the hardware store, so I thought I would try making some crawlers, at least the sugary kind. The spiders look all right." Grant's face was a conflicted mix of happy and worried. "Do you think we can actually win this case?"

Grant shoved his hands into his pockets. "We have to win for Caitlyn."

"For Caitlyn. Do you still feel guilty about what happened?"

"Wouldn't you?" Grant braced the counter and stepped back stretching his back, looking at the ground. "I left because I couldn't tolerate any more of my parents' suffocating control." His voice had dropped to almost a whisper. "But once I got to college, I realized she'd been left defenseless, and it was selfish of me to leave. She had no one. Her boyfriend was a jerk. She wasn't allowed to choose her friends."

Grant rubbed his chest and released a heavy breath. "If I could turn back time, I would. But I can't. Kyle's her son, and I want him to grow up happy. I don't want my parents anywhere near him." His hand covered hers. "Kyle belongs with us."

Caitlyn had no one. "I've asked before, but can you think of a reason Caitlyn would not just run, but want to hide?"

He shook his head. "After we found out

Caitlyn had died, Carmelita, our housekeeper told me Caitlyn was pregnant before she disappeared. I've done the math. She was four months pregnant."

And starting to show. "Why didn't you tell me?"

"I don't know. I guess I assumed you'd already guessed. You knew when she disappeared, and you had Kyle's birth certificate. If my parents had found out Caitlyn was pregnant, that would be enough to scare anyone into leaving town."

"I always thought of my sister as delicate and fragile. I guess I was wrong."

"There are so many things I wish I'd done differently."

Jenna reached out to touch his arm. Grant had been her rock—her stable, predictable, never-changing rock. She could feel the emotions berating him, corroding his positive nature and self-confidence. The frustration surged with every breath, beating at his soul. Eroding. Driving in a wedge, creating cracks.

She understood regret, understood the consequences of avoiding the words held so tightly, the words she found difficult to get past her lips, the words held in her heart. Her hand tightened, trying to give encouragement to a man who'd also lost a sister. He tried to pull back, but she didn't want to let him go. Not yet. She held on. Finally, he wrapped his arms around her. She synchronized her breath with his until the rise and fall of his abdomen slowed and his body relaxed.

"I can't believe she's gone," she said, not knowing what else to say. Placing a hand on his face, she gently smoothed his worry lines, as his jaw muscles rippled beneath her palm.

"We'll be okay," he offered with more confidence than he probably felt. "Once the custody issue is settled, we'll be able to figure out next steps. If you still want to leave Elkridge, we'll pack and move—go wherever you want."

"Like you said, one thing at a time." She took a deep sniff of the sugary sweetness of the half-decorated tray of cupcakes, then let the air out slowly. "You'd better get out of here so I can finish these."

"How much baking do you have left to do?"

"The bread is done. I finished all the orders

at the café this morning. I just have cookies and bars left to bake."

He gave her a quick kiss. "Then we'd better get started."

He unbuttoned his shirt cuffs, rolled up his sleeves, and removed his tie.

"What are you doing?"

"Helping."

"Grant, you don't have to. Besides, after I get done all I'll want to do is sleep."

"Perfect." He said, waiting for instructions. "Baking, then sleep. I get it. Now, let me help."

Jenna had no doubt he could find his way around her kitchen. The meals he cooked were savory, using an unusual mix of ingredients, combining both flavors and textures. He took care with his presentation, using three-dimensional plate presentations and color to add to the appearance.

"You're wearing a suit."

"That's what dry cleaners are for. Now stop dawdling. We have baking to do."

She shook her head in wonder. "There's an apron by the door. I'll prep the mixers."

"Good. I'll wash my hands. Did you order the larger latex gloves?"

"I did. They're on the supply shelf."

When he disappeared into the back, she flipped on the old-fashioned radio. A medley of staccato brasses came blaring out of the small speakers, giving the bakery a lively kick of energy. For the first few minutes, Grant measured, beat and stirred while she observed. As she expected, his natural instincts surfaced. He listened, accepted instructions, and worked hard. Why that surprised her, she didn't know. After the first batch, she left him to find his own rhythm.

Since she usually worked alone, she figured a big man in her kitchen would cause problems, but surprisingly she found his company quite enjoyable. From time to time she glanced his way, always receiving a smile in return. With two people prepping, the racks filled quickly.

"Would you taste something for me?" She dabbed her finger into the buttery mixture and lifted her hand to his mouth. "I'm wondering if I got the consistency right."

His eyes twinkled while his jaw hinged open, allowing her to insert her finger. When she did, his warm lips clamped down. A moist warmth surrounded her finger and triggered the same sensation in her lower abdomen. Slowly, she pulled her finger out of his mouth while a sizzling sensation rolled from her finger up her arm and exploded in her body.

"Tastes fantastic. Seriously." Grant stepped behind her, circling his arms around her waist. "Those look great as well."

The small-tiered cakes resembling birthday-wrapped gift packages were her newest creations. Grant's praise made her swell with pleasurable pride. "Thanks. I'm thinking about making red velvet cake with chocolate chips and green frosting to resemble a watermelon, but red cake may not sell."

"Don't second-guess. You've got great instincts. Follow them."

Instincts. Honed to a sharp edge since she was a little girl. She did trust her internal alarm system, so why did she have such trouble with Grant? Her heart said to trust him, but every time he got closer, she pushed him away. *Was it habit? Instinct? Fear?* She wanted—no, needed—to let him in, but...

A timer buzzed. She backed out of the circle of his arms, pulled on oven mitts, and retrieved the final batch of cookies from the oven, sliding the coconut-chocolate chip rounds into the cooling racks, next to the pies.

"All done, Fred," she said. "Good work today." She patted the oven door, then lifted her arms above her head and stretched. Grant turned off the radio and removed his spotless apron. Hers was covered in flour, sugar, and who knows what else.

After taking one step toward her, Grant stilled. His head tilted at an odd angle. "Did you hear that?"

"No." She turned toward the backroom.

"I smell gasoline. Something isn't right." He opened the alleyway door and fell back when a whoosh of flames engulfed the entryway. A scream lodged in her throat, and every muscle froze. Grant grabbed the fire extinguisher off the back wall. "Go call the sheriff."

She couldn't move. The stench of fuel burned the inside of her nostrils. "Who would do this?" she asked, but Grant's face had turned cold and hard while he battled to put the flames out.

"Go call the sheriff—*now!*" The barked command pierced the helplessness consuming her. She rushed to the back room to grab the phone and dial.

"911, what is your emergency?"

"I need to report a fire."

Her heartbeat pounded in her ears while she provided details. What if Grant hadn't been there to hear the sound?

Grant had managed to get the fire out before the volunteer fire department arrived. The building was charred and the dumpster was toast, although Nellie wasn't harmed. And thank goodness, Grant had parked in front.

While the fire crew spread kitty litter on the ground to absorb the gasoline, Jenna looked on. Grant dropped the empty fire extinguisher inside the door and placed an arm around her shoulder.

"I'm glad I heard something," he brushed sweat from his forehead. "We caught the fire before it could spread."

"I could have lost everything." *But maybe that was the point.*

A threat.

And there was only one person who'd threatened her lately—Vivian.

And he wondered why she didn't trust people.

Grant pulled her closer. "Everything's going to be fine."

Fine? Since when had anything in her life turned out fine?

CHAPTER TWENTY-FIVE

When the priority box from Duke arrived at her store, she practically accosted the postal carrier. Finally, her sister's diaries had arrived.

It took everything she had to not open the box until she'd picked up Kyle from preschool, gobbled down dinner, and rushed back to Grant's place. Dropping the brown parcel on Grant's kitchen table, Jenna ripped and yanked on the package like it was a much-anticipated Christmas present.

She dug through old newsprint stuffed in the box as filler to get at the gems.

Kyle climbed up on a chair to peer inside the cardboard box.

On the top of the stack was a delicate silver chain with a pressed penny from Yellowstone in a small plastic bag. She released the worn chain from around her neck and placed her sister's medallion next to hers in the palm of her hand, and extended her arm to show her sister's son.

"Your momma and I took a trip to Yellowstone National Park when I was a little older than you are now. It was a beautiful place, full of animals, beautiful flowers, and great big bugs. Bugs the size of your hand." She emphasized the word bug and crawled her fingers up the sleeve of Kyle's shirt to tickle his ear. He responded with a shrug and a giggle. She tapped his nose with her finger. "I'd like to take you there someday. Would you like to go?"

Kyle's gaze searched hers, and his little head nodded. His fingers traced the etched edges of the wolf imprinted on each coin.

"I think we should match." She straightened the chains on each medallion, trying to plug the leaking dam of sentiment.

Kyle's eyes shimmered with tears when she placed the most important thing she owned around his neck.

"From this day forward, no matter what, you'll always know we match. You and me—we're family. We belong to each other, because we match."

The sparkle of his silent tear frayed the corners of her heart a little more. She wished Kyle would give her a clue what to do. Was his tear sad? Happy? Both?

Abandoning the box, she pulled out the kitchen table chair and sat, arms open, hoping, pleading, wanting Kyle to talk to her—trust her. His bottom lip quivered, as the tears fell in earnest. Then he took a step, then another, finally crawling into her lap. He curled into a ball in her arms, letting the burden no child should have to bear fall from his little body.

Looping her arms around him, she pulled him closer as her own tears began to fall.

The memories of surviving for two days without her parents, not hearing from them, came tumbling back.

Jenna had managed to get Caitlyn dressed like every other day, fed her breakfast, made her a lunch like the one her momma always made. And she kept Caitlyn occupied to avoid answering her sister's questions about their parents' whereabouts. She'd been certain they would return home shortly—after all, it was Christmas. When they didn't arrive, she didn't know what to say. Hour after hour, she gazed out the front window, waiting for their car to pull up the snowy driveway.

On the third day, a knock at the door created a frightening sequence of events. Two strange men in uniform opened the front door. Her first thought was to run, and she would have if her sister could have kept up. She should have run. She should have lifted Caitlyn in her arms and run as far and fast as her scrawny legs could have carried them.

She could fully empathize with Kyle's paralyzing fear of losing a mother, and then a father-like figure—the only other person he considered family.

Rocking back and forth, she hummed Caitlyn's favorite lullaby, letting the tears and emotion drain from both their hearts. She combed her fingers through her nephew's silky hair, massaging his scalp. The child clung to her like her sister had in the children's home. When the lights were turned off for the night, and no one was there to beat them for disobeying the rules, her sister would climb into her bed. Jenna had promised to take care of her sibling, protect her, but she'd failed.

She couldn't fail Kyle.

She just couldn't.

The innocent face made her ache with sympathy. His delicate lashes rested on his cheek, exhausted from the struggle of the day. She lifted the long, thin body, careful not to wake him, and moved down the hall to place him in the middle of the bed before pulling his tattered handmade quilt, one of the few items he brought with him, over him to provide warmth and security.

The setting sun sent streams of colorful rays through the window. Kyle's hair, so fine, resembled strands of spun sugar.

If she was going to keep her promise, and avoid failing him, she needed to find the miracle Mr. Gertt recommended. The opened box of journals beckoned.

She retraced her steps, lifted the brown cardboard box, and settled on Grant's leather sofa. Sorting the six books, she placed and stacked them on the coffee table in chronological order.

Reaching for the first book, she hesitated.

You can do this. You need to do this. Caitlyn, please forgive me for intruding, but I need to understand what happened.

She pulled at the penny medallion, rubbing her thumb against the metal, before placing the worn leather journal in her lap, then flipping through several pages before turning back to the beginning. Skimming might allow her to bypass the emotional impact of reading and studying her sister's words for clues, but life never offered simple answers.

Plus, her sister liked to tell stories.

Wait. That's what her sister always said.

Her sister would draw pictures of fairies and animals and then make up stories. She'd weave in little details that would seem insignificant at the time, but would reveal a hidden meaning over time if the audience waited long enough.

No. She'd read every word. Scrutinize one page at a time. After all, what choice did she have?

She studied the first line.

"I BOUGHT *this journal with my birthday money. It's my secret. I'll have to find someplace safe to keep it. My parents are always going through my things, but I'll find a place, because I have to write. I can't sleep with all this stuff bunched up inside my head."*

THE FLUID HANDWRITING—THE fanciful loops and swirls—looked so familiar. While the cursive was more sophisticated, Caitlyn's style wasn't too much different from her early drawings. Jenna touched the inked pages, wanting to connect.

Caitlyn. I miss you. I should have tried harder to find you. I'm so, so sorry.

Her shoulder muscles tightened and her eyes stung from the threatening tears, but she refused to allow emotions to distract her from the task of finding answers. She lifted the journal higher.

Okay. Focus. There's no time for weakness. Not now.

After three hours and two books, she'd managed to blow and sniffle through an entire box of tissues. Good thing Grant had a late client dinner, because her crybaby face couldn't look pretty.

She stretched to pick up the next book from the wooden table.

In the first couple pages she could feel the shift.

The earlier books were mostly a mishmash of random drawings and thoughts—thoughts about finding Jenna, hopes of fitting into her new life, an instinctual knowledge Caitlyn would never be able to confide in anyone.

At twelve, Caitlyn included a photograph of a summer vacation, and wrote about learning how to ride horses and ways to avoid practicing her violin.

At thirteen, there were mentions of her parents' lavish parties, books she'd sneaked out of the library to read, a classmate she thought was cute.

This journal began pretty much the same way, but a few pages in the tone became progressively moodier, almost desperate, with each turn of a page. She'd turned fifteen and started high school. Jenna glanced at a passage, then started at the top to read more slowly.

THE POLKA DOT girls cornered me in the locker room today. It's not my fault boys like to stare and make fun of me. This morning, I taped my breasts down the best I could. Still, one of the girls threatened to chop off my hair. My BFF came in just in time, and threatened to have her senior friends kick some ass. They knew it could happen. The girls left and didn't bother me again. I've never been so scared. Ashley made me promise never to go into the locker rooms or bathrooms alone again. It's stupid, really. Why can't everyone just get along?

ASHLEY'S WORDS REBOUNDED, *I was her friend first.*

Jenna tried swiping the statement away, but the words continued to nag at her.

A few pages more, and there was another disturbing entry, then another, and another, every one about the teasing and bullying. Her smart, cute, yet shy sister probably got more than her fair share.

Jenna dropped the journal to her lap, not wanting to read any more. She rubbed her chest, trying to scrub the anger and ache away.

Deep-seated feelings of betrayal prevented Jenna from reaching out to her once-best friend. The raw hurt ached. She supposed Caitlyn's death wasn't Ashley's fault, but, darn it, she needed someone to blame.

Guilt seeped into her and pummeled her sense of righteousness.

Ashley had stopped by the bakery the day after the funeral to talk about Caitlyn, but Jenna didn't want to hear excuses. Not then. But now, even though the wound hadn't healed, she was beginning to understand Ashley's perspective. Besides, Jenna needed a miracle to ensure Kyle's safety.

Jenna took a moment to check on her nephew. His sprawled body, still in his school clothes, and his rosy cheeks and lips forced her to realize her bullheadedness had lasted long enough. She brushed his hair off his forehead, gently re-covered him, and then grabbed the wool blanket off the end of the bed. Quietly making her way back down the hall to the front door, she stepped into the cold night air.

The stars and moon peeked through the cloud cover to give her enough light to see, even though she probably didn't need the light. She sat on the top step before pulling out her cell phone and dialing by memory.

"Hello?"

"Ash, it's me, Jen." Uneasiness crept in, creating a stranglehold. Jenna held her breath, waiting, wanting her friend to say something, anything. "Are you there?" Jenna asked after a while, hoping to at least hear a few words to help her gage the temperature.

"I'm here," came the soft and tentative voice. "I'm trying to figure out what to say that won't make you hang up or never speak to me again. I've said I was sorry. I broke what's between us, and I know I'm responsible for that, but I don't know how to fix this. I've missed you terribly."

"You hurt me. You knew Caitlyn was in danger, and that I was her sister, but I shouldn't have reacted that way at the funeral. I'm sorry." She closed her eyes and inhaled a long slow breath. "But that's not why I called.

The Newhalls are petitioning for custody of Kyle."

"So it's true."

The anger emanating from the other end of the line provided some assurance Ashley was still on her side, so she continued. "My attorney has suggested I may not be able to keep Kyle if I don't figure out what happened to Caitlyn. And that scares the crap out of me. I have to figure out what made her run. I need you to help me figure it out. You were the one closest to her."

Ashley groaned on the other end of the phone. "I've been over the details a million times, and every conversation I can remember."

"I need you to go over it one more time. Maybe you'll remember something. I need to hear what happened. And I'm ready to hear it now, if you have the time."

The seconds ticked off, one by one, while Jenna waited for her response.

"It can't hurt," Ashley replied.

Jenna released the breath she'd been holding. Unlike others, Ashley understood what needing answers felt like. She'd spent an entire day reading her deceased mother's letters to her father to get closure. Somehow she doubted Caitlyn's journals would do the same, but then again…. "Let's start at the beginning," Jenna suggested, for lack of another alternative.

"Okay." She heard Ashley inhale deeply. "I met Caitlyn in school. She wasn't in my class, but something about her made me want to get to know her, protect her. She seemed so fragile. If that makes sense."

Jenna understood the sentiment completely. "I do get it, but we were both wrong. She was stronger than either of us gave her credit for."

"I discovered how strong she was when we had to keep our friendship a secret. Vivian selected her friends, and…surprise, surprise…I wasn't on the approved list. That's why I was shocked when Caitlyn invited me to go skiing during her college winter break. I'd recently returned to town to help my mom, and we hadn't seen each other in months. It was a bold move, and I was excited to know Caitlyn was finally taking a stand against her parents."

"I bet Vivian wasn't thrilled."

"You bet right. Her mom was way past angry."

"Did she make Caitlyn un-invite you?"

"No, but you know Mrs. Newhall. She can make things mighty uncomfortable. I do know she talked to my mom…who politely told her to mind her own business."

'Bout time Ashley's mother did something right.

"Anyway," Ashley continued, "Caitlyn planned for me to meet her and Grant at the house. The three of us were supposed to drive up together. However, as I was leaving the house, I got a text from Caitlyn telling me she'd made other plans."

"Wait. Did she really blow you off? That seems odd."

"You're right. Blowing me off didn't fit her style, but I remember being so furious about the last-minute ditch I wasn't thinking straight. This may sound selfish, but I needed a break from the 24/7 of taking care of my mom, and was really looking forward to a weekend of skiing."

"Hold on…I just thought of something." Jenna pushed open the front door, racing to the living room to grab a journal before sinking to the couch. She hurried through the pages, trying to find what she was looking for. *Got it...*

AT DINNER, he kept staring, like the boys at school, like I wasn't wearing any clothes. Then he started asking me questions—uncomfortable questions—but I refused to speak to him. After dinner, Vivian insisted I stop acting like a child, but I'm tired of her trying to control everything I do. I've never trusted him. Not after...gross!

AFTER WHAT?

Jenna considered the journal entry again, and scanned the previous entries.

"Ashley, think carefully, did the text you get sound like it was from Caitlyn? Or...could the text possibly have been sent by someone else using her phone?" *Like James Hunt?*

"That was so long ago. There's always that possibility. Why?"

"Just thinking. Before, you said you heard nothing from Caitlyn for a couple of years."

"Nothing, not a peep. When it happened, I didn't even know Caitlyn was missing until I heard it on the Saturday nine o'clock news. I tried to offer help, but the Newhalls closed ranks and refused to acknowledge me."

"You said something to Grant about getting a postcard."

"I did. It came around the time my mom died. I intended to save it, but I think I might have accidentally thrown it out in one of my tossing frenzies around the time I was getting ready to move out of my parents' house. I can't find it now."

Bummer. Jenna took a deep breath. "But Caitlyn never told you where she was, or that I was her sister."

"No. Never. After we started emailing back and forth, I began putting the pieces together. You never said much about your past. I figured you were just a private person until Caitlyn mentioned looking for an older sister. I only started to suspect you were her sister when birth dates, backstories, and other small details started to line up. It wasn't until Caitlyn mentioned the name Jenna Anne that I confirmed my suspicions and confronted her about it. In her next email, Caitlyn made me promise not to say anything to you. I got the impression she was afraid something bad might happen."

"Well, at least she was aware of what happened to me. Did she know I was looking for her?"

"I think so…" Jenna could hear a long, drawn-out breath on the other end of the phone. "She must've known. Think about it. What are the odds of you landing in Elkridge? This place isn't even within shouting distance of the top ten list of must-visits in the state. You being here communicated to your sister clearly you were searching for her."

"God, Ash. I hope you're right." She pulled on her sister's medallion. "I never stopped wanting to find her. See how her life turned out. Possibly connect again. I missed her every day." Jenna swatted at the tears welling in her eyes. "I still miss her."

"I miss her too." Ashley's croaked empathy provided comfort. "So what do we do now?"

Jenna took a long, slow breath. "Keep searching for answers, 'cause if I don't find them, I have a feeling not only will I have lost a sister, I may very well lose the only remaining family member I have left."

"Don't get mad at me for saying this, but I've discovered that sometimes you have to make your family. I love you like a sister, Jenna. We might not share the same blood, but you're as close to a sister as I will ever have. I know I hurt you, but I hope you can forgive me."

Jenna sucked in a gulp of air. She'd been surrounded by people all her life, and not once, with the exception of Kathy, did she ever connect with anyone until she came to Elkridge. Maggie, Harold, Ashley, even Grant, had so readily accepted and supported her, even when she'd given them no reason. Or, worse, made it nearly impossible for them to truly connect.

"I get what you're saying," Jenna shook out her fist and worked to release the backstabbing bitterness consuming her, but she couldn't do it. Not yet. She needed to win Kyle's freedom first. "Ashley, you'll need to give me time."

"I'll be here when you need me. And,

Jenna? Keep in mind...I need you too," she whispered.

"I think you might be forgetting about Chase. That man loves you down to your little toenails."

The ring of Ashley's laughter thrilled her. "Yes, he does...but that doesn't mean I don't need you. Get some sleep, Jenna. I have a feeling you'll need it."

Forgiveness, that's what she should feel, should do. Hadn't Kathy raised her to forgive? But she couldn't, not yet. Ashley's disloyalty still burned all the way down to her toes. Jenna disconnected the call and moved across the room to the picture window overlooking the valley below. The stars burned bright in the night sky.

"Caitlyn, if you're up there...please...if it's within your power, I could use a miracle."

The wind picked up, causing the branches to scrape across the window. The clouds brushed over the bright moon. The light and her mood dimmed.

"I think you sent Kyle to me, because you knew I need him as much as he needs me."

She turned and walked down the hall to

open the door quietly and study her sleeping nephew. She hated to wake him just to brush his teeth and put his pajamas on, but weren't those parental things what she was supposed to do?

Be a parent?

Make the rules to keep him safe, like never touching the hot stove or playing with the matches?

She took a deep breath and let out the slow exhale.

Oh, Caitlyn. How am I supposed to make this work?

CHAPTER TWENTY-SIX

J enna awoke with her face planted on one of Caitlyn's journals. She could hear Grant's even snores coming from the master bedroom. During the night, Grant must have covered her with a comforter. All the bits and pieces—a specific word, a particular phrase, a lengthy rant—all the clues began falling into place.

She didn't like the story Caitlyn's journals were telling. In fact, she hated it.

With each passing thought, a conclusion began to solidify in her mind—a conclusion her heart refused to believe, but yet she couldn't deny.

Grant was Kyle's father, not James.

All the facts aligned.

The height, hair color, birth date, the proximity. *Oh God.*

She didn't want to, but she'd reluctantly ruled out Caitlyn's boyfriend. The pictures of him she found on Facebook didn't match the physical features of Caitlyn's attacker.

Hadn't Grant admitted to loving Caitlyn? Spending time together? Feeling regret? Was he only with her because she reminded him of Caitlyn?

Nothing Grant ever did gave her the sense of an underlying malice. Yet everything in the journals indicated her sister was being harassed, possibly sexually abused.

Wasn't Grant the one who told her Caitlyn was pregnant? Maybe he hadn't heard it from the housekeeper. Maybe Caitlyn had told him.

Did he rape Caitlyn?

She reread the last page—the Monarch Butterfly poem Grant had previously mentioned—with a different set of filters.

COME HITHER, *monarch of peace.*

Allow my troubled mind to cease.
Secure me upon your wings so fair.
Before you find your joy and air.
Fly away, fly away, with abundant delight.
Soar on the winds to an alluring height.
For I am weary and need to sleep.
I give you my soul to always keep.
Fly away, fly away monarch of peace.
Allow my troubled mind to cease.

Oh, Caitlyn. What happened to take you to such a dark place? She flipped back a couple of pages to the passage that had given her the best insight.

AFTER MY PARENTS' *dinner party tonight, I overheard someone in the library talking on the phone about getting rid of newborns and the fetal matter. The man demanded he get more of the cut, arguing he wasn't making enough to cover the costs and the risks. I moved closer to hear more, but Vivian entered the living room with a tray of drinks and the man, whoever he was, hung up the phone mid-conversation. Does he know about my baby? I hope not. He might want to take it too.*

SHE FLIPPED to the next page.

THIS AFTERNOON I caught him staring at me. He must know. I bet he knows, and that smile of his tells me he's happy about it. He's ruined my life, and he's happy. Oh, God, what am I to do?

LITTLE FOOTSTEPS CAME PATTERING down the hallway. She snapped the book shut and held it close.

Did Grant know what her sister had written?

Not wanting to take the chance of Grant finding the next-to-last diary, she shoved it beneath the couch cushions.

Her heart pounded in her ears. She needed to think, absorb what she'd read.

Still half asleep, Kyle crawled into her lap.

"Good morning, sweet boy. We need to get you ready for school."

He pointed to the master bedroom.

"Grant came home late. He must be tired. Let's let him sleep."

Kyle's many needs allowed her to push the jumbled mess of clues into the recesses of her mind to simmer, and hopefully allow her to formulate a different conclusion. The "facts," as she understood them, must be wrong.

She rubbed his back. "C'mon, let's get you ready for school. It's reading day. Your favorite. Remember?"

Kyle rolled his head back and groaned. Today she couldn't allow him the luxury of a casual wakeup. "Come on, buddy, we need to get going. How about I make you banana pancakes? Yummmm." She tickled behind his ear. He shrugged and shoved off her lap and turned back toward his bedroom, his slipper-clad feet scuffing against the hardwood.

She went to start breakfast, knowing he'd eventually shiver his way into the bathroom.

An hour passed before she and Kyle were showered, fed, with their teeth brushed.

Thank goodness Grant hadn't awakened from his late night out.

What would she say?

What would she do?

She pulled her hobo bag over her shoulder and grabbed Kyle's homework. "Grab your backpack and lunch, little man."

Kyle pulled the nylon sack off the kitchen table along with his brown paper bag. Like a zombie, he followed, letting the straps of his backpack drag along the floor.

Once he was locked into his car seat and they were on their way to his school, Kyle's silence forced her to digest everything she'd read.

Caitlyn had described her life, especially the unwanted attention. She shied away from all men, trying to avoid conflict, or any type of interaction, whenever possible. Yet Maggie told her Caitlyn never shied away from Grant. In fact, Maggie indicated Grant managed to make her smile. Jenna's throat tightened with confusion.

Jenna wished Caitlyn had used names. Then she could be sure, but mostly she noted physical descriptions. Based on the height, hair color, and personality traits of Caitlyn's abuser, a clear image had formed in her mind.

The image fit Grant's description almost

perfectly. She gripped the steering wheel tighter. The attacker had a birthday in March —just like Grant. *What were the odds?*

Grant would've had access to her room —to her.

Hadn't Grant said he felt guilty about Caitlyn's disappearance?

Hadn't he described Caitlyn as her mother's little doll?

Wasn't he the last to see her before her disappearance?

While the facts pointed to Grant, something about the clues in her sister's journal didn't fit.

Was it because she didn't want to believe?

Then again, the speech pattern descriptors didn't match Grant's way of talking. He never used the terms baby or darling. Plus, he had never physically forced Jenna to do anything she didn't want to do.

Then again, maybe Grant had changed. He did call her J-Bird on occasion.

Thinking back over the past several weeks, Jenna had pushed him away, and he'd never complained—not once—or gotten angry. And a lurker? Never. He always gave her privacy when she needed it. Never once had she caught him leering at her...well, not a disrespectful kind of way. He was always a gentleman, and sex was never expected.

Yet the evidence in Caitlyn's journal pointed to Grant, and was possibly the reason she ran away. Only Jenna's heart challenged the facts.

Grant couldn't have molested Caitlyn. Could he?

There was only one way to find out...ask him.

Jenna lined up with the rest of the parents dropping off their kids.

"Ready to go, buddy? Almost there." Kyle put his book and lunch in his backpack and waited for her to get to the front of the line. "Here we are."

Jenna set Nellie's parking brake and opened the door to allow Kyle to jump out. "See you this afternoon. Okay?"

Without a backward glance, Kyle ran to the nearest group of kids. "Okay, then."

Admiration trickled into her heart. His capacity to adjust, to trust—trust in a way she couldn't—made her respect her little man.

But could she respect the big man in her life?

Grant, I hope you have an explanation.

GRANT FOLDED HIS BUTTON-DOWN SHIRT, placed it in the garment bag, and pushed the organizer pod into his suitcase.

He glanced at his watch for the third time, wondering why Jenna hadn't returned from dropping off Kyle.

Setting the black travel bag in the hall, he went to check his briefcase to ensure he had all the necessary documents.

The front door opened and he heard the familiar sound of footsteps. Just in time. He grabbed his phone and keys and turned to say something, but Jenna's scowl instantly erased the thought.

"Is Kyle okay?"

"Yes, why?"

"What's wrong?"

He took a step toward her, but she scooted

around the edge of the couch to the other side of the room and pointed at his bag.

"Are you going somewhere?"

A swirl of dust motes dancing in the stream of light from the picture window made Jenna look like an angel, except for the rage pouring out of her demon-possessed body.

"I finally got an offer on my condo and need to go to Chicago for a few days. One of the partners at my old firm wants to buy a place for his daughter. He's made a no-contingency cash offer, but now I have to get all my stuff out by the end of the week."

"What about Kyle's court case?"

"That's why I'm leaving now. I promise I'll be back in time for the hearing."

"Stay as long as you want."

What the hell? "What's wrong?"

"Nothing is wrong."

"Something's wrong. You're acting like someone pissed in your cake batter."

Oops, wrong thing to say.

She walked to the couch and pulled out a journal from beneath the cushions and waved the book in her hand toward his face. "What happened between you and my sister?"

"What happened?" He forced himself to remain calm. He squinted, then opened his eyes a centimeter wider, trying to quiet the bass drummer having a gay ol' time beating on his brain box. "Explain what you mean, by *happened?*"

"Did you have sex with her?"

"No." Acid burned its way up his throat. "That's disgusting."

Jenna raised the book in her hand, flipping open to a marked page to read aloud.

"I KEPT TELLING HIM NO, but he wouldn't listen. He said I was such a tease, I always wanted it. I didn't know what 'it' meant until he pulled up my skirt and jammed his hand up inside me. He held me by the throat, and I couldn't breathe. Couldn't scream. Couldn't move. He told me I was his little doll, and he could play with me whenever he wanted. After he was done, I ran to my room and locked the door, but I knew it wouldn't keep him out. Nothing would ever keep him out."

. . .

JENNA'S ANGRY, accusing eyes turned to him. "Is she talking about you?"

"No. That's not about me." His knees began to shake. His entire being shivered—the fiery heat of anger sending waves of chills across the skin.

"You think I could do that? Is that what you think of me? That I could do something so disgusting to *my sister*?" A wave of revulsion cut off his air, and he couldn't catch his breath. If he hadn't had years of people pushing him in the courtroom and in his life, he'd take the book out of her hands and rip it in two. "How could you think so little of me," he turned away from her.

"But you said you were the last person to see her alive—that you felt guilty. Why is that, Grant? Why do you feel guilty?"

"God. I've already told you a thousand times, because I left her here to deal with my parents. I should've stayed to protect her. I didn't know I had to protect her from her boyfriend as well."

"Whoever attacked her wasn't her boyfriend. The facts don't fit."

His stomach again lurched and sent acid

bubbling into his throat. "Don't look at me like that. What? Do you want me to sign an affidavit? I didn't hurt Caitlyn, Jenna. And you should know me well enough by now to know I couldn't do something like that."

Maybe if he didn't need to leave for the airport, he'd have pulled his punches like he always did, but damn it, he couldn't. Not today. He was sick and tired of putting up with her bullshit.

Why couldn't she trust him?

Why? Damn it!

He picked up his briefcase and walked toward the front door.

"Grant? Did you marry me because I remind you of my sister?"

He turned so fast the room kept spinning. Revulsion burned up one arm and down the other. "No, Jenna. That's not why. I've done everything in my power to help you—to earn your trust—and this is what you think? I'm leaving now, before I say something I totally regret, but hear me, Jenna. This conversation isn't finished." His hands bunched into fists. "I love you, Jenna, and I will do whatever it takes to protect Kyle. If you can't believe me when I tell you that, get the fuck out of my house."

She stepped in front of him and shoved the book in his face. "Someone impregnated my sister. I want an explanation."

"Let me say this again, for the last time. It. Was. Not. Me."

The pain in his head pounded a heavy beat and grew louder and louder by the minute. He had the sudden premonition he was about to throw up. He pushed forward, knocking her with his shoulder. "I've got to go."

"If it wasn't you, then who?" She asked.

"I don't know." *But you've given me a clue.* He opened the front door. "I'll see you in a few days. While I'm gone, I suggest you think hard about what you want, Jenna, because I'm not going to spend the rest of my life with someone who can't trust me."

"Maybe we shouldn't have gotten married."

God, he wanted to hit something. Hitting Jenna wasn't an option so he took a step back. "When will you start taking responsibility for your actions?"

"I don't know what you mean."

Grant closed the distance between them in

three steps. "Yes, you do. You're so petrified someone's going to hurt you, or leave you, that you push them away. In your heart, you know I didn't hurt Caitlyn. I can see the doubt in your face, but you haven't learned to trust your heart yet."

"I told you I wouldn't make a good wife."

His fingers closed into a steel ball, before he caught the frustrated reaction and forced them to relax. "That's an excuse, and you know it. You're a fighter. So fight for me. For Kyle. For us. I love you, but I can't do this alone. I thought I could, but I can't. You're going to have to decide."

"Then maybe it's best if Kyle and I move back into the cabin until we sort this out."

"Kyle needs to stay here. He has his own room and bed here. We can discuss this when I get back."

"Fine."

She might be okay with the living arrangement, but he wasn't.

She'd pulverized his heart into pieces the size of grains of sand. All the days and weeks and months of effort were shattered. He worked to put one foot in front of the other until he reached his car. He dropped the bags in the trunk, then slipped behind the wheel. He couldn't move. He didn't want to leave, not while knowing when he returned home, she—and Kyle—might not be there.

He rolled his wrist to check the time, then searched for the address of the clinic his parents went to. He'd have just enough time to stop at the diagnostic lab center off Hwy 70 on his way to the airport.

How the hell could she think he'd raped Caitlyn? *God, that cut, cut to the center of my soul.*

He should have told her his alternative conclusion. The explanation was simple. Too simple, actually.

However...after the crap she just pulled, he'd let her stew awhile.

CHAPTER TWENTY-SEVEN

A lady in a blue dress with a lovely smile escorted Jenna and Kyle through an oversized courtroom door. Finding the right key, the woman unlocked the room where the Honorable Judge Volz presided. The stale air wafted toward Jenna and forced her to hold her breath. Kyle squeezed her fingers as she pulled open the massive door.

Thank goodness the Elkridge court system didn't have the capacity to hear child custody petitions, or Kyle's case might already have been decided. The extra driving miles helped ensure she and Kyle got a fair shot. The judge had ordered her nephew's appearance for the custody hearing, and she was terrified to imagine what it might mean. Last week, Mr. Gertt warned her not to be late, so she and Kyle arrived a half hour early to review the tax returns, birth certificates, and other important documents.

The large open space with oak paneling and benches and rust-colored carpeting was most likely designed to provide an ambiance of majesty and calm. The décor didn't work. Not for her. The elevated judge's bench loomed in front of her, looking more like a hanging platform, minus the noose.

Having to air her personal affairs for others to hear was akin to hanging out her threadbare bra and torn panties for everyone to see.

Kyle's little fingers touched each bench as he passed the rows. He stopped and squatted to look underneath the seats. She instinctively understood.

"This place is sorta like a church," she said, "only it doesn't have hymnals, or places to kneel, huh?"

His eyes met hers, and the explanation seemed to satisfy him.

After a few minutes, Jenna pulled on his hand to get his attention. She walked him up the aisle to a wooden gate.

"Doesn't this remind you of a pasture gate?"

Kyle shook his head and giggled.

"No?" she asked, relishing the giggling happiness and not wanting it to end. "Hmmmm. Maybe you're right."

On the other side of the gate, Kyle bent to look under the table.

"Nope, no chickens or pigs. Not here. Seems like a mighty big waste for such a nice gate, doesn't it?"

"There you are."

Jenna turned to see Maggie hurrying toward her. Her friend's bossy, predictable nature eased the tension. "Sorry I'm late. I went to the wrong room."

Kyle stood on his tippy-toes to see Maggie, who'd slid onto one of the benches where people could sit and watch a trial. "I need to make a phone call," Maggie said. "I'll be just a minute."

Jenna acknowledged Maggie and released Kyle's hand.

"Kyle, this is where I'll sit with Mr. Gertt."

Trepidation and sorrow attacked her. Hardly anything good comes out of being in a courtroom. She should know. She'd been in plenty of similar rooms as a foster.

She touched the back of the chair. "Mr. Gertt is the man who will be talking to the judge. The judge is the man who will be sitting up there." Jenna pointed to the oak podium with the Colorado flag on one side and the United States flag on the other. "He's an important man, and makes hard decisions."

Kyle tilted his head way, way back to study the microphone snaking up from the desk he couldn't see. His expression held a mixture of fright and worry. Jenna wanted to scrub his little face until his cute, happy smile reappeared, but their nighttime routine wouldn't help. Not today. So she turned away. She knew exactly how he was feeling, only she had to hide her worry.

She walked across the room to the other table. "This is where the Newhalls will be sitting." Kyle's face matted into a dull expression. "You'll be okay. Maggie will be with you. They also will have a man sorta like Mr. Gertt who will be talking to the Judge."

Kyle took a place beside her and stared at one of the chairs.

"Yes, Grant will be here." She hoped. "You like Grant, his tickles, riding on his shoulders." She used her fingers to spider-crawl up his back until he bunched his shoulders around his ears and giggled.

The more she thought about Caitlyn's journals, the more she was convinced she'd been wrong. Grant wouldn't rape her sister. He wasn't the type of man who could hurt a woman. But, holy bejeesus, the evidence sure looked damning.

I want answers.

Grant loved Kyle, just as he had loved her sister. There wasn't any doubt. Even if she doubted his feelings for her, she didn't doubt his demonstrated loyalty towards Caitlyn's son.

Every minute Grant spent with Kyle, he'd showed a patience even she didn't possess. He fulfilled the role of uncle perfectly.

Jenna passed through the gate and allowed Kyle to explore on his own, and get comfortable with the place. She selected a seat on the far left side of the room, next to Maggie. At a quarter till the hour, court employees arrived, then other petitioners, then lawyers, who randomly checked in with the clerk who'd also just arrived.

"Are you doing okay?" Maggie asked.

"This place gives me the heebie-jeebies. I want to get this over with."

After several minutes, Kyle came to her and crawled onto her lap, and she hugged him to her, wanting to wrap him in her feelings of protective, mama-bear ferocity. Feeling the sting of tears, she gritted her back teeth to prevent emotions from penetrating through her calm façade. Today of all days, she needed to stay strong.

During the past few days, as soon as Kyle fell into a boneless sleep, the night's silence removed the daily distractions and opened up a way for doubts to smother with fear. In those early morning hours, when the night made her invisible, she could cry. But the raw emotions never helped solve her problems. The tears had one purpose—to cleanse the soul of hurt and the pain of living.

Seconds later, a commotion at the door caused her to rotate in her seat. The Newhalls arrived with such a high-and-mighty attitude, the room's temperature rose several degrees.

"Look at those peacocks strutting their stuff." Maggie added an eye-roll to the heavy layer of disgust.

Buck and Vivian's arrogant air and clothing spoke of wealth. The expertly tailored suits, shirts, and shoes could have funded Denver's homeless soup kitchens for an entire year.

Jenna pulled at her blouse, uncomfortable with wearing the tightly fitted shirt. She locked her hands together to keep from pulling at her collar, while Maggie continued grumbling under her breath.

The Newhalls didn't even look at her. She didn't exist to them. Never had.

Jenna urged Kyle to nestle between her and Maggie while they waited for the judge. Time ticked by.

As the courtroom clock struck the hour, the judge's chamber door opened. A foreboding feeling swept the courtroom like a horde of locusts across the plains.

A surprised exhale got stuck on the way out. "What's happening?"

Mr. Gertt exited first and motioned for her to join him at the table in the front of the room. "You're here. Good, good, good." He dropped his briefcase on the table and pulled several thin files from the brown leather satchel. Clearly he hadn't taken as much care with his wardrobe. The yellow mustard stain on his shirt stood out like a neon sign.

"We're first up." He picked up a pen and began quickly reviewing his notes.

"Is something wrong?"

"No, no. We're good. All's good."

As she lowered into the chair, a tall man wearing an exquisitely tailored suit exited the judge's chambers and strode toward the Newhalls. His features were angular, his expression blank. He whispered something to Buck Newhall as he shook the man's hand.

The biggest surprise was Grant. He walked out of the chamber last.

He looked awful. Contrary to his normally pristine appearance, he looked rumpled and exhausted. His fingers drummed against the side of his leg as he scanned the courtroom.

When he found her, he marched her way, his strides deliberate and elongated.

"You made it." Jenna greeted him with a smidge of cheer, in an effort to counterbalance their last conversation.

"I've been up all night and took the first flight out of O'Hare this morning. Why didn't you return my call?" he asked as soon as he was within a few feet. His quiet voice had a hard, accusing undertone.

"When did you call? There wasn't anything on the answering machine."

"I left a message on your cell phone."

"Ah. My phone ran out of minutes, and I didn't have a chance to add time." *'Cause I have to wait until I have the extra cash.* "Why didn't you call the house or bakery?"

Grant shoved his fingers through his hair. "I needed to talk to you about my plan, in private, but it's too late now. I don't have time to explain, but please believe that...whatever happens today...you need to remember I'm keeping my promise. I'll protect Kyle one way or another." He leaned closer, "and I haven't told anyone we're married."

"What's that supposed to mean?"

He scanned the people standing nearby, his parents, their lawyer, the clerks, then leaned closer to her ear, his breath warming her skin. "I can't explain here. You'll have to trust me."

When he pulled back, she nodded.

The muscles in his jaw twitched like he wanted to say more, but without another word, he turned, made his way over to his parents' lawyer to shake the man's hand. He didn't address his parents or look at the judge.

He looked ready for battle.

She turned to ask Mr. Gertt what was happening, but "Quiet in the court. All rise," boomed throughout the room while the Judge exited his chamber, and silenced the crowd only briefly.

"Please be seated," the Judge said after he took his seat. He didn't look up, just sorted papers and rearranged files. "Mr. Mapes, Mr. Gertt, and Mr. Newhall, thank you for meeting with me." His deep, steady voice calmed the noisy crowd. "For the record, I would like to repeat for all parties what was discussed in my chambers. Are the lawyers in agreement?"

Jenna tried again to get Mr. Gertt's

attention, but he was busy shooting Grant a poisonous glare. The knot in her chest began to tighten, squeezing her lungs and heart to the point of pain.

"Mr. Mapes, let's start with you. I understand you are representing the Newhalls. Is your party ready to present their case?"

The tall, handsome man on the right stood and buttoned his expensive suit jacket. "Yes, Your Honor. The Newhalls would like to petition for sole custody of Kyle Graden, on the basis that Jenna Dolcy cannot provide a suitable environment for him."

Jenna sucked in a gasp of air. *Not even partial or shared custody.* The churning in her stomach made her queasy.

The judge, still studying the paperwork, didn't look up while he asked, "And what is the basis for this claim?"

Mr. Mapes selected a piece of paper from his pile. "If I may direct your attention to the home study, Your Honor. It has recently come to my attention Ms. Dolcy has alternative living arrangements. The home study is no longer valid."

"And, where is she living?" The judge peered over the top of his wire-rimmed glasses.

"With Mr. Grant Newhall. Both she and Mr. Newhall are seeing to the welfare of Kyle Graden."

Vivian Newhall stood, but before she could say a word, Buck Newhall pulled her back down.

"In addition, Your Honor," the Newhalls' lawyer continued, "it should be noted that Ms. Dolcy is a diabetic. We have several documented statements from residents indicating her diabetes isn't well controlled."

"I don't see how this is relevant, if she is not living alone. Do you have anything else?"

Isn't that enough? Jenna shifted uneasily.

"Yes, Your Honor."

You're kidding, right? Jenna looked toward her attorney, whose expression was unreadable.

Mr. Mapes picked up another piece of paper, and Jenna started to wonder how many pieces of paper he brought with him. "Here's a letter from Mr. and Mrs. Newhall indicating they are willing and have the financial security to provide for education, clothing, and medical services for Kyle. An additional document from their accountant supports the letter's feasibility."

The judge waved for the additional documents to be handed over by the court clerk. The air grew thick as the minutes ticked by before the judge turned to Jenna's lawyer.

"Mr. Gertt, what have you to say?" Jenna noted her lawyer stood but didn't tuck in his tie, or button his coat, or do any of those things Mr. Mapes had done to provide a level of confidence.

"Your Honor, Caitlyn Graden before her passing made her wishes clear. She would like her sister, Jenna Dolcy, to raise her son."

"Anything else?"

Say something. Jenna begged silently.

"I'm in agreement. The housing arrangement and diabetes are not relevant."

About time.

"We have a letter here from her doctor indicating her diabetes is within the controlled range, and is easily controlled with diet, exercise, and insulin." He offered the piece of paper, but the judge appeared uninterested.

"Let's move on." The judge continued to look at the papers in front of him, then paused. "It's interesting Ms. Dolcy is diabetic, yet owns a bakery. What is Ms. Dolcy's financial condition?"

It doesn't mean I eat the stuff. Jenna's lawyer refused to acknowledge her beckoning gestures.

Mr. Gertt cleared his throat. "Ms. Dolcy has recently opened a bakery, so the store's income isn't yet stable enough to provide a financial statement. However, I have a purchase order here from a Ms. Margaret Conroy, who has guaranteed future purchases from Dreamy Delights."

"So there is no history of stable income? No other income source to support Kyle?" The judge peered over the rims of his glasses.

"Other than W-2s from her prior employment, no, Your Honor."

"I see." The prejudice in the judge's tone, while it shouldn't exist, spelled the word *inadequate,* and came across clear as the bell on a cloud-free morning.

Jenna wanted to stand up and rage at her lawyer, compel him to say something, anything that would sway the judge, but she'd been warned speaking out wouldn't do her any favors.

"Let's move on to the DNA testing." The judge shuffled some papers. "According to the DNA testing. Kyle Graden is in fact Jenna Dolcy's nephew. Is that agreed?"

"Yes, Your Honor."

Told you. I didn't need a DNA test as proof. Jenna breathed a sigh of relief.

"Mr. Mapes and Mr. Newhall, based on the DNA evidence presented by Mr. Gertt, do you agree with the findings?"

"We do, Your Honor," Grant responded.

"Mr. Newhall, I've received your paperwork for sole custody of Kyle Graden as well, is this correct?"

Jenna's gaze locked on Grant as rage burned in her core. *Why? Why would you do this to me?*

"Yes, Your Honor." Grant confirmed.

"For the benefit of this court, please respond to the following questions. The DNA evidence indicates with a 99.7 percent accuracy that you're the father of Kyle Graden. Do you agree?"

No! Jenna gasped.

Vivian Newhall gasped, and clapped her hand over her mouth.

"I do." Grant responded.

"And, based on the evidence, Caitlyn Newhall was not your biological sister, but a sister by adoption, is that correct?"

"Yes. I loved Caitlyn, as I love Kyle."

"And Caitlyn Newhall was aware of this fact at the time of her departure."

"Yes."

"Do you know why she decided to leave Elkridge?"

Grant shook his head. "Any answer would be pure speculation, Your Honor."

"Indulge me."

Grant hung his head, measuring his words before addressing the judge. "There are several factors which might have come into play. The fact she turned eighteen several months earlier. Her wish to become a veterinarian, and my parents' adamant determination for her to become a lawyer. I suspect she seized the opportunity to leave. It doesn't entirely surprise me she ended up on a farm. She'd have plenty of animals to care for."

"Did you know Caitlyn was pregnant at the time?"

"No, I did not."

"But you do confirm you're Kyle's father."

"As I said before, I loved Caitlyn, and the DNA provides facts."

Jenna didn't want to believe him, but his expression, his body language, the tone of voice revealed the truth. Hopelessness welled up from the black depths of her being.

The judge studied Grant, then the papers again. "What I still don't understand is why Caitlyn wouldn't have contacted you after she left."

Good question, Jenna wanted to scream.

"I'm not certain, but I believe she thought it best to protect Kyle. My parents can be controlling, and I assume she wanted to raise her child in a more relaxed environment."

Jenna struggled to get air into her lungs. She was losing Kyle. Losing everything she ever wanted. Grant was taking him from her. Her family was being yanked out of her arms again. The stabbing hurt was so deep, and so vivid, she could hardly breathe, and was afraid she might vomit.

"A biological parent is always my number one choice for custody." The judge's voice exploded across the courtroom. "The fact that Ms. Dolcy has been living with Mr. Newhall for only the past few weeks is not relevant to this decision. Future visitation rights for Ms. Dolcy, or the grandparents, can be worked out separately." The judge's voice boom-boom-boomed like a cannon going off. One bomb after another exploding midair. "Mr. and Mrs. Newhall, your petition is denied. Ms. Dolcy, your custody of Kyle Graden is now terminated. This court grants full custody of Kyle Graden to his father, Mr. Grant Newhall."

Oh, Kyle. No. No. No. No. NO!

"Since Kyle Graden is in court today, he will be placed in Mr. Newhall's custody immediately." The judge's gavel sounded like a nail being hammered into a coffin.

A court officer the size of a NFL linebacker moved in her direction.

"Wait. He won't understand. Let me talk to him," she pleaded.

The officer ignored her and kept walking.

She took a step, but Gertt blocked her path. "Let me go."

She yanked her arm back, and reached, arms stretched toward Kyle.

The officer pushed through the gate, and all she could think was, *Kyle run.*

Streams of tears tumbled down her face.

Please. No. "No you can't take him," she screamed.

This can't be happening.

Please don't take him from me.

He's all I have.

A wail so soulful, so desperate, so devastating, filled the courtroom.

The child's crushing cry for help stabbed at her selfish grief. He stood in the aisle with hands over his ears, his face red with terror, tears pouring down his face.

I did this. I broke my promise.

She climbed over the wooden barrier and pushed other parents and observers out of her way.

The judge's gavel pounded and pounded, decimating her heart. "Order in the court," he shouted.

She ducked around the officer and ran toward her nephew, collapsing on her knees to wrap him in her arms.

"Kyle. Oh, baby. Shhh." She smoothed his hair from his face. "Shhh. Kyle. You're okay." She pulled Kyle into a tight embrace, cuddling closer to protect him. "I'm so sorry." *How could I have let this happen?*

Kyle's little body hitched, trying to get air, as she tried to gather strength enough for them both.

"It'sokay-It'sokay-It'sokay...shhh, It's okay." She rocked the boy back and forth, one hand on his head, the other holding him as close as possible.

"Miss?" The authoritative question was more a statement.

No, please don't take him. Jenna ignored the security officer.

"Ma'am, you'll need to release the boy, now."

"Officer, please let me handle this," Grant said. The tenderness in his voice burned.

Instant hate filled her. A hatred so razor-sharp she wanted to lash out and shred him mercilessly.

She hated him.

He did this. He took Kyle from her.

A loathing formed in her gut. Her muscles

bunched. "Don't," she jerked away from the warm hand Grant had placed on her shoulder.

Slowly she unwound her body from around Kyle's, although she wasn't ready to release him. She bullied her seething anger into a corner to twist it and draw on its strength.

"Kyle? Kyle, look at me." She reached for his quivering chin, trying to soothe his emotions. "That's it. That's my good boy." She reached for the familiar metal chain around his neck and pulled it from under his shirt to hold it where he could see it. "Remember, what I told you?" She reached for Caitlyn's medallion. "We match. Remember?"

The torrent of tears paused as Kyle reached for the pendants in her hand.

"We match. You and me. I promise, I'll never be far away. I need you to remember that. I'm right here." She placed the pendant against his heart with her hand. "I'm here. The same with your mom. We're both here—in your heart. You can talk to us both, and we will hear you. Okay?"

A warm hand touched her shoulder again,

and she held out a hand to ward Grant off for a few more precious seconds.

"Kyle, you need to go with Grant. He'll take good care of you. He'll take you hiking, play ball with you, and maybe go fishing. You'll like that. Right? Remember all the fun you have with him?"

Kyle nodded, and she pulled a tissue from her pants pocket to wipe his eyes and nose. She kissed his forehead before standing and shoving the snot-filled wad back in her pocket.

Fear. Anger. Hatred. All those and more rose out of that black pit to consume her as she turned and visually dismembered the man she'd almost loved. The man who'd only a few weeks ago professed his love for her.

"Take care of him, Grant. Love him."

Grant lifted Kyle into his arms. The boy threw his arms around Grant's neck, burying his face against his shoulder.

"Jenna, let's go home." He extended his hand.

"I'm *not* going anywhere with you." The smoldering hatred she'd tackled and cornered threatened to come out swinging. "I trusted you, and you lied to me."

Her world ceased to spin.

Everything in her life ended.

Her search for Caitlyn.

Her fight to protect Kyle.

Her will to breathe.

She'd failed...failed them all.

Worst of all, she failed herself. She should have known to not trust anyone. Wasn't that the rule? The safe bet? But she'd been destroyed by the sweet hope that someone believed in her. Loved her. Wanted her. She gave into the temptation, and brought on her own destruction.

All her dreams, her reasons for fighting through life were gone.

Grant had created a living paradise. A fantasy world of what could have been. A wonderland of what-ifs...now lost. Forever.

"Since you lied about Caitlyn, did you lie about loving me as well? How could you do this?"

Grant glanced around the courtroom, then back at her. "We can't discuss it here."

She couldn't breathe. She didn't want to breathe.

"Then just go. Take care of Kyle."

Maggie wrapped an arm around Jenna and pulled her toward the door. A tidal wave of tears, rage and grief overwhelmed her ability to stand. Maggie's arm tightened. Jenna leaned into her embrace.

Her family was gone.

Grant had destroyed her dreams.

CHAPTER TWENTY-EIGHT

"You have to be the most selfish person I've ever met," Grant's voice carried through Jenna's bakery, resounding wall-to-wall.

"After what you've done, you dare to call me selfish? You got your wish." She shoved a baking pan in the sink to soak. "You got Kyle. Isn't that enough?"

"My wish? No, Jenna. You have it all wrong. If I'd gotten my wish, Caitlyn would still be alive, and Kyle would still be with his mother. I understand you're angry."

"You don't know the half of it." Jenna fought the urge to peel him with a sharp knife all the way to the core.

"You want someone to blame. I get that, but I'm tired of being that guy."

That's not true...or is it?

Grant paced away a few steps and back. "This conversation isn't getting us anywhere."

"Why do you think I haven't picked up the phone? Unless you're willing to grant me full custody of Kyle, nothing you say to me right now will make a difference."

"Nothing?" Grant raked his fingers through his hair. "Maybe not, but there are a few things you need to know about Kyle."

"Kyle? Where is he?" she asked, looking behind him, and then outside.

"He's at the library for story time, and then a group of parents have planned an ice cream social."

"I can't talk to you here. Customers could walk in."

"Let them walk in. I'm going to talk, and you're gonna listen." Grant stopped at the counter. "Kyle needs you. You need to come back to the house. You can't shirk your responsibility."

Jenna wiped her hands on her apron. "How dare you." She walked around the edge of her counter. "When you went behind my back and took full custody of Kyle, you took away my ability to take care of him. I don't even have visiting rights."

"Jenna, if your damn phone had been working, you would have known what I was planning for us."

"*Us*? There is no *us*, Grant. *You* filed for full custody of Kyle all on your own. *You* took him from me."

Grant's eyes grew darker. "What do you mean there is no us. Are you saying you don't want to be married anymore?" Every inch of Grant's frame screamed with tension as he paced back and forth.

"I won't allow you to put this on me. You lied to me."

"I've never lied to you."

"Oh, yeah?" She crossed her arms to keep the vibrating anger from shaking her entire body. "You said you didn't touch Caitlyn. If that's the case, then why does your DNA say you're Kyle's father? Huh? Tell me that?"

"I didn't lie to you. And if you'll calm down enough to listen, really listen, I'll explain."

"Calm down? You want me to calm down?

You can go to hell. You raped my sister, got her pregnant, and then abandoned her. There is no way I'll let you touch me again. So unless you are here to tell me you're giving me custody of Kyle, you need to leave."

"You know I can't give you custody of Kyle. If I did, my parents would have us both back in court before the month is out. Plus, I'd be breaking the law." The air around them grew thick with strain. "Jenna, come on. Don't do this. Let's go someplace and talk. Better yet, come home."

Her rage took another step up the incensed ladder. "Home?" A knot formed in her back and pinched between her shoulder blades. "I don't have a home. Home is where my family is. You took the only family member I have from me."

Jenna leaned sideways when the bakery's front door opened. A customer she'd seen on occasion walked into the store. "We can't do this here. If you ever cared about me, let me see Kyle, but leave me alone."

"Kyle, right. This has always been about Kyle."

She let her irritation sink deep into her

tone. "Yes, and I'd like to see Kyle today, if you'll let me."

"And, if you'd let me, I'd pick you up right now, drive you back to my place, prove to you how wrong you are about me, and make love to you until you can't move. All I want is to hold you in my arms for the rest of my life."

"Stop! Would you just stop?" She hissed through gritted teeth. She turned to the woman standing at the end of the counter, turning up the charm full blast to avoid having her customer run for the door. "I'll be with you in a minute."

"Jenna, listen to me…"

"Don't you think you've said enough? Anything else you need to say, you can say to my lawyer."

The expression on Grant's face was a mixture of anger, remorse, and frustration, and that was a good start, but it wasn't a tenth of what she was feeling. "Fine. You can pick Kyle up, but please have him back by bedtime. He has a big day tomorrow."

"His school play. I remember. I promise not to be too late. Now…I really must ask you to leave. I've got a customer."

She lifted her chin and moved behind the counter, her brave face locked in place, because if the devastating emotions weren't screwed down tight, she might burst into tears.

Grant turned and made his way out of the bakery. She closed her eyes for a few seconds to gain her balance. Grant always calculated more than one chess move at a time. How could she win against such a master?

She boxed the dozen treats for her customer. Normally, she would offer samples, or try to get the customer to try something different. Not today. Today, she merely rang up the order and wished the customer a nice day, just so she could cry in peace.

Frustration, resentment, and disbelief created a hurricane of emotions and made her nauseous.

She returned to her baking station and poked at the dough on the counter, then began pounding her fists into the dough over and over and over again until her fists felt bruised.

The bakery bells announcing another customer made Jenna drop her hands to her sides in defeat.

She expected to see Grant, but was surprised when Maggie strolled in.

Jenna groaned and braced for another lecture.

Maggie walked around the end of the counter. "Come here, you. You look like you could use a hug."

Jenna released a heavy sigh as Maggie wrapped her strong, comforting arms around her shoulders. "Hon, I'm so sorry." The sympathy on Maggie's face added more pity to her already overindulgent self-made pity-party.

"I've lost Kyle, and it's all my fault," Jenna hated hearing herself whine. "You warned me about the Newhalls, and I didn't listen," she added with a dreary note. "There is a reason I don't trust people. When I do, I get hurt."

She hated the tears stinging her eyes. Maggie's arms tightened a bit more until Jenna pulled back. Her friend pulled a napkin from her apron. "Here. You need to dry those eyes before a customer sees you."

"You're right. I need to focus on my bakery, and more importantly, on helping Kyle adjust to his new life." With her hands, Jenna swiped the falling tears off her cheeks and then accepted the napkin. "I've given myself twenty-four hours to grieve. That's it, and then I'll get back to dealing with my pathetic life. I feel so betrayed. Why would Grant do such a thing?"

"He must have his reasons. He's a smart man, but I don't want to get between the two of you." A heap of conflict flickered across Maggie's face. "Have you eaten anything today? Maybe you should come over to the café. I'll have Ted fix you something nice."

Jenna's cheeks warmed. "I had a cup of soup an hour ago. Besides, I need to stay busy." *Take care of my responsibilities. No more running.*

The dessert case filled with a rainbow of delights seemed shadowed by various shades of gray. "Thank you for always being there for me. It means a lot." She looked at the list of baking she intended to complete. "Plus, I need to leave in a half hour. I have an appointment at the sheriff's office to go over my case."

"Case?" Maggie rounded on her as soon as the statement rolled out of her mouth. "What's this about a case?"

"I didn't want to worry you, but Sheriff Joe

called yesterday to tell me he thinks the bakery fire might have been arson, and the evidence points to the Newhalls' housekeeper's son. I wanted the custody hearing settled before I went poking at the Newhalls again."

"Holy crap. If someone in this town is lighting things on fire, I'd better make sure my insurance policy's up to date. I'd lose everything."

Everything...that's what she'd already lost. At least Maggie had decided not to sell her land or the café to Clairemont. Jenna had a place to stay...for now. "I'm sorry, Maggie. If I'd never gotten involved with Grant, none of this would have ever happened."

"Now don't you go putting this situation in the bag of sorry you like to carry around. You have plenty enough on your plate at the moment."

"Grant will protect Kyle, and Kyle adores him. I've been thinking, maybe it would be easier for Kyle if I left town for a little while. You know, allow him to settle in with Grant without all the confusion."

"Oh, hon. I know you're hurt, but Kyle loves you. He needs you. You have to figure out how to put all this hurt behind you, because Kyle needs all the love he can get. Besides, I'd miss my sugar-girl."

Sometimes love isn't enough.

"Don't you give me that doubting eye-roll," Maggie chastised. A warm hand cupped her chin. "Kyle needs you. You have to keep fighting for him."

"Then why doesn't Kyle speak to me? Tell me that."

"I know you believe Kyle's silence is a trust issue. You need to give him time. He'll come around."

"I can understand him wanting control—control over one of the few things he can...but why can't I get him to open up—to trust me. It hurts. Hurts a lot."

Maggie swept Jenna's bangs aside. "Maybe you have to trust him first."

"I love him like he's my son. I didn't ever think I could tell someone I loved them, but I do. I love him more than my life. He comes first. I need to do what is best for him."

Maggie shook her head. "Love and trust are two different things, hon. Love is something you give. You've got a beautiful, loving heart,

Jenna Dolcy, but you need to open your heart to receive love, and to learn how to trust."

"Maybe I'm not deserving of love."

"Woman, I'm gonna whack you in the head —you're more than deserving. You've got a solid gold heart. Now, get your fanny in gear, and get your baking over with, so you can go see your little boy."

"I'm supposed to take Kyle to dinner, but what if I get there and he doesn't want anything to do with me, or refuses to go to dinner?" She couldn't help the tears welling in her eyes. "I remember sitting for hours in a corner when I refused to do something the nuns told me to do. Kyle must feel like he's being jerked around."

"Oh, hon. Don't you see…that's why you're the best person to help him. You can empathize. Everything will work out. You need to stay positive."

Losing custody of Kyle reminded her again how fast life could change. She looked at the woman who'd become like a mother to her. "I love you, Maggie," the foreign words somehow managed to dribble off her tongue. "I know

I've never said it before, but while I'm at it, I thought you should know."

Maggie gave her a stern glare. "Don't you dare make me cry. I've got a hard-ass reputation to maintain. I don't want people thinking I'm a pushover."

Jenna stood on her tiptoes and gave the big woman a noisy kiss on the jowls. The look in Maggie's eyes provided more than enough satisfaction.

"It will be all right," Maggie reiterated. "You'll see. Have a little faith, and believe in miracles."

Miracles.

"I've tried everything else, so I guess doing the wishful-thinking thing couldn't hurt."

"That's my sugar-girl." Maggie brushed the back of her knuckles across Jenna's cheek. "You know where to find me if you want to talk."

Jenna nodded while Maggie made her way to the front entrance.

A miracle.

Too bad there wasn't a recipe. She'd bake up a dozen.

CHAPTER TWENTY-NINE

The next day, Jenna relived moment by moment the awesome dinner she'd had with Kyle while pulling his favorite sweet bars out of the oven. She slipped the tray into the cooling rack, then danced back to the prep-table to Carrie Underwood's song *Blown Away.* When the storefront bell rattled, she automatically pulled two new disposable latex gloves from the box and turned. Her recovering customer-facing smile automatically faltered.

"Rachelle, what brings you in? Are you thinking about getting another box of brownies?" *Or have you finally figured out Grant doesn't like chocolate?*

The blonde slowly shifted her sunglasses to the top of her head. The woman considered her for several seconds before approaching the counter.

"No. Well, maybe yes, but not for the reasons you're thinking."

Odd. Rachelle, always one to be articulate, seemed unsure. *Very odd.* "And, what do you believe I'm thinking, Rachelle?"

"Something about Grant, I suppose, but you'd be wrong."

Busted.

The town's socialite pushed her expensive phone into her purse. "I'm here to ask if you would be willing to design something unique. I got my residential real estate license and want to start a business."

"What did you have in mind?"

"During open houses, I'd like to have nibbles with my logo on them. People like your stuff the best, so I thought I would ask if you would be willing to help me design something."

Rachelle's asking for help. Something's definitely up.

"You're not running your dad's office anymore?"

For an instant, Rachelle's expression was unsettled, then eased back into her typical haughty calm. "I suggested he find an experienced project manager if the land redevelopment deal is approved by the city."

"You don't think you can handle the job?"

Rachelle flipped her blond hair over her shoulder and her eyes narrowed with indignation. "Of course I'm capable, but I have different ideas."

In other words, you disagree with your dad, but would never admit it openly.

"I'm not sure your father's plan will work anyway. Maggie assures me she won't be selling her property."

"My father has ways of making people change their minds," she said, while studying the intricate floral design on her manicured nails. "But I'm not here to talk about my dad."

Jenna retrieved her order pad and a pen. "How can I help, Rachelle?"

For the next ten minutes, Jenna and

Rachelle discussed and discarded several ideas before settling on miniature brownie cups, pecan tarts, and ginger snaps, all with a branded logo to be approved by Rachelle before the end of next week.

"Will that be all?" Jenna asked.

"Not quite." Rachelle shifted her purse from one arm to the other. "I talked to Tiffany the other day, and your name came up. Quite unexpected."

I suppose she had a lot to say about our bathroom conversation. "And how is Tiffany?"

"She called me from a drug rehab clinic in Arizona. She asked me to pass along a message." Rachelle ran a finger across her brow to straighten the already perfectly aligned hairs. "She said you were right. She deserves better."

Surprise eased the tension. Authentic hope seeped in. "I'm glad she reached out for some help. If you talk to her again, would you let her know I wish her only the best? She has a lot going for her."

"I don't know about that." Rachelle rolled her eyes in an almost dismissive way, but her cynical jealousy told a different story. Jenna had the impression something had recently rocked Rachelle's world. Never had the confident woman seemed so unsure of herself.

Jenna pushed her order pad aside. "Ashley filled me in about your engagement to Jason. For the record, I want to say how sorry I am. No one should be treated that way. No one. Ever."

Rachelle's jaw muscles quivered with unspoken words, and hurt crisscrossed her face. "I must have gotten something stuck in my contact." She poked at her designer violet lens. "I have some contact solution in my car. I must be going."

"Rachelle? I didn't mean to upset you."

In the process of settling her sunglasses across her face, Rachelle paused.

"I'm sorry." Jenna took a step around the counter to face the tall blonde. "It was insensitive of me to bring up the subject. However, if we're going to do business together, I want to start with a clean cookie sheet—so to speak. No crumbs. Just good, solid ingredients to build a professional relationship. So, what do you say?"

Rachelle deliberated, nodded and then

turned toward the door. At the exit, she paused with her hand on the handle, before turning back. "You know, I saw Grant in the park yesterday playing with your little boy."

"If you're here to gossip, please don't. Grant loves Kyle. He'll be a good dad."

"Grant's good that way. He'll love Kyle even if he's not his own."

Jenna grabbed a rag and twisted. "Like his own? This town is so small, I'm sure you've already heard Grant's DNA matched Kyle's —right?"

"That's what I heard, but I also know Grant isn't Kyle's father. He's been cleaning up after Jason all his life. At least, this will be the last mess he'll need to take care of."

"Jason? I'm not sure what you're trying to tell me."

"You must know." Rachelle's default haughtiness slipped right into place. "Kyle *is* Jason's son, *not* Grant's."

Jenna shook her head. "Don't listen to the rumors. Grant's DNA tests show he's the father."

"Yes, and if Jason was still alive, his tests would show the same."

Jenna's muscles tightened. "You're not making sense."

Rachelle rolled her eyes, and clicked her tongue, "Maybe you don't watch enough television. Everyone knows twins' DNA would both match. Grant may be Jason's identical twin, but that's where the similarities end."

Jenna gripped the counter as the room began to spin. *Grant's a twin. Oh, God. He's a twin. How did I miss that?*

The cackle of Rachelle's laughter drew her gaze. "You didn't know Grant was a twin? How odd." The woman struck a superior pose, then at the last minute her body softened. "Then, again, Jason was gone before you arrived." Rachelle huffed out a puff of air. "Jason. The narcissist no one talks about. He'd be so disappointed."

"I didn't know. There are no pictures of them together, nothing in his house giving me a clue. Grant only talked about his brother as being older."

"Jason was older, but by minutes." The stunned realization on Jenna's face must have been the cause for Rachelle's smile. "That's okay. The only thing you need to know now is

Grant's bullheaded, and protective, and loyal. When he loves, he loves wholeheartedly. And for some odd reason, he loves you and Kyle. Grant's a good man, Jenna. You won't find one better."

Jenna, not quite sure of Rachelle's purpose, remained silent.

"My goodness, do I have to spell it out?" The blonde's eye-roll was a nine on a scale of ten. "Don't be stupid. Go after him. You couldn't possibly find a better man and husband and father than Grant." With a wave and a waggle of her fingers, Rachelle slipped out the door and was gone.

Stupid? Probably. Wait. Did that mean she could get Kyle back? If Grant wasn't Kyle's father...the thought lasted precisely two seconds before dissolving.

She refused to put Kyle through the legal tug-and-pull again. Besides, she didn't have the funds, or want to deal with the Newhall garbage.

Why didn't I trust Grant? If she'd been more open, then maybe people would have told her about Jason. Keeping secrets from her friends. Not being honest with herself. All the result of her insecurities and ingrained habits.

Easy excuses. Behaviors which had led nowhere but to unhappiness. The problem was, she didn't know how to fix a relationship, or show love, or trust someone. She'd never learned.

A loneliness so deep and so dark engulfed her, clogging her throat until she couldn't breathe.

The future she had once so clearly envisioned was gone.

She no longer could just be the baker, and, on occasion, a café waitress. She had responsibilities. She was a business owner. She had friends. She was part of this town.

She needed to get better at showing she cared.

She needed to do some self-evaluation and make some changes…learn to do things differently.

And she'd start today.

CHAPTER THIRTY

J enna walked down the hall of Mountain Valley Medical toward the pediatric wing, carrying a pink teddy bear, a balloon, and a box of Ashley's favorite baked goods. Her heart pounded with anxious trepidation. She peered through the closed door's window. The scene made her heart sigh with a heavy dose of wonder and a light dusting of jealousy.

Just say you're sorry, Kathy's recommendation popped up like a Jack-in-the-box, reminding Jenna again why she'd come.

Chase, Ashley's husband, sat in a chair next to her bed holding a tightly bundled child. The baby looked so small in the big man's arms. Beside him, his wife slept peacefully. Thinking twice about disturbing the couple, she took a step back.

"Don't tell me you've come all this way just to turn around and leave," Maggie accused, the gruffness in her voice making the embarrassment dig deeper. "I think Ashley would like to see you."

Heat brushed up her neck and cheeks for being caught getting ready to sneak off without making the amends she'd planned so carefully. "I'm not so sure about that."

"Come on," Maggie gripped her shoulders and turned her around. "We'll go in together." Maggie pushed open the door, and Chase looked up, then held a finger to his lips.

"I'm awake." Ashley's groggy voice matched her tired eyes. She flinched as she pushed up on her hands to gently shift her sore body. "I'm so glad you both came." She looked at Maggie for an instant, but then turned to Jenna. "I was especially hoping you'd come, Jenna. I've got a surprise for you."

Ashley lifted the hand with an IV needle

attached, beckoning her husband. "Chase, would you—"

"Got it." Chase stood and walked toward Jenna. "I think Ashley wants you to meet our daughter, Caitlyn Anne Daniels."

"Oh…" Instant tears filled Jenna's eyes. "I…ah…um."

"I hope you don't mind," Ashley said.

"No. No, I don't mind. It's lovely. In fact, I'm grateful." *Grateful for your forgiveness.*

Jenna swallowed back powerful feelings and held her breath as Chase laid the precious baby in her arms. Never having held a newborn, she didn't dare move. Her arms and shoulders were stiff. The little girl's face grew serious, then relaxed back into slumber. Chase hovered before returning to his wife's side and taking her hand.

"She's so perfect." Jenna's soul filled with a gentle peace.

Ashley's smile broadened. "I think so, but then again, I'm biased."

Baby Caitlyn's little pink hand stretched open, and then the five little fingers, complete with tiny little fingernails, curled in and relaxed. The baby's minute eyelashes. The peach fuzz hair. The button nose. All perfect. Hesitantly, Jenna stroked the child's plump cheek with her index finger. The baby stirred, not quite opening her eyes.

"Welcome to the world, Caitlyn." Jenna's chest ached with sentimental longing. She moved to the rocking chair Chase had vacated and slowly lowered herself into it. She looked up to see Ashley's kind face. "Thank you," was the only thing she could say to push past her remorse for the way she treated Ashley.

"She was my friend too, you know," Ashley reminded her. "After she disappeared, I was so lost. I was dealing with my mom, and then you showed up. I should have guessed sooner you were her sister. You both have such kind and giving hearts."

Jenna could only acknowledge her friend's compassionate gesture with a nod.

"Okay. Enough of this weepy crap. Healthy babies are something to celebrate." Maggie came to stand over her shoulder. "Besides, it's my turn, so hand her over."

Jenna instinctively cuddled the baby closer, not wanting the moment to end, but then realized there would thankfully be other moments.

Maggie switched places with her, and she went to sit on the bed beside Ashley.

"Are you okay?" Jenna asked, though more curious to know if their friendship was back on solid ground.

"I'm all right, but I think Chase needs a little TLC. He was on the verge of going down about the time Caitlyn decided to pop out."

Chase crossed his arms, looking indignant. "I hadn't thought about what it was like pushing a seven-pound ball through such a small opening." His whole body winced.

"All women heal as soon as they have a baby in their arms. If it's any consolation," Maggie added, "having babies gets easier, the more you have."

Chase pointed over her shoulder. "I need to find Ashley's dad." He took several steps toward the door. "He went for coffee about a half an hour ago and hasn't returned. He took it harder than I did. You know...seeing his daughter having a baby, and all." He rubbed his hands down his jeans as the loveliest shade of pink splotched his face. Two seconds later he disappeared from the room faster than Flash Gordon on a mission. When the door closed behind him, all three women started giggling.

"Poor Chase. We shouldn't be so hard on him. He's a good dad." Ashley's voice softened. "Speaking of new dads, Chase told me he saw Grant at the baseball field teaching Kyle to hit. I'm still surprised the judge awarded him full custody. Will you fight the decision?"

The vibration in Jenna's right leg caused her to take a deep breath to push off the growing frustration. "I don't think so." She swallowed the bitter pill of regret. "I won't put Kyle through that. Not again. Besides, Grant is the only one who can stand up to his parents. Kyle needs protection and a stable home. And money." She let out a slow breath of resolve. "The Newhall money can give him a life I can't."

"Money doesn't buy happiness or love." Ashley's sincere loyalty made Jenna feel a smidge better.

"Grant knows how to love. I was so blinded by fear and past hurts, I didn't trust him enough to accept what he offered." She lifted her gaze to Maggie's. "That's a burden I'll have to live with."

"He shouldn't have blindsided you like that." Maggie's gruff response tickled her with guilt.

"No, but then again, I didn't give him a chance. He tried talking to me before court was in session. He said something about protecting me, but I was angry and wasn't really listening. That's on me. That's my stupid stubbornness. I should have listened to him. I mean really listened."

"Really?" Ashley's sarcastic expression made her want to roll her eyes.

"Go ahead and make fun. I deserve it."

"Yes, you do," Maggie agreed.

"What is this, gang up on Jenna day?"

"Let's get real. Jenna, you've been pushing Grant away since day one—all because you took exception to his last name. You've tossed your cookies at him, and he still stuck around. He's a decent man. Guys like Grant don't come around too often, just ask me. What is it with you two, always pushing away the good ones?"

"I figured it out...eventually." Ashley's defensiveness made Maggie scoff.

"With only seconds to spare, and if Chase hadn't crashed your dad's snowmobile, things might have turned out differently." Maggie turned on Jenna. "So when are you gonna figure it out? Grant's a good man. He cares for you, and he's good to Kyle. I've never seen a man who took his responsibilities so seriously. Go talk to him. Clear up any misunderstanding you two might have."

"Talk about misunderstandings. Why did neither of you tell me Grant was a twin?"

Ashley looked at Maggie and vice versa. Ashley opened and closed her mouth several times, and Maggie cocked her head to the side. Then she shifted. "Well, 'cause...well, I don't know. Those boys looked identical, but were as different as two different sides of a rock, one smooth, and one as jagged as they come. Plus, I keep forgetting you haven't lived here forever like the rest of us."

"Thank you." Jenna breathed out slowly, clearly to make sure Maggie heard the sincere sentiment. "I'll take that as a compliment."

"What difference would it make anyway?"

A huge difference. I wouldn't have accused him of raping my sister, for one. "It doesn't matter now. I doubt he'll have anything to do with me."

"I wouldn't be so sure about that. Grant's a reasonable guy, and he did everything but stand on his head to get your attention when you were around. Besides, he truly cares about Kyle, and I know Kyle loves you."

"At least Grant managed to get his parents to stop pursuing visitation rights...that's good enough for now."

"Bah. It's not good enough, and you know it. I've seen what scared looks like, and you have it tattooed to your face."

"Scared?" Jenna sat up straighter.

"Yep. Scared. Scared someone might hurt you." Maggie only waggled her finger, but the gesture felt like a woodpecker hammering a hole in her chest. "I've spent every second on my feet working. One of these days, you'll wake up and wonder where the time went. When you get to be my age, you don't want to be alone, with your kids living in different corners of the world. For once, listen to this old woman, would ya?"

"Maggie's right." Ashley chimed in. "When Chase came along, I did everything I possibly could to push him away. If I'd succeeded, I wouldn't have my sweet baby, or the lovely husband who created her with me."

"I never thought I'd have kids, but Kyle changed all that." She loved him more than she'd ever loved anything, even Caitlyn. His innocence had opened her heart. But trusting Grant?

"Kids certainly can provide a different perspective." So many emotions piled up and smooshed together, like a pastry tube ready to squirt frosting. "It would be nice to have kids."

"I hope you do, for selfish reasons." Ashley nudged her with a hand to get her complete attention. "Chase doesn't have any friends his age in this town. I think he'd like to hang out with someone who doesn't talk his ears off. Harold and Bill Mason, over at the hardware store, don't know how to have a quick conversation."

Maggie snorted, then smiled, then a full-out belly laugh took over, which in turn woke up Caitlyn. The little wail and waving of fisted hands brought their attention to center on the beautiful bundle in Maggie's arms.

"Someone's hungry," Maggie stood and placed the baby in Ashley's arms.

The way Ashley admired her baby filled Jenna with an aching need. She automatically put her hand on her stomach, newly aware of an already-existing emptiness. The sensation of Grant placing tender kisses along her neck and shoulder followed it.

Tender. Patient. Kind. She missed him.

Her breath hitched. She'd loved him. *Wow. Love.* The realization hit her like a hammer upside the head.

Could she learn to love again?

Was she worthy of his love?

Her heartbeat pounded against the chains of the past, fighting for release, fighting against the fear.

Ashley opened her gown and held her baby to her breast. Caitlyn's eyes opened and rolled around before Ashley helped her make the natural connection.

She watched the new Caitlyn the same way she'd observed Kyle as he slept. The wonder. The singularity of the moment. The raw protectiveness.

Not knowing what to do, Jenna moved to

the end of the bed. "I'd better get going. Say my good-byes to Chase and your dad."

Maggie leaned back in the visitor's chair. "I think I'll stay a while. Be careful driving home. The roads are wet from the thunderstorm."

Ashley glanced her way. "The doctor said I'll be released tomorrow. Would you stop by?"

"Yeah, I think we should talk some more. Plus, if you'll let me, I'd like to plan your baby shower. I was even thinking I might test a new kind of cookie for Caitlyn's shower to celebrate her birth. You'll have to try out the samples."

"That sounds perfect." The tension in Ashley's expression transformed into relief. "Our mutt will be happy to see you. Lucky's missed his fresh-baked treats."

The normality of the moment reminded her of how much she had missed during the past couple of months. Going forward, she committed to not wasting any more time. Jenna waved as she walked out the door. Once outside the hospital's main entrance, she pulled out her cell phone and dialed.

After the second ring, she heard, "Hello? Jenna. Are you okay? What's wrong?"

She smiled at the concern in his voice. Always so protective. "I'm fine. Can I come over? I'm hoping it's not too late to take you up on your offer. I was hoping we could talk."

"I'm not sure that's a good idea." The pronounced pause scorched. "I've got a lot of work to do," His hesitation gave the impression walls were being built, ones that would be very hard for her to climb.

A semi-smile formed when the dozens of excuses she'd given him over the months whipped through her mind. She'd learned from the master how to navigate through the barriers. Grant was the best at getting answers. "So…when is a good time?"

In the silence, she could practically hear his wheels spinning. "Kyle and I'll be at the house tomorrow," he said, sounding reluctant. "However, if what you have to say is contentious, I'd prefer to talk someplace else. Kyle's still not talking, and I'm working hard to provide a stable, safe environment."

"I won't fight with you, Grant. I just want to talk, maybe work out a visitation schedule with Kyle."

"That may be a problem."

She tried, but couldn't help swallowing. "Does this mean you won't let me see him?"

"I will never stop you from seeing, Kyle. You're as much his family as I am. I've made you his emergency contact if I'm not available."

"Oh, wow, that's kind of you." She shouldn't have been surprised, but she was. She picked up her pace, almost running toward the parking structure. "Then, what's the problem?" She managed to choke out past her growing apprehension.

"I wanted to be sure before I called, but I think Kyle's somehow gotten the impression you don't want to be in his life anymore. After you dropped him off the other day, he started covering his ears every time I mentioned your name."

"I don't know why he might have…Oh, God." *Behave yourself, little man.*

"What just happened?"

Jenna leaned against Nellie and bowed her head. "Before I left I told Kyle to behave himself. Actually, I said 'behave yourself, little man,' the exact same words Duke used before he left. He thinks I've abandoned him." She closed her eyes, her heart pummeling her with regret.

"Jenna, it's okay. I'll talk to Kyle and let him know you'll drop by tomorrow—that you want to see him."

"Thank you. I would appreciate the help. Oh, and Grant? Ashley delivered her baby this morning, six pounds, ten ounces. They named their baby girl Caitlyn Anne."

The silence on the other end of the line extended.

"Grant, are you still there?"

"Yeah, Yeah. I'm still here. I'll have to send a note or gift or something, to thank them." She didn't miss the raw, tender emotion in his voice.

"Maybe you can stop by in a day or two. I'm sure Chase would like a visit…you're both dads, now. It will give you something to talk about."

"I don't know, they might not appreciate seeing me."

Not once in the many months she'd known him had he ever been unsure of anything. She hated hearing his lack of confidence, knowing it was largely her fault. He'd saved Kyle, and, in a way, he had protected her as well. She needed to change his perceptions, make things right.

"I'll see you tomorrow."

"Jenna?"

She heard the rawness in his voice, and she understood. "I promise. I'll be on my best behavior." There was that silence again. She opened Nellie's door and hopped in. Jenna released a steady breath of air she hadn't known she was holding. "See you tomorrow."

CHAPTER THIRTY-ONE

"Hey," Jenna put on her best happy-to-see-you smile when Grant opened the door, and then worked to keep it there when his skeptical frown greeted her.

Kyle stood behind Grant, leaning sideways to peek at her from behind his legs. His former gentle, curious expression had been replaced with a weary, untrusting stare.

Realizing she was the cause of the distrust birthed an excruciating ache.

She showed the box of baked goods to the boys knowing the contents wouldn't help. Not this time. This time she'd stepped into a big ol' pile of crap, and the only way out was to work her way forward, one small gesture at a time.

Grant swept his arm toward the living room. "I wasn't expecting the doorbell. Did you lose your key?"

"No. I have it. It's just...I wasn't sure. You know, I...um..."

"Come inside. It's seems weird talking on the front porch."

Awkward. Tentative. Reluctant. *She* had caused this mess.

She pulled her bag higher on her shoulder, nervously took a deep breath, and stepped into the mosaic tile entryway, wiping her feet on the area rug, then continuing across the aged wood floor to the kitchen. Her fingers tingled from fisting her hands out of a nervous habit. She set the box on the counter and turned to face the males she'd come to care about more than she ever thought possible.

"You both look great." She scanned the room, noticing the subtle changes. Picture frames with Kyle's drawings, toy cars on the ordinarily clean coffee table, Kyle's favorite travel cup sitting next to Grant's coffee cup, and dozens of other small changes deepened the ache in her heart. She missed those huge, insignificant things.

"How was school today?" she asked, her pitch escalating toward clownish in her attempts to entice a response.

Her nephew stared at her, his brows crumpled together.

"Kyle, your aunt asked you a question. You need to at least respond." Grant's kind yet stern statement made her aware he'd also changed. He'd become a real dad—a man who took his fatherhood seriously.

Kyle's shoulders scrunched toward his ears in an I-don't-know kind of way.

"Thank you, little man." Grant laid a hand on his shoulder. "Now, why don't you go finish your drawing in your room? Jenna would like to talk to me for a few minutes."

Kyle turned and took a couple of steps before glancing back over his shoulder, his expression still uncertain. Every few steps he repeated the look until he disappeared around the corner.

Jenna placed her hands on the counter to anchor her feet in place and to keep from wringing her hands. Grant's body language provided a gauge to measure his mood. For the first time since she'd known him, he shuttered his emotions. Gone were the friendly smiles and interested glances. He wouldn't make this easy, and rightly so.

She'd screwed up. Big time.

"Before the custody hearing, you said something about keeping your promise to protect me and Kyle," she stated as a way to get things rolling. "I still don't know what you actually meant by that." Jenna stumbled over every word, each becoming harder than the previous one.

"I promised you two things. One, I wouldn't tell anyone about our marriage, and two, I would protect Kyle. Without your permission, I couldn't tell the judge we were married, so I went with Plan B—using the DNA results to claim I was Kyle's dad. After you accused me of raping Caitlyn, I figured there was only one explanation."

Grant moved to the opposite side of the counter before turning toward her.

Then Rachelle was right. You're not Kyle's father.

"Why are you here, Jenna?"

"I don't know, really."

Grant shifted and blew out a heavy breath.

"Wait that's not true," she responded before the lawyer in Grant could verbally object. *Take responsibility for your actions. Say you're sorry.* She swallowed a couple times to muster some courage. "I came to apologize for accusing you of harming Caitlyn. I had no idea you and Jason were twins until Rachelle stopped by to see me."

"Rachelle? So…you believe her and not me? No. Don't answer that. I don't want to talk about Rachelle." The muscles in Grant's jaw pulsated. "Let me reemphasize. I never touched Caitlyn inappropriately. I loved her like a sister. I never lied. Not to you. Not to the judge. Caitlyn might not have been my biological sister, but she was my sister, nonetheless. You have to understand."

"I want to. I do. I haven't been a very good listener. Please tell me what I need to know so I can understand."

"Before I left for Chicago, I put a call into Mapes. I couldn't tell if he was bluffing or not, but he said he had a strong case. I realized if I didn't at least come up with a solution and fast, my parents would get custody. I couldn't allow another child to suffer. When you accused me of raping Caitlyn, there was only one explanation, and that was Jason. He'd always been infatuated with Caitlyn. In a way, you gave us what we needed to keep Kyle safe."

"I wished I'd been there for Caitlyn."

"I'm not sure it would have made a difference. Caitlyn never said anything about Jason. She was always private. All I knew was she didn't trust him for some reason."

"Then how did you know for sure Kyle was Jason's son?"

"I didn't, but if my hunch was right, my DNA would match Kyle's. It was a gamble I was willing to take to prevent my parents from getting custody."

"So you gambled Kyle's future on a blood sample." She paced back and forth across the wooden floor, rubbing the back of her neck, her mind whirling with bits of information, trying to fit together all the revelations of the past weeks.

"If things didn't go our way, I was willing to risk your ire and produce our wedding certificate. I hoped our age, financial position, and our marriage would add enough to tip the scales."

Her stomach lurched, and she stopped and turned. "Do your parents know?"

"That I'm Kyle's biological uncle? Or that we're married?"

"Either."

Grant's mouth tightened, and he shook his head. "They haven't said anything, and I doubt they will." Grant pointed to the books lovingly organized on the built-in bookshelves. "While you were away, I found and read Caitlyn's diaries. I was able to connect some of the information to certain events, so now I have enough to ensure their silence. My gut tells me there is more to the story, though, and I'm going to keep digging until we have answers."

"Thank you." Jenna's finger traced a wood grain on the butcher block island. "I feel stupid for missing the twin thing. I thought he was your older brother."

"He was older, by seven minutes. I never thought of him as my twin because we were vastly different, even though physically we looked the same. People always got us mixed up for reasons I still don't understand. Even our parents mixed us up, but Caitlyn never did. She could always tell us apart. I'm flabbergasted no one told you, but I realized after you accused me of raping Caitlyn that you had no idea I was a twin."

"I'm really sorry for what I said. I was scared. Can you forgive me?"

"Jenna, it's not about forgiveness. It's about trust, and you don't trust me."

The thought of fully trusting someone produced a drowning panic. She didn't trust anybody. It wasn't him. She trusted no one.

"I'll work on that." She committed with a bagful of determination, a cup of purpose, and a tablespoon of readiness. "Where do we go from here?" She bit her lip and hoped he didn't say nowhere, even though he had every right.

"That's a good question." Grant shoved his hands in his pockets and rocked back on his heels. "To be honest, I don't know. I've only thought far enough ahead to make sure Kyle is safe. He deserves a stable home. Jenna, you must know, I never meant to hurt you."

"I've been a little slow, but I'm beginning to catch on. You've been so patient. Do you think you can hold on a little bit longer?"

"I think I can manage." Finally, the curl of his mouth matched the smile in his eyes.

Jenna pulled out a chair from the island and lifted onto the stool. "How's Kyle?"

"He's confused. I'm trying my best, but it's hard. There's been so much change in such a short period of time. I think it will take time before he learns to trust again. He's still not saying anything."

"Is there something I can do?"

"I need to show you one of his drawings." Grant opened a drawer and pulled out a crumpled piece of construction paper, handing it to her. It was a crayon drawing of mountains and sun and flowers framing the picture. In the foreground were two males and two females. Everyone but one man had a red X through the figure. She held the picture against her heart, crossing her arms to hold the treasured drawing in place, and allowed the welling emotions to surface.

"What does this mean?" Knowing full well what it meant. Kyle didn't believe she was a part of his life anymore.

But it wasn't true.

Hadn't she stayed away to protect him from her anger?

Crushing guilt pulverized any excuse she could have made.

He wouldn't know why she'd stayed away, just that she'd left him. She stared down the dark hall.

"Do you think he'll talk to me?" Her question held only a thread of hope.

Grant walked around the counter. "I doubt it, but he might listen." He reached a hand toward a strand of hair falling across her eyes but at the last second he halted the action and dropped his arm to his side. "He's a good listener. You should try."

"Grant, I'm sorry. I'll do my best to fix this." *If only I knew what to say. What to do.*

Jenna moved toward the room, her feet dragging like she was wearing cement clogs. Grant placed a hand on her forearm. "Before you go, I think I should tell you the rest."

"The rest?" Her innards cringed. "I don't know if I can handle more."

"It's not about Kyle, it's about my family." Grant chewed on the side of his lip. "I had a talk with Sheriff Joe this morning. I believe you already know the housekeeper's son's been missing since the day of the arson."

"Yes, he told me." Jenna turned to face him. "Did he tell you I pressed charges?"

"He did. However, I don't believe Javier would have planned an arson. Not on his own. I can't prove it, but I have no doubt my mother is behind what happened. I gave the sheriff what information I had. He's checking into the details, but admitted it's unlikely anything could be done about my mother or her threats. Not unless she threatens someone again."

Jenna placed the picture on the counter. "Your mother is vindictive." She leaned closer. "What can I do to help?"

"Kyle will never be in her presence alone. Ever. I'll limit visitations, get a restraining order, or move if I have to, but I don't want it to come to that. Elkridge is my home. This is where I want to stay. But I can't be with Kyle all the time. It would be easier with two."

Two. *What a beautiful word.* "I'll help." Jenna fussed with the bow on the bakery box. "I need him, too." Her whispered confession came out with such a quiet strength, the statement felt true, solid. "I'd better go see Kyle. See what I can do to help him understand I haven't abandoned him."

She picked up Kyle's sad cry-for-help drawing and walked down the hall, stopping at a partially closed door. Kyle sat at a newly purchased drawing table, busily drawing on a piece of paper the size of the picture in her hand. She knocked on the solid wood door.

Kyle whipped around, his pupils dilating. His lip trembling.

"May I come in?" Jenna made sure to keep her voice friendly and calm.

After he nodded, she took several steps into the room, set the picture on his desk, and pointed to the female figure in the grass. The other in the clouds she knew represented Caitlyn. She tapped on the picture and crouched beside him. "Kyle, I want to talk about this red X. I think it's here because you believe I'm no longer in your life. Is that true?"

Her breathing stalled when he nodded. She laid a hand on his knobby little knee to reassure him that telling the truth was good. "I understand why you feel the way you do. Or at least I think I do. I want you to know I love you. Since the day we first met, I've loved you more and more and more. Just because you don't see me every day, doesn't mean I'm not thinking about you, or loving you."

She pushed to her feet, walked over to sit on his bed, and held out her arms. Kyle ignored her gesture, picked up a blue crayon, and pulled at its paper label.

"Kyle? Do you want to come sit with me?"

The little boy shook his head, and slumped further into the chair.

Well, crap. Those long-standing insecurities about never being loved, of being unwanted plagued her. Voices of doubt filled her head. Kyle wasn't rejecting her. He believed she'd rejected him. She searched for a way to make him believe in her love, and asked herself what Kathy or Maggie would do. Kyle had always responded to Maggie. Then she remembered.

"You may not want to sit beside me, but I have something in my pocket I'd like to show you."

He didn't look up, but his head tilted slightly sideways to peek when she pulled the small gold pendant out of her pocket and held it out for him to see. Then he looked right at her, his eyes inquisitive.

"I bet you recognize this. It was your mom's. You sure you don't want to come sit by me?" She patted the bed beside her. "I can tell you a story."

Slowly Kyle leaned forward and stood, then came and wriggled up onto the bed. He turned and folded his hands in his lap. The tension in her shoulders relaxed, but she dared not reach out.

"Look." She opened the tiny locket. "It's a picture of me and your mom. The pictures aren't so good. I copied them off our drivers' licenses."

Kyle reached his little fingers toward the two faces, caressing the images, before his dejected eyes met hers.

"If I give it to you, will you promise to take good care of it?" Giving him something so priceless almost made her hesitate. But when his big, tear-filled eyes met hers, all worry disappeared. She turned his hand over and placed the locket and fine gold chain into his palm.

Then she reached into the top of her blouse and pulled out the thick silver chain. "I want you to be able to see our images whenever you want, but just because I'm giving this to you, doesn't mean we don't still match. We will always match, you and me. I love you, Kyle. That will never, ever change."

Kyle bunched his feet beneath him and crawled into her lap. He settled before pulling his matching chain from beneath his shirt.

Jenna didn't have to wonder what winning the lottery felt like. She just won the biggest prize of her life.

In silence, she held Caitlyn's son, her beloved nephew, until he grew heavy.

He'd given her forgiveness when he didn't have to, and taught her a valuable lesson.

Her life was far from perfect. But perfection didn't matter.

Now if she could just figure out how to earn Grant's forgiveness and trust again.

CHAPTER THIRTY-TWO

As Jenna entered the café, Bill Mason stopped to tell her Grant had stopped by the hardware store to buy a little tool belt for Kyle. Cindy Harris mentioned the day before that Grant and Kyle were out taking pictures together.

"Where have you been, stranger?" Maggie's voice rang out over the café noise. "Are you here for Customer Appreciation Day?"

"Hey, Mags." Jenna slid onto a stool at the counter and grabbed the pepper container to help fill the tray of shakers. "I got your baking done early, so I wouldn't be in your way." Jenna looked around. "Where are your kids?"

"I loaded them up with fresh lemonade and sandwiches and sent them off to tube down the river. What's up with the grump?" Maggie chided, "If you don't cheer up, that scary face will become permanent. Then again, it would be perfect for Halloween."

"That would be perfect, since I scare kids speechless," Jenna pulled at her jeans, trying to get comfortable on the leather seat. "I've been researching ways to help Kyle start talking again. I'm so frustrated. I feel like a monster."

"Would you listen to yourself?" Maggie grabbed another saltshaker to fill. "I'm going to get my violin in a minute and play along to your sad song. You've got to put yourself out there to get the good things back."

"Listen to you being all optimistic. Do you have a new boyfriend I don't know about?"

"Maybe."

Maggie walked away. If the extra swing in her friend's curvy hips was any indication, Jenna might be the only person in Elkridge spending the upcoming holidays alone. At least she had her work. She picked up the menu for something to occupy her mind, even though she'd memorized the menu the first week she started work. Only the specials changed.

"The usual?" Maggie asked, walking toward her with a water in hand.

"Nah. I was aiming for something different. I promised myself I'd start eating better, to be a good example for Kyle. How about a salad, dressing on the side. Let's say I turned over a new leaf." She chuckled at her little joke while Maggie rolled her eyes.

"I'll put chicken on top. You need your protein, especially since Ernie said he almost hit you out on Route 16 by the Gradys' place. I can't believe how far you run. That's a good eight miles from here."

Jenna grabbed her glass of water and took a long, deep swig before setting it down. "That's nothing. In high school, I used to run sixty, seventy miles a week. I thought it was time to get back in shape. I'm even considering signing up for an adventure race. What do you think?"

"I think you're nuts." Maggie set the pepper tray aside and began working on the sugar containers. "Grant ran track in high school."

Here we go again. Jenna dropped her hands to her lap and released a frustrated huff. She wished Maggie would leave the scab alone. Over the last several days, every conversation led back to Grant.

Her conversations with him these days were stiff and formal. She half-expected him to ask her for a divorce, and she wouldn't blame him. She hadn't been a good wife. Heck, she hadn't even been a good friend. God, she missed him. If only she could figure out how to repair things. She was to blame. This was her fault.

The nights were the worst. When she closed her eyes, she could almost feel him snuggled around her body, his breath tickling her neck, his confident lips on her skin.

The memories were painfully sad. It didn't help when everywhere she went, townsfolk asked after Grant and Kyle.

Maggie paused while wiping the counter. "Maybe you should call and make sure Grant's bringing Kyle by for his free root beer float. I bet your nephew's never had one."

"Look, Mags, I appreciate your

matchmaking attempts, but you don't need to keep pushing." *Especially since we're already married.* "I hurt Grant. I can't repair the damage. My hope is that someday we'll learn to be friends."

"Did he give you that impression?"

"No, but...he needs to focus on Kyle right now. Kyle's still not talking, and I'm worried."

"Well, at least Grant's managed to keep him away from Vivian."

"If they arrest her, that will be one less thing Grant has to worry about." *Sweet fudge.* The look on Maggie's face made her want to find a key to lock her mouth. The words slipped out, lickety-split, and she couldn't chase them down and reel them back in.

Maggie moved closer and leaned in. "Arrested? I told you, you needed to be careful with that woman. From what you're not saying..."

Maggie trailed off as her attention moved toward the front of the café. Jenna looked over her shoulder to see what had stopped Maggie mid-lecture.

Grant stood in the doorway, giving Jenna's heart a pump of energy. An unsettled half smile rested uneasily on his face. She wished she could take an eraser and redraw the smile she was so attached to. Grant leaned over, cupping his hand, to whisper in Kyle's ear, and then he pointed toward the counter. Kyle's new bump-toed, sandaled feet took small, tentative steps toward her. She wanted more than anything to sweep the little boy into her arms and squeeze the snot out of him, but she waited, and waited, till his shuffling feet stopped beside her. She dropped into a squat beside her chair to greet him and give his ball cap a gentle tug.

"Hi, little man. I wasn't expecting to see you. What are you up to today? Are you here for your root beer float?"

He said nothing, only held out his hand without attempting to look at her. A red construction paper envelope dangled from his fingers.

"For me?" she asked, disappointed he still hadn't found the courage to use his voice.

He nodded and released the paper. Her shaky fingers pulled the card from the outer envelope. Big, block, red-crayon letters spelled the words "you're invited." A date and time also told her she'd been invited to a birthday party.

She placed the card in her lap and reached for Kyle's hand. "You want me to come to your house for a birthday party?"

Kyle nodded, refusing to meet her eyes while continuing to stare at the rungs of the chair behind her.

"But, it's not quite your birthday. Your birthday is in May." She angled her head down so she could see his face. He pointed at the card with the big girl stick figure holding hands with the little boy figure.

The date. Her chest muscles gave her heart a tender squeeze.

Caitlyn's birthday.

He remembered.

The skittish way he pulled away, refused to look at her, provided a bigger, and more important understanding. Kyle didn't think she would come. All her previous actions had created an impression, the wrong impression, in this darling boy's mind. He didn't understand why she wasn't there for him every day, any more.

Oh, Kyle...

How could she explain loving him, caring for him, was more important than most anything? How could she show him every second was devoted to helping make sure he had a stable environment?

Yet, there he stood, in front of her asking her, pleading for love. Hoping she might be able to come to a party, be with him, love him, even though he'd already convinced himself she still didn't want him.

"Kyle, please look at me," she begged. His sweet eyes flickered to hers, then away again. "Kyle, please?" His gaze locked on hers. "I would be honored to celebrate your mom's birthday with you. I love you with all my heart, little man. If I have to call and tell you every day, I will. Don't you know I would climb a mountain if you asked me to?"

She opened her arms wide. With only a moment's hesitation, Kyle stepped into her embrace. She curled around the fragile little body, cradling him in her arms. Her gaze met Grant's as he stood by the door. Waiting. Watching. He couldn't fix this. No one could fix it but her.

"Thank you," Jenna mouthed to him. *And, thank you for being so tolerant.*

Grant must have understood her message, because a hint of a smile flickered across his stoic face before disappearing.

When Kyle began to squirm, she released him and looked into his face.

"I'll be there with my party hat on," Jenna reached out and tickled Kyle's tummy, knowing the perfect spot to make him laugh, and was rewarded with the most magical giggle. He doubled over before stepping back.

"You'd better go. Your dad's waiting."

Without hesitation, Kyle ran to the door with a skip in his step. Grant turned and followed the boy out, never looking back. Only since Grant came into her life, had she finally learned how lonely she'd been, all her life. He and Kyle made her life full and beautiful, and she'd been too stubborn to see it.

"It's never too late to create a miracle," Maggie said peering over the top of the counter.

Jenna straightened. "Miracles, huh?"

Jenna grabbed her purse.

"Wait," Maggie said. "Where are you going? You haven't had your root beer float yet, and what about your salad?"

"I promise I'll eat." Jenna waved, halfway to the door. "I'm off to see if I can bake me a miracle."

CHAPTER THIRTY-THREE

Nellie's tires pulled and tugged up the slight incline to Grant's home. She expected twitchy nerves, but as she drove up the drive, a peaceful calm settled in her soul. Birds chirping their evening songs and the setting sun added a cheerful note which further soothed her apprehension.

Stepping out of the Jeep, she took a deep breath, inhaling the smell of pinesap and a meat smoker. She reached in and across to the passenger seat, pulling a stack of boxes into her arms. Gathering her courage, she took a determined step toward the door. Halfway there, Kyle came rushing out, wearing his little cargo shorts, an "I'm cute" T-shirt, and a big smile on his face. He grabbed her arm and pulled.

"I'm coming." She glanced around at the driveway. "Am I early? Where's everyone else?"

"You're it," Grant said from the doorway.

When she got close enough, he lifted the packages from her arms, and for a second their eyes met. The intimate interest had returned.

He shrugged. "Don't look at me. I'm innocent. You're the only one Kyle wanted to invite. It's his party." He leaned in, his breath sizzling hot on her skin. "You'd better go on in," he whispered, "Kyle's been waiting by the front window for you all afternoon."

Grant Newhall was many things, but innocent wasn't one of them.

She took a moment to brush the dirt from her sandals on the foyer rug before entering the house. Kyle gave her arm a tug, his body half-turned down the hall.

"Hold on a minute," she laughed, trying to unload her purse. As soon as her bag hit the wooden pegs, Kyle grabbed her hand and pulled her into the living room. She gaped at the room's splendor, genuinely impressed, but hamming it up a notch for Kyle's benefit.

Around the room's edges were lit candles, interspersed with new pictures. Jenna lifted Kyle into her arms and settled him on her hip. "Did you make these?"

She touched a pinecone dipped in green wax, and then a pressed flower ironed between two wax paper sheets. Kyle nodded and pointed at another picture frame. Awww. Her heart performed a triple pirouette. "It's a picture of you and your dad."

"Kyle took the selfie." Grant chimed in from the kitchen.

"You did?" She placed a hand on Kyle's heart. "It's a wonderful picture. What about this one?"

She asked, hoping for a word or two, but a shrug was all he was willing to give. She hugged him anyway. "You're getting too big for me to carry around. Ready to get down?"

He slid down her body and ran off to bring her something else for show and tell… only Kyle still couldn't manage the telling part.

Grant offered her a glass of wine, and then

made himself scarce, doing make-work in the kitchen. Anything to give her space.

She was grateful for the private time to reconnect. For the next hour, Kyle pulled out his newest finds, and surrounded her with books, puzzles, and race cars. When he brought out his racetrack, Grant put a halt to the jubilant sharing of toys.

"Kyle, maybe we can put your racetrack together after dinner. Right now it's time to eat." Kyle acknowledged Grant by disappearing around the corner toward the bathroom.

Grant wiped his hands on a dishtowel, then tossed it over his shoulder. "You taught him to wash his hands and face before dinner. He still remembers." His mouth curved and gave birth to a ray of hope. "Would you like to help set the table?"

Grateful for something to do, she began transferring plates, silverware, and glasses from the kitchen island to the table, careful to stay two feet out of range of the man she wanted to touch. She didn't dare allow herself to feel the heat from his body soaking into hers. Her skin ached to be in his arms. *I shouldn't have accepted the wine.* His magnetic aura pulled at her, and she fought and pulled in the opposite direction.

Concentrating on not making a fool of herself in front of Kyle, she didn't hear him return until he almost slammed into her. She reached out a hand to steady him.

"Hands and face washed?" she asked leaning in. "Any dirt bugs back here?" she automatically nuzzled his neck to make him giggle. "Looks clean to me. Where do you want me to sit?"

Kyle raced around the table and pulled out a chair. "Why, thank you, sir."

Grant moved behind her chair, dropping her purse by her side, and then moved back to the kitchen. She glanced at the bag, her testing kit resting on top.

Maybe he does still care. A miracle? Maybe? The realization hit her with the speed of light and gave her love seed a touch of fertilizer. After testing her blood, she waited for dinner to be served.

"Ohhh, myyyy." She took in the gourmet splendor of buffalo brisket, homemade potato salad, and baked beans. "This looks yummy,

Grant. When will you be opening your restaurant?"

"Someday." The appreciation in his expression made her want to climb in his lap and snuggle, but she had to remind herself those days were gone…but maybe not forever.

For the next half-hour, Grant spent every minute trying to make Kyle giggle or eat his food. He didn't ask her personal questions. As he'd promised, he was investing all his energy into making Kyle happy, and had put his life on hold. "Eat one more bite, then you can show her your surprise."

A spoon whipped in and out Kyle's mouth so fast the three of them broke out laughing. Kyle pushed from the table and disappeared, then reappeared a few minutes later with a white frosted layer cake with candy-coated chocolates scattered randomly on the top. The whole thing was tilting to the left.

"Did you make this?" Jenna glanced big-eyed at Kyle. His bobble-head response made her laugh.

"He pretty much made it all on his own." Grant added. "I helped with a few things, but Kyle did the rest."

"Wow. You have a cook *and* a baker in the family. I have some mighty stiff competition." She pushed away from the table. "Be back in a minute."

She took a detour to the living room and brought back the medium-sized box. "Kyle, I think you might like to open this one." She handed her nephew a cross-eyed, goofy-face gift-wrapped box. He tentatively took the box from her hand and sat on the floor to rip open this present. As soon as it was open, he smiled up at her while he pulled out matching navy blue aprons. He ran his little fingers over the white embroidered threads. After a few seconds, he stood to take Grant his.

Gotcha, little man! You do know how to read and write, not just mimic letters.

"Thanks, buddy. Thanks, Jenna."

The memory of Grant in all his glory making her breakfast with nothing on but an apron warmed her cheeks. A second later, Kyle returned and gave her a hug, thankfully interrupting her decadent deliberations.

Jenna tied the strings of Kyle's apron. "Grant, if you ever decide to open a restaurant,

I think you're going to have a partner. Kyle has your passion for cooking."

"Or baking."

"Kyle, do you want to get the other box?" Jenna pointed to the last one.

The scampering of feet filled her with happiness, a sensation so complete and full and satisfying, it almost took her breath away. He gently pulled at the paper until it slid away and he could open the box. Inside the box he pushed away the tissue paper and gasped. He tentatively touched the antique fame, and stroked his fingers over two little girls' faces.

"Kyle? Do you know who those people are?"

His gaze traveled between her and the picture. "That's me and your mom. She's only a little older than you are now."

He skimmed his fingers lightly over the glass surface. A single splash of a tear hit the glass and spread.

"Kyle?" Only a half a breath passed before she pulled him into her arms. His little body collapsed against her as a flood of silent tears poured down his face and soaked her shirt. She began to rock back and forth to soothe this precious child, who could no longer be innocent. Grant placed a hand on her shoulder, and she pushed her shoulder up to her ear, cradling his hand, drawing strength from his presence.

When the tears had run their course, Jenna whispered, "Kyle. Hey, little man. Aren't you going to cut your cake so I can have a piece? You worked so hard to make it."

Sad eyes with long blond lashes blinked up at her. He sat up and then slid to the floor, picked up the framed picture and placed it on the table, and then moved to the butcher block island.

Grant lifted the small camera on the counter and handed the device to Kyle. "Do you want to take a picture of your cake before you make a slice? It's a great cake."

The compliment made the boy smile. Kyle picked up the camera and beckoned them closer.

"You want us in the picture?" Jenna asked, welcoming the opportunity to get closer to Grant. An inspiration made her stick her tongue out at Grant as the camera flashed.

"Oh yeah? Take this." Grant's arm slipped

around her waist, and he gave her a cross-eyed, scrunched face look. She didn't notice anything else, because melting into a puddle right there on the kitchen floor seemed perfectly natural.

Kyle snapped a picture, capturing the moment, and set the camera down.

She couldn't remember the last time she laughed so honestly and completely. The need to stay right where she was expanded, and she embraced the joy, but the moment ended too soon.

"Time to brush your teeth," Grant said, and stepped back, instantly getting a stuck-out lip from Kyle. "We agreed this morning that you could stay up an extra hour, but now it's wayyyy past your bedtime. Go get into pajamas and maybe, if you hurry, Jenna will read you a quick story."

That got him moving.

After Kyle rounded the corner, Jenna turned to Grant. "I want you to know how much I appreciate this. I've given you no reason to be so generous. Spending time with both of you...I...um...thank you."

Grant reached out his hand and swept her

bangs aside. "My pleasure." He searched her eyes for some answer while he moved closer. He wanted to kiss her, she could tell. The tingling across her skin indicated she welcomed the idea. Apparently, her body would no longer allow her to deny what her brain refused to believe.

Grant was a generous and giving man. Good for her in so many ways.

As she began to rise onto her tiptoes to meet him halfway, a giggle stopped her from pursuing the urge. Kyle rushed into the kitchen. Instead of carrying a book, he brought another envelope and handed it to Grant.

Grant shot her a worried look before lowering himself to Kyle's level. "Hey, buddy. We talked about this before. If this is what you truly want, I'm good with it, but you'll have to ask her yourself—that was the deal."

Kyle looked at her and then the envelope in his hand, then swallowed hard and fidgeted with the envelope.

"What's going on?" Jenna broke the silence.

Grant stood and eyed the envelope nervously. "A couple of days ago, Kyle asked me about the Tooth Fairy. I told him when he loses a tooth, the Tooth Fairy grants a wish, or leaves money under the pillow in exchange for a tooth. The Bartlett boys lost a tooth the other day at school, and got a dollar from the Tooth Fairy. Later that night, I caught him trying to pull out a tooth."

"Ohhhh. What happened then?"

"I explained the Tooth Fairies don't accept pulled-out teeth. They only accept ones that fall out naturally. However, I did suggest if he wrote to the Fairy, maybe he could make a deal and get his wish early, and when his tooth did eventually fall out, then he could deposit the tooth and possibly ask for another wish."

"I see." Jenna glanced between the two males. "And did he write to the Tooth Fairy?"

"As a matter of fact, he did. But his request was a tough one. It wasn't something the Fairy or I could give him based on the letter alone. I suggested if he truly wants what he asked for, he had to ask with his voice. Because if he is brave enough to ask, the Fairy might grant his wish."

"I see. So Kyle's deciding if he is brave

enough and really, really, really wants his wish to come true."

"Yep." Grant shoved his hands in his pockets. The tension spread across the room like frosting on a cake. "Your decision, Kyle. But you know what this means."

Kyle took the envelope from Grant and slowly turned and raised the crayon-covered white square. His nervous energy made her want to pull the little guy in for a hug, but she forced herself to concentrate on opening and unfolding the card inside.

She read and reread Kyle's single wish.

Tears burned her eyes and tightened her throat as she lowered herself to eye level. "Is this truly what you want?"

Kyle nodded.

All sorts of emotions swirled through her, and her mind was spinning around and around, searching for answers, but when she looked at Kyle, the answer was in his eyes. His blue eyes reflected what she wanted, but she had to do the right thing. "I think your dad's right. If this is something you want, then you have to be brave enough to ask for it out loud." Jenna clamped her teeth together so she couldn't say another word.

She placed the card back in the envelope and handed the priceless gift back to Kyle.

His lips began to quiver.

Sliding the back of her knuckles gently down his cheek, she then placed her hand over his heart.

"Remember what I told you?" He nodded and reached for the chain around his neck, pulling out the medallion. She pulled hers from the top of her blouse and held it at an angle for him to see. "We match," she whispered. "We will always match."

Those big blue eyes studied her for a long, silent moment before he asked, in a small, wobbly voice, "Will you be my mom?"

Jenna pulled her beloved boy into her arms. "Oh, Kyle. Thank you for asking. Of course I'll be your mom. I love you with all my heart. I'll always love you."

"Will you live here with us?" the small voice asked.

Tears welled in her eyes. "That's up to your father." She looked up and pleaded with her eyes for Grant to forgive her.

"He already told me you can."

She blinked. Between the two of them, she'd be reduced to a raging river of tears. Then Kyle lifted onto his tiptoes and kissed her on the cheek. That tipped the scales. A tear slid down her face.

"He did?" The blurred confirmation on Grant's face provided hope.

"Yep." Kyle nodded vigorously. "He thinks your house is a furry-sword."

"I believe he means fire hazard." Grant corrected with a tinge of embarrassment in his voice.

Jenna laughed. "Of course."

Grant lowered himself and placed an arm around Kyle. "So, Jenna, what do you say? Will you stay with us?"

Both of them looked at her with childlike anticipation. Negative what-ifs plagued her, but she shoved the standard self-rhetoric into a dusty corner of her mind, because her heart had already decided.

"Yes, Kyle, I'll be your mom. And, I'll live here with you, if that's what you want."

Kyle threw up his arms and yelled, "It's fish-all."

Jenna gave him a squeeze. "Yes, it's official," she said, before setting him on his feet. "Now, your mom says it's time for bed."

He raced around the corner. "You'd better go," Grant recommended, but she noted a tinge of disappointment in his response. "He'll be out here again in thirty seconds if you don't go with him. It took me several days to get him to sleep in his bed. He's still afraid I won't be here when he wakes up."

Jenna wanted to stay, find out why Grant was less than enthusiastic about her accepting Kyle's offer, but didn't have time to think before rushing down the hall after the scampering feet.

As she neared Kyle's bedroom a thought occurred to her. She remembered telling Maggie miracles didn't happen for her.

Sometimes little boys who truly believe can make wishes come true.

She wondered...if she truly believed... would she get her wish?

CHAPTER THIRTY-FOUR

Grant stared into the darkness. A spark from the log in the oversized river-rock fireplace floated up the chimney. In the corner, the Christmas tree lights twinkled. He should feel contented. The past months with Jenna and Kyle had been pure heaven, but would it last? He'd learned to be less controlling, and more accepting, but he couldn't help wondering whether Jenna might leave again one day. And the thought of losing her was so painful he pushed the thought away...again.

"I'm glad this year is almost over." Jenna handed Grant a glass of wine before sitting and cuddling up next to him on the couch. She pulled a throw over their legs and curled her feet under the wool blanket, nuzzling closer.

Grant twisted his wrist. "Looks like you have eight minutes to wait. Are you going to make a New Year's resolution?"

"No."

"No? Don't you believe in them?"

"It's not that I don't believe, but I think I've reached my limit. While I didn't find my sister, I have closure, and in Kyle, I still have a part of her."

But, what about me? Us?

He swirled the red wine in his glass, trying to breathe past his disappointment. Even though she'd moved into the house, not once in the past four months had she commented on her future.

He'd promised himself he wouldn't push. It was part of his resolve to avoid turning into his parents, but he wasn't comfortable with the status quo, and waiting was gnawing at his soul.

"What about you? Any New Year's resolutions?" she asked.

"I'm not sure yet. My dad got a clean bill of health. He wants to split the practice."

"You were going to sign up for some adventure races. Enroll in a cooking school. What happened?"

"I'm still not sure practicing law is for me, but until Kyle fully trusts we aren't going anywhere, I don't want to make any significant changes. I'll keep my promise and finish out the six case files I've taken before deciding what's next. Besides, Peggy Sue's been reorganizing the files, and my dad didn't object when I mentioned hiring a paralegal. I can make it work—for now."

"But you're staying here. Right? You aren't planning to move?"

He closed his eyes, starting to count, and ending around six or seven. He didn't want to play this game anymore. He lifted his arm from around her and stood.

"Where are you going?" she asked.

He turned, drawing on every ounce of patience he had left. "Jenna, I get your parents died, and your child-self feels they abandoned you. I get my parents took Caitlyn away from you, when they should never have parted siblings. I even get there might have been others in your life who haven't treated you as they should have."

He rubbed his forehead and dragged his hand down over his face. "And, call me a fool, but through all your doubt, in spite of all the times you've pushed me away, I still loved you. I know you've promised Kyle to be his mom, but I still want you as my wife. I want us to be a real family."

She sat up and set her drink aside. "After I accused you of raping my sister, and told you I hated you...you still want to be married to me? That this, what we have here, isn't just for Kyle's sake?"

Spontaneously, a bundle full of hope floated to the surface, a submerged hope he'd believed was lost forever. He paced a couple of steps, then stopped in front of her again.

"For me, this is as real as it gets."

Jenna jumped to her feet, then shoved her hand into the Christmas tree and pulled out a little box and thrust it his way.

"What's this?"

She jumped up on the couch, looking him in the eyes. There was the childlike glint in her eye he'd come to cherish. She placed a hand on each of his shoulders "So, what you're saying is..." she swung her arms to encompass the room, "...this is real? Like, possibly a forever-family type thing? It won't end when Kyle's grown?"

"Yes, absolutely, one hundred—no, one thousand percent."

"Holy crap." She jumped into his arms and wrapped her legs around his waist. "I found my miracle." She reached for the medallion hanging around her neck and squeezed. "There's only one problem."

He turned and slowly lowered them both to the couch, choking on a sliver of panic before grinding his trepidation down to a silent squeak. "By now you should know we can solve any problem, big or small."

"Good, because I think it will take both of us to resolve this one."

He gave her a squeeze. "Well? Will you tell me what it is, or do you want me to guess?"

The look in her eyes gave him the impression she wanted to run again, but then the look shifted, and he realized that, for the first time since he'd met her, she was starting to fight. Fight for what she wanted—what she needed—but didn't feel she had a right to ask for.

She looked away and whispered. "I want us to get married. I want to have a real wedding —to say 'I do' in front of the whole world. I want everyone to know I love Grant Newhall."

A thrill shot up his spine and blasted him off the sofa to spin her in a circle. "Hell, yeah!"

He pumped his fist in the air, dancing around the room...until reality made him pause to study her again for confirmation. "Really?" He slowly set her on her feet.

Her eyes brightened with a splash of joy. He wondered if she might be on the verge of deciding she was living with a lunatic.

"Yes! There's no one in this world I want more than you and Kyle." She laughed. "What do you say? Will you marry me again?"

"That's a yes, yes, and a hell yes." He leaned forward and planted a hot, juicy on her lips. "I'll marry you right now. Today. Tomorrow. I don't care. I'll marry you every year for the next hundred years if you want."

"Why is it you never had any doubts about

us?" Jenna placed a hand on his face, her expression serious.

"The first time I saw you, you were working at the café, and the place was packed, but I only saw you. Your smile. Your generosity. You stole my heart the day I first saw you, and I've never, ever wanted it back."

"Not once?" She teased, and he leaned in. The heat from his physical response warmed her insides to 350 degrees, perfectly done. She pushed the box into his hand. "This is for you."

He slowly opened the box. Inside the worn burgundy velvet box was a plain gold band nestled in a white cushion pillow.

"I hope you don't mind something used. This ring was my Dad's. He adored my mom. In all my life, I've never seen a happier couple, and I want us to be that happy." Jenna's eyes brightened with unshed tears. "I love you, Grant Newhall. I think I always have, but I was afraid if I loved you, you would leave, or disappear from my life."

"And now?"

"I've been wrong about so many things. I'm sorry. Truly, I am. I promise, I'm done running. Done doubting. I've already asked a lot from you, but I have one more request."

"Name it."

She stood onto her tippy-toes to wrap her arms around his neck. "What do you think of the last name Graden? I was thinking, since Kyle decided to adopt us as his parents, we could both change our names, start fresh."

He pulled her into his arms to feel her finally, fully in his life. No hesitation. No what-ifs. "For you, anything. I love you, Jenna Dolcy Graden." He kissed her soundly. "Just remember, I loved you first."

He kissed her again, a slow, sensual kiss, putting every ounce of his passion and love into the connection. When he pulled back, he held her chin gently in the palm of his hand. "And, don't you ever forget," he pointed to her heart, "Kyle and I both need you."

She placed her hand across his heart. "I love you, Grant Graden. You're the only man in this world who is devoted enough to calm my fears. I've always known you were a good man, and I want to be the wife you deserve. I will always love you…I have to love you, because you're the one who taught me how to love again."

I'm so glad you could join Jenna and Grant on their journey to their happily ever after.

THOSE OF YOU who have read my books or been part of my newsletter have heard my explanation for why Authors never see their Star Ratings requested by Amazon, so thank you for allowing me to share the information once again.

When Amazon asks a reader to "Rate this book" on their Kindle, Amazon is the only one to see these ratings.

I'm left clueless about how you feel about this book. Your input matters.

Book reviews help me decide what kind of books I write. Plus, the more people who leave an review, the more likely Amazon is to move a book up in the rankings? Written reviews help other readers find and love a series.

Please continue to rate the book on your Kindle or reader as this helps Amazon, but take an extra moment to pop over to the review section and leave a few words!

Seriously, a few words like, "great story," is enough.

If you have not read my Elkridge Series or the Lonely Ridge Collection, and have no idea why authors keep asking you as a reader to take a few minutes to leave even a couple of word reviews, here's the break down of how reviews work in this crazy business.

Reviews (not ratings) help authors qualify for advertising opportunities. Without triple digit reviews, an author may miss out on these valuable opportunities. And with only a "star rating" the author has little chance of participating in specific promotions, which means authors continue to struggle, and many talented writers give up writing altogether.

Readers aren't the only ones who use reviews to help make purchasing decisions. Producers and directors use your reviews when looking for new projects.

This is why I'm asking for your help.

A few kind words make such a massive difference to me. Your words give me the encouragement I need to continue writing because honestly, I write my books for you, and I'd like to keep delivering the types of stories you want to read.

And, yes, every book in a series needs reviews, not just the first book. Even if a book has been out for awhile, a fresh review can breathe new life into a book.

So, please take a few minutes to leave a short review. Even a couple of words will brighten my day.

Lastly. Thank you for reading this book. I hope to see you again soon. Cheers!

More Books By
Lyz Kelley

Elkridge Series

BLINDED
ABANDONED
ORPHANED
RESCUED
UNMISTAKEN
ATONEMENT
BITTERSWEET

DO YOU WANT A FREE BOOK?

I've got a present for my readers, your very own ebook exclusive: *Regrets, the prequel to BLINDED* when you sign up for my newsletter.

DO YOU WANT A FREE BOOK?

http://lyzkelley.net
Sign up to start falling in love today!

DEDICATION

To Mike.
My husband, partner, and friend.
For your uncompromising love, determined
patience, and stubborn resolve. There are no
words to express how much
I love you.

AUTHOR NOTES

Dear Readers,

In 1941, the world was at war, my grandfather had died a few years earlier, and my grandmother was struggling to care for her three small children. My sixty-eight year old great-grandmother who lived in La Junta, Colorado, came to retrieve my aunt, age eight, and my mother, age five. My infant uncle was placed in the foster care system. In 1945, my uncle contracted polio. In 1946, Chicago's Shriners Hospitals for Children accepted his case and enabled him to get the physical and emotional care he needed.

On any given day, there are over 400

thousand children in the United States foster care system, and over six percent languish there for five or more years, according to childrensrights.org.

What happens to these children? Where do they go? What shapes their lives?

Orphaned is a story about a healing love, a belief that even with a shaky start, a child can find a love, one that creates a belief in a happy ever after. I know my aunt, uncle, and mother each found a healing, lasting love—a love that changed the course of their lives forever.

~Lyz

ACKNOWLEDGMENTS

Over dinner this story was plotted with the amazing attorney, child advocate, and writer Grace Burrows, and Robin Kaye, a beautifully gifted writer and mother. Without their seeds of support this book, or my writing career, may not have not been formed.

My sincere thanks goes to Aidy Award for her beautiful developmental edits and constructive suggestions for improvement. Faith Freewoman, my amazing content/ copy editor, who demanded I put the emotion on the page and worked tirelessly to make the best book possible. To Rachelle Paige for her input and to Carol Agnew who crossed every

T and dotted every I. To Rogenna Brewer, who created a great cover for my story.

Also, to the sisters at the Mount Saint Vincent's home for your endless patience and grace in serving the children of Colorado who face severe emotional challenges due to trauma and neglect. Thank you for allowing me to coordinate the holiday pajama and teddy bear exchange. I'm truly humbled to be in your presence, and praise you for the difficult path you have chosen.

You all have my sincere gratitude.

~Lyz

THANK YOU FOR READING: ORPHANED

Award-winning author Lyz Kelley mixes a little bit of heart, healing, humanity, happiness, honor, hope, and honor in all her books that are written especially for you.

She's is a total disaster in the kitchen, a

compulsive neat freak, a tea snob, and adores writing about and falling in love with everyday heroes.

Please also consider leaving a review on Amazon Goodreads and/or BookBub. Reviews help readers find new books to read, and authors find their footing.

You can also find Lyz on Facebook and Instagram for news, contests, giveaways, and more exciting stuff!

COPYRIGHT

ORPHANED Copyright © 2017 Belvitri Services, LLC

Email: Lyz@LyzKelley.com
Newsletter Sign Up: www.LyzKelley.com
Facebook: www.facebook.com/LyzKelley
Instagram: https://www.
instagram.com/lyzkelley/